TREASYRE HUNT

BOOK III OF THE TYRNING CYCLE

TIM FOX

TREASYRE HUNT
BOOK III OF THE TYRNING CYCLE

COPYRIGHT

INTRODUCTION

I'm beginning this "Introduction" with a mind-felt thank you. Work, family, friends, life. Time's Wheel turns as the writer spends untold hours cloistered from everything, everyone. Turning words on days when they fit. Conceding impasse on days when they don't. Never knowing in advance whether the day's effort is going to be immensely rewarding or leave the feeling of having spent the entire day listening to an audiobook of fingernails scratching slowly down a chalkboard.

The thank you is to every one of you who took a moment of your time to let me know you enjoyed my efforts and you couldn't wait for me to get this volume finished. Kindness is so soft-spoken and unassuming, it is easy to forget how immensely powerful it truly is. Thank you.

Now, on to Book III. I began the initial research for the "Tyrning Cycle" almost a decade ago. "Scavengyr Hunt" was published in 2015. "Wytch Hunt" followed in 2017. When you add in the approximately 134,000 words in "Treasyre Hunt," the completed trilogy weighs in right at 400,000 words.

As I've told you since day one, my favorite narrative framework is the "hero's journey" as described by the late Joseph Campbell. The "Tyrning Cycle" follows that paradigm. It is a heroic fantasy woven from the fabric of well-known mythemes, albeit they've been cocked more than a little cattywampus. The trilogy has three polestars: True Hero, True Love, and True Choice.

Are the books any good? That's totally your call. There is no quantitative measuring tool to determine whether a book is "good." Reading is one of the most democratic activities we can undertake. Every reader is entitled to their own personal vote as to whether they enjoyed the experience.

My goal is to write stories that would draw me in as the reader, narratives that would make me want to stay up reading an hour past my bedtime on a work night because I couldn't wait until the next evening to find out what happened. Stories that are clever and complex, that let me use my mind's eye to populate the tale well beyond the printed words.

If you liked "Scavengyr Hunt" and "Wytch Hunt," I think you are going to love this volume. Some previously introduced secondary characters find new depth as they get their turn in the limelight. There is an assortment of super-fun new characters and Realms. And yes, if the characters have succeeded in reeling you into their reality, there are also several instances of, "I'm not crying, you're crying." I'm extremely proud of how the words turn in Book III.

I'll conclude this "Introduction" with two of my favorite Joseph Campbell quotes. The first is, "We must be willing to let go of the life we planned so as to have the life that is waiting for us." The second, "The privilege of a lifetime is being who you are."

Thank you for spending some of your valuable time with Taliesin, Väst, Myrddin, Elle, the smart mouthed Air Hose, and all the rest of the inhabitants of the Folk universe.

Smile and enjoy the privilege of being you today. Oh, and remember to pause and look over your left shoulder. Repeatedly.

Tim.

ACKNOWLEDGMENTS

To Mom and Dad. Mom and Dad were both with me to share my joy when I completed "Scavengyr Hunt." Heroic fantasy wasn't their preferred genre and my writing lexicon was a little "gritty" for them. However, they always made a point to tell me how proud they were of their second son (c'est moi) and of his accomplishments and told every one of their many friends they needed to read my books.

Dad wasn't with us by the time "Wytch Hunt" was published. Mom was and she made sure every person listed in her substantial address book knew I had finished Book II…and that they needed to read it.

Mom and Dad are together again and not here physically to celebrate the release of "Treasyre Hunt" with me. Much of the best parts of who I am are because they both chose repeatedly to be the Heroes of my story. I think of them both most every day and I am genuinely thankful to have been blessed with such loving and supportive parents.

To my brothers. Thank you for at least acting like you read (and enjoyed) the first two books. As proof that no good deed goes unpunished, I would like to take this opportunity to remind you that boxed sets (sans box) of the entire trilogy are now available and would make rocking client gifts. (I'm not kidding, there really aren't any boxes.) Purchased at rack rate, of course. You know the rules. Baby always needs a new pair of shoes.

To my *Treasyre Hunt* Encouragers, Aiders, and Abettors.
Karla Burnett, Holly Davis, Christie Greer, Laura Haynie, Diane Holitik, Amy Joyner, Sharlee Purdom, and Tyler Thompson. Thanks for your constructive criticism, your encouragement, and

your mad skills at proof reading. To KHT, thanks for enlightening me as to the magykality of "Y"s.

To The UnFading Spirit. I am convinced You are the author of dozens of miracles every day, all of them happening just over our left shoulders. We simply need to train ourselves to pause and let go long enough to look for them, to look at them. Well, that and to make sure we remember to look over our left shoulders.

I did a little research to see if there was a name for a "group" of miracles. Like, *e.g.*, a parliament of rooks, an ostentation of peacocks, or an asylum of loons. The Google indicated there wasn't one. I'm claiming naming rights and I'm going with a "beneficence." A beneficence of miracles has the Ring of Truth to it. (That's right longtime readers, I absolutely went there.)

We, Your children, call you by many different names and we have widely disparate views on a bazillion details: about Your name, Your nature, and how You want us to worship You. The one constant in our multitude of ideologies is that You love us. All of us. Unconditionally.

Thank you for the blessings and miracles in our lives, both noticed and unnoticed. My personal version of "Seeking the Center" includes trying to appreciate my blessings a little more every waking day and earnestly trying to be kinder today than yesterday. I believe if we each do our best to "Seek the Center," we will ultimately find You waiting, waiting with open arms to gather all of Your children safely home to You.

PANTHEON OF THE MOIETY

AMARANTOS

PRINCIPES

CHRONOS

AURORA

SOL

LUNA

RULING COUNCIL OF THE MOIETY

ARCHON

The Alberich
King of the Tuatha Dé Danann

SENESCHAL

The Marid
Suleyman of the Djinn

PARLIAMENTARIAN

The Raja Jinn Peri
King of the Malay Faeries

The Márku
Empress of the HuldreFolk

The Proteus
Regent of The Olympians

HUNTS SCHOOL ADMINISTRATION AND FACULTY

PRINCIPAL

Chiron

HUNTSMISTRESS

Lilith Empousa

HUNTS TEACHERS

Professor Daedalus Hardcastle
Doctor Delphi SilverTongue
Professor Sprite Elphinstone

HUNTS FINALIST TEAMS

AYLLU
Incan/Mayan Realm
"clan"

YAXKIN
"Center"
Allyu Prime Direction

XAMAN
"North"

NOHOL
"South"

LIK"IN
"East"

CHIK"IN
"West"

KABILA
Swahili Realm
"tribe"

KATI
"Center"
Kabila Prime Direction

KASKAZINI
"North"

KUSINI
"South"

MASHARIKI
"East"

MAGHARIBI
"West"

OMADA
Greek Realm
"party, group, or team"

BORRAS
"North"
Acting Omada Prime Direction

NOTOS
"South"

ANATOLIA
"East"

DYSI
"West"

QUINT
"Five"

PLEME
Serbo-Croatian Realm
"tribe"

SREDINA
"Center"
Pleme Prime Direction

SEVER
"North"

ISTOK
"South"

JUG
"East"

ZAPAD
"West"

SHUZOKU
Japanese Realm
"tribe or family"

CHUUSHIN
"Center"
Shuzoku Prime Direction

KITA
"North"

MINAMI
"South"

HIGASHI
"East"

NISHI
"West"

SLÄKT
Swedish Realm
"group of people related by blood, marriage, law or custom"

NORD
"North"
Släkt Prime Direction

SÖDER
"South"

OST
"East"

VÄST
"West"

FEM
"Fifth"

"When mortals were infants, both the Principes and the Folk regularly trod the Earth plane. Chronos is Amarantos's Seneschal, her First Born. Even Sol, Luna, and Aurora must bend their knees to Time. She has always held herself apart from all other living beings."

LEX IMMORTALIS

CHAPTER UNUS

What in the Five-Hells is the human doing?

He looks like he's…no way, that isn't possible, even for him. Is it? Apparently, it is. He's heading straight toward the nearest exit. Leaving? He's leaving? Are you kidding me? He knows the Hunts ceremony starts immediately following the Imbolc Feast. Which begins as soon as all of the non-Hunts School delegates of the Areopagus have walked downstairs to the Prime Omphalos chamber.

The HuntsMistress hasn't announced the team order but it's not like the talysman presentation is going to take very long for each of the teams. Quint knows our talysman is branded on his mortal ass. If he's not present when the Omada's name is called we won't be one of the three teams competing in the third and final Hunt. Which means my chance to be part of the Ruling Council with full access to the Hunts School campus for the next three centuries is over and I'll have to go home as soon as this school year concludes.

Home. Bound there until the end of Time. Without having found the answer. Without having discovered the key to free my mother.

It's been almost a hundred years of unrelenting, unceasing

pain. I'm not bitching. I mean I knew what was going to happen when I bargained with my father to be the only Folk representative from my Realm to ever attend Hunts School.

I assumed I would eventually get used to it, that it would become background white noise. I've never been more wrong. Something about my body chemistry and this plane resets my pain acclimatization level every morning when I wake up. Some days it's been all I could do to make myself focus on schoolwork. I know everyone thinks I'm the biggest jerk in all of the known Realms but I was doing the best I could.

My father knew what would happen to me. The bastard. He knew the pain would be unceasing. He's been to Hunts School on his official duties many times throughout the centuries. I'm sure part of the reason he agreed to bind the contract with me was to teach me a lesson. Fine, Pops, lesson learned. Every agonizing minute would have been worth it though if I'd been able to find the magyk words needed to free her from his damn enchantment.

The answer is here. The fabled Hunts School, the one place where all of the known information from every Realm is replicated and available. He guaranteed me the words were in plain view. What were his exact words? That he'd, "hidden the key in plain sight where any moron or fatuus could find it." Which was kind of interesting. In several respects. Although he had me tutored in any number of languages I've never known him to deign to speak Latin. The word choice was also interesting. Fatuus is Latin for "idiot." "Moron" is the same word, both in Latin and English. Why the redundancy?

I've searched as diligently as I could, spent every free moment researching. Looking. Listening. I've scoured the campus, all of the easily visible places. At least twice. Stood on the top of every one of the structures, at all different times of day and night, looking in all directions. Pushed on innumerable odd stones or pieces of furniture looking for hidden doors or compartments. Pretty sure I found them all. One thing's for sure, if the key is in a book, it's not in the library. I've combed all of the archives from top to bottom, including bribing my way into the restricted area.

If Quint leaves now all of my effort will have been in vain. I can't go home. Not yet. Not without doing everything within my power to try to insure Omada wins the Tyrning. Which means not letting that ass—with our talysman on his ass—desert the team now.

Decision made, Notos spun clockwise on his left heel, turning so he could reach up and grab a handful of Borras's shirtsleeve. "Prime, Quint is leaving. You have to stop him." As the Omada Prime glanced down, Notos saw his group leader's shoulders were slumped, his eyes already tracking Quint's travel to the far end of the ziggurat.

"It is his decision to make, Notos." Borras's normally booming voice was now soft as the rumble of ten-second distant thunder.

"That's not true," Notos replied quickly. "Not if he's putting all of our futures at risk. That makes it official Omada business. The Rules allow you to use the binding on all team related matters."

Borras slowly turned his massive frame so he was squarely faced with his Second Prime. In an instant the Omada captain's face reformatted from despair to somber. "Your statement is a valid interpretation of both the contest rules and of my authority. If I am being completely honest, it is taking all of my willpower to prevent myself from using the binding to stop Quint."

Borras sighed, before drawing a long, measured breath. "There is no question our talysman is the most powerful and that it was received from the most powerful wytch who has ever lived.

"I need do only one small thing to ensure Omada remains in the Hunts. One short command will keep me personally in the running to become the next Archon. If I say the words I still have the chance to become the most powerful person in the universe for the next three hundred years.

"Think of all of the good I could do, Notos. I have. The Omada could build on the monumental works that have occurred all the way from Arthrys's reign through Alberich's. With the team's help and the almost unlimited individual magyk bequeathed on the Archon, I could become a force for good, unparalleled in the entirety of Folk history. I only have to do one small thing to guarantee I might still be able to accomplish all of that."

Borras stopped talking as he bent his left leg until he was kneeling on his boulder-sized kneecap. From there he could look Notos directly in the eyes. "That one small thing is to abandon my personal search for the Center. Just this one time. For only the briefest of moments. Turn away from what I believe Amarantos would have me do and look only to myself for guidance. After that I can return to following the UnFading Spirit in the manner in which I have always believed I have been called to follow Her."

"Prime…"

Borras emphatically shook his great, shaggy head as he slowly stood. This time he was no longer slumped but stood fully erect. "Then what, Notos? After I stole Quint's free will this time, what would I have to be willing to do next for Omada to win?" As he saw Notos was about to interrupt him again, Borras raised his hand. Softly, not angrily. Softly, one comrade to another. Softly, as the first among equals but the first nonetheless. "Forgive me my friend, it was unfair for me to weight you with my decision. Leadership demands not only the making of decisions but also the willingness to carry their weight, so that others might complete the tasks that they themselves are called to perform.

"For better or for worse, I am Omada Prime and I have made my decision. We are charged not merely with winning the Hunts, but winning by Seeking the Center. I have long believed that is the only way for any team to ultimately prevail."

Borras placed his ham-sized right hand gently on Notos's shoulder. "Stop. Be still a moment, Notos. Look inward, not to the event horizon of your heart's want but to the one Truth that is your heart's need.

"I will not abandon my faith at this juncture just because everything is on the line. That is when faith is the most important, when faith can perform it's greatest work. It is why She has called us to Seek the Center always. Every decision we each make, every choice, large or small, they all bear consequence."

The giant paused a moment as they both watched Tal finally reach the ziggurat's threshold and step out of sight. "Notos, we all saw what just happened to Quint. He is mortal and he is in a strange Realm. In only a few months he has suffered far more, has lost far more, than any of the thousands of us who have been students here for the last hundred years. It is understandable that at this moment he is grieved beyond our ability to understand. Or his. I believe if he is given the opportunity, both Quint's heart and his mind will ultimately lead him to Seek the Center."

"And if you're wrong, Prime?" Notos asked.

"If I am wrong I will be sorry we did not win but I will never regret not usurping his free will."

Notos watched as Borras paused a moment, a moment in which the broken landscape that was the Omada Prime's face transformed into one of his trademark humongous smiles. Smiling, Notos, asked himself, starting to get genuinely pissed. What in Five-Hells is there to smile about?

"I am due to check in immediately at our feast table," the Omada Prime announced. "Ana and Dysi can go with me but there is no Rule which requires all team members to be present for the entirety of the feast."

Borras must have seen Notos still wasn't understanding why he was smiling because the left side of his mouth twitched a little further up as he continued. "Squad security is traditionally one of the responsibilities of the Second Prime. Our Fifth Prime is hurting badly right now, Notos. I don't believe he is focused on the real and present danger he is in now that everyone knows our talysman is branded on his body. Seems to me the team's security chief would suggest that any team member in such a position be provided with a friendly protective shadow."

Understanding relief finally washed over Notos's face. "As Omada Second Prime I am charged with team security. I am strongly recommending our Fifth Prime be afforded immediate close-distance security."

Borras put his catcher's mitt sized paw on his teammate's shoulder. "Permission granted, Second Prime. You are only to follow and protect. DO NOT interfere in his actions, whatever they might be. If someone, anyone, attempts to harm him you are permitted to use whatever means necessary to protect him. Understood?"

"Understood," Notos confirmed, as he began fast walking after Quint.

CHAPTER DUO

Väst gasped as she felt her left leg spasm, then watched helplessly as, on its own initiative, it took a small stutter-step forward. No, she thought to herself, please no. Please Amarantos, not now. Please don't let this be happening again.

The compulsion geas had physically controlled her body many times in her early years at Hunts School. Particularly during the genesis of her involuntary seduction of Kentro. It had been years though since the relentless magyk had ripped physical control of her body from her. Väst knew in the back of her mind the compulsion had been steering her since the moment she arrived at Hunts School, but she had repressed how helpless it made her feel. Helpless and ashamed.

The scope of her geas went far beyond any magyked compulsion she'd ever read about. Both in duration and effect. Unbelievably, it had lasted almost a hundred years now. Also unprecedented was the aspect where it not only made her perform such actions, the geas also influenced the response of its target. Väst had spent hundreds of hours looking, poring through every book and scroll on compulsions in the library. There was not a single word, not even a hint, that such a thing as a "reciprocating compulsion" geas was even possible. On top of everything else, this third-party interference affecting Hunts contestants was occurring on the Hunts School campus itself. The single most heavily warded place in all of the known worlds.

There was no question what the geas wanted of her at this moment. She felt it now seize control of her right leg, trying to forcibly pick it up to follow the now completed left step.

In the past it would have been impossible for her to resist the compulsion. Now, because of Quint's wish, Väst could tell that if she exercised her will she had the ability to resist, to stop it. If she did though, whoever was attempting to use her as their marionette would know something was wrong. At this point they couldn't possibly know about Quint's wish that she be made whole but if she disobeyed they would know she now had the power to override the compulsion. Which would undoubtedly precipitate a massive shit storm of other unpleasant actions. No, that piece of information needed to be kept secret as long as possible.

So she yielded to the compulsion, allowing it to pick her right foot up, then her left for a second step, and then her right again. As she looked ahead she saw Quint. Where's he going? The feast is going to start shortly. It looks like...damn, he's leaving. Not that I blame him, given what's happened to him in the last twenty-four hours.

The Omada talysman is branded on his skin. If he's not back for the post-feast ceremony they're out. Which answers why I'm being forced to move in that direction. But not the underlying reason. Either the geas wants me to follow him...or it doesn't want Quint to leave unnoticed.

Why? Well, his team has left him alone and we aren't wearing our Pucas. If he leaves without backup there are any number of contestants who would be willing to take him out. If I get too close the reciprocal compulsion might try to make me do something to him or even him do something to me. If I don't at least act like it's working on me though, that's its own brand of trouble.

Shit! Now Nord's staring at me. His next move will be to ask me where the hell I think I'm going and then he'll see Quint. If he sees Quint leaving by himself, he will absolutely send someone or someones from our team to kill him and take the Omada out of the Hunts.

Stop it, Väst! She scolded herself. Put together a plan of

action. Quint is distressed beyond his breaking point. Who wouldn't be? Clearly he'd been in love with the human female. Elle, she reminded herself. The mortal had a name and there is no reason to be disrespectful, or jealous, of the deceased. Quint had watched the girl die in his arms and had then been blamed for her death. Regardless of what actually happened, he obviously blames himself and is going to continue to do so.

On top of that, only a few minutes ago, Emet, the simulacrum golem, sacrificed himself for Quint when he offered to become the bloodpryce Equivalynt. Which meant Quint lost yet another part of himself. Not even to death though, even worse. To eternal exile in the Five-Hells Realm. As they had so often been reminded here at Hunts School, there are fates worse than death.

Nord was too busy gloating over Quint's loss to realize the full import of the golem's existence. His creation by one of the Omada meant that unlike any other team in Hunts' history, the Omada were not limited by Alberich's Bane on Earth Realm. The Hunts School wards against the use of magyk were apparently a different matter. It was obvious from recent events the school's wards still effectively restricted Omada's magyk.

Conclusion—the Big Bad either doesn't want Quint leaving this building or if he does leave, it wants him to die before he gets wherever he's going. Which means the Big Bad wants Omada to lose. For some presently unknown reason. It's also obvious whoever is behind the geas doesn't know absolutely everything—he, she, they or it had been caught off-guard by the existence of the golem.

Fact One—I can't count on what Quint feels for me and what's left of the geas to reign him in right now. Fact Two—I can't take a chance the reciprocating geas might make him do something to harm himself. Fact Three—I can't let whoever is running the unknown evil empire know their power over me has been negated. There's too much at stake and I don't have enough information to make smart choices. Fact Four—my own contract binding to Släkt will limit me in taking actions which might have a direct negative effect on my team's chances to win the Tyrning.

As she looked she saw Quint was almost to the door.

Väst allowed the geas to make her stumble another few halting steps at an angle toward Quint. That's good, she told herself. If someone's watching it'll help if it looks like I'm trying to fight the compulsion—and losing. She followed up with another few stutter steps before beginning to take slow, regular strides. I can't get too close to him but I can't stop moving in his direction. Luckily, Nord hasn't looked past me yet to see Quint heading out.

After another couple of steps, it came to her what needed doing. I gotta take myself out of the game, buy Quint some time to regroup, and try to keep him safe. Give him a few minutes respite, to remember he is supposed to Seek the Center. He doesn't have to be here now, he only has to show up for Omada's turn at the post-feast ceremony. Whether he does or doesn't, that's on him. I just have to buy him time to make a clear-minded decision.

Dammit! Nord just looked past me and saw Quint leaving alone. Time for fast action, she told herself. But what? I can miss both the feast and the ceremony. All of my Släkt teammates are healthy so we'll have the required four-person minimum. Nord will be presenting our talysman, so I'm not needed for that either.

Keep walking, she reminded herself. Whatever I do it can't look intentional on my part. She looked around, saw Nord and the rest of Släkt were headed toward her, about fifteen steps behind. I can't take a chance on my binding preventing me from involving my team, she decided.

Right, then. What are my other options? She looked ahead as the other teams milled around, waiting for the hall to clear so the banquet tables could be placed. The Archon would allow magyk for the feast setup so it wouldn't take five minutes once all the non-Hunts School Folk cleared the Great Hall.

Got it! Got it!

Damn, I can't believe I'm actually going to do this to myself. Fast, Väst, you need to do it quickly, she told herself as she saw Nord delegate the Släkt's Second and Fifth Primes to hightail it after Quint.

If I'm out of commission, Nord isn't going to be able to take a chance on something happening to even one of our teammates, she told herself. He'll have to call them back from chasing Quint.

Damn, this is going to hurt, she told herself the moment she realized what needed to happen. Lots of pain. Who's the meanest, most foul-tempered, itching-to-fight girl left in the Hunts? Sredina, First Prime of Pleme. Absolutely no question about it. After the Pleme embarrassment with Cassandra, Väst had watched Sredina on several occasions practicing her combat skills. She was, in a word, vilicious—the perfect melding of vicious and malicious. Plus she was mad as hell at herself for not positioning her team better. I'm really not excessively vain and I realize this human form is only temporary, but please, please, please—no permanent damage to my face.

Väst yielded to the impetus of the compulsion and quick-stepped up behind Sredina, before intentionally treading heavily on the girl's left heel. As intended, Sredina's foot came out of her shoe, causing her to stumble. Väst immediately snapped at the Pleme Prime, pitching her voice low so only the two of them could hear. "Watch your step you stupid cow. Everyone knows you totally blew it for your team. If Pleme had even a half-ass First Prime it would make the third term Hunt. But not with your sorry ass fucking things up."

She barely had time to congratulate herself on the successful execution of her plan before Sredina regained her footing, cocked her right arm back, and rocketed a haymaker upward and through Väst's nose. Väst felt more than heard the splintering sound, her last cognitive moment before her head caromed off the marble floor.

CHAPTER TRES

Kati stood silently. As she had for the last half-hour. Impassively observing the labyrinthine drama continuing to unfold in front of the entire Areopagus.

I am Kabila Prime, she reminded herself. My highest duty is to position my squad to win the Tyrning. To make that happen we have to be one of the three teams to make the final Hunt. They agreed to bind their contracts to me, placed their fates within my hands, trusting I would do everything within my power to make Kabila the next Ruling Council.

Technically speaking my obligation is to steer Kabila to a win while "Seeking the Center." An archaic, amorphous concept. Her perspective had always been the "Seeking the Center" proviso should be interpreted more as practical guidance than a hard-cornered theological requirement. Thus far it had meant limiting any wet work, drawing a line at intentionally killing or permanently maiming any of the other contestants. Thus far.

While the Quint-centric rollercoaster of chaos had been careening throughout the entire Areopagus, she alone of the remaining Primes had been dispassionately observing. Observing, triangulating, vectoring, calculating—in any and every manner conceivable—how any of the almost unbelievable twists and turns occasioned by Omada's Child of the Divine Spark might be used to gain an advantage for Kabila.

As Kati checked her personal perimeter she proudly noted Kabila was the only team standing in combat formation. The other four members of Kabila were in a tight defensive position around her. Mashariki, her Fourth Prime and lover, was a half step back off her right shoulder, guarding her six.

The mortal, Omada's replacement Fifth Prime Direction, had obviously been close to falling into shock when his sentence of eternal damnation was announced. Who wouldn't have been? Then boom! There was the over the top spectacle of the Five-Hells portal opening in mid-air. Next, the unimaginable happened—the Lord of Darkness himself stepped through the opening and into the assembly hall. Yep, Veles, the King of Five-Hells himself. In all his freaky ice and fire musculature.

Shit! It'd taken every bit of concentration Kati could muster to keep from screaming like some scared ass toddler, even though she knew Veles wasn't there for her or any of her crew.

Just when she'd thought today's bag of surprises was empty, there'd been more. A simulacrum golem? Really? Holy hell! Someone on Omada has royal-level creationmagyk. Strike that. Once in a generation royal-level creationmagyk. Kati had already dismissed the possibility any unauthorized magyk had been used on the Hunts School campus. Which meant, as improbable as it was, at least one of the Omada had the ability to access their magyk on Earth plane proper. That conclusion had been duly noted and filed in the folder of possible threats to her team.

The fact that someone on Omada was a brilliant tactician was also filed in the danger folder. If Quint had gone to Five-Hells the Omada would have been eliminated since their talysman was branded on his ass. No Quint, no talysman presentation at the post-feast ceremony.

Someone had been smart enough to review the rules and pull out the Equivalynt clause. Kati was just guessing, but she was pretty sure no one had used that clause for many, many Tyrnings.

She subtly brushed her right hand across her crotch. Even though she knew it was there, she still felt the need to double-check. Yes. Strapped snugly up against her junk, crisscrossed tightly with a double thick band of spydersilk was Kabila's talysman, the beaded bag containing corpse dust. Spydersilk had the tensile strength of Alfar steel. Anyone seeking to steal it would have to kill Kati first.

Her thoughts turned to the third Hunt. The Ruling Council would review the talysmen at the conclusion of today's feast. The top three teams would go on to the third term Hunt. Kati's calculations left Kabila solidly in fourth place. The Omada wytch strength was the highest as was the power of their talysman. Släkt was next. As much as she hated to admit it, the Shuzoku's Scabbard of Many Names, received from Morgaine, was going to knock her squad out of the competition. Absent an alteration of the present dynamic, Kabila was going home.

She'd noticed immediately when the mortal started walking toward the exit. The Omada Fifth Prime was leaving the ziggurat by himself, with the Omada talysman branded on his body. Kati felt more than saw Mashariki's twitch moments later, his body requesting permission to go take care of the foolish human. She'd subtly dropped two fingers straight downward, their team's hand command to stand down.

No, she had quickly decided, that would be a foolish play. Let someone else make that mistake. After the whole golem blood-pryce equivalynt scene, the human was the focus of way too many people. Anybody stupid enough to mess with him now stood a good chance of getting caught. Which would mean disqualification. Which also works for Kabila, she reminded herself. Because that team would be out and we would stand a better chance to make the cut.

It was Väst of Släkt who unexpectedly made the next move. Kati initially assumed the girl was moving to eliminate Quint on behalf of her team. But as she watched, she saw Väst deliberately step on Sredina's heel.

The wytch Morgaine had ruined Kita, the Shuzoku Second Prime, mentally and emotionally, effectively turning her into a zombye. Even if the Shuzoku won the Tyrning, Kita would never be able to effectively take her place on the Ruling Council. She had paid a heavy price to earn her team's talysman and was now easily the weakest link in the entire ziggurat. It had been a sloppy, emotional decision for the Suzoku Prime to allow Kita to continue holding their talysman. But there it was, loosely strapped to Kita's back.

NOW! Kati screamed to herself. Worry later about why Väst is intentionally picking a fight to create a diversion. Seize the opportunity. Quick hand gestures to each of her teammates to move into place behind each of the other four Shuzoku, as their entire attention was diverted to watching while Sredina beat the hell out of Väst. Another quick succession of hand signals conveyed Kati's instructions to Mashariki, who nodded his understanding.

Kita, mouth agape, was numbly watching the fracas. Kati quickly flashed a five-signal hand sequence and her team leapt into action. Three of her four teammates gently manipulated three members of the Suzoku two to three steps forward, pushing them even closer to the conflict area. They then giant-stepped backward, effectively blocking Kita from her teammates' view. Mashariki feather-stepped immediately behind Kita while Kati moved behind him, this time blocking the view of Chuusin, the Suzoku Prime Direction. Mashariki silently slit the leather straps crisscrossing Kati's back. As the scabbard began its free-fall, he grabbed it in midair, turned, sidestepped around Kati, and quickly mingled with the thousands of members of the Areopagus as they made their way out of the Great Hall to wait their turn at the Prime Omphalos chamber.

Kati smiled to herself, as she signaled Kaskazini, Magharibi, and Kusini to resume defensive positions around her. There would be time to relax after the Ruling Council named the three Finalists. They only needed four team members present for the Ceremony. Mashariki was smart enough to know he needed to stay well gone until after the HuntsMistress announced her decision.

I'm going to call my interpretation of Amarantos's instruction, "Practically Seeking the Center," Kati decided. Yes, that version of religious philosophy might just help me become Archon for the next three hundred years.

CHAPTER QUATTUOR

Tal felt like he'd been standing at the threshold of the Gas Station Crossing for at least one eternity, maybe as many as a handful. Stacked end to end.

His internal chronograph reported it was probably more like only about five minutes. That can't be right, Tal thought, disputing the accuracy of his Logic Center. I'm a newly minted expert on eternities. It's been at least one eternity since I sat on the Nemeton High gym floor, holding Elle's lifeless body tightly to me. It's been another eternity since Emet chose to be my Equivalynt, paying the bloodpryce for me, after which that monster Veles took him to Five-Hells.

That's incorrect, Logic Center quickly replied. It was only last night Elle was murdered. Emet sacrificed himself for you only about fifteen to twenty minutes ago.

"There's no clarity," Tal whispered to himself. "My entire life has become a tragic blur."

No, it hasn't, Frontal Lobe advised Central Processing. Although that last statement was maudlin as hell, it added. Central Processing touched base with various departments to confirm Frontal Lobe's position. Sensory Imaging checked in as fully operational. Synthesization, however, was experiencing overload failure and was presently off-line.

Makes sense, Tal thought, as he worked his way through the information. My brain is basically now serving the same function as the black box on an airplane. It is continuously recording and retaining raw data but it's waiting for someone to read and interpret the information. Without a set of interpreted conclusions, the data doesn't provide a narrative.

Tal could almost see in his mind's eye the information being keyed into the black and white screen of what for a laptop would be called the "safe startup mode." An overload had occurred and his brain had gone into a shut down survival mode.

Sure he'd felt overloaded before but never anything remotely like what had happened in the last twenty-four hours. Guilt had doggedly, relentlessly pummeled him into submission. Elle was dead. Emet was damned for all eternity. Thea and Pell were no doubt being hounded by the police who wanted information on their murderous son's whereabouts. Without a miracle, the twins were going to grow up with the indelible stain of an older brother who would spend his entire life either as a fugitive or behind maximum security bars.

Tal realized he now knew exactly how a boxer felt when matched against someone he knew was going to pulverize him. From the initial bell, accepting blow after punishing blow, repeatedly being jackhammered until he was forced to retreat to his corner. Once there he was trapped. He first raised his gloved fists in defense, before even that effort became too much and his arms inevitably dropped uselessly to his side.

Besieged, beaten, surely the poor schmucks finally reached the point where they begged their opponents to hit them so hard they had no choice but to drop unconscious to the canvas. Oblivious—even if only for a ten count—to the unmanageable pain of their sentience.

Safe mode startup did allow isolated gray scale images, purged of the color of any emotion. Like images of Väst. Tal's mind flashed to a freeze frame of how genuinely distraught she'd been at what had happened to Emet. It had taken every bit of discipline Tal had to walk by her a few minutes ago. Sometimes he felt like he did when he first saw her in Orientations class on that first day of school. It was as if she'd had a tractor beam or exerted her own unique gravitational force on him. Which was ridiculous. Everyone knew there was no Folk magyk permitted on Hunts School campus.

He'd been able to keep his shit together somehow, so as not to draw undue attention, until after he'd exited the ziggurat. Then he'd begun running. Down the steps. Crying. Around the main building. Sobbing. Running past Fountain Flow. Weeping. Across Grass Green, to the very edge of the Hunts School campus. Dead stop.

Tal understood his mind was exercising a form of "fight or flight" in an attempt to save itself from permanent damage. He'd been desperately trying to outrun his internal mental dialogue about the consequences of his decisions to date and the certain consequences of the present important decision. With every step he'd felt the branded talysman burning on his hip, reminding him Omada would be out of the Hunts if he left now. Burning through his skin as if to remind him his leaving meant he was probably sentencing the known universe to three hundred years of Släkt rule.

Was leaving selfish? Or was leaving actually the right decision for his family, and his friends, both here and on Earth plane proper? Tal knew if he took one more step, if he stepped across the Gas Station threshold, it meant he'd made the decision to give up.

He did.

CHAPTER QUINQUE

Notos stood at the edge of the meticulously manicured Grass Grow. His next step would take him into what appeared to be endless rows of waist-high cotton. He knew that bucolic field wasn't where he would end up. He and the team had been through this when they'd gone to Quint's house the first time. When he'd almost busted himself out by telling the Omada he'd smelled the Crestfallyn. The experience had repeated last night when everyone had come this way for the Hunts School field trip.

Notos knew the drill. Right before stepping off of Grass Grow, a wall of the Gas Station Crossing would materialize. In that wall would be a door, framed up like it was some tired old badly in need of a coat of primer back door out of a random deserted gas station. But today? Nothing.

What in Five-Hells is going on? He'd tried to step forward off of Grass Grow five times thus far and each time he'd ended up only taking a giant step sideways. Not only was there no doorway, it was physically impossible for him to step off of the Hunts School property. As an experiment he tried sticking his hand across the line. Nope. No part of him could even cross the air space between Hunts School and Earth Realm proper.

Notos took a step back. If there's one constructive thing I've learned from that idiot mortal, it's to stop, then think my way around any problem. There's something different going on with Quint this time.

Notos reviewed the facts. I did what Borras instructed me to do. I gave Quint plenty of space, he had no idea I was stalking him. As he crossed Grass Grow I started closing the distance between us. Then right as he disappeared I started running. In case it was important for me to be close enough to count as being "with" him. I was only maybe fifteen feet behind him when he went through the door and now there isn't a door for me.

Wait, rewind it. Quit assuming things happened, he told himself. Quint did step off of Grass Grow. Quint did disappear. I assumed there was a doorway like the other times but I didn't actually see a door today. That's right. No Gas Station Crossing wall, no door. It's almost as if he didn't go into the Gas Station Crossing. But where the hell else would he go?

CHAPTER SEX

In Tal's admittedly limited experience, the Sol's Gas Station Ladies' Room had never looked even remotely like the present tableau. He was standing in the epicenter of a pool of light about six feet in circumference. Tal instinctively looked upward to ascertain the light's source. It emanated from a single naked incandescent bulb, which was apparently operated by a well worn, raggedy-ass on/off pull string dangling about a foot above his head. He knew it wasn't really an incandescent bulb, that it was magyked to look like one. The light hurt his eyes exactly the same though. Semi-blinded, Tal squeezed his eyes closed for a couple of seconds then looked downward so that when he opened them he could hopefully engage in a more comprehensive site assessment.

A sea of shadows encompassed the puddle of light. Or maybe it's all one giant amoeba shadow with a doughnut hole of light in the middle, he thought. Or it could be that shadows themselves are actually like a coral reef, having billions of individuals with separate shadow lifetimes of undetermined duration but together comprising a humongous life form. It's possible that shadows die and are resurrected every time a light switch is flipped on and off. Is there a name for a group of shadows? Never heard of one, Tal concluded. Might as well coin one while I wait for my eyes to finish adjusting. Gang of shadows? Swirl of shades? A susurrus, he decided. A susurrus of shadows.

That might not be a perfect name for all shadow groups, but it fit perfectly for the present company. Tal heard murmuring from dozens, maybe hundreds of voices. Did shadows have voices? Whoever or whatever was talking was speaking so softly he couldn't identify exactly how many different voices he was hearing much less what was being said.

Tal took a small step forward and slowly, cautiously slid his left hand outside the light's zone of influence. Nothing bad happened so he stepped back, stood on his tiptoes, reached up and pulled the pull chain. The light vanished.

Smooth move you doofus. Now you can't see anything at all. As soon as his eyes readjusted, Tal looked up. His mouth fell open. He couldn't help it. A jaw-drop was the only acceptable response to what he saw. Central Processing issued a directive for the lower jaw to close.

Suspended high in the sky, hundreds of feet above the now darkened light bulb, was a ginormous horizontal stain glass window. Well, because of its horizontal orientation it might more technically qualify as a stained glass ceiling. The stain glass design stretched hundreds of feet in each direction. The construction was backlit by about a squillion stars.

The ceiling masterpiece was configured in a rose window design, with north, south, east, and west designated in block letters, and a huge white "C" in the middle of a center circle of red. The light bulb hung suspended in the air, its cord attached to nothing at the other end but located directly below the "C."

While Tal's mind continued to process the visual information, he looked down. He was standing in the atramentous center of an expansive sand garden. At first glance, except for the red center, it appeared the sand sculpture floor mirrored the stain glass ceiling.

As Tal continued looking down it seemed the entire design rotated almost imperceptibly the smallest tick of a tick in a clockwise direction. Familiar, he told himself. This floor is familiar. How can a ridiculously large sand floor in the middle of absolutely nowhere seem familiar, he asked himself.

When his eyes finished adjusting to the minimal amount of refracted starlight Tal observed there were hundreds of indistinct figures, completely encircling him, immediately outside the parameters of the sandy floor. Shadow figures. They all seemed to be whispering to themselves while they busily worked. It was them—they were making the indeterminate shadow noises he'd been hearing.

What were they? Maybe who were they, was a better question. What were they doing? What were they saying? One question was quickly answered, they were weaving. Every one of the shadows was warping and wefting on their own separate tapestry. He quickly scanned a half dozen of the weavings and saw the figures were consistently repeating a basic design. Each of the designs was only minutely different from its neighbors and each of the designs was an echo of the floor upon which he stood.

Familiar? He asked himself again. Yes it is, his brain quickly replied. The floor, the tapestries, they're all kalachakras. The shadow figures were all working on time wheels.

They're not just any old kalachakras, he noted. They're working on my kalachakra. The one Mertin Wilt showed me at Nemeton High. The same kalachakra on the tawdry beat to shit Wheel of Fortune in Atlantis. Tal looked down at the floor again for confirmation. Yes, exactly. The time wheel I'm standing on at this precise moment.

Tal squinted, looking at several of the tapestries just a bit farther away. His initial assessment, that there were only small differences was incorrect. Some of the tapestries were radically different, some had thick color columns in the same places where others had thin ones. Some of the works had large black centers, while in others the center was a tiny black pinprick. Others had wide areas of totally white yarn woven into the design.

His brain rolled out another piece of freshly quantified data. The shadow figures, they're all talking in my voice. Tal strained to hear, to sort the indistinct amalgam into specific, individual strands. That one over there is Me, talking about whether I'm going to have a second helping of chicken spaghetti for dinner. That's Me over there weaving tears because my ass is raw, my diaper is wet, and I had no other way at the time to communicate with my mom. All the way over there, that one is Me musing out loud about calling Elle to get her input before I accept a full ride Presidential Scholarship to Hendrix based on the conclusions reached in my award winning nonverbal communication study.

Tal continued scanning. There were innumerable other Hims. One Him was muttering about dusting his clothes off and trying to make it back to the highway to get back to Nemeton High for his belated lunch date with Elle. A few hundred yards to Tal's left there was another Me/Him shadow Tal giving a eulogy at Pell's funeral. On and on and on. Where am I, Tal thought? Why am I here?

A voice chimed a response to his unspoken questions, a voice much more the notes of a song than spoken words. "You should know where you are, Taliesin. The Lailoken specifically questioned you about this place."

"HOLY CRAP!" Tal hollered. If it is literally possible to jump out of your skin I would have done it right then, Tal thought. Even though the voice was warm and not the least bit threatening. A female voice? Yes. Young? Not particularly. Old? Definitely not old. Ageless? Yes, check that box. And familiar, he added. On it, he heard his data processing neurons respond, as they kicked information retrieval into overdrive.

"Hello?" Great, his voice was now taking the opportunity to turn quivering traitor on him. "Sorry about the cursing, ma'am. I was looking for the Gas Station Crossing Ladies' Restroom and I, umm, I seem to have taken a wrong turn."

"Did you? Are you sure which turn is correct, which is incorrect? It seems that decision and its resulting conclusion is entirely your call. It was you who asked for and received my permission to sit in the Siege Perilous," the voice replied.

Okay, the unembodied wraith in the darkness sounds sympathetic, Tal decided. Or was it pitying? There's a difference, isn't there, he asked himself. Between sympathy and pity.

"Yes," the voice again answered his unspoken question. "There is a material difference between sympathy and pity."

Great, another mind-reader has made an entrance. Whoa, back it up a few verses. Lailoken? Did whoever is out there say Myrddin told me about this place? And what's up with that whole me asking to sit in the "Siege Perilous" comment?

The voice continued, "Seek the Center, Taliesin. Worlds depend upon you."

"You know, you're not the first person, well first something, to tell me that. A whack job out of order Gas Pump first told me that a couple of months back.

"Listen whoever it is I'm talking to, I'm really going to need a little bit more direction," Tal said, waving his hands frenetically to include every bit of the bizzarity that encompassed him round. "Because all of this, this is some seriously freaky shit."

"If you wish to become the hero of your own Journey, Taliesin, you must first choose to be the hero of someone else's." With that Tal saw, in his peripheral vision, a hand grasp upward out of the darkness. Tal jumped sidewise, about a half a split-second after the precise moment his brain conclusively determined the hand was not his own. The hand reached overhead, pulled the chain one time, and absolute darkness overtook him.

CHAPTER SEPTEM

"Five Hells!" Notos exclaimed, leap-falling backward. That's different, he told himself, as he sat on his ass watching as wisps of the Gas Station Crossing appeared and then joined their nearest brethren, finally coalescing into a solid structure. Complete with the previously expected hard-worn back door.

Something has changed, Notos concluded. Wherever Quint was—or wasn't—he's now in the Crossing. Or he's entered it and moved on through to Earth plane proper. Either way, as his team member, I get to go to him.

Notos picked himself, up, brushing grass off the seat of his pants before grasping the doorknob. Which didn't turn. Not a bit. He then pulled. Nope. Pushing was next. Nada. He even tried propping his right leg up on the doorframe and twisting. Still nothing. With apologies to Sol he kicked the holy shit out of the door. Repeatedly. The cumulative net result was that he was pretty sure he might have stress-fractured his right big toe.

What gives?

The simple fact I can even see the gateway door means Alberich's Bane still isn't operative against the Omada. Something very unusual is going on with that damn mortal. I need to figure this out. Time is not in our favor.

Stay or go? That's the immediate question. I'm sure Borras would like to have a report and our team currently only has three present for the post-feast Ceremony. Whether we have enough members for the Ceremony is immaterial, he finally decided. Quint bears the talysman. Without him the Omada is out of the Hunts competition and I'm heading home without finding a way to save my mother. Stay it is then. Until Quint either returns or Borras comes to give me the bad news.

CHAPTER OCTO

Kati and the Kabila sat at their place of honor at one of the Finalist feast tables. Occurring only once every three centuries, the Tyrning Imbolc Feast honored both the arrival of spring as well as the second-term winnowing preceding the third Hunt. The feast setup had been the same for tens of thousands of years. The Ruling Council, together with their significant others, sat at a head table on a raised dais. Arranged in a semi-circle were the five Finalists tables. Their tables were also on risers, but not as high as the head table. Today, for the first time in Hunts School history there would have been six Finalist team tables. Yesterday's concession and subsequent departure of the Allyu had restored the customary status quo.

Behind the Finalists' tables and arrayed in an expanding fan-shaped design were the remaining Feast invitees. Even though the thousands of regular members of the Areopagus had used the Prime Omphalos to return to their home planes following the earlier convocation, the number of Feast attendees was still staggering. The Archon had magyked in tables, seats, and place settings for the thousands of Hunts School students, together with the even larger number of faculty members, support staff, and grounds crew. The cafeteria staff had been working nonstop for well over a week preparing the food.

Principal Chiron, the HuntsMistress, and the rest of the Hunts professors were seated at a center table sited immediately behind the Finalists.

As Kati quickly detailed the layout, two matters caught her attention. First, there was a six-guard detail standing at full attention just inside the entryway. Second, there were only three students seated at the Omada table. They're still missing their Second and Fifth Primes, she mentally noted.

Kabila's table was dead center in front of the head table. Omada was at the table farthest to her left. The two Omada females looked anxious. Borras, Omada Prime, was impossible to read. As gifted a leader as Kentro had been, Väst of Slåkt may have done Omada a huge favor when she took him out of the game. Something still doesn't add up about the way that whole Kentro thing went down, Kati mused. Stay on task, she demanded of herself. No question it was a net positive that Omada ended up with the mortal as its new Fifth Prime. Well, no question until the events of this morning.

Per her established possible threat assessment protocol, Kati's mind immediately began addressing the multitude of possibilities. She glanced quickly to the Slåkt table. It was all the way to the right far end of the Finalist tables. Smart move by the Ruling Council to seat them as far from Omada as possible.

All four able-bodied Slåkt were present. Väst, their fifth member, had been stretchered to the infirmary following the beat-down she'd received from Sredina. The Slåkt body language combined with their inane banter evidenced extreme relaxation. Makes sense, Kati thought. They have the required minimum of four present for the Ceremony and their talysman is powerful enough for a guaranteed ticket to the last Hunt.

Even though Nord wouldn't hesitate to kill the munedan, he had obviously decided now was not the best time or place. Kati moved her gaze to her immediate right, to the table between Kabila and Slåkt. The Pleme. They'd met Cassandra, a powerful, high-points wytch but failed to garner a talysman from her. Without divine intervention they were headed home. Like Slåkt, their body language was relaxed. It was a different kind of relaxed than the Slåkt though. It was the slump-shouldered, forced conversation relaxed of disappointed but resigned. Nope, Kati decided. Pleme isn't the reason the two Omada members aren't here.

Which leaves Shuzoku as the only possible agents of nefariousity. Well, besides me. They were seated to her immediate left. One quick peripheral glance told Kati everything she needed to know. Shuzoku was down and out for the count. There had been a few minutes of frenzied action when Sredina realized their talysman had been gone. Then there was yelling and screaming. Not at each other but at the other teams accusing them of theft and major rule violation. Then total meltdown as Chuusin realized he'd been totally played and he had screwed up in the biggest way imaginable.

No, Shuzoku had nothing to do with Omada's predicament. They weren't up to anything, not even feasting. Every serving salver on their table remained heaped with the same amount of delicacies as when they were first delivered. The wine decanters were all still brimming. All of the dining cutlery remained in its original place-setting configuration, surrounding the solid gold chargers that were set beneath the spotlessly shined china plates. The Shuzoku were sitting quietly at their table, a point of stillness within the riotous tempest that was the Imbolc Feast. Their heads were lowered to their chests and it looked to Kati like they were holding each other's hands under the draped table.

I did that to them, she thought, pulling her gaze back to the three members of her team sitting with her. Hey, you. Pity has no place in the Tyrning equation. It was either them or us, she confirmed to herself. I am Kabila Prime and it is my contractual obligation to do everything I can to win this Tyrning. While Seeking the Center. Practically, or course.

Mashariki was still gone, disposing of the stolen Shuzoku talysman. He was savvy enough to know he shouldn't be seen until after the Ruling Council confirmed the three teams that would compete in the final Hunt. I'd better not see him until Third Hunt Orientation class. Class was scheduled to start an hour post-Ceremony. By then it wouldn't matter if there were any hard questions asked of Kabila.

Marid, Seneschal of the Ruling Council, stood, took his ceremonial staff, and banged the dais floor three times. "The

Imbolc Feast is concluded," he intoned in a ritualistic cadence, his voice magykally amplified throughout the now tomb-quiet Great Hall. "The second term Hunt was a Wytch Hunt. Pursuant to the Hunts Rules governing that type of Hunt, the Ruling Council makes the final decision concerning weighting of wytches and talysmen. It falls to us then to determine the three teams that will advance to the final Hunt. We shall stand in recess for thirty-minutes, after which the five remaining teams will make their presentations."

CHAPTER NOVEM

Blackness…

Again.

Dammit.

But this time instead of shadow voices I hear…

Skittering?

At least my head doesn't feel like its ground zero for a Manhattan Project detonation. Tal tentatively stretched his arms outward, first to the front, then peripherally. Nothing. Nothing to assist in orienting him where he was in the Ladies' Room. Or if he was even in the Ladies' Room.

The noise, however, isn't skittering. Chittering, maybe? That's it, isn't it? It's chittering. No, that's not quite right, either, he decided.

If it's not chittering, what is it? Tal took a cautious baby-step shuffle forward with his left foot, before again fanning his arms out to the sides. No toilet. No stall walls. Nothing.

I got it!

The noise.

It's chattering.

Crap! That's not it either.

Okay, Tal, just chill. You're letting your fear of the dark freak you out. Run through the Omada deductive reasoning drill. He cocked his head to his left and focused. It's more metallic than organic. Definitely not an animal sound. Thank goodness.

Tal then moved his head to the right, listening that way. The noises had a machine-like repetition, in both frequency and duration.

Clattering, maybe? That's it, he resolved, that's what it is…the noise is clattering.

Next issue. Which would normally be which way to the light switch by the damn door. Not today, he told himself. Nope. Today the next question is…

Do I really want to know what kind of machine is clattering in a women's restroom?

"Damn it," Tal yelled, as he stubbed his right foot on something hard. And immoveable. He baby-stepped his way forward, cautiously stretching his hands out until he could touch whatever the thing was. Don't worry, he told himself. It's not going to chew your fingers off. Well, I'm pretty sure, it's not going to chew my fingers off. He slowly felt all around the thing.

What the hell? A recliner? Really? Who puts a recliner in the middle of a pitch-black girls' bathroom? And what happened to that cute little decorative curio table with the seasonal potpourri?

Maybe it's some type of delaying tactic, Tal thought. If it was at all possible he would suspect a certain mouthy little Air Hose was behind the present shenanigans. The Gas Station Crossing is Sol's avatar, placed to assist the Hunts School. Which means it's a piece of him. "Sol, look I don't want to be disrespectful but I'm only here for a quick minute. Show me the way to the door and I'll be out of your hair. Won't ever bother you again. Promise."

There was no response, not even any change in the clattering. Tal started to feel his way around the recliner. "If anybody thinks I'll change my mind because they made me cool my heels for awhile in the girls' powder room, that's not happening. Just saying." Might as well sit while I wait, he decided as he eased into the chair. I'll just sit here until my eyes finally get used to the dark and I can see which way to the door.

CHAPTER DECEM

One of Väst's eyes was completely boycotting opening and the other was only amenable to halfway. "Well, hello again, Infirmary…" Väst mumbled from her swollen lips as she glanced around. Hell, I can't even understand myself. This must be what collagen lip plumping gone wild feels like, she decided.

"She's waking up," a voice announced.

"Good," another voice stated before its corresponding face suddenly occupied the entirety of Väst's limited field of vision.

"I know you—you're the Chief Physick." The out of focus balloon face nodded up and down. "You've juiced me up with human painkiller, haven't you?" Another nod.

"Yes," the Chief Physick replied. "As you know, we are not permitted to utilize magykal intervention until after the results of the present Hunt are announced."

"Got it," Väst confirmed. "So what's with giving me the blubber lips, bub?" she asked. "I would like my factory issued set back, please."

For a split second the Chief Physick actually grinned. The smile was quickly replaced with the usual and customary neutral but solicitous face of medical health care professionals throughout the known universe. "Släkt Fifth Prime, in addition to a broken nose and three cracked ribs, you also received substantial soft tissue damage to your face. Additionally, you almost certainly sustained a major concussion. As the Hunt is not yet concluded, the prudent course of treatment would have been to place you into a medically induced coma until we were able to magykally heal you."

"Let me guess. The Släkt Prime Direction put the kibosh on that plan."

"Yes, we received a note to use whatever measures get you back to non-maimed status the fastest. Regardless of whether it means you suffer unnecessary pain and physical damage."

"The note was from my Prime Direction?" Väst guessed.

"Yes. He wanted to make sure you would be in attendance for the post-feast class."

"Without even knowing whether we made the cut for the third Hunt or not," Väst confirmed.

The Chief Physick nodded, before adding, "The excessive plumping of your lips is an unavoidable side effect of the balm used to minimize the most serious tissue damage. The swelling will only last a few hours. We have chosen to wait until the last minute possible before attempting to nonmagykally repair your other injuries. Even with anesthesia, the pain…"

"Do it," Väst demanded. "I'm not getting you and your staff involved in this. That bastard may end up as the next Archon and there's no telling what he might do to you if he finds out you didn't follow his orders."

"Acting Fourth Prime, if we're going to make sure you're awake in time for class we can't give you a general anesthetic. The pain will be…"

"Do it, Chief," she said, interrupting him. Then groaning as she rolled sideways in the bed, to look at the floor. "I'll need my clothes after you're done. Where are they?"

The Chief Physick paused before answering. "I will see that a blood free set is here when we finish treating you. We haven't had sufficient time to assess the severity of the blows to your head. Even when we get to do magykal intervention, it may not be safe…"

"When you got the note from my Prime, you replied explaining the severity of my injuries, didn't you?"

The Chief nodded.

"You received a response back from him?"

The Chief nodded again.

"Well?" Väst asked.

The Chief Physick paused before continuing. "I believe the exact words of his reply note were, 'I don't give a shit what happens to her long term. You'd better have that sow upright and in class or you and your staff can be my special project next term'."

"Seems like neither of us has a choice in the matter, then."

The Chief Physick bowed slightly. "If you will excuse me, I will go assemble the surgical instruments necessary to effectuate the repairs." With that he walked toward the outer door.

When Väst was certain she was alone, she gave herself permission to cry. For just a minute.

CHAPTER UNDECIM

As Tal impatiently waited, his left hand grazed the top of a table. He felt around a bit and ended up touching what was clearly a lamp base. Great, he thought, another single light bulb scenario. Working his fingers up the lamp he found the switch, squeezed his eyes closed, and pushed the switch.

The light this time was low-level. As his eyes adjusted, the first thing he noticed was there was another recliner on the other side of the table. No occupant, just a twin to his chair. As he turned his head back to the front, he noticed there was now a second light source.

The Ladies' Room usually left him typewritten notes, reminding him to wash his hands or turn off the overhead light. This time the message was markedly different, both in medium and substance. On the door itself was a small neon sign, like a building code mandated type of sign, the kind that stayed lit even when all of the power went out. The sign, in vivid red neon, advised—"EXIT ONLY."

It wasn't until his pupils finally shrank to their proper aperture setting that Tal could finally see the source of the clattering. There were hundreds—check that, at a minimum there were hundreds—of old-timey ticker tape machines. He'd realized on his previous trips that the interior size of the bathroom didn't necessarily correlate to the exterior dimensions of the Gas Station but this visit took that disconnect to a whole new level.

There may actually have been thousands of the machines. The kind with the little glass bubble on top. Each of the machines stood atop its own separate waist-high stand, with scarcely any navigable distance between each of the units. All of the devices were spewing printed tape ribbons at ninety to nothing, with the serpentine tapes curling around the foot of their respective stand.

Tal squinted to get a better look at the machine closest to him. Etched into the wooden base of the machine itself were the words, "Instrument Furnished By The Shambala Telegraph Co." Immediately below those words was a small, green-tarnished brass plaque. There were only two words inscribed on that plaque—"Taliesin Smith."

Okay, this place is always a mite outré but this is taking freaky weird to a whole new level. As the talysman branded into his buttock pulsed pain, Tal told himself not to freak out. This is nowhere near the weirdest thing that's happened to you in the last few months. Maybe even the last ten minutes, he decided.

Tal took a moment to finish a three hundred and sixty degree assessment of what had always been a nicely appointed washroom. The machine stands were different colors. Not multi-colored like a rainbow, each stand was one solid color. Reds, yellows, greens, blues, of every hue and gradient seemed to be represented. Machines of the same color were grouped together in patterns. The stands of the hundred or so machines in a circle closest to the center—to the two recliners—were all jet black.

Tal's far right peripheral vision reported a slight movement. He quickly turned his head that way. His left peripheral receptors reported motion from that side of the room. As he rapidly moved his head left and right it seemed as if all of the machines, except the ones on black stands, were moving in an almost imperceptible clockwise direction.

Let it go, Tal, he told himself. You're done with this ridiculousness. Remember Elle? Remember Emet?

There's the door. What the hell difference does it make if it's an "EXIT ONLY" door now? That's what you want. A one-way ticket back to your old life. Whatever's left of it that you can salvage, that is. All you have to do is jump up out of this chair and walk through that door.

You're exactly right, he replied to himself, as he pushed his recliner to an upright position and began to stand…

CHAPTER DUODECIM

The entire crowd grew silent and resumed their seats as they saw the Seneschal of the Ruling Council stand. He pounded his staff on the floor. Once, twice, three times. "Five teams remain in the Hunts competition. They are Kabila, Omada, Pleme, Släkt, and Shuzoku. The second semester Hunt was a Wytch Hunt. Pursuant to the Hunts Rules, the Ruling Council is given the authority in Wytch Hunts to rank the team results. The Släkt representative will step forth at this time to provide an account of Släkt's Hunt accomplishments."

CHAPTER TREDECIM

"HOLY CRAP! MY EYES!"

"BLOODY HELL! MY EYES!"

Tal screamed and instinctively crossed his arms in front of his eyes in a failed attempt to shield them against the unexpected fireworks-bright blinding light. In that same instant Hearing processed some additional aural data. What's up with that? Tal wondered. I only yelled, 'Holy crap! My eyes!" Does the Ladies' Room now have an automatic American-British echo module?

With his eyes squeezed tightly closed, Tal now heard—over the constant clattering—an additional sound. Rustling. Coming from his immediate left. From the direction of the other recliner. Funny, last time I looked I was the only living being in this bathroom.

"Um, well, hello?" a deep, mellifluous male voice asked.

I'm not sure if its British or some other European accent, Tal decided. Whoever is now in this bathroom with me is definitely not from around these parts. He sounds...urbane, Hearing suggested. Yes, that's a good description.

There was a moment's silence before the owner of the urbane voice spoke again. "Okay, good, now I can at least see some details..."

Next, Tal heard, almost as one, a series of short staccato

sentences.

> "ARE YOU KIDDING ME?
> "YOU?
> "IT'S YOU?
> "ACTUALLY, THAT SHOULD HAVE BEEN, 'IT WAS YOU?'
> "HOW COULD I HAVE BEEN SO DENSE?
> "OF COURSE IT WOULD HAVE BEEN YOU."

As his unknown bathroom companion took a moment to catch his breath, Tal kept rubbing his eyes, trying to get the sparks to stop arcing all the way across his vision. "Umm, excuse me, Mr. Stranger Danger. I'm not trying to be rude but can you tell me— WHY YOU'RE SCREAMING AT ME AND WHY THE HELL YOU JUST FLASH GRENADED ME?" Tal demanded, his voice rising from both pain and frustration. He gave up on trying to see and closed his eyes to focus on listening.

"Sorry about that," the now recomposed and still very mellifluous urbane voice said apologetically. "Sorry. Really. The Stytch isn't in control of any aspect of the tyme-transition. Sometimes, like just now, the whole supernova-type lightshow thing happens. Other times there are no extraordinary visual clues but I do get the mother of all migraine headaches. There have even been some transitions with zero indicators. The shifts then were so subtle it took me a few minutes to realize I'd even been translated into othertyme." There was another brief pause. "Or, as in this case, that I'd been shifted back into realtyme."

Still blind, Tal had to rely on his other senses. His voice is familiar, Tal thought. No, not the voice itself, it's the speech cadence. Like a stranger is using the same syntax and syllable emphasis of someone I know well.

His companion continued, hesitating often, as though searching for words or about to be overwhelmed by emotion. "Please excuse my outburst. You'll have to forgive me for being surprised. I had long ago lost faith...not in Her but in myself... in my own ability to come to a place where I could forgive myself... to allow myself to ever feel that way again. I was taken

48

off guard when my time to choose finally came…and despite all my assurances to countless others over the centuries that it really was my decision to stay or to go…

"Now…I'm here in this place…and I can't believe it was you…that you would be…I mean, it never entered my mind that… well, clearly I should have seen it… and I'm not sure why I'm surprised it was you. Just goes to show that even after all of these centuries the UnFading One remains a total mystery to me."

Cryptic much? Tal thought. I am totally clueless about what this guy is babbling about.

After a couple of heartbeats, the stranger added. "Your eyes should have adjusted by now, Taliesin, if you'd like to try again."

Okay, the familiar sounding stranger knows my real name, Tal thought quickly, as he slowly, carefully opened his eyes. As the black dots ceased tangoing across his vision, he observed the voice belonged to a young man, who was now comfortably seated in the other, previously empty, recliner.

The guy appeared to be in his late twenties. He was dressed formally, as if he was going to a black tie dinner or some toney charitable gala. Tal noted the dude's sharply creased black tuxedo pants, white French cuff shirt with black onyx buttons and matching cufflinks. The jacket was an always in style notch-collar black satin. The man also had a handkerchief, which he was using to wipe moisture from each of his eyes. Lots of moisture, Tal thought. Either he's bad allergic to naugahyde recliners or we're talking substantial tears.

The mystery continues, Tal thought. Total stranger with familiar speech patterns who knows my real name. He does have a really great voice though, Tal thought. With a voice like that the boy could probably sing opera. Or do the "mind the gap" messages for the London Metro. Maybe both. Focus, Tal, he told himself.

Since the man was now sitting quietly with his arms folded, Tal took the opportunity for a second assessment. His first thought was the man was jaw-dropping handsome. A full head of luxuriant but closely cropped dark blonde hair, detailed with sun-bleached highlights. Steel-gray eyes, that even though they were red from crying, nevertheless exposed a soulful clarity well beyond anyone Tal had ever met. Well, almost everyone, he corrected himself. Dude must exfoliate regularly, Tal decided. Even his skin seems radiant.

In a word—beautiful. If it's possible for someone to be ruggedly beautiful. It was as if a three-D printer from a studio art department had woven him out of the fabric of every heroic legend. A "man's man but women know instantly he is fully conversant with his emotional self" handsome. Like Robert Redford. Not when he wore the guise of the insouciant devil may care Sundance Kid. No, this guy is the heir of the intrinsically suave young Hubble Gardiner from "The Way We Were."

Who is he? Tal wondered. How did he just appear? Alberich's Bane prevents Folk from utilizing their magyk on Earth plane proper. I realize we're in the Gas Station Crossing but none of the Folk except the Omada have any juice in here. And even then only if I'm on this plane with them.

Which reminds me, now that I'm making my list of questions. What's up with the hundreds of ticker tape machines? Emet could have probably parsed the answer out for me in no time.

Five-Hells! Emet's gone, Tal remembered, as he felt himself starting to slide once more down into the despair crater. And Elle...

Tal's reverie was interrupted when the man began speaking again. "Thank you for allowing me a few moments to compose myself," he said, as he finished daubing his eyes, before carefully folding his handkerchief, and laying it on the table between them. "It's been a very long time since I've been caught off guard like this."

The stranger paused a moment before smiling broadly. Tal could tell the smile was merely a forced overlay for whatever sadness was threatening to overwhelm the guy. "I, of course, had no way to know this would occur now nor that you would be him." The man reached over, picked his handkerchief up off the chair's arm and wiped several fresh tears from each eye.

I feel sorry for the guy, Tal thought. Unless he turns out

to be some Robert Redford handsome psychopathic killer with mad social skills. If that's the case, then empathy is out the door. Empathy and me, he added. The poor guy's obviously struggling with something though.

"You see that's the thing about othertyme. Well, you don't see now but you will have seen by the very first time we meet each other. I've been the Stytch for more than a handful of centuries of realtyme. I honestly can't tell you how many hundreds of times Amarantos has sent me othertyme."

The boy is definitely cray but at this point in time doesn't appear Hannibal Lectorish, Tal thought, as the man took a breath in his soliloquy. And what's a Stytch?

The young man continued. "Time, realtyme to you and me, is referred to as the fourth dimension by the Children of Dust. Human physicists believe there are eleven possible dimensions. Of course, with compatification in and around the higher dimensions, everything above time is subatomic in size. But mortals don't understand the intricacies of magyk or the existence of its many additional dimensions."

The dude took a moment to shake his head. "Sorry, about the digression. It's been a long day. Actually it's been a long night, which might still be night or which I guess could be day. Only Amarantos fully understands othertyme. Even the Principes are bound to the linear plane of realtyme.

"Anyway, the two tymes have only a tenuous relationship one to the other. Which is not to say there aren't infinite intersections in the interstices between them. It's because realtyme has a linear timeline and othertyme doesn't. But you know that. Well, you don't know that yet, but you will."

Tal had heard enough to realize the male version of Helen of Troy seemed to be bat guano crazy. Unhinged is unhinged, he reminded himself. A turn toward violence is always a possibility. Get yourself to a safe defensive place, he decided, as he slowly pressed his forearms against the padded arms of his chair and began standing up.

"I didn't realize she would be the one who would help me to find my way to finally forgive myself…and, of course, I had zero reason to believe you were…" The stranger stopped and looked squarely at Tal. "You might as well sit back down, Tal. We have much we need to go over before I have to leave and I'm sure you have plenty of questions."

Tal ignored the suggestion and rose the rest of the way to his feet. Who is this guy? he asked himself. Why does he have a voice I know? Might as well take the bull by the horns, he decided. "Excuse me, weird stranger person but I'm going to go ahead and do the whole leaving right now thing. It's why I'm here. I was just heading out," Tal said, pointing to the door, "when you dropped in and blinded me."

The man steepled his fingers in front of his face. "Oh, I see…it's been more than three years for me but for you it's only been, well, actually I'm not sure how long it's been." The man leaned over looking closely at Tal. From his sympathetic look Tal realized that "clueless" must have been writ large across his face.

"I can see you've made your decision. If, for whatever reason, you've decided you need to leave Hunts School, that's your call. Every choice you make has always been yours to make. Every single decision.

"We humans have always misunderstood the concept of destiny. Because of our mortal event horizon, we believe destiny to be the antithesis of free will. It isn't. In the Big Scheme there is no pre-determination, there is no post-rehabilitation. For each and every one of us there is only our unfettered right to make our very own 'in the moment itself' realtyme choice."

The man continued as Tal thought about taking a step toward the door but didn't. "All of the UnFading Spirit's children operate under the same rules, All, without exception." The man paused, his physically still youthful eyes suddenly looking at Tal with hoary-oak ancient wisdom. "I had genuinely hoped you'd moved beyond your desire to throw away every day of your now, Taliesin Smith." With that statement, his unknown companion again motioned to Tal's presently unoccupied chair.

It's him, Tal realized. The blossoming reality of who he was talking to physically wobbled Tal. He didn't so much sit as free-fall backward into his chair.

"Myrddin." Tal uttered the name as soon as his brain resumed coherent operations. Myrddin said those exact words to me the first time I met him, when his physical form was teenage Dr. Mertin Wilt.

What gives, though? Why does he look so different? He doesn't look like any version of Myrddin I've ever seen. To start with, for the first time ever, he's not wearing a single damn shade of purple. Tal leaned forward and peered closely at the man. The dude's eyes were now a normal gray. A striking steel-gray I'll give him that, Tal decided, but definitely not Myrddin's centuries old purple.

"Of course, it's me." Myrddin paused again, confusion now creasing the space between his eyes. Slowly, comprehension caused the vertical line to disappear. "I'm sorry, Tal. I'm a little tyme-addled. This is the first time you've seen me when I am as Amarantos created me." Myrddin paused again, "This trip was the longest I had ever spent in othertyme, almost three years. Actually, I was right in the middle of an extremely important dinner date, and…"

Tal interrupted him. "That can't be right. We've seen each other any number of times this school year. I mean, come on, the first time we met was at Nemeton High, less than six months ago."

"I told you othertyme is not tethered to the present."

Tal leaned forward in his chair. "Oh, I get it. You were on one of your time missions and Amarantos called you back to make me change my mind about quitting the Hunts."

"No," Myrddin replied. "That's not at all what happened. You have no idea…"

"You can save your breath. My mind is made up and no amount of guilt-laying by you or Amarantos is going to make me change my mind."

"I wasn't recalled here to…"

"I appreciate you're only doing as you're told, but I…"

"Stop talking!" Myrddin commanded. The authority in the Traveler's voice elicited immediate compliance from Tal. "Now sit back, Taliesin. Take a deep breath." Tal did as commanded.

After he saw that Tal was settled, Myrddin continued. "First, and most importantly, Amarantos doesn't force anyone to be the Stytch. I asked to be the Traveler. That was my choice, my decision. There has never been, nor will there ever be, a situation in which Amarantos interferes with any of her children's exercise of Free Will. Never. It's not going to happen."

"That's not true," Tal answered, his voice rising. "There has been any number of instances…"

"You are wrong," Myrddin calmly replied. "I presume you want proof. I can give it to you." Tal watched as Myrddin pointed. "There's the door," Myrddin said. "You can use it whenever you wish."

Tal looked up, past the rows and rows of ticker tape machines, each busily killing trees one extremely narrow strip of paper at a time, to the door that now had a sign reading, "EXIT ONLY." "What gives with that, anyway? Why does it now say that?" Tal asked Myrddin, motioning with his thumb to the sign.

"Before I can answer, you'll have to tell me what you see," Myrddin responded softly.

Okay, even for Myrddin that's a little weird. "Umm, same as you, I'm sure. It's a bathroom door with a neon sign that reads 'EXIT ONLY'," Tal replied.

Myrddin grinned in response. "Interesting. That's not what I see. I see a sign that says, 'ENTRANCE ONLY'."

Tal paused several beats to give his deductive reasoning assets an opportunity to deliver. They finally reported back that they had zilch. "What? How is that even possible?"

"The best way to answer you is with a series of questions."

The Socratic method, Tal thought. Damn I hate the Socratic method.

Myrddin continued. "Tell me, is the fact there is a door over there with an 'Exit Only' sign intimidating or coercing you, in any manner, to make you exit through the door?"

"Seems like a silly question, but that's a hard no."

"A one-eighty of the same question, then. Does the existence of that door make you feel pressured to turn around and go back out toward Hunts School?"

"Again, no." If people are going to be administering pop quizzes in his Ladies' Restroom, Sol really needs to add a Tylenol dispenser, Tal thought.

"Is the door's presence in any manner twisting your arm to make you sit in that chair and have this conversation with me?"

"Of course not," Tal replied. That was unnecessarily snippish, Central Processing informed Speech.

"Last question, which will complete the logic circuit. Is the mere fact there is a door over there with an 'Exit Only' sign on it making you take any action of any nature?"

"That's a negative," Tal replied. Speech proudly noted there was no snippitude in his last response.

"Well and good then," Myrddin gently replied. "Now, use that vaunted gigantic intellect. Tell me why the door has a different message for each of us."

This time Tal scrunched his eyes together in the universal facial expression of concentration. He'd never been sure if that particular muscle configuration actually helped with data analysis but he'd decided it couldn't hurt. Finally, the answer came to him. "Because that damn Ladies' Restroom door is a brick and mortar representation of the philosophical concept of choice."

Myrddin smiled broadly. "That is correct. Every door presents a choice. Sometimes the choice is a physical one. In or out. Right or left. Up or down. Sometimes, however, the door presents the opportunity for a metaphysical choice. In the Realms where magyk reigns, a door can be both.

"So, you see, it is not of the UnFading Spirit to intimidate, nor to coerce. We each make choices every day. We step through a door with every choice we make. We use some doors frequently, many, many times throughout our entire lives. There are some choices, though, some doors, that once you pass through there is no returning. One door closes..."

"I don't get it," Tal interrupted, more than a little irritated. "I've been in and out of that bathroom door any number of times already."

"The rules have changed, Tal."

"Why?"

"Because of the choices you've made. The rules changed when you chose to replace me."

"And now I'm firmly back to 'you lost me,'" Tal replied.

"What was your third wish on Aurora's ring?" Myrddin asked.

Tal paused, thinking back on his request. "It's a little hard to remember. Things were pretty dire. I was butt naked, my ass was pretty much literally on fire, and if I didn't immediately kill the most powerful wytch who ever lived she was going to murder everyone on my team. I'm not sure even Toastmasters has a prepared speech addressing those contingencies."

"Focus, Tal. What were the precise words you used?"

C'mon buddy, Tal prodded himself. What's the use of a photographic memory if you can't total recall something so important? "I asked…I asked…, 'If it is of the Center to restore Baba Yaga's humanity, let me not just be named Taliesin, but allow me to become the Taliesin of this time and place.' Then I also asked that she grant me the magyk of Taliesin and I thanked Aurora for my wishes."

Myrddin's face spread into a broad smile. "It was that choice—your choice—that changed many things. Including the Ladies' Room rules."

"Still doesn't make any sense to me," Tal quickly replied as his frustration chafed into anger. "Assuming you're correct and the rules changed, why is the door 'EXIT ONLY' for me but it's 'ENTRANCE ONLY' for you?" Tal didn't even wait for Myrddin to respond before he continued. " 'ENTRANCE ONLY' is nonsensical, anyway. While we're on my ever expanding list of questions, I'm used to you looking different every time I see you but this time, this time you look 'different' different. What's up with that?"

When Myrddin didn't immediately respond, Tal opened his mouth to continue, even though he realized he was pretty much babbling at this point. Pretty much. Tal felt his mouth close in response to an order from Central Processing. Analysis had just completed unknotting a large block of realization. "No," he whispered. "That's impossible."

Myrddin sat silently, his body motionless, giving Tal's epiphany time to gestate. Which it did—into a mushroom cloud. As his comprehension went nuclear Tal felt every muscle go rigid, saving only the facial musculature necessary to form words.

"It's one of the simplest of cause and effect logic equations, isn't it?" he asked Myrddin, before answering his own question. "The values of 'x' and 'y' have been transferred. The door, 'x,' is different and you, 'y,' are different because I'm different. I'm different...because...because I'm now the Traveler. Which means you're not."

CHAPTER QUATTUORDECIM

"Thank you, Nord, Släkt Prime Direction, for your excellent presentation," Marid stated, continuing his role as emcee for the Ceremony. "You may be seated. Let the official Hunts records reflect Släkt met Hecate and was able to somehow obtain the Hecatic Strophalos. An extraordinary accomplishment I might add."

Damn, they're impressed, Kati admitted to herself. All of them. Let it go, she told herself. Nothing to worry about. You already analyzed the results. Baba Yaga, Hecate, and Cassandra are the top three wytches. You knew Släkt was going to be number one or two. That ranking depends on whether the Omada Fifth Prime makes it back with his team's talysman. Nothing to worry about, Kati told herself.

CHAPTER QUINDECIM

"In what kind of screwed up world am I equipped to be Amarantos's time-traveling hit man?"

Myrddin remained sphinxlike in his recliner, fingers steepled, not looking at Tal, instead staring directly ahead, toward the bathroom door.

"Did you hear me?" Tal asked. "You've stepped up to the plate innumerable times. You're not merely the stuff of legends, I mean, you are actually the stuffing of legends. The innard parts of untold myths. Your actions have made you into many of the greatest heroes in recorded human history. Well, a lot of the Earth myths are seriously wrong on the specifics of certain events, but regardless, you've got substantial champion chops. I'm only a run of the mill dumbass idiot teenaged Dust Child. Granted, I do have a brand magykally seared on my left ass cheek that hurts like hell pretty much nonstop, but I don't know that I put painful ass tats in the catalog of potential hero assets."

When Tal got no response from Myrddin, he kept going. "How the hell am I supposed to know what the UnFading Spirit wants me to do? Look at me when I'm talking to you, dammit! How? How?" Tal pleaded, his voice cracking.

In response Myrddin unsteepled his fingers and slowly turned his head toward Tal. "What I have done every day for centuries now is simply the same thing we are each charged by Amarantos to do every day."

"I know what you're going to say. We are charged by Amarantos to 'Seek the Center'."

Myrddin nodded his response.

"See, there's another problem. How am I supposed to direct other people toward 'Seeking the Center' when I have absolutely no idea what that means?"

Myrddin laughed. "Taliesin, you are a brilliant young man, you truly are. But you are also incredibly dense sometimes. Have you heard anything I have said to you? Ever?"

Not knowing the correct answer, Tal went with the non-committal ambiguity of a shoulder shrug.

Myrddin shook his head slowly from side to side. "It's okay, Tal. I know it's been a lot. We will cover what I can tell you in the time we're given. Now that the transition has been completed, my time in the Gas Station Crossing is limited. You'll have to learn the remainder as you go. On the job training, as it were."

Tal raised his hand. Myrddin grinned, as he replied, "Ask, but quickly."

"Where will you go from here, since you're no longer the Traveler? You said that for you, the sign on the bathroom door says 'ENTRANCE ONLY'."

Myrddin gave Tal a small smile. If Tal were required to put an additional modifier on the facial expression, he would have described it as a small, wistful smile. "As always, it is my choice. The door presents the opportunity for me to return to Earth Realm to live out the rest of my days. It is clear to me though that such choice would be chasing the past.

"There is an evil which has long threatened Amarantos's Stytch. As I am no longer the Traveler, I will no longer be in constant danger. However, I also no longer qualify as human suspended so I cannot live on any of the Folk Realms. I am not even allowed to remain on the Hunts School property because unlike you, my name has never been in The Book."

When he saw Tal was about to interrupt him, Myrddin hurriedly continued. "I am content, Taliesin. The world has turned too many times for me—both in realtyme and othertyme. I have done the best I could in the service of the UnFading One.

The Lady Aurora told me several centuries ago that when I finally gave myself permission to be healed I would always be welcome in the Pentacle. I intend to join she and Arthrys there for my remaining days. Who knows? I may even do some writing."

"Could we maybe rewind back to the part about the Traveler being in 'constant danger'?" Tal asked.

"Yes, that is as good a starting place as any. Taliesin, do you remember the first time we met?"

"Yeah, you were Dr. Mertin Wilt, a know it all British Doogie Houser wannabe."

Myrddin smiled, "I told you then your sense of humor would be crucial to your survival and it has been. Think back to that conversation, Tal. Without giving the Adversary a context to understand our conversation, I very specifically gave you all of the hints and the information you would need to survive, and to Seek the Center."

"Now comes the part where you're going to ask me to repeat those things back to you. Right?" Tal asked.

Myrddin nodded slightly. "I'll help get you started. Seems like we had a discussion about how many cardinal directions there are."

"Fine, fine, fine," Tal interjected. "You were right on that one. I was wrong. There are five not four."

Myrddin leaned forward. "Now that I've primed the pump, tell me the rest, tell me everything else you remember me telling you."

Tal sent the request to Archives for all mental images. They started popping up but in random order. "You told me you wrote, 'The eyes indicate the antiquity of the soul.' "

"Correct," Myrddin confirmed, "and you argued with me that Ralph Waldo Emerson wrote it."

"Because he did."

"Yes, I did," Myrddin replied.

"I guess you still don't have any extra-strength Tylenol?" Tal asked, rubbing his forehead.

The immediate past Traveler shook his head no.

"Didn't think so. I remember the entire floor of the room was completely covered with sand. Colored sand that was in geometric patterns. You told me it was a sand mandala." Tal paused as a mental snapshot of that statement materialized. "Actually, you told me it was a specific type of mandala, called a kalachakra.

"Correct. On many Realms, kalachakra means 'Wheel of Time'."

"Right. You told me to use my memory to fix the details in my mind, because it would be important." Tal paused in his recitation. "I'd almost forgotten but that kalachakra was the same as the one on Fortuna's Wheel of Fortune on Atlantis plane.

"Wow. I guess, I'm the one who's slow to the party today. The design of the sand kalachakra on the floor of that room at Nemeton High is the same kalachakra I was standing on only a little while ago in...in...whatever that plane was where the shadow weavers were getting busy." Tal halted when he noticed his reference to the shadow weavers surprised Myrddin. That's twice today he's been surprised by somewhere I've been or something I've done, Tal thought.

"Taliesin, am I correct in assuming that before you stepped into the Gas Station portal you had decided to abandon the Hunts?"

I'll give it to him, Tal thought, the dude is one hell of a good guesser. "Correct."

"And you had also decided you no longer wanted to accept the responsibility of being responsible for whether other people lived or died?"

"Correct, again."

"When you thought you were stepping into the Gas Station Crossing this time, you went somewhere else, didn't you?"

"No," Tal replied. "Well, maybe. Ever since I first met you it's really hard sometimes to tell what's real and what may simply be the pseudo-events of an extended concussive delusion. I'll commit to this. I'm pretty sure I got detoured to some freaky place with no walls and a humongous stain glass ceiling. It had kalachakra flooring and thousands of shadows weaving fancy bath rugs. Oh, and their lighting budget was woefully inadequate. The entire place was lit by only one light bulb."

Myrddin's laugh this time was a short but gleeful bark. "Come now, Taliesin, you know exactly where you were. We specifically discussed that place in our first conversation."

"We did?" Tal asked. He waited to see if Archives had an image for him. Nope. "We couldn't have, Myrddin. It wasn't even somewhere, it was really more of an absence of a place, more of a 'no place.' Not trying to be funny but it was really no place at all."

"Exactly," Myrddin confirmed, while crossing his arms.

"What? Wait a minute. I do remember you gave me some college lecture speech about Sir Thomas More combining two words. I think it was the literal translation of two Greek words."

"And?" Myrddin asked.

"Utopia!" Tal yelled. You said 'utopia' literally meant 'no place'."

"So, I did. We will come back to that. Now we must hurry through the rest. What else do you remember?"

"You also told me everyone's universe has its own Barton Sellars, or worse. And that, 'Every person, in every lifetime, has a choice: concede to the darkness or fight for the light. Sometimes they win, sometimes they don't'."

Myrddin grinned. A little. "You know, there are times I even amaze myself with my ability to turn a phrase."

"You told me 'fighting for the light' begins when a person finally chooses to 'Seek the Center.' You also rudely told me I was directionless." Tal paused at this juncture. It's not that you don't remember the rest, Tal found himself telling himself. It's that everything Myrddin told me at our first meeting was absolutely spot on. And you're scared, aren't you? Damn straight I am, Tal mentally replied to himself.

"Finish it, Tal," Myrddin prompted.

"You know the rest," Tal snapped in response. "I'm sorry," he said, holding up his hands in apology. "It's been a long couple of days. You told me I would gladly throw away every day of my 'now' to be 'then' and once I was 'then' I would promptly find a new 'then' to throw away my 'then now'."

Tal hesitated as he looked at his mentor. "You were right, you know. I would have fast-forwarded through years of my life to jump to the place I thought I wanted to be."

Myrddin smiled as he looked directly at Tal. "We all have to learn in our own time, Taliesin. Which for some is sadly not in time."

"It's what you said," Tal continued. " 'A destination is only an ending' and that we can never find the destination we desire until we learn to 'Seek the Center.' And to 'embrace the journey—both the pain and the joy'."

Myrddin smiled, wanly this time. "That's a lesson I myself have had to learn many times over the centuries. The most painful lesson being this last trip as Stytch."

Tal watched as Myrddin struggled, clearly reliving anew a sizeable dose of brutally fresh pain, some extra value meal order sized anguish which hadn't even had time to congeal into a scab. "Very well done, Taliesin. You have omitted only one detail. The single most important thing—my first words to you when you entered the room."

Tal paused and let the whole photo album of that day's meeting scroll past him. It would be nice if these things were in chrono-order, he thought to himself. Nope, I've looked at every one of the mental images. Nothing. "No, I'm sure I've repeated everything."

Myrddin's face clouded as he spoke, "No, Taliesin, you haven't. The first thing I told you was the name of your Adversary. The identity of the one who has tried to kill me innumerable times since I first became Amarantos's Stytch. The same entity who has tried to kill you and those who care about you repeatedly since you first stepped on the grounds of the Hunts School."

"Well, maybe you could go back over…"

"I CAN'T!" Myrddin yelled, before catching a calming breath. "What I told you, in the manner I told you, was safe then. Any further explanation at this juncture might prove life threatening. Think, Taliesin. I told you you should remember it. That it might be important."

DAMMIT! Tal screamed internally. I can't believe I've misplaced that information. If what Myrddin is telling me is true—and he's never been wrong before—he told me the name of the sonofabitch asshole who's responsible for every horrible thing that's happened to me, and those I care about, since I got to Hunt's School. Bati—brutally murdered by the Keres. Väst—who's only still alive because I used one of my three wishes granted by Aurora's ring. Emet—who paid the bloodpryce for me for Elle's death. And Elle—a true innocent, Tal thought, as he choked up. She knew nothing about the Hunts School, had nothing to do with this quest for ultimate power for the next three hundred years. All dead, or worse, because of me.

Yeah, Tal you have to figure out what you're missing, because whoever that motherfucking piece of shit is has to be stopped. Trying to buy some time to find the information while he also got himself under control, he was finally able to croak out his next question. "The staff?" he asked. "Do I also get the power of the Traveler's staff? You know the one with the glowing gargantuan amethyst?"

"Thank you for reminding me. I almost forgot," Myrddin said as he began haphazardly rummaging through his coat pockets, then the pocket of his shirt.

As Tal watched, Myrddin scratched his head and began excavating his pants pockets. "I think you must have misunderstood me," Tal said softly. "I was asking about your staff. It's about nine feet tall so I'm really thinking it's not in your watch pocket."

"Thank goodness!" Myrddin finally responded, as he pulled a small, rectangular piece of ivory colored paper out of his front left pocket. "Please take this," he added handing the paper to Tal.

Tal looked at it. On one side in purple flowing script it said, "M. Ryss." On the other side, in the same embellished font it read, "HC SVNT DRACONES—Royal Stationers & Cartographers, 777 Shamb Hala Court, New York City."

He flipped it back and forth a couple of times before extending it to give back to Myrddin. "Hello? I was talking about the staff. I don't need the phone number of your map maker," Tal replied. "Or whatever communication device was being used about three hundred years ago when you had this business card printed."

"No, you keep it," Myrddin replied. "Where were we?

Oh, um, right. The staff. Sorry but that's a hard no. I'm keeping it as my retirement present. You know, like a gold watch. Well, it's only like a gold watch symbolically because you and I both know the physical properties and composition of a staff have very little in common with those of a gold watch."

Tal held the card between his left thumb and forefinger. "What exactly am I supposed to do with this?"

Myrddin patted him on the wrist. "You'd know better than me. Actually," Myrddin said, pausing to scratch his head, "at some previous time—which hasn't yet occurred—you apparently did know better than me."

"Confused," Tal mumbled. "I am sorely confused."

Myrddin smiled gently. "I know, it really does take some getting used to. There's a reason the Folk call tyme-travel Conundrum. The first time we meet you need to give me that card. It will give me the opportunity to make a proper goodbye for the decision I have already made. Well, which I will be making."

Tal's response was a slack-jawed stare. "I'm not sure I have ever been more clueless in my entire life."

Myrddin chuckled. "Welcome to my world. The choice to be here was mine. Remember the card, Taliesin. It's important."

"I will," Tal replied, then watched as the now Traveler Emeritus shook his head as if to clear it.

"Right then, it's time," Myrddin finally said, as he pointed to the side of the bathroom that usually contained the bathroom stalls.

Tal turned his head to follow Myrddin's arm. There were no stalls this trip, only the inside of the tired planking of the outside wall of the Gas Station Crossing. Across the weathered boards there was a vibrant, freshly painted stencil of a large multi-colored arch. It described a parabola almost ten feet high at its apex. "It's a rainbow. Aurora has made an express route for you to her Pentagram, hasn't she?" Tal asked.

"Yes," Myrddin confirmed, as he stood, motioning for Tal to do the same. Two short steps closed the distance between them. Tal realized he was only a little surprised as Myrddin pulled him close and embraced him.

"You are a good man, Taliesin Smith. Seek the Center in all of your decisions. I am very proud of you." With that Myrddin disengaged himself and walked briskly to the arch. Before he stepped through he turned back to look at Tal. "Oh, and if I were you, I'd spend some time thinking about the first thing I told you. You know, it…"

"I know, I know, it might be important," Tal said.

"Exactly," Myrddin confirmed before turning and stepping through the arch.

CHAPTER SEDECIM

"THAT HURTS!" Väst screamed in agony.

"I'm sorry, Acting Fourth Prime," the Chief Physick replied. "We are doing the best we can while limited to human medical practices. We've sent our fastest intern to the ziggurat to let us know as soon as the Ruling Council has made a decision. The first team was scheduled to start a short time ago. They should be about ready to begin with the second squad.

"You need to prepare yourself. We're going to have to shift several ribs back into proper position and we've already given you more morphine than was prudent."

"Just do it," Väst growled from between gritted teeth. "Do it now.

"AAAAAAAH!"

CHAPTER SEPTENDECIM

"It's just little old me again," Tal mumbled, as he fell back into his recliner He wasn't sure if he was talking to himself...or to the Ladies' Room...or maybe to one or more of the hundreds of ticker tape machines.

It's go time to make a decision. A choice. Why does it always have to be my choice? As long as I'm asking, why does every choice I've made since I first walked into this bathroom seem like it's a monumental decision? An earth-shattering choice for someone I know and care about?

Is every choice we make a critical choice or are there choice categories, he wondered. Like small, medium and monumental ramification choices? If so, someone should create a choice categorization flow chart so all of us confused choosers will know which choices are potentially life changing.

Which raises another point. Regardless of the category of one person's choices, can it be raised, or lowered, by a different category choice made by someone else? Is your choice to give your loved ones a hug and tell them you love them before leaving for work in the morning in the same choice category if you make it home safely at the end of the day, as it is if you're involved in a fatal collision and never get the opportunity to make that choice again? Can the subsequent intervening choices of others retroactively make your choice more consequential than it otherwise would have been? Is it even all on me, Amarantos? Are the choices I make truly my decisions or am I walking your pre-determined Taliesin Smith life labyrinth?

CHAPTER DUODEVIGINTI

Marid stood after Chuusin concluded his presentation. "Thank you Shuzoku First Prime Direction. Your story was compelling. Without question Morgaine is one of the most powerful wytches in the Cult of Nyx. Her talysman, the Scabbard of Many Names, would unquestionably have positioned Shuzoku to continue forward in the Hunts. It is a shame the talysman was misplaced."

The immediate grumbling from the crowd let everyone present know the word was out that the absence of the scabbard was not an accident, that there had been unattributable foul play involved in its disappearance. Kati whispered to herself, "Play it smart, Masha. Something bad will happen if you show up before the Council's decision is announced."

Marid turned his back to the audience and whispered with the Archon and the rest of the Ruling Council. "The Ruling Council grants Shuzoku special permission to immediately take their Second Prime to the infirmary to see if there is anything the physicks can magykally do at this point to repair the brain damage she has sustained. This is, of course, without prejudice to the right of the Shuzoku to remain in the Hunts if they are determined to be one of the top three teams."

Chuusin grimly nodded his appreciation, walked over to Kita, helped her to stand, and the Shuzoku processed single-file out of the ziggurat.

Well, that's that for Allyu, Kati told herself. They would

never have given Shuzoku permission to leave if they thought it would be one of the top three teams. From the look on his face as he marched out, Chuusin knew it too.

We're down to four teams now. Maybe only three, she thought as she glanced over to the Omada table. Still no sign of panic from any of the three Omada team members present. Call Omada next, she prayed. Call Omada next.

CHAPTER UNDEVIGINTI

Never in a million years would I have guessed I'd be in this situation. Hanging out in a barcalounger in some pocket dimension between two planes of existence attempting to conclusively resolve the eons old discussion between free will and predestination.

It's not like I have to start from whole cloth, Tal gently chided himself. Ninth grade Western Civ curriculum had contained a scattershot smattering of the major tenets of a number of the better known philosophers. Like Immanuel Kant, who'd had a very distinct position on predestination. He'd been liberally quoted in the textbook.

C'mon, Tal, use your eidetic memory. Visualize the page. The Kant quotes were on a right-hand page, top half. That's right. The first Kant quote was, "Live your life as though every act were to become a universal law." Doesn't really help with resolving the free will issue. I'd say that quote though puts Kant clearly in the "every choice is a critical choice" camp.

The textbook said Kant is generally defined as a compatibilist. If I put that theory into musical language it would be the same as that earwig by Donnie and Marie Osmond, "I'm A Little Bit Country, She's A Little Bit Rock and Roll." I was never able to buy into Kant's position that we have free will because although our bodies are restricted by time, our souls are making decisions "outside of time." Which now that I think about it sounds like a human being trying to describe realtyme and othertyme.

Thomas Hobbes was also a kind of a "hedge your bets" type of philosopher. Hobbes said we have free will because of "actional liberty." Whatever the hell that is. Then he turned right around and said "volitional determinism" set restrictions on our "actional determinism." Seemed like a bunch of three-dollar words. Like obfuscation.

There it is, Tal finally remembered. The major thing that stuck with me as making the most sense, was the "Principle of Alternate Possibilities." Surely, we can only be held morally responsible for our actions if we were free to choose otherwise.

Predestination or free will? Is it either/or? Or is it a mix and match deal? The religious philosophers have never been able to conclusively argue the answer to that puzzle either. What normal person's head wouldn't spin when asked to discuss the differences in the theodicy of Pelagius, Erasmus, and St. Augustine?

Speaking of deep mysteries of the universe, is there never any Tylenol in girls' bathrooms or is it just this one that never has any in stock?

CHAPTER VIGINTI

Here we go, Kati told herself as Marid stood once again to bang his staff on the floor. It's either Omada or us.

"As most of you are aware, there were an unprecedented six teams in the second Hunt this year. One of the six teams, Allyu, suffered the death of a teammate during the Wytch Hunt and has formally withdrawn from the competition. The remaining members of Allyu have returned to general curriculum studies for the balance of this school year. We thank them for their honor, their dignity, and their effort. We mourn with them the loss of their Fourth Prime and pray that Amarantos may gather him swiftly unto Her."

That's a little different than the HuntsMistress's outpouring of affection for us when we fail, Kati thought.

"There are two teams remaining for presentation of talysmen to the Council. Would the Kabila First Prime Direction please step forward to make Kabila's presentation?"

It's go time, Kati told herself as she reached underneath her blouse and pulled the quick release on the spydersilk straps she'd used to secure their talysman. She reached down and grabbed the beaded bag containing the corpse dust before standing up and confidently striding forward.

CHAPTER VIGINTI UNUS

Focus, Tal. Focus. Make your choice. Imbibe the "Drink Me" potion or consume the "Eat Me" cake. I'm sure Daedalus blamed himself for his son's fall. It's what parents do. The simple truth, though, is that Icarus is Everyman. Each and every one of us has been told repeatedly what will happen to us if we fly to close to the sun. But it's our choice, no one else's.

In the immortal words of the post-modern philosopher Morpheus to his acolyte Neo: *"You take the blue pill, the story ends. You wake up in your bed and believe whatever you want to. You take the red pill, you stay in Wonderland, and I show you how deep the rabbit hole goes. Remember, all I'm offering is the truth. Nothing more."*

CHAPTER VIGINTI DUO

Tal stared at the "NO EXIT" sign. There are many immutable facts on the other side of that door. Elle is dead. She's gone and there is absolutely nothing I can do about it. On Earth Realm I am a fugitive from justice, wanted for her murder. If I walk through that door I will either be a fugitive for the rest of my life or I will have to turn myself in to be charged and tried. Odds are I'll be convicted and receive life without parole. My little brothers will have either a ghost on the run or a convict for a big brother. Neither ranks particularly high on the good role model scale.

The best argument for walking through that door is that if I'm locked away there is no way I'll be responsible for anyone else's death. On the flip side, I've told Mom and Pell I'm safe, and they don't have to worry about me. What possible benefit can I be to the people I love if I walk through door?

If I turn around and go back to Hunts School I have the chance to help Omada win the Tyrning. I can help make sure the Släkt don't become the Ruling Council. I can, maybe, figure out a way to get Emet out of Five-Hells. Of course I may also cause more deaths and more disasters to further bloody my hands.

Damn, I miss the days when my biggest decision was thick or thin crust.

CHAPTER VIGINTI TRES

Decision made. At the end of the day we have one life. Every waking hour of that life is replete with a multitude of choices. I must, we must, each of us must, simply do the very best we can. Every choice. Every day.

Tal finally opened his eyes. The Ladies' Room was now back in its original configuration. Stalls, a cozy sitting area, two sinks with a counter and mirror above it. There were only three differences between the room now and the room as it appeared on his first passage to Hunts School.

First, the door to Earth Realm still read "EXIT ONLY." Guess that makes sense, Tal concluded. Even with today's decision that path remains open to me. It is, however, from this time forward always going to only be a one-way trip through Sol's Gas Station Crossing.

Second, there was a single remaining ticker tape machine. As Tal stood and walked over to it, it coughed up its last message before sputtering to a halt. Tal ripped the tape off its reel and held it up to read.

> Now that you've made your decision, you should proceed with some measure of alacrity. The Ceremony is well underway and Omada has been issued First Call. You only have about four hundred forty-three seconds until Omada forfeits. Oh, and please don't step on Notos when you exit.

The third difference became apparent as Tal turned back toward the wall on the Hunts School side of the room. There was now a trompe l'oeil mural, painted in amazing verisimilitude. The wall painting was an honest to goodness stereotypical set of Wild West saloon double swinging doors. They were so realistic Tal could have sworn he heard them creaking in some non-existent breeze. The doors even contained some knife carved words of wisdom—**'holster 'em tite, pard. it's gunna be a hellofa ryde.'**

Oh well, I guess it's Mary Poppins' time, Tal thought, as he strode over to the painting. Just as he was about to step through his subconscious populated an agenda of important but still unresolved matters relating to he and Myrddin's *tete a tete*. The single bullet-point on the list was a question—"What was the first thing Myrddin ever said to me?"

CHAPTER VIGINTI QUATTUOR

"Thank you Kati, Kabila Prime Direction. Please let the official school record reflect Kabila obtained corpse dust, an excellent talysman, from Kanka, one of the lesser wytches of the Cult of Nyx."

That's okay, old man, Kati thought to herself as she walked back to the Kabila table. I've done my job better than any of the other Primes so far. We're going to ride our talysman from that "lesser wytch" all the way to victory lane.

Once, twice, three times, Marid struck the dais floor with his staff of office. "Omada, you are now called to present your talysman."

Kati watched, along with the entire assembly, as Borras remained motionless at the team table, one teammate on either side. The crowd began murmuring almost immediately. What is he doing, Kati wondered. Then it hit her. He's a smart son of a bitch that one is. The Hunts Rules provide for three calls by the Seneschal. Between the first and second call, there is a mandated two-minute wait period. Following the second call, the required wait period is three minutes. The named team has one more minute to respond following the third and final call.

He's giving his teammates every chance to make it back before he steps up to the podium. Damn him, he's clever, but where are they?

The clicking, clacking, snuffling, and trumpeting from the

assemblage continued to grow as Marid waited the prescribed time period. At a nod from Alberich, he stepped forward and banged his staff three more times. "Omada is summoned for the second time," he pronounced, before stepping back and reclaiming his seat at the head table.

CHAPTER VIGINTI QUINQUE

With his left leg extended completely parallel to the ground, Tal hurdled over the Omada Second Prime. Even with Tal's beautiful form, Notos would probably have sustained at least a small concussion if he hadn't thrown himself flat to the turf.

"Hurry up, Notos!" Tal yelled backwards over his left shoulder. "We only have about five minutes until Omada is cooked." Tal wasn't sure if it was the rush of the wind burning his ears or Notos hurling epithets.

CHAPTER VIGINTI SEX

All noise of any kind had been sucked out of the Great Hall. It was so quiet Kati really thought some of the attendees might even be holding their breaths, afraid they might miss something. It had been almost the full minute since Marid had banged his staff and announced third and final call for Omada. The Omada Prime remained motionless.

Then, just as Marid was tensing his legs to stand once more, Borras stood and walked very slowly to the front of the room. "Good day. I am Borras, Omada Prime Direction. As you can see, Omada only has three team members present at this time. Our Fifth Prime has the talysman in his possession. He was having some severe medical issues and I sent our Second Prime Direction to check on him. I feel certain they will both be in attendance by the time I finish telling you who the Omada met and what talysman we received."

He's stalling, Kati thought, as she decided whether to stand and protest. No, Omada is screwed and I don't want to draw any attention to Kabila since Mashariki is still off ditching the Shuzoku talysman. Besides, that idiot Nord will blow a gasket if this keeps up. He can't help himself. Let Släkt be the assholes.

CHAPTER VIGINTI SEPTEM

Tal grabbed Notos's arm, pulling him up short just outside the ziggurat. They were both winded but Notos had enough breath left to blast Tal. "What the hell do you think you're doing, human?"

"I just needed a quick breath, Notos. Plus, I'm not sure I'll be able to disrobe once I'm face to face with Alberich and Aine. And everyone else."

"The talysman is branded on your ass, you idiot. I'll rip your damn clothes off of you if I have to. What is it you propose?"

"This," Tal replied, kicking off his shoes, before quickly pulling off every article of his clothing. "Problem solved. Let's go win!"

CHAPTER VIGINTI OCTO

"And so, ladies and gentlemen, Omada survived an encounter with the most powerful wytch in all of history. Unfortunately she had to be killed for our Fifth Prime to obtain our talysman."

Marid stepped forward. "Omada's accomplishment this Hunt will receive special recognition in the official Hunts School record books. It is truly unfortunate that at the conclusion of such a brilliant, successful team effort, your team does not have the minimum four members present for the Ceremony. Nor is your talysman present."

Kati couldn't help herself, she started beaming and leaning over to congratulate the rest of her team. At that moment there was a huge commotion from the Great Hall's main entrance. There were hundreds of people standing and flying and leaping so Kati couldn't see what was going on. Not until the disturbance reached the front of the Great Hall.

"Don't be so hasty, Mr. Seneschal, sir," the human yelled as he ran up the stairs leading to the raised dais. "Omada, party of five? Last call for Omada, party of five. Look sharp, people. Winning talysman on display."

A collective gasp from the congregation confirmed what Kati was seeing. The Dust Child was running right across the top of the Ruling Council's table, on top of their plates and dishes. No, not just running. He was completely naked. With both his junk and his admittedly tight Cult of Nyx branded ass right at eye level of the Archon, his wife, and the rest of the Ruling Council.

Holy hell, Kati told herself. Omada is still in the game because their human mooned the Ruling Council of the entire known universe.

CHAPTER VIGINTI NOVEM

"What's going on, where am I?" Väst asked, disoriented.

"Relax, Acting Fourth Prime. You're still in the infirmary," the Chief Physick replied. "Our runner returned a few minutes ago with word the second term Hunt has been officially declared concluded. We immediately used healmagyk to knock you out while we magykally finished repairing your broken bones. Because of the delay, there is nothing we can do in the short term about the majority of your facial swelling and bruising. It had too long to set up."

"The Hunt is over?" Väst confirmed groggily. "Who? Who…"

"Kabila, Omada, and your team," the Chief Physick replied.

"I'd better get going, then," Väst said feebly, as she attempt to roll over.

The Chief Physick put his hand on her shoulder to restrain her. "We have confirmed with Principal Chiron that class doesn't start for an hour. We just now got through fixing you, you need to take as much time to regain your lyfeforce as you can before you go. I'll deny I ever said it, but we all know your Prime is a total jackass. We'll make sure you're out of here in time for class."

CHAPTER TRIGINTA

Alone, finally, he unlocked his desk drawer and withdrew his dagger. Closing his eyes, he began his calming ritual by placing the knife's tip lightly at the top of the disfiguring scar. He slowly drew its razor sharp edge diagonally downward, not caring whether he pressed too hard and drew blood. Her glamour would cover it in case anyone walked in his office.

Downward, slowly, through the white scar in his black eyebrow. Calming himself, focusing his thoughts. The knife bumped its way across his puckered, empty left eye socket before climbing the ridge of his shattered nose. On the downhill side it wobbled back and forth in the finger-width trench traversing his lips. Taking a long, deep breath he pulled the knife down into the hole under the right side of his chin, the place where the Sword of Many Names had carved a chunk of flesh from his once perfect face.

Excalibur. The Sword of Many Names. I should have been the one who claimed it, not Arthrys. It would have been mine, except for that damned mortal's interference. She promised me. She promised I would be Archon for life and that she would restore me to my former physical countenance. She promised me I would have my vengeance.

He'd learned as powerful as she was that She didn't know everything. First, his teammate, one of the Crestfallyn, hadn't been allowed to take the mortal's face because one of the Omada had royal level deathmagyk. Her order to release the Keres, the Hell Hounds, had been a disaster because the Cooshies unexpectedly came to help the human.

Finally, She'd told him to kill his teammates to thrice-blood a weapon. After he'd used the magyked blade to kill the human female, it looked like Her plan to have the Dust Child sent to Five-Hells was going to succeed. Until a damned simulacrum golem showed up and spoke. Never in the history of the Moiety had a golem spoken. The Creature had been created by yet another one of the Omada gifted with royal level magyk, this time creationmagyk. She obviously hadn't known about the golem, either.

No question She is powerful but there is much She doesn't know. Maybe I should… "Ach, Ach…" Mordred gasped, as he dropped his dirk and grabbed his throat with both hands. "I can't breathe."

'Maybe you should what, Malebranche? Go ahead, I'm interested in how you planned on finishing the very last sentence of your execrable existence.'

"Ach…ach." She's here. I didn't feel Her come in this time.

'You only sense me when I let you, fool. Go ahead and finish what you were saying. You have about twenty seconds left to live.'

"I can't breathe…"

'You would have been dead centuries ago except for my grace. On your knees before your Mistress.'

Hands still around his throat, Mordred felt his legs give way at her command, knees cracking as they hit the travertine floor. Floating black dots were moving across his vision. "Please, Mistress. I meant no disrespect."

'Forget yourself again, worm, and I won't be so merciful,' She whispered in his mind.

Mordred felt the stranglehold ease. As soon as he gulped several mouthfuls of air, he continued. "Thank you, Mistress."

'I think you need a permanent reminder,' She said, right before Mordred felt a mass of tissue in his eyeless left socket pop loose, tissue and blue blood erupting from the open wound.

Screaming in agony, the last thing he remembered before mercifully passing out were her final words. *'Yes, there are things I don't know but I know everything in due time. Do not dare doubt me again. The Dust Child will suffer as no other mortal has suffered. And if, for some unknown reason, he does not spend the rest of eternity in Five-Hells, I shall give you both permission and opportunity to exact vengeance for the both of us.'*

CHAPTER TRIGINTA UNUS

Tal watched as the classroom door slammed shut behind the HuntsMistress. Huh. She didn't even touch the door. Couldn't have used magyk to make it happen. The campus is a zero-magyk zone, unless the Archon specifically authorizes it. Maybe the hallway air was simply calling "no backs" on Our Lady Of The Immeasurably Bad Attitude. If I was some good clean air, I wouldn't want to be spending any time inside that body either.

Today's full body, long-sleeved outfit was red leather, sewn together with thick black leather stitching. Her thigh-high four-inch stiletto heeled boots were the inverse color scheme, black leather with scarlet laces. The entire ensemble looked like somebody had used a giant seal-a-meal to shrink-wrap a high-end demon dominatrix outfit on her.

Bandoliers containing at least a dozen wicked-sharp short knives crisscrossed her chest. I recognize that style from the "Weapons" textbook, Tal told himself. They're a miniaturized version of a Japanese tanto. Tantos have extra strong points, designed for piercing hard objects. The HuntsMistress had also taken the time to add extra arrows to the quiver strapped to her back. She must have left her bow in the saddlebag attached to her broom, he decided.

"Well, here we are," she began. "Normally, I call this session 'winners and losers.' Seeing as how you are all the most pitiful crop of Hunts Finalists in probably a hundred Tyrnings, it's more appropriate to call today's session, 'losers and even bigger losers'."

A hundred Tyrnings, Tal thought. That would be thirty thousand years. I mean, that's some serious disrespect she's dishing out here.

"Because of Omada's lowlife mortal, I was stuck with six teams instead of five for the second-term Hunt. By showing that yellow is their team color, Allyu previously reduced that number to the traditional five squads.

"I have now received the official written ranking list from the Ruling Council. Pleme?"

"Yes, HuntsMistress," Sredina, their Prime Direction responded as she stood to attention. She signaled the rest of her team to stand as well.

"I don't know why you're even still here wasting my time," Ms. Empousa snapped quickly in return.

To her credit, Sredina didn't back down. In fact, if anything, she stood straighter, evidencing her pride both in herself and as the leader of one of the Finalist teams. "Because members of Pleme have worked diligently for almost a hundred years to stand here today. Because Pleme, out of the thousands of teams to begin the Hunts two years ago now, remains as one of five Finalists. Because Pleme has always followed the rules, and has always sought the Center…"

"Blah de blah blah blah," the HuntsMistress said, her lip snarled in the universal contempt configuration. "You met one wytch and failed to obtain a talysman. I'd call that abject failure.

"On my orders school staff has already removed all of your personal possessions from what were formerly your Hunts' Finalist dorm apartments. Your crap is now sitting on your respective bunk beds. In the general population dormitories, along with all of the other mediocrities who are basically wasting oxygen here at Hunts School.

"This classroom is for Hunts Finalists only. You and your teammates were only wannabes and guess what? From now on you are officially 'never-wases.' Leave before I call security and have you taken out in shackles."

Seeing the HuntsMistress was finally through with her

tirade, Sredina slowly turned her back on Ms. Empousa, directing her comments to the remaining teams. "Pleme wishes for you all a safe, successful last Hunt. May you always Seek the Center."

"GET OUT, NOW!" the HuntsMistress snarled. Sredina turned to her team, ordered them into single file, and proudly led her squad out into the hallway.

The HuntsMistress glared at Pleme's backs until they were out of sight through the glass inset of the classroom door. "Good, that removes some of the stench in the room. Let's see, what's next? Oh yes," she added as she looked down at a sheet of official Hunts School stationary. "The order rank as determined by the Ruling Council. In third place, a team replete with mediocrity, who if I had the power I'd be sending home with the rest of the losers, Kabila. In second place, Släkt..." The HuntsMistress paused and lifted her eyes as she heard some low-level noise come from the Släkt table. "I'm sorry, Släkt Prime, did somebody on your second place team—a team I might add that lost the second term Hunt to a team that has a Dust Child as one of its members—have something they wish to discuss with the class?"

Nord was so embarrassed he couldn't even look the HuntsMistress in the eyes. "Look at me when I'm talking to you, Nord of the Släkt." Nord complied, lifting his eyes, as the rest of his facial muscles tightened into a rictus. "Good, now I'll be able to tell that you mean it when you say what I'm going to tell you to say."

No, Amarantos, please no, Tal pleaded silently. Not again. Please let it stop. Nord has been right at the boiling point since the last time she pulled this stunt.

But it didn't stop. "Now repeat after me. 'My team came in second...' " She stopped there waiting for him.

It looked like Nord wasn't going to do it until Söder grabbed his arm. "My...team...came...in...second..."

"Very good, Prime. Now that you've admitted you weren't good enough to win, the rest shouldn't be difficult. 'Because I was outsmarted at every turn by a munedan'."

Nord refroze. Harder this time than mere seconds ago, if that was even possible.

"I guess this is the moment where I remind you I have the authority under the Hunts Rules to bump your team for violation of a direct order given by the HuntsMaster or HuntsMistress." She turned around, placed the stationary on the desk, and grabbed a pen.

"Because...I...was...outsmarted...at...every...turn...by ...a...munedan," Nord finally growled.

"Good boy. I thought by now you'd be tired of learning that lesson. Apparently not. It's starting to look like the only way Släkt could win this Tyrning would be if Quint of the Omada was its leader."

Tal had to make an effort to keep his jaw from dropping. *The bitch isn't even trying to conceal what she's up to anymore. Right here. In front of the entire class. She's trying to goad him into killing me.*

The rest of the class watched as Ost and Fem had to physically restrain Nord. "What's the matter, Prime? Cat got your tongue?" Ms. Empousa asked disparagingly, as she casually flipped her hair over her right shoulder while she turned to address her next victim. "Ahh, and here we have Shuzoku."

Please, Tal thought to himself. *They've suffered enough. The bitch must have demanded that Kita be brought back from the infirmary specifically for this. Please just tell them they're losers and send them away.*

"Shuzoku Second Prime." Tal watched as Kita sluggishly responded to being addressed directly by the HuntsMistress. "How does it make you feel, Kita? To have irrevocably bartered away the most intimate personal part of yourself. For absolutely nothing. Oh, that's right you can't feel anything. Ever again."

Kita might couldn't feel anything but she could still pretty much dissolve right before their very eyes. Damn, Tal thought. *She looks lost. Really lost. Like she's been desperately clinging to the last vestige of her humanity with fingernails bleeding emptiness and now even that final shred is being torn away.*

"Stop it," Chuusin screamed.

The HuntsMistress did stop—for a couple of seconds Long enough to draw herself almost impossibly erect, after which a malignant smile metastasized from her black heart to her face.

If it was possible to catch cancer from a smile, Tal thought, we'd all have stage four.

"Oh, yes, Chuusin, Shuzoku Prime." In an instant, every bit of the facial malignancy evolved into a black saccharine coating on the HuntsMistress's well-modulated voice. "What was it Morgaine Le Fay, the second most powerful wytch in all of recorded history, said to your team?"

I hate the Socratic method of teaching, Tal thought. I absolutely hate it.

"Ah, yes, I remember now. She swore to you on the mark of Nyx that the Scabbard of Many Names would 'see you qualified for the last Hunt.' It would have too if you had been worthy to lead the Shuzoku. All you had to do to be in the final Hunt was to secure your talysman. I guess you're feeling really good about yourself right about now, aren't you."

Chuusin shriveled under the verbal onslaught. Kira, now frothing at the mouth and muttering incoherent syllables, fell seizing out of her seat and onto the cold marble classroom floor. Minami and Nishi leapt out of their chairs to help their stricken friend.

Head down, Tal, cautioned himself. Omada needs you to keep your head down. This is no concern of yours, Shuzoku is out of the Hunts, however this goes down. Let it go.

"Umm, excuse me, Ms. HuntsMistress, ma'am. I was wondering if we're about through. I really need to go to the little boys' room." Tal hadn't even realized he'd spoken words. Words. Out Loud. Until after he'd spoken them. Words. Out loud.

Ms. Empousa's hair lashed sideways as she fixed the high beams of her Medusa-class glare upon him. Tal didn't even need to turn his head to know Notos was also powering up his Death Star laser stare, to incinerate whatever ort was left of Tal after the HuntsMistress incinerated him.

"As much as we would all enjoy watching you soil yourself Omada Fifth, I don't have time to deal with making sure you cleaned it up properly. Luckily for you, we're out of time for this period. Professor Elphinstone will fill you in on the details of this term's Hunt in your next class.

"Oh, by the way, it's a Treasyre Hunt. Just so we're all

clear, the rules of the Treasyre Hunt say the comparative valuation of any treasyre collected is in the sole and complete discretion of the HuntsMaster or HuntsMistress. There is no appeal. Not to the Ruling Council. Not to the Archon. My decision this term will determine the Ruling Council for the next three hundred years."

The ramifications of her last couple of sentences hadn't even had a chance to begin sinking in before she spun around and flew out the door. Leaving the Släkt both high-pissed as well as gloating, Chuusin and the rest of the Shuzoku organizing a two-person arm carry to get Kita back to the infirmary, Kati of Kabila watching every movement made by the other two remaining teams, and Notos looking to crawl all over Tal's ass as soon as they got back to their team room.

CHAPTER TRIGINTA DUO

Professor Sprite Elphinstone paced nervously across the width of the classroom as the members of the three remaining Hunt teams took their seats. They had again chosen tables as far away from each other as possible. Tal remembered thinking the classroom was huge on the first day of school, when there were nine teams and over forty students. Now it seemed as if there was a vast distance separating the squads. I guess there is, he decided.

Tal stole a furtive glance to the Släkt table. Yep, she was back from the infirmary. Must have been against medical advice, he decided. Even the quick glimpse made him a little nauseous. The splint on her nose was a pretty good indicator it'd been broken. She already had the beginnings of a pair of first-rate raccoon eyes. Why would she pick a fight with Sredina? Everyone knew from Combat class that, with or without her Puca, Sredina was a take no prisoners scrapper.

Tal turned his attention back to their teacher, watching as he began mopping substantial moisture off of his forehead. Bitch has done it to the professor again, he decided. The HuntsMistress has laid it off on Elphinstone to give us some genuinely terrible news. I really hope a handkerchief allowance is part of the Hunts School's remuneration package.

"Ahem," Professor Elphinstone began tentatively. "Ms. Empousa has deman...has requested that I be the designated faculty member to cover all of the rules and details of the

Treasyre Hunt with you. As it's already been a long and emotional day," with that Tal saw the Professor look sympathetically in his direction before continuing, "I've decided to cover only three main topics with you today. Since this is the only class course you'll have this term, I've scheduled two special sessions tomorrow, one at nine bells in the morning and the other at fourteen bells in the afternoon.

"One of the three teams in this room will be the next Ruling Council. Navigating complex inter-plane rules and regulations is a major component of effective governing. The HuntsMistress has therefore absolutely loaded this Hunt with all kinds of requirements, limitations, and potential penalties. I'm not going to take questions in this session but will be happy to do so tomorrow."

"First, there is this," the professor said as he walked over to the chalkboard and began underlining the last three words written in large print. FOREST FELL IS NOT PART OF HUNTS SCHOOL. IT IS UNWARDED. TRESPASSING MAY RESULT IN DEATH [OR WORSE.] The words had been there since Tal's first day at Hunts School. "This statement that there are things worse than death has been proven several times over since the start of this school year." The professor tapped each word for emphasis.

"Please, please be careful," he added. "The second topic is a general overview of the terms and conditions of your third and final Hunt. The third topic...well, why don't we address the matters one at a time."

Borras scribbled something on his notepad. He pushed the tablet into the middle of the table where all of the rest of Omada could see the words. "This means there is something abnormal, possibly life-threatening about both topic two and topic three. GIVE NO INDICATORS, VISUALLY OR VERBALLY, OMADA IS CONCERNED. We will address the issues later in our team room." He looked quickly at Tal for confirmation before moving the pad into position for Anatolia, Dysi, and Notos to see and acknowledge they understood.

The Professor moved quickly from the board back to the front left corner of his desk, where he tapped a two-foot tall stack of books. Well, it's really only three books, Tal thought. I don't know the minimum number of books required to constitute a stack, but surely three books...

"This stack of books—"

And there's my answer, Tal told himself.

"—contains the only three known originals of 'The Definitive Compyndium of Folk Treasyre'." He paused to look around the room, his face suddenly serious. "If it were up to me, these volumes would not be entrusted to students. Particularly students in a winner take all competition."

Professor Elphinstone reverently stroked the cover of the uppermost book. "These books are normally housed in the most secure portion of the school library. Each of the tomes was created millennia ago." The professor paused, his face grave. "The Compyndium were made using certain practices and procedures that are now quite rightly deemed barbaric and outlawed. Some among us say the books should be destroyed because of the manner in which they were created. Others counterpoint that destruction of the books would make the authors' sacrifices meaningless.

"It took the joint fused magyk of seven times seventy scholars working nonstop for an entire Tyrning to create each original of the Compyndium."

Wow, Tal thought. Three hundred years times four hundred and ninety people equals a total of one hundred forty-seven thousand person years to make each of the books. Okay, fine, but what's the big deal? You make the original and then you magykally xerox as many copies as you need. Wait, did the professor say, "each original?"

"Numerous attempts have been made in every Tyrning following the making of the third original to create additional Compyndium. Every one of those efforts, by some of the most powerful royal-level recreationmagyk Folk in recorded history, yielded books containing only gibberish. To this day, all efforts at copying the books have failed as have any additional efforts to forge new Compyndium originals. We do not know if it is because of the change in our societal rules or whether it is evidence of a lessening of Folk magyk."

Tal wrote down pretty much every word the professor uttered. Obviously the books are ancient. I get that but aside from being antiques I still don't get what all of the foofaraw is about. When he looked back up, the professor was attempting to sponge the moisture beading on his lip with his now saturated handkerchief. If today's class goes much longer, Tal thought, we're going to have to get that boy some fluids with electrolytes. Or an intravenous drip.

"This is the first time in many generations the Compyndium have been taken outside the confines of the library vault. It is also the first time the Compyndium have been utilized in a Hunt.

"Seshat, the Head Librarian, originally vetoed even removing the books from the secured vault in the library. Her position was that although the books have their own potent self-defense magyk, there was no need to take unnecessary risk with such irreplaceable artifacts. The HuntsMistress, as you might imagine, argued she didn't care two cents about the Head Librarian's position, contending her authority under the Hunts Rules superseded Seshat's decision.

"It wasn't until Principal Chiron intervened that the matter was resolved. In addition to being Principal, he also holds the title of Chief Archivist of the Moiety. He told Ms. Empousa if she could come up with a suitable plan to address Seshat's legitimate concerns that he would overrule Seshat and allow the Compyndium to be used. The HuntsMistress came up with an acceptable plan so the books were brought here from storage earlier this morning."

If it was that mean-mouthed bitch's idea I'm sure the plan allows for the possibility of death or maiming, Tal thought to himself.

"Each team will be given the choice whether or not to accept or reject the terms for taking possession of one of the Compyndium. You should know though that if your team does not have access to the information contained in a Compyndium, the odds are prohibitively against your team winning the Tyrning."

So it's a no-brainer to take one for the team, Tal mused.

"Once each book has been attenuated—"

Hold on now, Tal thought, as Central Processing pulled the alarm cord attached to the emergency mental brakes. "Attenuated." Yeah, I don't like the sound of that.

"—only Principal Chiron and the respective members of that Finalist team will be able to touch that specific book."

Why is Chiron in the "authorized to touch" mix? Tal wondered.

"Principal Chiron required that he be included in the arrangement. As a...well, you know...as a fail safe in case something unfortunate were to happen to all of the members of a team."

I guess that makes sense, Tal decided, as he watched their teacher visibly squirm before continuing. Of all the terrible things Empousa has made him tell us so far this year, what's next must be the worst.

After again futilely mopping his water-laden brow, the professor continued. "In order to have access to one of the Compyndium, the Prime of that team will be required to blind consent to binding a contract."

Even though there were now only fifteen competitors remaining, the excited utterances by every one of the other fourteen rose to an almost deafening level. Tal looked at Borras who was noticeably paler than his customary healthy brown hue. The giant was biting his lip to keep from saying anything else and was using his right hand to send a series of one-word signals to the rest of the Omada.

'Quiet.'
'Terrible.'
'More.'
'Much.'
'Worse.'

As Tal watched, both Dysi and Ana blanched until their skin almost twinned Notos's normal fish belly white pallor. Borras pointedly looked at Tal before discreetly moving his head backwards, then to the left. Tal knew that signal well. Not a word, of explanation or otherwise, until they were in their team's eavesdropping-proof safe room.

"Quiet, please." Tal noticed the professor wasn't demanding the students be silent. He was asking. Damn, a blind contract must be a truly terrible thing. "Quiet, please. Thank you," he said as the rumbling ceased. "I realize blind consents are extremely rare."

As several voices rose again in further protest, he held up his right hand for silence. "Fine. They are never used and are in fact illegal in almost every situation on almost every plane. The fact remains the HuntsMistress has substantial discretion in the management of the Hunts and she has decreed they will be used in this Treasyre Hunt.

"At this point I'm going to have to insist that you all not interrupt me again. The third task I have been given is to complete distribution of the books prior to the end of this class period or else all three teams will be penalized. Randomly and at different penalty levels."

Taking a deep breath, he continued. "The blind consent will involve bloodmagyk." Tal felt Borras grab his right wrist and squeeze it. Like a vise grip squeeze. After looking at his Prime's face Tal realized the squeezing was for Borras's benefit. So that he could keep from screaming, "NO! The deal is definitely not acceptable." About the time Tal decided he would have to learn to be left-handed for the rest of his life, the pressure abated. His right hand throbbed as the blood rushed back into it. When Borras finally let go he quickly wrote one word on Tal's notepad. 'Sorry.'

The other two teams were now either too stunned for any type of verbalization or their Primes had been able to maintain control of their teammates. Professor Elphinstone signaled to Kati of Kabila to stand and approach the front of the classroom. Before leaving her table she looked to each of her four teammates. They each gave her a small affirmative nod. She then slowly walked the length of the room until she was right in front of their teacher. At that point the professor drew a gleaming stiletto from a hidden ankle sheath. The professor mimicked a slashing motion across his palm before handing the knife to the Kabila Prime. Kati followed his instruction and slashed her left palm. Blue blood immediately welled up and out of the entire length of the razor thin wound, thoroughly coating her palm. She handed the bloody weapon back to the professor who wiped it on his pants leg before laying it on his desk.

Whoa, this shit done got real, Tal thought. Bloodmagyk! Obviously with the approval of the Archon or else it wouldn't work on Hunts School campus. But why? What was going on?

Professor Elphinstone motioned for Kati to extend both of her hands. Again, she did as directed. He then picked up the topmost Compyndium and placed it in her cupped hands. Kati grimaced. Something about even simple physical contact with the book caused significant pain.

In a slow, ritualistic cadence, Professor Elphinstone said, "A blind blood contract is offered. Do you consent?"

"I consent," Kati replied.

The professor continued in the same monotone voice. "State your team name, followed by the names of all of your Directions."

Still holding the book at arms length, Kati responded. "Kabila. Kati, First Prime Direction. Kaskazini, Second Prime Direction. Kusini, Third Prime Direction. Mashariki, Fourth Prime Direction. Magharibi, Fifth Prime Direction." As Kati finished her litany, the blue blood welling from her palm was abruptly sucked into the tome. Her entire body went rigid. The rigor was brief and was quickly followed by a violent tremor that shook her entire body. Tal's peripheral vision informed him all four of the other members of Kabila simultaneously jerked violently in their seats. As if they'd all received a significant electrical shock. It would have to be a magykal shock, he thought. It'll be electrical when it's my turn.

"The contract is bound." The professor motioned for Kati to return to her seat. As she began walking down the aisle, he motioned to Nord to approach. Tal noticed Nord didn't even look to his Släkt teammates for consent. Elphinstone repeated the ritual with Nord.

After finishing with Nord, Professor Elphinstone motioned Borras forward. Before leaving their table Borras looked each of his teammates in the eye, seeking their approval. Dysi and Ana were still white as twice-bleached linen. It was, of course, difficult to tell if Notos was whiter than usual. But all of them, including Tal, nodded permission to their Prime.

The entire ritual was repeated for the third time. As soon as Borras uttered the words, "I consent," every nerve ending in Tal's body fired at the same time. It took every bit of control he had to maintain control of his bladder. That hurt as bad as getting ass-branded, he thought. It really hurt. At least I'm not walking out of here with urine on the front of my pants. Sometimes you have to focus on the small victories, he reminded himself.

The professor indicated Borras should return with his Compyndium to the Omada table. As soon as Borras reclaimed his seat, the lecture continued. "As you have all agreed to blind consent of the blood contract, all three teams will now enjoy the privileges—and the obligations—that come with the bargain.

"As I mentioned earlier, the creators of the Compyndium were all chosen because they each had royal-level creationmagyk. It took careful scouring of all of the known Realms to find sufficiently gyfted Folk to complete the task. They were required to work until their magyk was completely exhausted. A dedicated team of physicks was onsite here at the school to insure their lives would be maintained for the balance of the natural lyfe expectancy of their Folk species."

Ana leaned over and whispered to the rest of the team, "What kind of 'lyfe' would those people have on artificial magykal lyfe-support? They drove those Folk until they completely exhausted their magyk and then they found some way to simply prolong their lives."

The Professor's explanation continued. "The result of the creators' collaboration and sacrifice is that the three Compyndium are unlike any other books in the entire known universe. As you can see, the books are extremely large, each containing several thousand pages. The books, as physical objects are finite, yet because of the collaborative magyk used to create them, the entries in each book are potentially infinite."

"Huh?"

Tal turned his head to see Mashariki of Kabila was the now somewhat embarrassed author of the ineloquent utterance.

Professor Elphinstone smiled for the first time of the entire class session. "Now that I've completed my required list and we still have a couple of minutes before the bell, I'll try to answer a couple of your questions. To answer Kabila, it is the *sui generis* magykal property of each of the Compyndium that make them priceless—and irreplaceable. Your Primes blood-bound themselves to the Compyndium and because of their authority, they also bound the rest of you.

"We will address procedure tomorrow, but this is generally what you can expect. When you each return to your secure team rooms and your Prime opens your assigned Compyndium, you will find that all of the pages are blank. Once the Journeys begin, each book will have the ability to show every single piece of treasyre you can imagine.

"This is where your time hard spent for the last hundred years will be of use. Every person you've met from a different plane. Every stray fact you've heard from one of your classmates or in a lecture. Every myth or legend you've ever heard in your entire lyfe experience. Any of these sources of knowledge may yield the name of the treasyre that might win the Hunt. Once you think of the name of an object, that object will appear in your Compyndium. There will be detailed artistic renderings of every variation of its physical appearance, together with a detailed description of the relative value of the object as treasyre, and perhaps most importantly, the book will also provide the name of the Realm in which such treasyre is currently located."

A low whistle from the Släkt table interrupted the teacher. It was followed by a question from Ost. "So what you're saying is the minute one of us opens our book it will be completely different than it was before we opened it?"

"Yes."

Ost wasn't done. "Which means that each of the three books will be different than the other two?"

"This is what I have been telling you. Each of these books is an irreplaceable original."

Again the low whistle, this time accompanied by some quiet murmuring at all of the team tables.

The professor's smile now turned upside down. "Okay, turning to the negative. I think you all realize now why each original of the Compyndium is irreplaceable. We will talk about the books' defense mechanisms in depth tomorrow but here's the bottom line. Principal Archon, Seshat, and the HuntsMistress have agreed to use of the books. Terms of the use will be enforced by the bloodmagyk blind contract. If a Compyndium is lost or destroyed, the mandated penalty is that one of the team members will forfeit their principal magyk. For the rest of their lives they will only have whatever secondary gyfts Amarantos has given to them."

There were no smart remarks. No deep breaths. No movement of any nature. The classroom had suddenly taken on a funereal pall.

Professor Elphinstone gave the class a couple of minutes to regain their composure before he crossed behind his desk to the classroom blackboard. Tal noticed his handkerchief was now back in full mopping mode.

"I'm directing that the Primes maintain control of the books until class tomorrow morning. I'll begin going over the remaining terms and conditions of the Hunt then and finish tomorrow afternoon. Primes, store your book either in your dorm suites or in your team room this evening. Be careful, be alert, and there shouldn't be any problem. Remember, class at nine bells in the morning. Bring your Compyndium. Class is dismissed."

CHAPTER TRIGINTA TRES

Tal, as Omada Fifth Prime, was last to enter the secured team room. The Omada Prime held his finger to his lips until he heard the hiss of the door magykally sealing behind Tal.

"What in Five-Hells?" Notos demanded. "What is the matter with Empousa?"

Borras raised both his arms, palms down, signally everyone to take their seats and take a moment to chill. "Second Prime, you know better. Naming has the ability to draw unwanted attention, even in this room."

Notos ducked his head slightly and raised his hand, the two-gesture combo comprising the universal acknowledgement of "my bad."

Borras continued. "We're all anxious. We'll find out more at nine bells tomorrow. Until then we all follow protocol and hold fast." With that he sat down in the only chair big enough in the room to accommodate him. "I'm not going to keep you. It's already been a long day and we're better served resting or relaxing than driving ourselves crazy playing head games about what the remaining terms and condition of the Hunt will be."

"Quint," Borras said, as he turned directly toward their replacement Fifth. "The rest of us have been here for almost a hundred years now. Away from our families, away from those who care about us...away from those we love and cherish. We have all suffered hurt, injury..." Borras reached across the table with his great right paw to softly cover Dysi's hands, "Grievous loss." Making eye contact with each of his teammates in turn he continued, "Past experience tells us that more, perhaps even greater, sacrifice may be required of one or more of us. That said, we all chose this exile, this opportunity, with full knowledge of the pluses and minuses. We weighed all of the factors and still volunteered to come to Hunts School to try to win the Tyrning."

This time he turned directly toward Tal. "You didn't. You shook my hand in good faith when I asked. You, who have no magyk, have time and again proven yourself an indispensable member of Omada. We would not still be in the Hunts if it were not for you, Quint. At every turn you have made the hard choices, the choices you believe lead you toward the Center. The last couple of days would have crushed any of the rest of us." Borras paused and smiled before continuing. "But not you. Somehow you bear the unbearable. Thank you for your sacrifice.

"You can lead us out today, Fifth Prime. We will meet again tomorrow as soon as class adjourns."

CHAPTER TRIGINTA QUATTUOR

"This morning's session will be the longer of our two classes. To assist in working our way through the Hunt details and requirements, I have written an outline on the board to cover all of the major bullet points."

Professor Elphinstone seems more relaxed today, Tal thought, as their teacher approached the top left side of the chalkboard. The HuntsMistress must not have dumped the delivery of any new life-threatening information on him.

"As you can see from the board, you will all be allowed to Journey with your Pucas this term."

There's some happy to start the day, Tal thought. The chance of me biting the big one goes down dramatically when Piras has my back.

"The Journey window will be five weeks. Ms. Empousa has declared the Journeys will be formatted as if they were independent studies. One team member at a time, for a consecutive seven-day period. Each week will begin at exactly midnight on day zero. The week will end at exactly midnight on day seven. Transfer will be made at that time from the outgoing member to the incoming member. Pickup and drop-off of the Compyndium will occur in Principal Chiron's office. He and Head Librarian Seshat will inspect the Compyndium for damage at each transition. Each of the Primes is authorized to decide

Journey order for their team. The default is in descending Prime order."

Tal was writing notes as fast as he could. *The default order has Fifth Primes going last. Since Slåkt has a replacement, Väst should move up to the fourth week and I'll be matched with that jackass Fem to bat clean up for our respective teams. Hopefully one of the rest of our squad will hit a home run and make my results superfluous.* He moved his head slightly to steal a surreptitious peripheral glance at the Slåkt table. *Yep, she was there, head down taking notes. She still looks like someone recently used her face as a punching bag. Which I guess they kind of did. Why didn't Nord let her stay in the infirmary to heal up properly? Central Processing promptly supplied the easy answer—because Nord is a dickhead extraordinaire.*

"A thesis will be required from each team member. The Journeys will not start for a few weeks, to give all of you time to pick a topic and then conduct research for your paper. It will be a violation to begin writing the paper before it is your Journey week. The HuntsMistress wants you to have the pressure of multi-tasking when it's your week with the Compyndium. You may pick any topic you like. Minimum five thousand words. The thesis requirement is a pass/fail. Any student who starts the paper early or who fails to submit their paper will be given a "fail," placed on the disabled list, and will not count toward the team minimum of four active players. The HuntsMistress has assigned me the task of determining whether the papers pass muster."

Thank goodness for small favors, Tal told himself.

"I have been asked to emphasize that when the final seven-day time period expires there will be no further use of the Prime Omphalos allowed during this Hunt. No exceptions."

Got it, Tal thought, as he wrote that detail down to make sure he'd remember.

"Exclusive control of—and responsibility for—the team Compyndium shall be with whichever team member is currently Journeying. If that team member is incapacitated, the team Prime will be allowed to handle the book."

Kusini of Kabila raised his hand.

"Question?" the professor asked.

"Who is going to determine whether someone is sufficiently 'incapacitated' to allow our Prime to handle the book?"

"It's a good ask. Best we can tell, the Compyndium's self-protection magyk will probably make that decision."

What the hell, Tal wondered.

"More needs to be said on that subject," Professor Elphinstone added. "For the last few centuries the books have only been opened under strictly controlled and warded situations. We have no reliable information as to what the Compyndium can do to defend themselves. We don't even have a good grasp of what type of actions the books might deem offensive. On this point I would remind each of you that there are things worse than death."

Got it, Tal told himself, as he wrote the warning down, underlined it three times and put a couple of exclamation points behind it.

A freshly laundered handkerchief made its first appearance of the morning. "There will be no automatic recall this term. If you do not make it back to the omphalos that is serving as your portal, you will not be returned to Hunts School. There is no time limit on making it back to your portal, with the following caveat—if your seven-day Journey period expires before you make your return trip, you will be stranded on whatever plane you're then on. Maybe for the rest of your life.

"The HuntsMistress is leaving to individual team strategy to determine how—and how much—you wish to keep each other informed as to acquired treasyre. At this point in the school year, you should assume the walls have ears."

Good point, Tal thought, as he made a note. Borras will undoubtedly have a plan addressing those details.

"As you will be wearing your Pucas, you may Journey as many times as you wish during your week. However, the HuntsMistress has declared that each teammate must secure at least a minimum of two level three treasyres. Any team member not securing the required minimum treasyre will be placed on the 'disabled' list."

Even with the best of luck that probably means a two Journey minimum per person, Tal realized. Shouldn't be a problem. I can't imagine a situation where I wouldn't take Piras with me.

"Ms. Empousa, although given wide discretion under the Hunts Rules in Treasyre Hunts, is still required to adhere to the MTVS as her baseline. In the extremely unlikely event a piece is not listed in the MTVS, she will then be allowed total discretion in determining treasyre valuation."

Tal raised his eyebrows at his Prime.

Borras wrote, "Magykal Treasyre Valuation System."

"The rating schedule goes from category one at the low end up to category five. Your team will receive credit for every item collected but please remember there are wide variations even within each rating category. For example, in some instances one category five treasyre might be worth more than ten category four items, while some category five treasyre might be worth only two pieces having a category four rating."

"The entire west wing of the library has been closed to all non-Hunts students. Släkt will have the exclusive use of the second floor, Kabila will utilize the third floor, and the fourth floor will be Omada's study territory. The HuntsMistress has implemented these precautions to help insure the safety of the Compyndium."

Yeah, to hell with the students, was Tal's initial thought. So what should be different about her position this term, he asked himself.

"If you write nothing else down this morning, every single team member needs to write this down. The library stairway and stairway landings are neutral territory. Other than utilizing the stairs themselves, during the five-week Journey window, if any member of a team is caught on a floor of the west wing of the library that is not their assigned team floor, that individual will be placed on the 'disabled' list."

Tal noticed that got the attention of the entire room. Figures, he thought. Even if they can't steal or mess with another team's Compyndium, some of the remaining competitors were no doubt already salivating about the chance to catch someone when they were all by themselves. In a situation where there would be absolutely no witnesses. Nord wouldn't think twice about it and I'm not trying to be unfair but Kati seems to be situationally maleable.

"We won't have any more classes this term after class this afternoon. You should all be researching both treasyre to target and term paper subjects when it isn't your week with the Compyndium. When it is your week, you should be Journeying and writing your papers.

"I will be available in my office during regular business hours for individual consultation. My availability is restricted to meeting with you only during your week to Journey.

"That is all for now. I will see you at fourteen bells."

CHAPTER TRIGINTA QUINQUE

Borras had decided that instead of meeting in the team room during the break between sessions, Omada should collect food and drink from the cafeteria, go sit in the sun, and relax. They would meet in the team room after the final class session at fourteen bells. It had been a good call, Tal decided. Tensions were high and it looked like the majority of this last term was going to be spent in individual work, not team effort.

They were now about an hour in on the afternoon class with a plethora of additional rules and restrictions having been added to the list for the Hunt. Professor Elphinstone was standing with his back to the class, reviewing his now labyrinthine Hunt outline on the chalkboard. "Alright then, I think we've covered everything I was told to address." He stopped to pull two fresh handkerchiefs out of his left front pocket and a third one out of his right inside front pocket before seating himself in his chair.

Wow! Tal thought. A "three-hankie all being used concurrently" requirement. The HuntsMistress has clearly outdone herself yet again with her assholery.

"Which brings me to my final assigned task of the day," Professor Elphinstone said wearily. "I have been instructed to administer an oral pop quiz to you right now. Whichever team wins today's test will have the exclusive opportunity to Journey to Earth Realm for treasyre collection."

"WHAT THE FUCK?"

CHAPTER TRIGINTA SEX

Tal glanced quickly around the room. He wasn't sure who yelled, he was so shocked he wasn't even sure if it was a guy or a girl. For a split-second he was worried it might have been him but concluded it wasn't. Nor was it any of his teammates. Thank goodness it wasn't me was his first thought. Notos would have knifed me was his second. As he looked at each of his teammates Tal could tell from their still-stunned expressions the prize was potentially a game-changer.

Professor Elphinstone cleared his throat with a soft "Ahem," but otherwise pointedly ignored the verbal ejaculation. "One member of the winning team will be allowed to Journey one time to Earth Realm using the Prime Omphalos. The winning team will be required to choose that individual before the start of the first week seven-day window. The Prime Direction for that team will notify me in writing of their team's selection." The Professor paused to wipe a little of the sheen off of both of his cheeks. "I strongly suggest you hold your decision in strictest confidence and not speak of it outside your secured team room."

Tal quickly drew a question mark on his notepad. Borras took Tal's pen and wrote his response. "Death!" What in Five–Hells? Then it hit him. The HuntsMistress was again baiting all of the Hunts teams to abandon whatever moral restraints they might still be clinging to. If someone on one of the other teams knew who the Earth plane delegate was, they might take whatever action necessary to make sure that person didn't have the opportunity to make that Journey.

Professor Elphinstone glanced down at his notes to confirm something before continuing. "Ah yes, that's how it goes. When it is the designated team member's turn with the Compyndium, that one book will have the ability to show the location of designated treasyre on Earth plane. When specifically directed the Prime Omphalos will send the designated competitor to the omphalos closest to the subject treasyre."

"Okay, that's today's prize. He picked up a large sealed envelope at the front left corner of his desk. He opened the envelope before quickly scanning its contents. "The HuntsMistress has written out an extremely lengthy series of questions on a wide range of topics. As the prize involves the Earth plane, the HuntsMistress has decreed all of the questions and answers will relate to that Realm. Each individual question will have the same value. Fifty points. In some instances there will be a series of questions relating to one general topic. In those instances whichever team answers the initial question correctly will have the first opportunity to answer the successor questions on that topic. If that team completes the series, it will receive the prescribed points for each correct answer. However, if that team misses a question in the series, then not only will the other teams have a chance to pick up all of those points but the initial team will have the aggregate points from all of that series' questions deducted from their cumulative score. Let us begin."

CHAPTER TRIGINTA SEPTEM

The "pop quiz" had become a marathon slog. All of the teams had been burned on more than one occasion by raising a hand too fast but thus far there hadn't been any of the potentially game-changing question series. There hadn't been any easy questions since the initial few rounds so team strategy for all teams had shifted to letting one or more teams answer incorrectly and then trying to poach with the narrowing list of correct possibilities. Tal had been able to help a little, but had to constantly remind himself the other students had an almost hundred year study head start on him.

Notos had been the Omada champion so far. Even with Notos's good work they still remained four hundred points behind Släkt. Kabila was in second, three hundred fifty points ahead of Omada.

Professor Elphinstone strode to the front middle of the classroom. "The next question is one of the question series. There are three questions in this particular series. Remember, each question is worth fifty points. If you guess wrong on the first question, your team loses one hundred and fifty points. However, whichever squad correctly guesses the first question gets to take a free shot at the next question. If they get that right then they get a free shot at the third question. Any questions?" He looked at each of the Primes in turn, beginning with Kati of Kabila, who shook her head no.

"Good. Let's begin. First question. Name the first Olympic event."

Tal watched as with zero hesitation Notos's hand began to shoot skyward. Short Term Memory flashed an image. Two, actually. First was Dr. Mertin Wilt. Well, Myrddin in othertyme the first time they'd met, but Tal hadn't know that then. Myrddin had told him, *"You would throw away every day of your now to be then. And once you were then, you would promptly find a new then to throw away your then now."* The second image was the pop quiz on his very first day at Nemeton High. Ms. Christie asked this exact question. If Tal hadn't experienced his then now back then he wouldn't know the answer in his now now. Damn it, I need some extra-strength Tylenol.

Faster than his conscious mind could even process his action, he grabbed hold of Notos's hand just shy of full extension and jerked it forcibly back down to the top of their table.

Notos immediately pulled his hand away from Tal. "What in Five-Hells do you think you're doing, you idiot?" he angrily whispered at Tal. "I'm on a roll and that's the easiest question in over an hour. Even an idiot could answer that question. It's the marathon."

"Wait a sec," Tal responded, tightly gripping Notos's arm again.

"Quint?" Borras questioned.

"Trust me, Prime."

Notos was scarlet-shading-into-purple livid as Fem's hand was the first from one of the other two squads to be fully raised. "You just cost us big time human. We're already four hundred points down. It's the first of three questions. When Släkt answers it correctly they'll pile another hundred and fifty points on their lead."

"Släkt was the first to raise their hand," the Professor declared.

"Too easy, Elphinstone. It's the marathon," Fem said, turning to smirk at Notos, rubbing it in that except for Tal's interference, Notos could have scored huge points for Omada.

"That is incorrect, Släkt Fifth Prime," their teacher replied.

"What? You're crazy!"

Professor Elphinstone drew himself up to his full height. "Släkt Prime Direction, I allow all of you much leeway given the stakes of the present contest and the unbelievable pressure that you are under. However, directly challenging the academic veracity of one of the Hunts School staff is not something that may be overlooked. As Prime you are responsible for the conduct of your team members. I will notify Ms. Empousa in the morning that the Journey window for the Släkt Fifth Prime should be shortened by one day."

Fem was still out of control. "You can't do that, you sorry..."

Tal wasn't sure which happened first. Professor Elphinstone opening his mouth to issue a further sanction or Nord's fist breaking his teammate's nose to make sure he didn't finish his sentence. As part of the transfer of force, Fem was catapulted out of his seat, landing appendages akimbo on the floor. Which was quickly covered with a rapidly spreading pool of dark blue blood.

Professor Elphinstone began again, now having to speak up to be heard over Fem's moaning. "We will take a short break as the Släkt seek medical attention for their Fifth Prime."

Nord stood up at his table. "Thank you, Professor, but Släkt isn't asking for any special favors. Let's proceed with class and we'll take our Fifth Prime to the infirmary after we win the quiz. Turning his head, he looked down at his Fifth Prime. "Unless you want a second helping, you'll suck it up and quit your damn caterwauling." The noise from the floor quickly diminished to what must only have been Fem's involuntary whimpering.

"One hundred fifty points is deducted from Släkt. Kabila had their hand up second," Professor Elphinstone said. "What's your answer?"

"We wish to retract our entry," Kati replied. It was clear from her face she'd also thought it was the marathon and she didn't want to eat a hundred and fifty points.

"I'm sorry, Kabila Prime. That's not the way the exercise is set up. Hand goes up, an answer must be tendered."

It was clear from her face that Kati had nothing. "Err, well, the javelin?"

"Wrong."

"Discus?"

"I told you you only get one answer. Violate the rule again and your team will be Journey-sanctioned. Kabila also loses one hundred and fifty points."

The teacher angled towards the Omada table. "That leaves Omada. Does your team wish to assay an answer?"

Tal looked at Borras first, who shrugged his shoulders, and looked sideways at Notos. Clearly, he was deferring the call to him.

"Last ask, Omada. Any other guesses?"

Tal directed his attention to Notos. "I know you don't think too much of me but I know this one. I promise."

Notos's nod was almost imperceptible. Tal immediately raised his hand.

"Omada. What is your answer?"

"The initial event of the Earth Realm Olympics was a running event, just not a marathon. It was a six-hundred foot sprint called the stadion. Legend says Hercules marked the distance himself by walking two hundred strides."

"Correct," Professor Elphinstone replied. "Omada will tentatively receive fifty points."

Tal heard a few "what the hell is a stadion" echoes resound throughout the entirety of the classroom.

"Second question. Remember you will receive another fifty points for a correct answer but still lose one hundred fifty if you're wrong. What was the second event added to the Olympics?"

Omada was now afforded the luxury of having time to confer by scribbling notes on their respective notepads. Tal gave them a moment before simply looking at Borras and nodding to let their Prime know he had this one as well.

"Omada, it is time for your answer."

Borras nodded at Tal, who quickly answered. "The diaulos."

Tal could tell from their teacher's reaction he was clearly impressed. "Another fifty points, for the moment, for the Dust Child and for Omada." There was grumbling from the other teams as well as Fem's soft sobbing from the floor under the Släkt table.

Elphinstone raised his hand to get everyone's attention. "Well, as they say on many planes, 'third time pays for all.' Final question in this subject series. How long is the diaulos?"

Tal didn't even wait this time before raising his hand. Professor Elphinstone nodded at him. "That's kind of a trick question as the tracks at the Greek stadia were not originally of uniform measure. So the length is a relative length, not an absolute. A diaulos is twice as long as the stadion in any given venue."

"Correct," Professor Elphinstone confirmed. "Omada is in third place with Kabila fifty points ahead of them. Släkt remains in first place with fifty points more than Kabila."

If anger had a voice the room would have been aroar. It didn't but pain did. In the form of a louder whimper, followed by a gurgling noise issuing from Fem's bloody lips.

Professor Elphinstone began walking toward the door. "One last question series is all that remains. Absent any possible legitimate corrective lesson, I cannot in good conscience allow the Släkt Fifth Prime to remain in the classroom. He needs medical attention immediately. This doesn't penalize Släkt as the Fifth Prime is obviously incapable at this time of participating in the team discussion."

The professor walked over, opened the classroom door, and punched a button on the hallway wall. Within seconds two physicks showed up. The professor held a short conversation with them, at which point all three entered the classroom. The physicks loaded Fem on a stretcher and carted him out of the room.

Professor Elphinstone gently closed the classroom door before turning to face the remaining Hunts competitors. "Let's finish the exam, shall we? Whoever answers the first question correctly gets first chance to answer all of the remaining questions. If you miss a question you lose all of the points for the entire series. Ready?" he asked as he scanned the classroom.

"Please listen closely to the entire question before raising your hand. What is the <u>most literal</u> translation of the phrase, *'tempus fugit'*?"

Tal had closed his eyes while the professor was reading the question. The professor had said "listen closely" to the "entire question." I mean, come on. What veteran of public school systems doesn't understand exactly what that specific phraseology means. Those are the usual suspect code words announcing a trick question. They're the verbal equivalent of a teacher's exaggerated wink.

Tal realized he was squeezing his eyes closed. What the hell, maybe it does help you listen better. And he heard it. There. Professor Elphinstone's cadence changed when he got to the words, "most literal." He overemphasized those two words.

Quickly opening his eyes he saw Borras was gearing up to raise his hand. Although everyone was gun-shy from the results of the last question series, one way or another this series determined who won the quiz. And the singular trip to Earth Realm. None of the teams wanted to act precipitously but on the flip side too much caution could also cost them the opportunity to win the day.

Tal caught Borras's eye and subtly shook his head to the left. Just the one time. So neither of the other teams would catch on there might be a trick. Borras raised his right eyebrow and acted like he was going to go ahead and raise his hand anyway.

Tal glanced around. Both of the other Prime Directions had their hands about halfway up. They'd paused though when they saw Borras hesitate. "Prime," Tal whispered. "Whatever you think the answer is, it isn't." Tal saw from the corner of his eye that it was Notos who caught on first. "Trick," he mouthed at Borras.

Borras nodded like he understood, right before immediately tensing his hand to shoot it to the roof. Kati of Kabila knee-jerk reacted to Borras's action by immediately raising her hand. At the exact same moment that Kabila Prime won the right to answer the question first, the Omada Prime Direction ever so slowly lowered his massive ham of a hand, while one of his trademark horizon to horizon grins began working its way, coast to coast, across his massive face.

"Well, well, well," Tal said admiringly. "It looks like Omada Prime's got game."

"Yes, Kabila Prime," Professor Elphinstone stated, formally acknowledging Kabila had prevailed in obtaining first shot at the answer.

"It means 'time flies'," Kati responded, while she raised her right hand to receive high-fives from her squad.

Professor Elphinstone smiled broadly. "I'm sorry Kabila but that is incorrect. It is true that is the most common translation of the phrase used on Earth Realm but that is not what the question asked. Kabila will be docked one hundred fifty points and is out of contention for the prize. The floor is now open for either of the other two teams to provide a correct response.

It was now between Omada and Släkt. Because of the point differential, Omada had to get it right to win the Earth Journey. Tal looked to his teammates. It was clear all four of them would have given the same answer as Kabila. He glanced back over his shoulder to the Släkt table. Tons of tension and fast hand gestures all the way around. They're having to regroup as well.

Tal turned his focus back to his Prime. Borras, per his usual, let everyone participate as he glanced around the circle. Ana and Dysi gave slight negative headshakes. Notos mouthed the word "out" before turning his head to Tal. "You came through big time a few minutes ago, mortal. But that doesn't mean squat if you cock this up."

Tal looked back to the Släkt, who were practically salivating at this point. Notos is right. "I know it, Prime," he told Borras. "I know the correct answer." The Omada leader inclined his head in response and Tal raised his hand.

"Yes, Omada Fifth?" Professor Elphinstone asked.

"The most literal translation is, 'time flees'," Tal said firmly.

Professor Elphinstone beamed the universal teacher smile utilized when a student has done well. "That is correct, Omada Fifth. The complete sentence in which it was first used was, *'Sed fugit interea fugit irreparabile tempus, singula dum capti circumvectamur amore.'* Literally translated it means, 'But meanwhile it flees: time flees irretrievably, while we wander around, prisoners of our love of detail'."

Time flees irretrievably? Tal realized he'd never thought about the famous quote in the context of its place in the entire sentence. He'd always assumed it referred to the mortal condition. What if it also meant Time was afraid of something? But what could that possibly be? His attention was summoned back from its wandering by a palpable increase in several dynamics occurring simultaneously in the classroom. There was the relief, coupled with pride, of his teammates. There was also a burgeoning anger from both of the other squads. The Kabila animus was noticeably higher at this juncture than Släkt. That was to be expected, he decided. Kabila had stubbed their toe and they had no chance left to win the prize.

Professor Elphinstone rapped his fist on his desk several times, signaling for everyone to quiet down. "There are two more questions in this series. If Omada gets them both correct, it wins by the narrow margin of fifty points. If it misses either of them, Släkt won't have to answer to be the winner. The next question is who is the Earth Realm poet credited with coining the phrase, *'tempus fugit'*?"

Tal let the words replay twice in his head before he concluded there was no trick to this question. He nodded at Borras, who promptly looked to the other three. They all nodded they were good with Tal taking a crack at it.

"The Earth Realm poet was Virgil," Tal stated.

"Correct again," the professor replied.

The grumbling from the other tables increased. Tal realized a large portion of it had nothing to do with the actual score. It was because a Dust Child was single-handedly beating them all. *Every time I turn around, my continued survival doesn't seem to be a given at this damn school.*

"The third and final question is a little harder. What is the name of the poem in which Virgil used the subject phrase?"

This is no good, Tal realized. This isn't a one-man show, Omada is a team. The other two squads don't need to be gunning for me, thinking if they can somehow take me out of the game, that Omada is no longer a threat to win the Hunts. We need for them to be afraid of our entire squad. Both individually and as a whole. Bluff, Tal told himself. Bluff and give Borras the chance to reforge us as a unified team.

Instead of responding aloud, Tal grabbed his notebook and scribbled, "I think I know it but I can't call it to mind at this moment." He pushed the tablet to Borras who reviewed it before passing it to Ana, then Dysi, and finally Notos.

Their entire group was sufficiently disciplined that there were no facial expressions that might alert the other teams to the Omada predicament. They had to know there was a potential problem since Tal didn't immediately answer. The air in the classroom now had a whiff of "eau de wolves immediately before they rip the faltering leader's throat out."

Borras retrieved Tal's notepad and wrote, "Suggestions?" He passed it to Ana. She took only a few seconds before writing, "I have absolutely no idea." She passed it to Dysi, who promptly wrote, "Ditto." She tried to pass it to Notos but he had his eyes closed. Concentrating.

Borras resignedly retrieved the pad, "Take your best shot, Quint. A guess has more chance than no answer at all."

Damn it, my play didn't work, Tal told himself as he slowly raised his hand. I guess I can act like it suddenly came to me, he decided.

Suddenly, he felt a hand on his shoulder. A cold, bony-assed hand. Notos's hand. Voluntarily touching him. "Pretty sure I know this one, teammate. Mind if I take a crack at it?"

Tal nodded, as he felt his face flush with relief. Momentarily, anyway. Because if Notos got it wrong…

"Yes," Professor Elphinstone replied in response to Notos's raised hand. "I see it's the Omada Second Prime this time. Your answer?"

"The Earth Realm poem is titled, 'Georgics'."

Tal was pretty sure everyone in the entire room was holding their breath at that exact moment.

"Correct," Professor Elphinstone confirmed. "With a sterling example of team cooperation, Omada wins the quiz and the prize. Thus ends your last formal class at Hunts School. Please leave your Compyndium on my desk as you exit. Your team's volume will be delivered to your first week Journeyer at midnight in Principal Chiron's office on their first night.

"Omada will need to tender the name of its teammate who will be taking the Earth Realm Journey at that time. We are adjourned."

Borras waited until both of the other teams walked out before motioning for Omada to stand and walk in single file.

Smart, Tal thought. This way he puts himself between his team and the last member of the preceding team, which also puts Omada's fragile mortal the farthest away from the enemy. As they walked down the hallway to their team room, Tal put his body on autopilot so he could think about Earth Realm. About Mom, Pell, the twins. And, of course, Elle.

CHAPTER THIRTY EIGHT

'AUTHORIZE BREATH!' Medulla demanded of Central Processing.

No response.

Medulla tried again, 'MAKE LUNGS EXPAND!'

'REQUESTS DENIED,' came the priority one override from Central Processing.

Tal couldn't hold his breath much longer. Someone had kicked him in the head with a boot heel and that someone was now standing on his neck, holding his head underwater. He knew what would happen if he inhaled, but his lungs were out-screaming his brain. Tal gasped a half-breath and immediately started choking on the sediment-filled water coursing through his nose and mouth.

Wait a minute, I've almost drowned exactly like this once before. The Journey when I found the Sword of Destiny. Hold tight lungs, if I'm right a hand is about to…snatch me by the collar and throw me up into the air.

As he flew up into the air like a Raggedy Andy, Tal's lungs began heaving as he gratefully sucked air. Central Processing began exploring some at least semi-rational explanations. Prefrontal Cortex urgently reminded Tal he needed to look to his right—NOW.

Yep, it's the armor-wearing soldier who saved me the last time. Just like last time, he's killed the guy who was trying to stomp-drown me. All of the terrible sounds are the same as before, horses and men screaming, together with all of the other sounds of injury, and death, and war. Tal retched, remembering the gore from the last time he'd experienced it. What's going on? I was with my team walking to our secured room, and boom! Here I am again, near death.

The solider was talking to him. Tal was still so discombobulated that at first the man's words didn't even register. "Snap out of it, soldier! I don't have time to babysit you, I'm expected back at the command tent."

That's exactly what he said to me the first time, Tal thought. What's next? C'mon, what's next? Right. He's about to send me over to those trees. That'll give me a chance to catch my breath and try to figure out what's going on.

"I have to go, but I'll stay and cover you until you reach those trees. Go!"

Right on schedule, Tal thought, as he attempted to haul ass toward the trees. Attempted being the operative word. It seemed as if the driving rain had been specifically oriented so as to pummel him to the ground, where its co-conspirator muck could try to ensnare him. How did I ever make it last time, Tal wondered, as he sidestepped a couple of slow motion swordfights, before finally making it to the safety of the thicket.

Last time I spent about fifteen minutes hiding in here trying to figure out what was going on. Clock's ticking, Tal, figure it out. We just won the pop quiz and were all headed to our team room to discuss strategy.

Now I'm here again. Back on Earth plane for the series of events that culminated in me giving Excalibur to Arthrys. The first time around Borras thought it was a Conundrum—an impossible time travel. I left the Prime Omphalos chamber but the rest of the Omada didn't. Or maybe I just thought I left.

I didn't go to the Prime Omphalos chamber this time so this isn't a Journey. When I was here last time I didn't know I had been here before like I do now. Turn the Rubik's cube, Tal. Use that memory of yours.

HOLY SHIT! Amarantos sent my ass othertyme. It fits. Borras was right, a Conundrum is impossible—except for the

Stytch. Which was Myrddin but now is me. I didn't remember being here last time because this hadn't happened yet. But it has now. Damn this time paradox thing is a bitch to cipher. This is an actual physical case of déjà-vu. Well, a little different. I need to do everything exactly the same. So it will be a case of déjà-vu-redo. Otherwise I might not make it out of here alive, Arthrys might not get the Sword of Many Names, and that asshat Malebranche might win the Tyrning.

Damn, I let my mind totally wander when I should have been keeping a rough track of my total elapsed time. Think, Tal. That's it. There was a point in time where the downpour seemed to double and you knew visibility would be limited for anybody who might want to hack you to pieces. Wait for that moment.

Although partially sheltered by the dense shrubbery of the thicket, Tal heard the rain begin to hammer harder. This is it. Out this way a short distance and then I have to lay down in icy water accumulated next to that low wall over there. He ran to his spot by the wall. Now I'm going to have to watch two guys savagely kill each other. Again. No, this time I know what happens so I only have to listen. He did. To metal crunching bone, to blood gurgling in their throats as both men tried to breathe. He knew it was over when he heard their death breaths rattling out of their mouths and smelled the overwhelming stench of them shitting themselves as their bowels, no longer restrained by life, voided their contents. Even though he knew it was coming, Tal threw up again. Just like last time. Actually this is the only time. I just have to recreate it. But how can that possibly be the case? How is it possible I could do it right last time and then maybe screw it up this time? Stupid time travel. It's stupid.

Tal didn't waste the effort putting on the armor this time, except for the mail hauberk to protect his head and neck. The rest had ended up being too heavy and he'd had to take it all off without it apparently having been needed to guarantee his safety. Instead he stayed still and spent the time by using the minutes to try to remember exactly everything he'd done and said.

Okay, time to go. You crept along this wall about half a mile and then two groups of fighters came toward you. You stuck your face in the mud and played dead last time. Do it again, just don't fall asleep this time. He quickly carved a little air cavity in the mud so he could turn his face a little to the left and still get air while it appeared from above that he was taking the final dirt nap.

Both sets of soldiers finally gave up their fight and he heard each side retreat to their respective armies. Now what? Oh yeah, this is where I used my first wish and the Sword of Power rose up out of the water.

Wait a minute. If I can save that wish I'll have one to use to save Elle's life at the Winter Formal. I'm sure Excalibur is just hanging out there in that field. I can go feel around in the water until I find it. That's actually a good plan, he decided.

It's a shit plan was his very next thought. This is what Myrddin told you about. Free will in this moment, in every moment of your life. There is no such thing as predestination. I can choose not to use the wish this time. I have no idea what the consequences of that one decision might be. Maybe I find Excalibur, maybe I don't. Maybe Arthrys becomes Archon, maybe he doesn't. Maybe Elle ends up living, maybe she dies in some other manner. "Worlds depend upon me," according to Gas Pump Unus.

I'm sorry, Elle. I feel like I'm killing you all over again but I can't take a chance on Arthrys not getting Excalibur from me. Tal turned his ring one time, it turned into a rainbow band illuminated from within. It seemed almost alive the way the colors flowed over and through and around each other. What were my words last time? Memory supplied the answer. "Amarantos, please help me 'Seek the Center'."

Okay, this is where you thought you got a defective magyk ring and you followed the wall as it angled up toward the fort. Right about here, where the threshed wheat field has been turned into a shallow lake.

The rain finally let up and the rainbow appeared. Here we go, Tal thought, as he stepped across the field toward where one end of the rainbow terminated in a stone hand rising from the water. A stone hand holding the Sword of Many Names.

Bingo. Knowing what he had to do, Tal walked around the back of the stone block and read the inscription:

Through countless choosings,
across legions of lives,
I am the Sword of Many Names.
Eversore the Destroyer.
The Flaming Blade of Uriel.
One day I shall be called Dies Irae—The Day of Wrath.
Given freely I may be, by force never taken.
Take me up— if you 'Seek the Center'.
If not, leave me stay—else your soul I'll take.

Alrighty, I survived grabbing that bad boy last time. But it's been almost an entire school year since then. Do I still qualify as 'Seeking the Center," or have I gone south in some meaningful measurement?

This is a stupid discussion. This time is last time. It's the only time. I've actually only been here this one time. Well, maybe that's a correct interpretation of the vagaries of time travel and maybe it's not, he told himself. For absolutely everyone else in the universe this is the only time. For you and you alone—it is the second time which will occur simultaneously with the first time, except still occur after the first time because you had no idea the first time what choices you would make during this simultaneous second time.

STOP IT, TAL. "That way madness lies," is what the Bard would tell you if he were here. Okay. Fine. Good conversation. You've already used your first wish. Grab the sword and let's giddy up, he finally resolved. Despite his just completed discussion with himself, Tal noticed his hand was shaking as he reached out to take the Sword of Power. He closed his hand right above the hilt, the stone hand released the weapon to him, and it and the boulder sank into the water. Which was crazy because the water was only eighteen inches deep.

Because of his prior or simultaneous or whenever real time experience, he was prepared for the sword's power this time. Somehow the Sword of Many Names had a mind of its own. That's not accurate, he decided. It has a will or a purpose, it doesn't mean that it's sentient. In any event, he ignored the seductive thoughts it was engendering. There is only one person who can safely and properly wield this sword—Arthrys.

Tal started walking until he reached the wall. I laid it right here, he reminded himself. Then the soldiers showed up.

"Who dost thou battle for?"

Right on cue. Oh shit, I forgot. I'm going to have to stand here and let them knock the crap out of me. Right after I have a conversation with them and mention Arthrys Pendragon by name so they can repeat it in the tent. Which is after I wake up with a shit-rope gag stuffed in my mouth. Tal remembered his words and their words and dutifully repeated his lines like it was rehearsal for this year's senior play.

Okay, now Victor tries to pick up the sword of power and can't. Tal watched that event. The captain then ordered him to pick up the sword. Tal complied. Sorry, not sorry, Victor, he thought, as the sword seized control of his arm, slicing through the air at Mach speed, cutting off a chunk of Victor's left ear lobe. The Sword of Many Names continued its dance on autopilot, cutting Vic's sword in half before ending up with the point at Victor's throat.

"Yield! I yield to the magyk sword," Victor whispered, his greasy shoulder length hair falling over his face as he fell to his knees.

Okay, Tal just stand here while…damn, that hurt, he thought, as he fell to the ground from getting knocked in the back of his head. Just lay here because it's going to happen aga…

Gaugghh!! I swear that rope is even nastier than the last time…first time…same time. To hell with time travel. You know the good stuff is coming so it's less fun and you know the bad stuff's coming so it's even worse. At least I know I'm not blind this time, he reminded himself. He started moving his head up and down on the tent pole until the cloth blindfold slipped down his neck.

Damn, my head really hurts. He listened to the ongoing argument in the tent about what to do with him. The entire thing took on a different meaning since he now knew these weren't his Släkt opponents, they were Arthrys's Släkt from five Tyrnings past. Now they were finished arguing about whether to kill him, and had moved on to their discussion about the Sword of Many

Names. Here comes the critical part…Arthrys hearing his psuche name. And there it is, and here comes Nord to get me.

As he was being manhandled into the tent, Tal reminded himself this upcoming part was critical. He needed to repeat it word for word. Maybe he could just add a little additional bit. If he told Arthrys that Malebranche survives their duel and becomes the leader of the Crestfallyn, maybe Arthrys could make sure he kills him. Then Tal wouldn't have to deal with that faceless spook that haunted him until his eighteenth birthday. His mom wouldn't have to move all the time.

Great idea, Brainiac, because if y'all aren't hounded by the specter then she doesn't have to keep moving and she won't be in that Starbucks to meet Pell. Say goodbye to the twins. Oh, and your family would never move to Nemeton.

Okay, right. Fine, I get it. I get it, Amarantos. I finally understand that just because you're omniscient that doesn't deprive any of your children of their Free Will. Now into the tent.

"I am Mitt, Prime Direction of the Släkt."

Man I forgot how regal the dude is, even in his Hunts School disguise. Tal dutifully played his part in their colloquy about Hunts School, about Tal being human and finally about the Sword of Many Names. Now he's going to ask for me to hand him the sword to look at. Steady as she goes, Tal. He doesn't kill you. Well, he didn't the other same time at this moment of earlier but actually the same time. "This sword belongs to Arthrys, Pendragon of the Alfar."

Arthrys's sword was at his throat. Now comes our dialogue about how all of this came about. We're almost to the end. Holy crap! Last time it was the Recall that terminated our meeting. Or was it?

Okay, it's time to gyft him the sword. Done. Now he's telling me Lailoken has been whisked away to do Amarantos's bidding. Except that's not what's happened. I've taken his place as the Traveler and he is human once more. Now tell Arthrys how you got the sword, how it fulfills the prophecy and help him discover its new name. Excalibur.

Seems like there is something I'm forgetting about our conversation. Right, Tal's words of wisdom. "Excalibur it is, Arthrys Pendragon. Please remember when you are Archon, humans are Amarantos's children too."

"I will remember your words and your gyft. Is there no gyftpryce you would ask of me?"

Here comes my jumping off point. "Now that you mention it, there is a little something something. Do me a huge solid. Please, please don't cut my head off with Excalibur the first time you and I meet."

"Done," Arthrys replied immediately but then looked confused. "I don't understand. This is the first time we've met."

Right now, Tal told himself. Last time, right now is when the pain became almost unbearable, right now is when…

When I'm sitting in a chair in our team room doing my best bobblehead impression, while Dysi is shaking the holy crap out of me, yelling at me to "Snap out of it, damn it!" while Ana tells Borras they should probably take me to the infirmary to have me checked out.

Five-Hells! It wasn't a Recall last time, it was the back end trauma of being sent othertyme. This whole exercise of trying to parse whether my present is really and truly now or whether someone else's passed past is my present present is seriously exhausting.

CHAPTER TRIGINTA NOVEM

Five weeks. The period from their last class until midnight tonight. When Borras was due to check in with the HuntsMistress, Principal Chiron, and Seshat in Chiron's office.

At the outset Tal thought the five weeks was going to feel like an eternity, but it hadn't. It flew by. For everyone else, since they'd been students at Hunts School for almost an entire century, it must have seemed like the blink of an eye.

There are around twelve weeks and some change between Imbolc and Beltane. Which makes sense, Tal told himself, since they're both cross quarter feast days for a number of "pagan" cultures. The actual dates of each feast fluctuated from year to year. Like Thanksgiving. This translated to about ten usable weeks, give or take, each semester for school purposes. This term was broken down into around five weeks of research and independent study followed by the five consecutive weeks of Journeying. At the conclusion of that time block there would be a couple of days before the Beltane Feast and the investiture of the new Archon and Ruling Council.

Much of the waking portion of Tal's five weeks had been spent with his head in a book. First, in trying to figure out a worthy topic for his paper. When that goal was finally achieved, he turned his attention to a second goal. Attempting to diversify his knowledge concerning known world navels. His hope being there might be literary references to treasyre associated with such sites.

The list was large, there were substantial references in almost every culture. Tal knew enough now to understand that only some of the world navels physically exist on Earth Realm but all of them exist on one or more of the countless other planes of existence.

Tal had previously heard of many of the sites, although not necessarily in the context of being world navels. Places like the Oracle site at Delphi, the Foundation Stone above the Well of Souls on the Temple Mount in Jerusalem, Mount Sinai, and Mecca. These were all well known.

There were dozens of unfamiliar ones. Easter Island, Cuzco in Peru, Baboquivari Peak in Arizona, and the Temple lot in Independence, Missouri, to name a few.

After research, the next biggest block of time had been meeting with his teammates in their team room. Debating and deciding on many different procedural matters. Details Tal never would have considered but might be important. After the Journeys began, the teammates were not going to again meet all together, unless someone signaled an emergency. Togetherness presented an unnecessary opportunity for someone to take out two or more of their team, which would reduce them below the required four-person minimum.

They were not going to make any attempt to tell each other what specific treasyre they'd collected. Instead, they would use campus messengers to deliver necessary information. As the gossip conduit would quickly apprise the entire campus of a note's contents, Borras worked out an encryption for information concerning treasyre levels. Sometimes up was down, sometimes up was middle and down was down, and so on. Without the key Borras outlined for the Omada, any information would be completely misleading. A similar but separate pattern was developed for advising that a team member had made their minimum number of Journeys and acquired their minimum qualifying pieces of treasyre. Borras had even been sufficiently tactically prescient to mandate when the Compyndium was not physically present with that week's team member, that it should be stored in the team safe room. They all had access to the team room. This wasn't the case with their dorm suites, which were inaccessible to anyone else, excepting only senior school administration.

Being busy proved to be a huge blessing. His perpetual engine brain hadn't had much time to feel. Not to feel guilt about his family, about Emet, or about Elle. Not to feel self-pity concerning those or any other topics. Not to miss being with Väst.

CHAPTER QUADRAGINTA

The omphalos and its encircling henge were situated on a small hillock overlooking a near endless sea of desert dunes. Kati's targeted objective, Mount Kaf, was barely a smudge on the horizon.

That Compyndium was unbelievable. She'd been more than a little shocked when she'd first opened the book and every single page was still completely blank. Pissed off might be a better description. She'd been slow on the uptake about how to access its magyk, hopefully her teammates would catch on faster than she did. Once she'd figured it out though, the book's magyk had been everything and more than she'd imagined was possible.

She'd played it safe the first couple of Journeys. Picked up two level three treasyre pieces. Not enough to win but sufficient to satisfy Empousa's damn minimum collection requirement. After that she'd only tried for level five artifacts and had struck out all three times.

As Kati paused to catch her breath, she took a moment to recall the Compyndium's information about this Persian Realm. The planet on this plane, which was roughly Earth-sized, danced in a complex orbit determined by the gravitational pull of its three suns. With her boots on, she knew she stood about six feet, with her eye level being about four inches less. The math indicated an unobstructed view to the horizon for her would be right about three miles.

Three miles out and back, she thought, glancing up to fix the position of the three suns. None were anywhere near their zenith and the air temp already felt like she was being kiln-baked. Has to be a round-trip with no safety net this Hunt. Which means all the way to the destination and back to touch the local omphalos or I don't return to Hunts School. Ever.

I can't do it, it's not possible to get that far with this heat. What little flesh wasn't covered by her Puca already felt like it was broiling. That was despite the best efforts of Azar to absorb the majority of the heat and regulate Kati's internal systems to keep her as cool as possible. As she took another glance across the dunes she could see the heat waves undulating upward.

There has to be some method in which the mission can be accomplished, she reminded herself. The Compyndium identified this omphalos site as the one closest to the treasyre. It's late on my seventh day. This is my last Journey. I don't have another level five object identified and even if I did I'd have to be out and back before the exchange with Kaskazini in Chiron's office at midnight tonight. Plus, I have no idea how time would be measured on any other treasyre plane.

Nope, this is it. You know what you have to do, she confirmed to herself. You are Kabila Prime and you have an obligation to your team. You have to do whatever it takes to obtain the treasyre and make a timely return to Hunts School.

As if that thought had spun it into existence, Kati caught a glimpse of movement in her peripheral vision. She turned her head to the right. It was one of the Realm's fabled Zoba'ah. This one was a whirlwind so large its funnel was lifting whole acres of sand to fuel its upward spiral. In the otherwise clear cobalt sky it didn't appear to even have a skyward terminus. It spun closer, closer, until Kati wondered if she'd made an assumption she shouldn't have made. Stand your ground, she told herself. You couldn't outrun it now, even with Azar's help.

The sand tornado stalled in place about a hundred feet away from her, its sand quickly abrading her exposed skin. As was her way, Azar said nothing, but Kati could tell the maelstrom was hurting her as well.

Suddenly the Zoba'ah changed. It ceased contact with the

ground and slowly began spinning itself up into the sky, becoming smaller and smaller, until with a small popping noise it was gone. Floating in the place formerly occupied by the whirlwind was the largest kind of, sort of, bird she had ever seen in her entire life.

'Well not really a bird, more like a demi-bird,' Azar advised her.

It's a Simurgh, Kati told herself.

'If we are to be precise, Mistress, that is The Simurgh.'

Must be an important distinction if Azar is going to thought-speak to me, Kati decided. She's right, though. The Compyndium's dossier on the beast had been thorough. Its name, derived from a Persian plane language, literally meant "thirty birds" because it was at least as big as thirty birds. The creature's plumage was a breathtaking melding of a peacock and a flycatcher. The claws, however, were those of a lion not a raptor and as the Compyndium had reported it looked large enough to tote an elephant.

The Simurgh entry had mentioned its ability to prophecy. The life span of the singular creature was listed as "renewably eternal." Renewable in that each incarnation of The Simurgh lived a little less than two thousand years. Then it self-immolated, emerging anew from the embers. Kati knew that every Realm was different. What was absolutely indestructible, or fatal, or eternal in this Persian Realm might only be relatively indestructible, fatal, or eternal on another plane. It was the same with Time. A minute, an hour, a year was constant within every individual plane, but those were not universally equal measurements of Time.

The Compyndium entry stated The Simurgh had survived three entire cycles of this plane's destruction and rebirth. Which made The Simurgh truly an ancient of days. Kati knew from her hundred years of classes at Hunts School that mythologies about cycles of world destruction and recreation were common across many of the known Realms. On the Aztec Realm, the myth was known as the "Legend of Five Suns." Differing versions of world cycles of destruction and rebirth were also taught on the Navajo, Hopi, and Hindu planes.

Pulling herself from her reverie, Kati took a closer look at The Simurgh. This incarnation may be centuries old, Kati thought, but her human face looks to be that of a woman in her forties. A finely chiseled, classically proportioned woman in her forties.

"Peace be upon you and yours, sister-daughter of the Unfading Spirit."

"You're The Simurgh," Kati replied.

"In our present lyfe we are titled, Forever Rising Sun. On some planes, and to some Folk, we are known as The Bennu or The Phoenix. To others we are called The Firebird. How may we be of assistance to you this day?"

Wow, Kati thought. The Simurgh's voice, maybe actually voices, was like the human vocal equivalent of the musica universalis. Perfectly pitched, balanced, harmonious with itself and the entirety of its surroundings. "I am Kati, First Prime of Kabila. My team is one of the three remaining Finalists in this Tyrning's Hunts. I have Journeyed to this Realm to collect treasyre."

There was a pause before The Simurgh responded. If Kati had known the creature's mannerisms better she would have thought the body language indicated resigned sadness.

"Kati, Kabila Prime," The Simurgh replied, with a nod and a small but courteous bend of her neck. "A Treasyre Hunt? I was afraid that might be the reason for your visit. This is the final Hunt of the present Tyrning?"

"Yes, Simurgh."

"Whichever team prevails shall be the Ruling Council for the next three hundred years?"

"Yes, Simurgh."

A sigh, Kati thought. There was no question that both of the creature's wings lowered momentarily.

"It is beyond my understanding, now or in any of my prior incarnations, why the Folk do this to their beloved children. Why they subject them to death, or worse, as the path to acquire leadership. Kati, Kabila First Prime, you are aware Amarantos has charged all contestants with attempting to win by Seeking the Center?"

Now it was Kati's turn to pause a beat. "I am, Simurgh." There's no need for her to know I've decided to interpret Amarantos's commandment as a fluid concept. As "Practically Seeking the Center."

"You are surely aware bartering for treasyre follows the same laws as those governing gyfts and gyftpryces."

"I am," Kati replied.

"There is only one level five treasyre within this Realm."

"The Tablets of Destiny."

"The Tablets are unique in all of the known Realms. Whoever wields them has the ability to turn back time for up to one hour." The Simurgh paused her serious pause yet again. "The barter price for that relic is too high, nor is it yours to offer, Kati, Kabila First Prime. It would be best for you to return this minute through the omphalos. Once you return to Hunts School you can choose something else to collect."

"This is my last Journey, Simurgh. I am leader of the Kabila and I have thus far failed them. Is it true you possess the gyft of future sight?"

"It is."

"Will you use your gyft for me?"

"Answers to questions three are part of the Tablets' barterpryce, sister-daughter. Please ask wisely for I will answer only the question asked. No explanations will be made. Once you ask your third question, the barterpryce must be paid in full."

"Thank you Simurgh." Think Kati, she told herself, wiping her brow. Damn, it must be hotter than I thought. I feel like I'm roasting.

Azar interrupted Kati's thoughts with thought-speak. 'It appears the heat of this Realm increases exponentially as its three suns rise to zenith. Their combined heat will soon prove more than I am able to counteract for you.'

Frustrated, Kati snapped in reply. 'I do not need your input in this matter, Puca. Do your job. And don't ever interrupt me again while I'm thinking.'

Smallest to biggest, Kati told herself. Be careful of your questions, she reminded herself. Ask exactly what you need to know so there's no wiggle room. Okay, got all three. "If I continue with this quest will I obtain the Tablets?"

"If you continue with this quest you will obtain the Tablets," The Simurgh formally intoned in response.

"If I obtain the Tablets, will I safely return to Hunts School?"

"If you obtain the Tablets, you will safely return to Hunts School."

"If Kabila possesses the Tablets will it win the Treasyre Hunt?"

"I am unable to answer that question as phrased. You may try one more time."

Okay, okay, what did I miss, Kati asked herself. What was ambiguous? If I get the Tablets there's absolutely no set of circumstances where I'm letting them out of my sight until the Coronation Ceremony is over. That must be it, though. My question must have been too amorphous as to time frame. That has to be it. Well, that's an easy fix. "If I possess the Tablets at the time of the Coronation Ceremony, will Kabila win the Treasyre Hunt?"

"If you possess the Tablets at the time of the Coronation Ceremony, Kabila will win the Treasyre Hunt."

It all seems too easy for a kickass level five artifact, Kati decided.

"Kati, Kabila First Prime, you did not use any of your questions to ask what the barterpryce will be."

"I didn't need to Simurgh. Given the answers to those three questions, there is no barterpryce too high." Kati continued, "I do not know how few Earth plane hours remain before my midnight deadline. I must travel to the Tablets, obtain possession, and return to this place for my Recall before my time expires. Whatever the barterpryce is, it will be paid in full."

The Simurgh nodded her head slightly in acknowledgement. "So be it. You were warned it was not yours to pay. The Unfading One has given us each the unfettered right to choose as we will. I will ask the Zoba'ah to carry you safely to Mount Kaf. The treasyre you seek is on an altar atop the mountain's highest point."

'Please do not do this, Mistress,' Azar pleaded in Kati's

mind.

Kati chose not to even dignify Azar's objection with a response. "When we get there, is there a dragon or some other fell monster waiting to rip my head off?"

The Simurgh smiled. Briefly. "No, Kati, Kabila First Prime. You simply have to pick the Tablets up to make them yours."

"That's it?"

"It will be a sufficient test."

"Will the Zoba'ah bring us back to the omphalos?"

"I shall ask," The Simurgh replied. Stretching her wings to their utmost she flapped them. The wind buffeted Kati who had to brace herself and lean into the gale to keep from being blown ass over heels backwards. Now twenty feet above the ground, The Simurgh flapped her wings again, and then again. Now several hundred feet above the omphalos, she began ululating, summoning the whirlwind.

It reappeared, hundreds of feet in the air, looking like a swirling blackish pancake. Suddenly the bottom fell out of the pancake, becoming a funnel that zoomed toward Kati.

Deafened by the locomotive roaring of the great storm, Kati found she had to close her eyes to keep them from being shredded by the tens of thousands of spinning sand particles. She could feel Azar recoiling from the damage being done to the Puca.

Kati wasn't sure when her feet left the earth but she knew when they touched down. It was about one full second after the maelstrom disappeared, leaving her still about fifteen feet above the mountaintop.

Azar said nothing but she knew the Puca had taken a big hit, because without Azar, Kati would have broken both her legs after freefalling to the quarried limestone paving of the open air shrine. As if that wasn't enough bad news, it wasn't any cooler up here, even though they were thousands of feet above the blistering sand dunes. In fact, it seemed substantially hotter in the thinner air.

Panting, Kati surveyed the peak. About another hundred feet above her was a circle of a dozen Corinthian-style columns.

Each column was about twenty feet tall and appeared to also have been constructed with the grayish limestone that was underneath her feet. At the top of every column there was a large round polished metal mirror. Each of the mirrors was angled generally toward the interior of the shrine.

In the center of the circle described by the columns was a stone altar. It was about waist high to Kati. As was everything else, the altar was carved limestone. The two Tablets of Destiny were dead center in the altar. The artifacts were each about the length and width of a piece of notebook paper. Unlike their surroundings they were not made of limestone but rather of some deep red bloodstone.

'Rubies,' Azar advised her. 'Each of the Tablets is one large, fashioned ruby.'

Grinning, Kati took a giant step across the threshold of the shrine proper. A whirring noise arose from above. Looking up to see where the noise originated, Kati saw each of the twelve mirrors had angled themselves a little more toward the center of the shrine. Toward the altar. She cautiously took a baby step. Again, the mechanical noise. Again, the mirrors self-directed toward the altar. There were now twelve distinct circles of concentrated sunlight, each about ten feet away from the altar. It didn't matter that the suns had not yet risen to the center of the sky, the mirrors were catching the rays full on, amplifying the light, and projecting burning rays near the altar.

Kati realized why the flooring, the structure, the altar, why everything on the hilltop was unadorned, nonflammable limestone. The mirrors are the defense mechanism for the Tablets.

Kati took three steps in rapid succession. The mirrors refocused with each of her steps. She was now a little more than an arms length away from being able to lean over the altar and pick up the Tablets. What's up with this? she asked herself. The mirrors have had plenty of opportunity to focus on where I'm standing but they haven't zeroed in on me.

Her next step brought her thigh into contact with the side of the stone altar. The mirrors adjustment now placed all twelve of their beams on the Tablets themselves. The rubies instantly became like some type of gemstone volcano. Heat erupted from the Tablets, ashing Kati's eyebrows. She stepped backward. With her motion the beams left the Tablets and once again became twelve circles of light on the altar top.

'Mistress, I am begging you not to do this thing. I do not have enough remaining lyfeforce to both survive the return trip and keep your hands from being burnt completely away should you grasp the Tablets.'

Out of breath, her face and hands already substantially burnt, Kati growled in response. To both her pain and to the apparent impasse. NO! This cannot be. The Simurgh answered my three questions. I can take possession and I can survive. The Kabila will win the Tyrning with possession of the Tablets.

Oh, she realized, as sudden clarity provided the answer. The Simurgh said I can survive taking the Tablets. Me. Well, "Practically Seeking the Center" is the way to win the Tyrning.

'No. I do not consent,' Azar replied softly. It was clear she was already running thin on lyfeforce.

'We both know that's not how the Pucas' service works at the Hunts School,' Kati thought-replied. 'Once you bound the original contract with me your primary obligation became to keep me alive. At all costs. I'm sorry, Azar, but me being the Archon is much more important to the universe than the life of one Creature.'

Kati leapt forward and grasped the Tablets with both hands. The mirrors immediately shifted focus and Kati watched as the flesh on both of her hands began to melt away from the bone.

In the next instant Kati felt Azar using her remaining lyfeforce to heal her blackened hands.

In the second next instant the Zoba'ah swooped from the sky, enveloping Kati, lifting her up and away from the mountaintop.

In the third next instant there was screaming. She heard screaming. Hers. Blinded by the whirlwind, Kati suddenly felt the unmitigated furnace blast of the Realm begin burning her entire body.

In the fourth next instant, Azar's dead corpse silently slid down and off of Kati, to be spun away, forever lost in the fury of the Zoba'ah.

In the fifth next instant, the cyclone dissipated and Kati freefell through the scalding air, before hard bouncing off the unyielding omphalos stone. With the shred of consciousness still available she felt the welcome tingling of the Recall begin.

Kati clutched the Tablets tight to her chest while mouthing four words in an endless loop. "Practically Seeking the Center. Practically Seeking the Center. Practically Seeking…"

CHAPTER QUADRAGINTA UNUS

"Kat, you're crazy if you think I'm leaving your side."

"Masha, you don't have any choice. I've left too much to chance this week while I've been laying here. If Kabila is going to win the Tyrning we have to be the team that makes the fewest avoidable mistakes from here out. Do you understand?"

"Yes, Prime," Mashariki replied.

"Kaskazini's week ends at midnight tonight with the transfer to Kusini. I realize Kaz is Second Prime but you know how I want things done more than he does. I want you nearby and on alert as security tonight at the handoff."

"Absolutely not," Masha replied.

"You have to. It is one of the most opportune times for an attack by an opponent." The Kabila First Prime tried, for somewhere around the millionth time in the last seven days, to move. A little, a lot, it didn't matter. Her efforts met with continued failure. What'd you expect, she asked herself. You're in a full-body cast. Actually, both she and the Tablets were in the cast.

Despite Azar's sacrifice Kati's hands still received third degree burns. They could have been repaired with magyk but only non-magykal drugs and healing could be used until the Treasyre Hunt was officially declared over and a winner announced. Even then the Chief Physick had warned her she might never regain full use of her fingers. There's always a pryce to pay, Kati reminded herself.

Thank goodness for Masha. When they'd wheeled her into the infirmary the physicks had blown off what she was trying to communicate, thinking her ravings only screaming-level-pain-induced nonsense. Mashariki had understood, though. Masha knew Kati like no one had ever known her. He told her he hadn't specifically known what the two inscribed rectangular redstone tablets were, nor why it was so important they stay with her at all times. It was enough that even in her severely wounded condition, it was of foremost importance to her. So, he'd stayed with her in the surgical arena itself through seventy-two hours of surgery and when the physicks were finally ready to encase her entire body, Mashariki ordered the physicks to make a sealed pocket over her chest area for the treasyre.

She mentally reviewed the extensive list of her injuries. Five cracked ribs, several bilateral pelvic breaks, a compound fracture in her left femur, multiple factures of the left tibia, and they'd had to put three pins in her right ankle alone. Several of her internal organs had also been bruised. In the final few hours of the surgery they'd drilled four holes in her skull right above her eyelids and attached a halo brace to insure her neck fracture couldn't further damage her spinal cord. No question about it, she was seriously fucked up.

It had now been a week. A full week since the HuntsMistress summoned Mashariki to the Prime Omphalos chamber to retrieve her broken body. The Hunts Rules had prohibited any non-team Folk from assisting Kati or Kabila in any fashion to make the midnight transition.

She'd been out of it most of the time so at her request Mashariki had later caught her up to speed with the week's events. When he'd first arrived in the Prime Omphalos chamber, she'd been mumbling something over and over. Her face was so burnt and swollen he'd been unable to make out the words. Mercifully for both of them she'd screamed only once, when he bent to gently pick her up, before she passed out.

Luckily for Kabila, she'd left the Compyndium in the secured team safe room. I'm still not sure if that was foresight or accident on my part but I should have addressed that potential problem earlier. Non-return of a team member is a foreseeable risk. If it had been in my dormitory suite no one else would have been able to gain access to retrieve the volume. Not in time to meet the midnight deadline, which would have meant Kabila lost the use of the Compyndium.

Kati, the book, and her term paper had to be at the midnight handoff. She'd had a death grip on the tablets and tried to fight Masha when he attempted to take them away from her. So he carried her first to their team room to pick up the Compyndium and her thesis and then to Chiron's office. He'd said the trip was terrible beyond his ability to describe. Not having time to go to the infirmary for some pain relief, every few steps she'd wake up from the pain of being carried, only to pass right out again when it surpassed the threshold her conscious mind could tolerate.

The infirmary had been notified and physicks were waiting with a stretcher at Chiron's office. The moment the transition was accomplished they'd wheeled her to the infirmary. Even out cold she'd refused to release her grip on the treasyre.

Earlier today she'd had Masha hold a mirror up for her. Seven days after her return and her face still looked like a palette for an advanced class on the art of painting facial trauma. Based on the force necessary to create her physical damage, the physicks had estimated the Zoba'ah had dropped her from about twenty-feet above the omphalos stone, the pointed end of the stone bisecting her body. The whirlwind must have been sentient, she realized. It had to have known two things to drop her from that high up. First, that she had to make physical contact with the omphalos for the Recall. Second, that even another couple of seconds on the Journey to carry her lower might have been the difference in whether she survived.

"Masha, the tablets, are they still there?" she quietly asked her lover again. "Do they remain in my possession?"

"Yes, my Prime," Mashariki replied softly. "They remain within your cast."

Kati gathered herself. The physicks would be coming to flip her over soon and they always gave her another large hit of morphine before they turned her. "Listen to me. I am giving you an order as your Prime. I have neither the time nor the energy to argue with you. You heard Professor Elphinstone. Each member of a team has to obtain at least two level three artifacts.

"I have secured the winning treasyre. Kabila plays smart from here on, which means assuming full defensive mode. The team is only to seek the absolute lowest value level three treasyre. Those pieces should be easier to acquire and will have small barterpryces. Whoever has the Compyndium is to stay only in their dorm room, our team room, or the library. That's it, except for going to and from the Prime Omphalos chamber. Tell them that they are never, never, to go to the library or the ziggurat at the same time of day or by the same path."

"Yes, Kati."

"The Simurgh said if the Tablets are in my possession at the time of the Ceremony that Kabila will win the Tyrning."

"Surely one of the rest of us can carry them to the Coronation Ceremony, my Prime."

"NO!" Kati responded vehemently. "The Simurgh's prediction must be fully and completely followed. Even without magyk, I will be off the maimed list by the Ceremony."

"Kat; it's impossible. I've heard them talking. You won't be off the maimed list until magyk can be used to help heal you. You have substantial internal injuries and you're in a full body cast, for Amarantos's sake."

"I also have the winning treasyre pieces bound to me. Masha, you have to listen to me, believe me. This is the home stretch. Kabila won't win unless each and every one of us is willing to lay it all on the line. You and I know all of my fractures aren't going to heal nonmagykally in less than a month. That's fine. They only have to heal enough to where the physicks can pump me full of sufficient painkillers to allow the cast to be removed. I'll find a way to walk on my own power to the treasyre presentation.

"My heart, I cannot even imagine what type of addiction issues or further physical injuries might happen if you do this," Mashariki said, pleading with her.

"That's the point. Further injuries don't matter. Additional damage doesn't matter. None of it matters. As soon as the Tyrning is concluded and we win, the physicks can magykally heal any new injuries as well as the old ones. They can magykally cure any drug addictions."

"Kati…"

"It's not open for discussion, Masha. Now, we need to discuss the optics of me being in here long term. To win we have to have at least four non-maimed members for the final Ceremony. If either of the other teams or anyone working on their behalf thinks I'm permanently damaged and that it would only take something unfortunate happening to one more of us to get Kabila removed from contention…"

"I have been assured by Principal Chiron the medical staff doesn't, under any circumstances, discuss patients and also that the Infirmary is privacymagyked so that none of the other teams will find out any detailed information about your status."

"Excellent," Kati said, through a more pronounced grimace. They'd better hurry up with that next dose of meds, she thought. "We're going to fuck with the rest of the teams, let selected information slip. We'll get the word out I sustained substantial burns to my hands but that the physicks are ready to discharge me. Instead, I have vainly chosen to stay in the infirmary so that I'll be in perfect shape to assume my position as Archon when Kabila wins the Tyrning."

"Smart play," Mashariki replied. "A seed of truth always helps sell a full-grown lie."

"That's my hope. Still, you and the other three have to take extra care. If the others smell blood in the water, your lives won't be worth a plugged spesmilo. Each of you must take care of yourselves, and each other. I'll task Magharibi and Kaskazini to take first shift guarding me tonight after you leave. After Kusini gets some rest, I need you to set up eight-hour rotating shifts. One of you four will have the Compyndium, one will be on security here, one will take their turn catching some shuteye, and the fourth will fetch provisions and liquids for the Compyndium holder."

"Kati, I don't want to leave…"

"You will do as your Prime Direction commands."

Mashariki snapped to attention. "As you order, Prime."

"Inform the others the book is not to be left unattended in their dorms. It must either be with them or stored in our team room."

"I will tell them, Prime."

"Absolutely no unnecessary risks. All of you do the bare minimum possible. Stay safe."

"I understand, Kati. With your permission I will remain here until it is time to secure tonight's Compyndium transition," Mashariki said, before leaning forward, maneuvering his way around the halo brace so he could lightly brush his lips against hers. He then sat quietly, watchfully, in the bedside chair he'd spent almost every moment sitting or sleeping in for the last week.

When they came to flip her mattress-stretcher rig upside down, Kati asked for an extra dose of chemical nothingness. She knew involuntary blackout was the only way she could stop two memories from roiling in her head. The first was Azar, repeatedly begging her not to quest the Tablets. The second, well, the second was how she felt when a fragment of her soul spun away into the maelstrom together with Azar's body. Both dead. Both irretrievably lost to the living who love them.

CHAPTER QUADRAGINTA DUO

"Week four ends at midnight tonight. I've communicated with the HuntsMistress and Principal Chiron and let them know Släkt is changing our Journey lineup. Fem, even though you're the replacement Fifth Prime, I'm moving you to week four. Ost you'll hand the Compyndium over to Fem at midnight tonight. Väst will take the last week of Journeys."

"Why?" Väst asked, as she looked at the rest of her teammates seated around the table in their secure team room. "I'm ready to go. Got my thesis topic picked out and the research completed. It's my week." She'd been wondering why Nord had sent messengers calling them to a special, last minute called meeting. Now she knew.

"It's no concern of yours, Acting Fourth Prime. Maybe it's because it's your fault our team's original Prime Direction was murdered by that filthy munedan. Maybe it's because I think you need an extra week to study so that maybe, for once, you can actually help your team this term. Maybe it's because you think you're better than all the rest of us. Maybe it's all of the above. Doesn't matter. I hold your binding. I say jump, you jump. Now get the hell out of here. The rest of you stay for a few minutes."

CHAPTER QUADRAGINTA TRES

Dearest Queen of the Tuatha de Danann—

If you wish to see your meddling child live through the Treasyre Hunt, you will meet me in the astral plane. Immediately. And not a word to your husband, the Archon.

Fingers suddenly too numb to function, Aine watched as the note began fluttering its way toward the floor, only to spontaneously combust and burn away to nothing. Not even ashes remained. Who? How? How does this person know Alberich and I have a daughter on Hunts School campus? Who has magyk so powerful they can invade this school?

I am the High Queen of the fairy Realm, my royal-level awaymagyk is the strongest ever tested. This lowlyfe has threatened our child. There can be only one response she told herself as she walked over to her favorite chair. Once seated Aine took several calming breaths before launching her spirit into the aether.

CHAPTER QUADRAGINTA QUATTUOR

"Prime! Prime, please wake up. We need to speak. Immediately."

The combination of words and gentle shaking roused Kati from her narcotic induced rest. Even with the full body cast and the huge doses of IV painkillers, the shaking fired up a buttload of nerve endings. "Stop," she croaked through dry lips. "I'm awake. Don't touch me, it hurts."

"I'm sorry, Kati," Magharibi replied. "Mashariki told us a little about your condition but we had no idea…"

"It's okay, Ribi. The less said about my physical status, the better. What's so important?" Before her Fifth Prime could respond, she came to full alert. "Ribi, it's your week with the Compyndium. You were supposed to switch with Mashariki at midnight tonight. Why are you here? Where is Masha?"

"That's the problem, Prime. Mashariki is missing."

CHAPTER QUADRAGINTA QUINQUE

Väst realized she had been merely killing time since she woke up this morning. Why? Why did Nord move her to this week? What had he told the rest of the team last week after he'd told her to leave the team room? If there had been any more Släkt meetings, she hadn't been invited.

The transfer from Fem had gone according to schedule at midnight last night. There were times she'd like to punch that oily smile right off his face. As soon as she got back to her dorm suite she'd given the book a quick look over. That's all it took because she'd discovered the priceless, irreplaceable relic, which was allegedly worth more than her life, was still blank. Every single one of the hundreds, maybe thousands of pages, in the damn thing were blank. Well, to be truthful, she hadn't looked all the way to the end but the first few hundred pages were blank.

She'd turned the lights off to see if the book might have been inked with darkglow. Nope. Next she'd held a candle close to one of the pages to see if the contents might be disclosed by thermal reaction. That effort was quickly abandoned when the Compyndium somehow intensified the heat from the candle flame and used it to burn her fingers. Like really burn them, she thought, as she softly massaged the welts all up and down her right hand. Defensive mechanisms, much? I'll say. Obviously the volume has substantial defensive capabilities. Tired, a little scared, and in more than a little pain, she'd closed the book, determined to make a fresh start this morning.

After showering and slamming some breakfast calories she'd begun in earnest trying to figure the book out. Making little to no headway she'd packed the Compyndium together with a few other textbooks into her backpack and headed for the library.

It wasn't helping her focus that it was a beautiful spring day on the Hunts School campus. Flowers were budding and a warm zephyr caressed her cheeks. Nor was it the least bit helpful that the thousands of students no longer participating in the Hunts were now seriously enjoying their final semester on campus. For one hundred years, which included their mandatory summer residency, they had all lived and breathed Hunts School, the Hunts, and the Tyrning. Many hundreds of their classmates had either been killed or maimed during their time at school. For the remnant, the days of terror and angst were all in the past. The Hunts would be formally concluded in only a little more than a week, the new Ruling Council invested, and most everyone would travel to their home planes via the Prime Omphalos.

For everyone except the three remaining teams there were no more tests. No more possibilities of death (or worse.) No more freaking godawful HuntsMistress. Sure, several handfuls of non-competitors were still working the campus, toadying up to one or more of the remaining contestants. Their motivation was clear. They were attempting to ingratiate themselves, looking for minor court factotum positions, apparently preferring that life to permanently going back to their home Realms.

Those students were the exceptions though. Mirth was king now and it had decreed during its brief reign the entire campus would pay homage. When she cruised past the stadium, she'd seen dozens of students playing a variety of sports, while hundreds of others hung out in the bleachers, indolently enjoying the mid-morning sun.

Mirth's boon companion today was Music. Singing of joy and optimism for the nascent Tyrning, it seemed to spring from the walls themselves. Couplehood abounded as well. Around every corner it seemed there was a young twosome. Some were engaging in the bittersweet conclusion of a long-term romance. Others were hooking up, so that they might use their Hunts

School magyked human forms for one last minute senior year fling.

More than anything else though Väst heard Mirth's laughter. Ranging from soft-throated chuckles to rip-snorting guffaws, all iterations of laughter were well represented. And why shouldn't there be laughter? For the entirety of their voluntary exile at Hunts School they'd all had to be so serious, so intent. Pedal to the metal attention and effort trying to win the Hunts. Well, that and also trying not to die or be maimed.

For pretty much everyone else, their last few days at Hunts School were like a banana split sundae, complete with ice cream, hot chocolate syrup, whipped cream, and a cherry on top. "Pretty much everyone else" only excluded the fifteen students still feverishly trying to win the Tyrning.

Väst made sure all of the gaiety didn't distract her from exercising Code Red danger protocol from her dorm suite to the library. There was no question each of the remaining contestants had a target on their back.

Today, the Hunts School library building was more like a mausoleum with a substantial book fetish than a functioning center for intellectual pursuit. Apparently Mirth had ordered the library quarantined. The only other person Väst saw was Seshat, the head librarian, manning her post at the central desk on the ground floor. Easily recognizable by her cat-eye glasses, Seshat made a mark to note Väst's entry time but didn't in any manner disturb the graveyardish silence. When did that woman sleep? She was at the handoff last night and there's no telling how early she opened the library this morning.

Väst walked quickly up the winding staircase. Past the first floor landing, not stopping to look around until she was squarely on the second floor landing. She hadn't even realized she'd been holding her breath until she gasped for air. The competitors had all been warned the other teams' floors were out of bounds, and the penalty was substantial. There was no way she was going to the third floor or fourth floor landings, and she wasn't even going to tarry overlong on the first or second floor landings.

Väst saw no one and heard nothing, excepting her own

footfalls on the dark cherry hardwood floor as she walked to the broad open area in the middle of the second floor. The area's interior space was big enough for three rows of three large eight-person library tables. She took a seat in a chair at the midpoint of the centermost table in the pattern. That way she should have plenty of warning if anyone showed up.

After opening her backpack she carefully took out the Släkt Compyndium and placed it face up on the table. Her hand still hurt and she had no intention of unintentionally pissing the book off. Next, she took out the two other textbooks she'd brought, her notepad, and two pencils. Yielding to her OCDish nature she squared all of the objects with each other and also with her chair. Now I'm ready to get started thinking up some winning treasyre, she told herself.

CHAPTER QUADRAGINTA SEX

Kati's first thought was about her lover. "What do you mean Masha is missing?" Then, immediately, "Our Compyndium? What's its status?"

"The Compyndium is safe," Magharibi replied. "After Masha missed the midnight transfer, Principal Chiron and the Head Librarian accompanied me to our team room. The Compyndium, Masha's term paper, and his two level three treasyre pieces were stored there.

"We found Masha's Puca on the fourth floor landing. As for Mashariki himself, we've looked everywhere. He seems to have vanished."

"Thank Amarantos at least the book is safe." Stop, Kati, she told herself. You can't worry about Mashariki until you fulfill your obligations to your team. "What's the penalty damage?" She could tell from Magharibi's surprised look he thought Masha would have been, should have been, her next concern. I am Kabila Prime, she reminded herself.

"Transfer of the Compyndium was not timely made."

"Which means they've seized our volume and we forfeit any further right to use it this week. Okay, that's manageable. Ribi, go back through our textbooks for the last five years or so and pick out two or three easy level three artifacts. Take only enough Journeys to secure two of them and get your paper finished to turn in on time."

"Yes, Prime."

"Since Masha completed his paper, is he still on the active list if we find him or he returns before the Closing Ceremony?"

"Principal Chiron said he would turn the paper over to Professor Elphinstone for grading and if it met with his approval that Mashariki would remain on the active list. For now."

"Ribi, trust me. I'm worried to death about Masha but I can't let myself go there until I make sure Kabila is squared away. I've secured the winning treasyre. Which means our number one objective right now is to keep four of us on the active list."

Yes, Kati told herself. The Simurgh's prophecy is still viable. We are absolutely going to win the Tyrning. By "Practically Seeking the Center."

"I don't want you to leave your dorm room except to go to the Prime Omphalos chamber. Do you understand?"

"Yes, Prime," Magharibi responded.

"Tell Kaskazini and Kusini that one is to sleep and the other is to stand sentry over you and the sleeper. All three of you are to remain in your dorm suite. All three of you are to wear your Pucas at all times, asleep or awake. When it's time to get food and drinks, I want both of them to go so that one can guard the other."

"Yes, Prime."

"Now about Mashariki. His suite has been checked?"

"Yes. Principal Chiron used his master key. There is no sign of him. Kati, his Puca? The fourth floor?"

"You believe Omada did something to him?" she asked.

"It is their assigned floor."

"It's not Borras's style and he's too smart to leave evidence. I know none of the Folk can interfere with Hunt contestants until the Hunt is officially declared done. They are however required to confirm, upon our request, whether one of our teammates is alive or dead. So we can make sure we have the minimum number of teammates to remain in the competition. I believe in these rare cases that Queen Aine is asked to use her awaymagyk to scry for that information."

"Formal request of the Archon has already been made."

"And?"

"We were told the request was 'under advisement'."

"What does that even mean?"

"No one knows. Something about the Queen being presently indisposed."

Curious turn of a phrase, Kati thought, but we have enough problems on our hands without worrying about another mystery. I need to lock down this win for Kabila and then we can find Mashariki. I have to assume we're down to four now, Kati reminded herself. If the other teams find out about Masha, it will be open season on Kabila until the Hunt is over.

Which resolves one issue. However jacked up I still am physically, I can't defend myself at all while I'm encased in six feet of plaster. Even if my mobility is injury-limited I stand a better chance of surviving without the damn cast. Not a good enough chance, she told herself. You've done the best you can to make sure the other three are protected. The infirmary is a designated neutral zone so you're safe as long as you stay here.

"That's all for now, Magharibi. Be wary. Please ask the physicks to come in. This cast is coming off. Right now."

CHAPTER QUADRAGINTA SEPTEM

It's pretty obvious whatever is on the pages isn't moisture activated, Väst thought as she swiped at the string of drool stretching the couple of inches from her lower lip to the first page of the Compyndium. Thank goodness, the book didn't consider bodily fluid an attack. Well, saliva, at least. The jury's out on other types of bodily fluid. And oh by the way, ick, Väst.

She stretched. Well, tried to stretch. The rather substantial crick in her neck felt like it was going on her permanent record. I can't believe I passed out like that. This is what happens when you don't get your required rest. Time. What time is it? Only time mechanisms allowed in the library are the ones on the stairway landings. Great, she thought, as she tried to uncross her legs to stand. My right leg is asleep. Using her arms to manually uncross her legs, she stood and then hopalonged back over to the stairs.

Middle center rear on every landing was an oversized hourglass. They all stood on a low table but the hourglasses themselves were about eight feet tall. The instruments were actually twelve-hourglasses. On each end there were reciprocal marks notating the hours and half hours. Each of the glasses was magyked to automatically flip every twelve hours, with AM and PM inscribed on the opposing globes. There was only a dusting of sand in the bottom of the apparatus. It flipped only seconds ago, Väst told herself. Since its pitch black outside the windows that means it's only a hair past midnight. You'd of thought Seshat or somebody would come to check on me. Well, on the positive side, no one came to murder me either. That a girl, she told herself, be a twelvehourglass half full kind of person.

As the blood returned to the entirety of her right leg she walked a little more normally, although still stiff-necked, back to her seat. Back to the blank-paged Compyndium. She rifled a few dozen pages. All blank.

Great, just great. I only have six days left to get my minimum two Journeys in and score at least some medium value swag for Släkt. So asshat Nord can be Archon of the known universe for three hundred years.

I'm not going anywhere unless I can find out how to make the Compyndium show me some treasyre to collect. She slowly turned another ten pages thinking there might be some time delay appearance mechanism. Nope.

Väst's stomach growled, so she leaned over and rummaged through her backpack, on the outside chance there was some leftover water or a candy bar. Nothing. Her mind wandered to sneaking over to the cafeteria to load up her backpack with a midnight snack. The cafeteria buffet line was open twenty-four/seven. Surely it was a safe time to make a quick run over and back. Anyone still up now was engaged in more private pursuits.

Saliva gland production geared up to meet the requisite moisture required to properly salivate over the suddenly item specific caloric intake necessary to slake her hunger: a couple—fine, make it three—slices of pepperoni and anchovy pizza, together with a bowl of ambrosia. The instrument necessary to make that feast happen was located right at the end of the buffet line. The Cornucopia.

Instantly Väst saw with her own eyes, smelled with her nose, why the Compyndium were priceless artifacts. In mere seconds a multipage description about the Cornucopia appeared in the tome.

To describe the Cornucopia entry as exhaustive was an understatement. The writing on page one concerned the Cornucopia's origin story. It had been created on the Greek Realm by the then Zeus avatar, one of the greatest creationmagyk heroes of the Folk. Next followed a detailed listing of every plane in which the Cornucopia had resided, together with its owner at that time. The section concluded with its present day location at Hunts School, along with the info that the Prime Omphalos was the omphalos presently closest to the treasyre.

The book's illustrations took mind-boggling to a whole new level. Boggling times boggling. Whatever the word is for that. Boogling? Squaboggling? Each drawing was full-spectrum color and on the two-dimensional paper surface they were still somehow three-dimensional. When you flipped to a page and touched a drawing, it would rise silently from the leaves of the book to float and slowly spin in midair. If you touched it again, it would rotate on a number of different axes so the viewer could study it from every possible angle. Yep, definitely mind-squaboggling.

As Väst watched, several slices of pepperoni and anchovy pizza appeared from within the Cornucopia, flowing out to the edge and then out into open space. This visual was quickly followed by a bowl of ambrosia. Wow, just wow. I didn't even specify New York style and that's what the image is showing me. As she began, reluctantly, turning the page, the image descended toward its point of origin. But not before Väst got a solid noseful of a very specific odor. Pepperoni and anchovies. Okay, Head Librarian, I get it now. If I were you I would never have let these books out of secure storage. Certainly not to a bunch of uber-competitive students, at least some of whom would do pretty much anything to rule the known universe for the next three hundred years.

The last full page of the Cornucopia entry contained an exhaustive explanation of all of the factors utilized in determining its Treasyre Hunt level: intrinsic value outside of any magykal factor, magyk utilized in creation, magykal output from the object, *ad almost infinitum*. The actual score was the last piece of information provided by the Compyndium. Turns out the Cornucopia was only a level two treasyre. Not worth collecting even if there hadn't been a campus ban on stealing it.

I understand the mechanics now, she told herself. The user has to specify the object. Then the pretty much unbelievable magyk of the Compyndium presents all of the historical, as well as real-time, information about the artifact. Including its present location and even which omphalos in that Realm is closest to the treasyre.

She tested her hypothesis by mentally identifying several objects Hunts teams had collected during the first term Scavengyr Hunt. The entries were immediately created and populated. In every instance the Compyndium correctly showed the present location of the items as Hunts School. Once an entry was created, it remained in the book with all of the prior descriptions.

Everything the professor told us in class is starting to make sense. When the Compyndium leaves the possession of one user it returns to its native blank state. Why didn't my asshat teammates tell me how the book works? I wouldn't be surprised if the book's defense mechanisms prevented that type of disclosure.

There are more layers to this book's magyk than there are of filo dough in a piece of baklava. "Baklava!" Väst wasn't sure whether she'd actually mouthed the word or her stomach had growled it aloud. Regardless, her body's message was clear. She hadn't had any food or water in quite some time. If she was going to make a hard effort at locating treasyre, it was time for a sustenance break.

The entire expedition; packing, scurrying through the dark, snagging a ridiculous amount of food—including three pieces of pepperoni and anchovy pizza from the Cornucopia—together with a pitcher of nectar with a to-go lid, scurrying back through the still dark but getting lighter, unpacking, and commencing of face-stuffing had taken only a little more than an hour. Which had been about half an hour ago. I'm about to founder, Väst told herself. On the flip side, I'm fueled up and a couple of glasses of nectar are way better than a hundred cups of coffee. It's time to hit the books. Well, book and not literally "hit it" because who knows what the hell it would do to me in response.

After making a short list of items she concentrated on them one at a time. Even though Väst was allowed to wear Ardere, her Puca, on her Journeys this Hunt, she had no intention of unnecessarily endangering either one of them by going to some stranger-danger Realm to find treasyre.

First up was the Golden Fleece. The Compyndium listed it as presently on the Macedonian plane. Not a problem. It was, however, only a level three treasyre piece and to get it she would have to get past an insomniac dragon. Thanks, but no thanks. After the Snype Hunt she felt like she could speak on behalf of all students at Hunts School. They would give the finger to any great wyrm while maintaining a large and respectful distance. After that she called up the Girdle of Brunhild, which was located on a Norse Realm. With no dragon. It gave superhuman strength to its wearer. It was a level three piece which would help meet her required minimum but not contribute much to winning the Hunt.

Any thoughts this whole treasyre-seeking thing was going to be a piece of cake left the building. Not only were the higher-level pieces more difficult to obtain, part of the difficulty was identifying elite treasyre pieces.

Then there was the whole issue of lack of motivation. Väst closed the Compyndium and decided to take a few minutes to breathe and focus on possible sources and solutions of her ennui. Ultimately she realized there were three reasons her heart wasn't in this Hunt. First, by all accounts, her teammates had already scored substantial treasyre. Which might, or might not, make any items she submitted superfluous. Second, it hadn't been much of a team esprits de corp moment when Nord, their Prime, told the entire Areopagus he'd potentially sold all of his teammates into death (or worse.) What was even more bizarre was none of her other three teammates seemed particularly bothered by that minor detail. In fact it was almost as if they'd forgiven Nord. Maybe they were preternaturally certain Släkt was going to win and Quint would be the one given to the wytch for payment.

Third, perhaps most importantly, she'd become convinced it wasn't in the best interests of the known universe for Släkt to be the Ruling Council for the next three hundred years. She couldn't act directly against her contract binding but passive resistance in the form of half-ass effort didn't seem to trigger the bond. Still, and as much as she cared about the universe from a macro perspective, she also wasn't too down with being bartered to Hecate as chattel.

At a creative impasse she stood to stretch, before walking quickly toward the landing to look at the twelvehourglass. It was already past noon. Wow, time flies when you're going pretty much nowhere. I need a break, and a shower she decided after sniffing both armpits. It's not that I stink, she thought defensively but I am getting a little ripe. Broad daylight should be relatively danger free. I'll take the long way back to my dorm suite. Some sunlight will do me good. Plus I can get a few hours real sleep and pick up a couple of my class notebooks to jumpstart my imagination. She walked back to her seat and stowed her textbooks, pads, pencils, and left over food scraps—no one needs Seshat on their ass—in her backpack.

As Väst was about to close the Compyndium, the pages began slowly turning themselves, one by one. The turning moved quickly from first gear into second. Lickity-split the pages were turning in overdrive, as if blown by some invisible miniature ghost bellows. Riffling now at near supersonic speed they kept turning, halting abruptly when there was only one last leaf left unturned.

Väst found her hand gripping the top-left corner of the page, whether from some form of curiosity compulsion or basic Folk-nature, she didn't know. She shivered. From the soles of her feet to the crown of her head her body experienced an involuntary shake that left her in a clammy sweat.

I didn't turn those pages, she reminded herself. The incomprehensible strength of the magyk in this book did it. That same super-magyk deliberately stopped right before the last page. It turned thousands of its own empty pages and intentionally stopped on the penultimate page.

I'm guessing that means the last page isn't going to be empty, she told herself. She hesitated for a full two minutes. Not a compulsion then, she decided. Whatever game the Compyndium is playing, turning the last page has to be a voluntary act. For some reason I have to choose to either see what's on the final page or choose not to see it.

I can sit here all day driving myself crazy playing the "what can it possibly be" game, she told herself. Or I can follow my gut instinct. Which is telling me I need to know what's on the final page.

Decision made, she gripped the top left-hand corner of the page between her thumb and forefinger and slowly began lifting the page. As it rose toward the vertical, a soft keening began. As soon as the leaf crossed the top ninety-degree angle, the noise amped up into an almost deafening screaming. When it was finally laid flat open, she saw the entire last page contained an edge-to-edge exquisitely detailed full-color rendering. The image on the last page was of Mashariki, the Kabila Fourth Prime. Kati's lover.

The image Mashariki was naked, except for a dirty scrap of a loincloth. Across his entire body he was bleeding from hundreds of razor-thin cuts. He was cruelly staked, the stakes being wooden shivs pounded straight through the tendons in his wrists and ankles. The floor over which he was horizontally spread-eagled was a bed of glowing coals. The Compyndium's magyk that turned the pages had also used its ghost-bellows to heat the coals to Bessemer-furnace hell-hot. The drawing's eyes were squeezed closed. Agony was apparent in the detailed rictus of every muscle in his body as he attempted unsuccessfully to lift his blackened skin up and away from contact with the flaming coals.

Suddenly the three-dimensional illustration began rising from the page, just like the Cornucopia had done. Mashariki was still staked and the bed of coals rose with him. Väst could feel the heat wash over her. Much higher and it would singe her eyebrows.

Once the Mashariki image was completely free from the page, it opened its swollen eyes. The high-pitched screaming stopped as the image licked its charred lips. The eyes turned toward her face. Oh my god, the drawing is focusing on me, Väst realized.

"VÄST," the drawing's voice choked out from its parched throat. "VÄST, I SEE YOU. FOR THE LOVE OF

AMARANTOS, PLEASE. PLEASE SET ME FREE...OR KILL ME..."

Väst's right hand reflexively slammed the book closed at the same moment her mind finally understood what she'd just witnessed. This was the reason that son of a bitch Nord had moved her from the fourth week to the fifth week. That wasn't a magykal illustration of Mashariki—it was Mashariki.

CHAPTER QUADRAGINTA OCTO

"Archon, I'm sorry. If you want us to do any psychic probing or have someone brought to campus with royal level awaymagyk, we'll need to take the Queen to the infirmary."

"Thank you Moros, but that isn't an option. Even with Aine's power her spirit-self has already been away from her body far too long. If she is to have any hope of finding her way home, her physical form must be exactly where she left it. Thank you for coming so quickly."

The Chief Physick bowed deeply from the waist. "We would do anything for you and your Queen, my Lord. With your leave I shall return to the infirmary."

Alberich nodded and the Chief Physick left the Archon's chambers. When he was alone, Alberich, Archon of the Moiety, the most powerful Folk being in the known universe, knelt to the floor, and took his wife's hand in his. "Aine, what have you done? We talked about how dangerous it was for you to leave your body right now. So, why? What has happened? Beloved, I can't even imagine what has occurred that made you believe you needed to go astral without me here to protect you. Fight. Fight, to find your way home."

CHAPTER QUADRAGINTA NOVEM

"Acting Fourth Prime, can you explain to us why you're wasting time calling a team meeting instead of busily treasyre hunting to help Släkt win this Hunt?"

Knowing there was going to be a major confrontation, Väst had been desperately invoking every calming technique she knew. Her first action after leaving the library was to find one of the students who'd been toadying up to her squad and order him to go find Nord and tell him to assemble Släkt immediately in their team safe room. After that, while softly chanting a calming mantra, she'd gone to her dorm suite. There wasn't enough time for a shower but she washed her face, put on some much needed deodorant, and changed clothes.

Neither the time nor the relaxation techniques had helped in the least bit. She couldn't remember the last time she'd been so angry. Every time she'd thought maybe she was about to reduce her anger to a husbandable level, her next thought skyrocketed it once more. It was like somebody kept discharging emotional defibrillator paddles against her chest without first yelling "CLEAR! CLEAR!"

For a hundred years now the charge to all of the students, and now to the three remaining Finalist teams, was that they were supposed to win the Tyrning by Seeking the Center. Even though Nord held the contract binding her to Släkt, she had some leverage with respect to Mashariki. Not much but some, and she was going to use it.

"Hello? I asked you a question."

"YOU'RE A LUNATIC! What in Five-Hells do you think you're doing?" So much for my calming exercises, she told herself.

"Do I really need to remind you I am the Släkt Prime Direction and I have the sole and complete discretion to decide what strategy our team uses to win?"

Chill, Väst, just chill. That was a moderate and therefore extremely unNordlike response. He's baiting you, so just chill. "STRATEGY? Your strategy was to capture Mashariki within our Compyndium? He is being tortured, you bastard." Fine, put me down as a fail on the "chill."

Nord was again too calm, way too calm. "Our strategy was merely to use the book as a lure to take him hostage. We had no idea the Compyndium defensemagyk would suck him in. And the torture part, well, that's just a bonus."

Alright, at least I'm getting a little bit of a grip, she told herself. Be reasonable. "You're crazy, you really are. This is why you switched my week with Fem, isn't it? I guess you coopted your little Renfield into assisting you with your plan. Well, you can bet none of the rest of us are going to go along with it."

"We took a vote, Väst," Söder said. "It was unanimous."

As Väst's knees gave out on her she sank into the nearest seat. "A vote? Ost, you didn't vote for this, did you?"

"Yes," Ost replied. "Well, for the hostage-taking part, anyway. Like Nord said, we didn't know about the book's powers."

"And now that you know the Compyndium is actively torturing him every second he is held within the book's magyk?"

"It is actually Mashariki's fault he has been trapped by the book," Ost added defensively.

Has the entire world gone insane? Väst asked herself. "How can this possibly be his fault?"

Fem, the weasel, supplied the team's response. "Professor Elphinstone very plainly set forth the rules we were to all follow concerning accessing other teams' Compyndium and Mashariki violated the rules."

"How? How did he violate the rules?"

And now it was time for well-modulated Nord to step back in. "I'm sure Fem will be happy to explain it to you, Väst, if you will listen. It will be good practice for him in case he's questioned by the HuntsMistress. Fem?"

Fem beamed his gap-toothed unctuous smile. "Certainly, Prime," he replied, turning to address Väst. "As I told the Prime and the other loyal members of our team, I was over at the library minding my own business, you know, getting my thoughts together for the treasyre I was going to hunt.

"I had just summoned up an entry on the buckler of Iblis, which by the way is a major level five piece, when I began to experience a little gastrointestinal discomfiture…"

"Please, spare us," Väst groaned.

"Fine. Well anyway, I was so overcome I must not have been thinking clearly and I guess I totally accidentally completely by silly mistake left our Compyndium right in the middle of the third floor landing at the library. Open to the buckler entry, of course."

"You baited Mashariki?"

"I'm offended by your insinuation, teammate," Fem replied. "I mean how was I to know that when I accidentally left the Compyndium open on the landing for five days that Mashariki would just happen by?"

Nord took over the narrative. "Originally we were merely going to catch Mashariki violating the Hunt conditions. Kabila would have been assessed a major penalty, which would have been sufficient to remove them from serious contention."

"How did you know he would even be there?"

"I guess somebody might have ghosted a note from his girlfriend telling him that if Kabila was going to win she had to know immediately what treasyre Släkt was collecting. I'm afraid the note might even have said 'at all costs'."

"You tricked him."

"Hey, none of us told him to violate the rule, we just presented him with the opportunity to prove his character. He failed the test."

"So much for winning by Seeking the Center," Väst remarked resignedly.

"You can climb down off your damn soapbox. Mashariki had the same choices as all of the rest of us," Nord replied.

"What happened?" Väst asked, motioning to the Compyndium.

"He chose wrong," Nord said. "He made the mistake of actually touching the book."

Fem was so excited, he interrupted his Prime. "You should have seen it. The Compyndium, it like, well it flipped itself to its last page. Then it somehow stripped the Puca clean off of him. After that the dude got reduced to some kind of holographic image of himself. About that time he started screaming at the top of his lungs and then he got smaller and smaller until finally he flattened out on the page and the book closed itself."

Väst felt like she was about to be sick to her stomach. She'd been right. The Släkt had absolutely no business winning the Tyrning. "Well, you've obviously got him on an infraction, let's go see Principal Chiron about getting him out of the book."

"Not so fast, Missy," Nord snarled. "You don't throw a gyfthorse away by the mouth."

She felt like correcting Nord but decided the best move was simply to leave him to his ignorance. "We have to do something about it. If we don't say anything and I turn the Compyndium in at the end of this week he could remain in the book, being tortured forever."

"So?" Nord asked, with a shrug of indifference punctuating his response.

Väst looked at her other three teammates. None of them, not a single one, seemed to be troubled about leaving Mashariki trapped forever. "Why? What do we have to gain?"

"Well, the most obvious thing is Kabila is down to four and their Prime Direction is still in the infirmary. If she doesn't recover—or if something happens to another Kabila player—then they're out for good."

"No," Väst replied, the rigidity of her entire body communicating her resolve on the matter. "I'll go tell Principal Chiron myself."

Nord finally released his customary anger. "I think not, you worthless whore." He raised his right fist in the air, "By the binding I hold as Släkt Acting Prime Direction, I decree no member of Släkt shall in any manner, directly or indirectly, communicate to anyone outside Släkt that Mashariki is trapped within our Compyndium. Additionally, I command that the Släkt Acting Fourth Prime, while she has possession of the Compyndium, shall undertake no effort attempting to release Mashariki from the book." Finished, he slowly lowered his fist.

As Nord was talking, something that felt like steel phlegm slid backwards up Väst's throat, coating the inside of her mouth. Unable to stop herself, she vomited onto the team table.

Nord was smirking directly at her. "I see you now understand your place." He turned to address the entire squad. "According to that fool Elphinstone we can't use Kabila's treasyre as ransom for Kati's boy toy. Which means our only choice is to swing for the fences. Ost will use his nice but unremarkable penmanship to write another anonymous note. This one addressed to Kati, telling her Mashariki has been taken hostage. Kabila can secure his release by publicly announcing by noon on the last Journey day that Kabila is irrevocably withdrawing from the Hunts, that they are turning over all Kabila treasyre to the HuntsMistress, and that Kati has dissolved her team's binding."

"Kati is going to know it's us," Söder remarked.

"I already took care of that," Fem replied uber-smirkily. "I left Mashariki's Puca on the Omada stairwell landing."

"Could you be any more of a dumbass?" Väst asked him.

"Both of you shut up," Nord barked. "It doesn't matter. Kati's not going to say or do anything that might endanger Mashariki."

Having already forgotten he was supposed to shut up, Fem commented. "That's all well and good, Boss, but if Kati accepts the deal and we let her boy out, he knows it was us and he can tell Principal Chiron."

Nord snorted. It was probably supposed to be a laugh, Väst thought, but it was much too vile a sound to fit into any category of laughing. "What is the matter with you? Whether she takes the deal or not, we're not releasing Mashariki. Way I got it figured, once we turn the Compyndium in it may be hundreds of years before anyone opens that book again. Odds are Mashariki remains trapped in the book forever when the Head Librarian returns the books to the secured storage area."

And I thought I was nauseous before, Väst told herself, as a stronger wave of disgust swept over her. "You still have to beat Omada."

Nord turned his attention back to her. "Not a problem with the buckler of Iblis."

"Fem successfully obtained that piece?" Söder asked hopefully.

"No," Nord replied. "The bargainpryce for that piece is going to be astronomical. I can't take a chance on losing Fem. I'm going to need him on my Ruling Council for the next three hundred years."

Väst finally realized what Nord intended. "You want me to risk my life to get the buckler?"

"Anything for the team, right?" Nord asked.

"And if I fail, if I die?"

"Let's see," Nord said, gesturing as if he were counting, "1-2-3-4. Yeah, four. Whoo, that's a relief. We'll still have enough players to qualify. Even if you're dead—or worse.

"I already got us a piece of treasyre that's enough for the win. The buckler is for kicks and grins." Nord motioned to everyone except Väst to follow him out the door. When he reached the threshold he stopped and raised his right fist again. "Oh, damn," he said coyly. "I almost forgot. As your Prime I order you to eliminate the human from the competition. Without getting caught, of course. I also order you to clean up your nasty puke before you leave."

CHAPTER QUINQUAGINTA

Three of Kati's four teammates were gathered around her hospital bed. "Kusini, who delivered this note?"

"We don't know, Prime. It was taped to the outside of our team room door. The envelope said '*Urgent. To Be Opened By The Kabila Prime Immediately*'."

"I see," Kati curtly acknowledged.

"What does it say?" Magharibi asked.

"Not here," the Omada Prime responded before turning her head toward the attending physick. "Please bring me some street clothes. I need to leave immediately."

The physick bowed his head as he folded his hands together. "I'm sorry, Kati, Kabila Prime, but given the nature of your injuries we have been given special instructions that you may not leave the premises until the Chief Physick, the HuntsMistress, or Principal Chiron, authorize your departure."

"Physick, I do not mean to be rude but perhaps you misunderstood me. Answer this for me, please. Which would be worse for you? Some missing paperwork, or having to explain to your supervisor the reason the potential new Archon had to have her stitches resewn was because she ripped them while she was kicking the holy shit out of your ass?"

"I will bring the clothes immediately, Kati, Kabila Prime. Together with a release form for your signature."

"I will be happy to sign your form, thank you. Now if you'll excuse us, Kabila has urgent matters to attend."

CHAPTER QUINQUAGINTA UNUS

Seriously, there is absolutely no way things could be any worse, Väst told herself. None. After Kabila folds there will only be two teams left. The good guys and my team. Plus, I've been ordered to "eliminate" the guy I'm in love with. And yeah, I'm pretty sure about that last part.

Nord thought he was being cute with how he worded his order. Somebody must have thought the whole "plausible deniability" wording up for him, he's not that subtle. It doesn't even make any strategic sense. Omada has five healthy members. Removing Tal from the equation doesn't help Släkt one bit. Nord ordered me to do it because he's a dick. Although maybe he's not as clever a dick as he thinks he is.

Focus, Väst. You'd better find out about the buckler of Iblis. With its high level five status, there's a good chance you may be the next person eliminated. As she began carefully lifting the front cover of the Compyndium she heard a noise from the racks directly behind her. Whipping her head to the left, she scanned through the fully loaded stacks.

"Who's there?" she challenged. Little quavery there, Braveheart, she chided herself. And of course there's no response. What self-respecting skulker is going to voluntarily self-report? So, what's the play, here? If I identify the trespasser and try to report them, he or she will simply deny it. Surely if Seshat had seen someone else enter she would corroborate my story.

Not worth the risk, she decided. Nord may have assigned someone to spy on me and the stakes are far too high at this juncture for an unverified complaint against another team to be sustained.

So if attempted capture is off the table, what's the proper move? I think it's pretty clear at this point the Compyndium are perfectly capable of protecting themselves. Me, not so much. As Professor Elphinstone advised us, the book may or may not care what happens to whoever has possession of it at that moment. Still, I can't let somebody be spying on me through the shelves, finding out what treasyre I'm trying to collect.

Nancy Drew it, she decided. Knowledge is power, right? Slowly closing the Compyndium, Väst rose as silently as she could. Thinking she might could flank the peeper, she took baby steps over to and then down behind a parallel set of racks. She bent at the waist as she walked and every few steps, in a random pattern, she slowly crouched, so she could look through the stacks at ankle level.

Nada. She finally came to the railing overlooking the stairwell. Glancing over she looked down to the ground floor. Just in time to see Principal Chiron's back, legs and feet as he strode out of view. She didn't see his head but she was one hundred percent sure it was him.

Väst's first thought was, "What the hell?" Her second was that it actually made sense. The headmaster had probably been making routine rounds of the library west wing for the last five weeks. Trying to keep the possibility of misfeasance to a minimum. Anyway, mystery solved. Back to the Compyndium.

Väst could tell something was different as she re-entered the broad open area encompassing the nine tables. Her textbooks had been moved off to one side—and the Compyndium was open. I closed it. No question about it, I closed the book.

Väst stalked slowly across the open space separating her from the table. Her 'fight or flight' instinct had kicked in big time, she could feel every nerve was ready to activate its respective tendons or muscles. When she finally reached her chair she slowly pirouetted, first clockwise, then even more slowly counterclockwise. When done she stood motionless. Listening.

Listening harder. Nothing. No sound. No visual. No person.

Convinced but still wary she settled into her chair. It was only then she noticed the sheet of paper laying across the open Compyndium. The paper looked to be some high quality stationery but the weight of the paper wasn't what was remarkable. What was floating an inch or two above the paper most definitely was.

A small, swirling cloud composed of what looked like thousands of tiny grains of black sand was hovering above the paper. Actually, if a speck is smaller than a grain, they were specks of black sand.

As Väst watched, the miniature cloud formation developed a leading edge and dipped toward the paper. Wherever its swirling brought it into contact it left a momentary mark. The half-life of each dot was only a few seconds before the mark was subsumed down into the off-white of the paper. Writing, she realized. Shifting black sand is writing words on a piece of paper.

She had to follow along quickly because of the writing's transient nature. As soon as one or two words were completed, they began to be absorbed into the stationery. *Ignus fatuus*, she told herself. It's like a black sand version of a will o' the wisp.

'I don't...know how you...broke my geas...but it is of no moment...'

"Wait? Who is this?" Väst asked.

'Someone...you have...no power to...defeat...'

It's the Big Bad. I'm talking to the Big Bad himself. Well, we're pen pals anyway. "Why are you doing these terrible things?"

'Silence...you are not worthy...to speak to...me.'

Although taunting an unknown adversary wasn't the best strategy, Väst couldn't help herself. "Obviously you think you're all that but it looks like you're coming up on the short end of the stick this time."

The spinning motion of the sand cloud ceased. It was now rapidly shifting sideways across the page to print the words. *'I'm quite sure...your mother...feels differently...at this point...in time...you know,...Aine,...your mother?'*

Väst felt an ice-cold fist grasp her heart. Aine? How does this thing know she is my mother? That's super top-secret. Only a couple of people in the entire universe even know what species of Folk the Hunts School students represent, much less who their families are. Big Bad is lying. Mother is always with father. His Archon-enhanced magyk is more than enough to dust this shithead.

'Insolent cur...present circumstances...would indicate...he doesn't have... sufficient magyk "to dust this shithead"...'

Shit! Careful, Väst, she told herself. The asshole can read your thoughts.

'Yes I can...enough of this...I am weary...of you wasting me...'

" 'Wasting me?' What the hell does that even mean?"

Väst noticed the sand letters were cycling even faster now. *The Queen of...the Tuatha De...should not have...used her awaymagyk...to interfere in my business...'*

Väst felt the entire room suddenly become colder. "You're saying you have captured her astral projection?"

'Yes...'

Okay, it's panic time.

'Yes...it is... "panic time"...'

"Mom can't be away from her physical body more than a couple of hours. After that it will be impossible for her to find her way home."

'Her time now...is different...than yours.'

How is that even possible, Väst wondered. Never mind. Doesn't matter. This thing wants something. Get the dickering done so Mom can go corporeal before it's too late. "Let's get to it then. In exchange for my mom, you want me to do something for you."

'Yes...'

"I'm waiting."

The sand mini-particles momentarily changed back from shifting to swirling before rising into a cone shaped figure that looked much like an angry tabletop tornado. Wherever the tip of the funnel assaulted the page, another word briefly appeared. *'You will...tell the munedan...you found...a really old copy...of the Hunts Rules...that allows him to...take the golem's place...in Five Hells.'*

Väst was momentarily stunned. Quint? The Big Bad was after Quint? She'd been expecting something blunt like stealing treasyre or maiming or killing someone so a team might be out of the running. This was so oddly specific. Why Quint? "But, that's stupid. There's no such rule. All he has to do is look in his Rulebook and he'll know it's a lie."

The whirlwind tightened before lowering its tip once more. *'A remnant of...the geas remains...use your body to...make up the...difference.'*

Väst suddenly felt the need for a shower. Not a rinsing off. Not some casual soaking in a tub with bubble and lavender petals. A skin-needling shower with a loufa made of pumice. Surely if she scraped enough skin off she could dig deep enough to the place where pain stripped away stain.

'You balk?...I ask you to...only do with the Dust Child...something you have voluntarily done...many times...before. Enjoy yourself...and save your...mother's life. You have until...your time with...the Compyndium is done...to comply...' With that final directive, the funnel drilled itself completely into the sheet of paper. When it was fully absorbed the paper burst into flames, leaving the Compyndium unscathed.

Väst meant to put her head down on the table only long enough for sufficient tears to be expended to allow her to begin thinking rationally again. The events of the day proved too much. She failed to reach that threshold before she physically cried herself to sleep.

CHAPTER QUINQUAGINTA DUO

"Excuse me, but in this Realm it is considered ill-mannered to touch someone else's tuff without their express permission."

Startled, Tal found that with Piras's enhanced strength, they'd leapt more than thirty feet backwards from the omphalos…leaving them now precariously balanced on the last lip of a cliff.

"Mind the precipice, it is nigh on a two hundred meter drop to some rather large, rather hard, sea boulders. General consensus is that falls from that location are most unsurvivable."

"General consensus," a second voice chimed in.

"Consensus!" a third added.

'Piras?'

'I got us covered,' Piras thought-replied, before immediately helping Tal broad jump about fifteen feet back toward the omphalos. Tal hoped it was sufficient distance from any imminent threat posed by the as yet unidentified owners of the three voices.

"Well, don't stay back there behind us, show a little common courtesy and walk around where we can see you," the principal voice said.

"Common courtesy," added the second.

"Courtesy!" exclaimed the third.

Tal did a quick sit-rep. Behind him was an undulating cliff. The roar of the surf pummeling the rocks far below was clearly audible. In front of he and Piras, perched on some form of low stone dais with beveled edges, were twelve…no, Tal quickly recounted, fifteen oddly shaped free-standing stone columns. They were of varying heights, with the shortest being about twice as tall as Tal and the tallest looking to be about thirty to thirty-five feet high. Only one of the pillars had a capital. Tal guessed that's what it was. It was circular, with a diameter much larger than the column. Really kind of looks like a large stone basket-hat, Tal decided. 'Well?' he thought-asked Piras.

'Although the potential danger is as yet unquantified, I believe I possess the requisite prowess to quickly remove us from any potential grievous harm,' the Puca responded.

'Wow! Great answer. Did you pick up a thesaurus when I wasn't looking?' Tal thought-asked. 'Okay, let's go get busy with the mission objective,' Tal thought-added, as he began walking around the long line of stone pillars.

It wasn't until Tal stepped around the front corner of the dais that he realized the fifteen columns weren't stone pillars. They were stylized stone heads with torsos.

"Best not to stand there gawking."

"There gawking."

"Gawking!"

'Piras, the one with the funky basket-top hat, his lips moved first. The tallest one spoke second,' Tal quickly thought-noted.

'I marked that. The third was the one closest to us. Quint, they are animated stone Creatures.'

Without any facial movement, Basket-Top spoke again. "Young Master, I am Paro, Head of the Moai."

"Paro, Head," said the tallest.

"Head!" added the one closest to Tal.

Okay, surely somebody besides me thinks that's funny, Tal thought. I mean, c'mon, the dude's title is Head head.

"The Folk most commonly refer to our plane as Easter Island Realm. Its true name is Te Pito O Te Henua."

'Which means, "Navel of the World",' Piras thought-whispered.

Yeah, that can't possibly be a coincidence, Tal told himself. Omphalos is the Greek word for "navel."

Paro continued. "We are the Tongariki Fifteen and serve as the governing body for the Realm. To my left is Hotu, to my right is Tu'u. They are my principal advisors."

"Tongariki Fifteen."

"Tongariki."

"How many of the Moai are there?" Tal asked.

"Hotu, Tu'u, I give you leave for the remainder of this conversation to dispense with advising," Paro told the other two. He took another moment before he answered Tal. "Several hundred yet remain, Young Master, but we are a small remnant of our former glory. Mother Soil has reclaimed some, while Brother Sun and Sisters Wind and Rain have taken others. Fashioned of tuff, we are."

Tal was clueless about tuff so he went to something even better than Google. His know it all Puca. 'Piras?'

'Tuff is a porous volcanic rock. Easy to carve or sand smooth with tools of harder stone. It is, however, extremely vulnerable to degradation by the elements.'

"Why are your backs to the sea?" Tal asked.

"Your perspective is erroneous," Paro replied. "Our backs are not to the sea. Our faces are turned inward so we might share the blessings of mana with all of the inhabitants and creatures of Rapa Nui. At one time, standing on our ahu, we Moai completely circled the island."

'Ahu?' Tal thought-spoke to Piras.

'I believe those are the ceremonial platforms on which they stand,' he replied.

"Young Master, we have been courteous and introduced ourselves…," Paro stated.

"Right, right. Sorry, I'm terribly sorry. My mom would be all over me, it's just that I'm a little wigged out. I've never had a conversation with, well with…"

"A blockhead?" Paro asked, his comment being followed by chortles from his two advisors.

"Well, yes, actually," Tal answered. "I am Quint of the Omada and this is Piras."

"Well, well, honored guests indeed," Paro stated. "We have a Hunts contestant and the High King of the Puca here. Quint, I know it is a Hunts School secret as to what manner of Folk you are, but I also know it is permissible for you to tell us your principal and secondary magyks."

When in doubt, go with honesty. Thank you Baba Yaga for the lesson. "About that, I don't have any."

Tal wasn't sure how an expressionless carved stone column could express major disbelief but somehow Paro did. Without moving a single pebble. "There is no need to lie, Master Quint. All folk possess magyk. It is the lyfeforce that animates all—Principes, Folk, and Creatures alike. Only Amarantos's youngest children are possessed of the Divine Spark."

"Bingo," Tal replied.

"What, what? You are a Dust Child? A human? At Hunts School?"

"Dust Child!" Hotu exclaimed.

"Dust!" Tu'u exclaimed next.

"It's my understanding I'm the first mortal to ever be named in the Book."

"Brothers and sisters of the Tongariki Fifteen, hear me now, no matter how deep you may slumber. Long have we waited, long have we endured, but a mortal, Quint of the Omada, has come of his own free will to Te Pito O Te Henua. We will now treat with him to see if he might possess the key to our salvation."

"Key to."

"Key."

'So many questions,' Tal thought-messaged Piras. 'Why would mortals have been on this plane before? And what's up with the Key to Salvation thing? I don't have any keys. Why would anybody think I have the key to anything, much less their salvation?'

"Master Quint, given the time of year, you are here not only on a Hunt of some nature but you are a member of one of the three teams participating in the last Hunt?"

"Yes, sir."

"Your Omada is one of only three teams that may be the Ruling Council of the Moiety for the next three hundred years?"

"That is correct," Tal confirmed.

"What type of Hunt are you on?"

"A Treasyre Hunt, Head Paro," Tal replied.

"Hmm," came the deep basalt rumble. "As you can see, this Realm is a poor one. Where once there were tens of thousands of ancient coconut palms, there is now only barren terrain."

"I'm here because a super-old really dusty ass bock in the library mentioned there was such a thing as the 'Key To Your Heart's Desire.' Only source that ever mentioned the thing. I opened our Compyndium and thought about that treasyre. It was identified as an extremely high level five artifact. The whole entry was odd though. Every piece of treasyre, regardless of its value, has pages of information. Pictures, full descriptions, all prior owners, and the name of the Realm where the treasyre is presently located. There was nothing about that Key. Not a word. The entirety of the entry was one sentence. 'Go to the Prime Omphalos right now.' So I did.

"As it turns out, you, personally, are the omphalos nearest the treasyre. That is why I was touching your tuff when we arrived. Again, my apologies for that."

"The Key To Your Heart's Desire, you say," Paro replied.

That had to be some cracking wise inflection right there, Tal thought. Again, solid rock doesn't permit for much facial expression but somehow Paro gets his context across. "Yes, Head," Tal replied.

"It is good to know that as powerful as they are that those damnable Compyndium can't overcome Sol's magyk."

"Wait, what?" Tal asked. "Sol? The only guy Principe? The one with the extremely mercurial Ladies' Bathroom?"

"Yes, Sol, one of the Elder twins. Surely you didn't think Amarantos would leave the Key To Your Heart's Desire laying around unguarded, did you?"

"Well, since I didn't even know there was such a thing until about fifteen minutes ago, I'm going to have to say I hadn't ever given it much thought," Tal replied. "I guess it makes sense though. Paro, I would like to bargain with you for the Key. How much is it going to cost?"

"We had almost forgotten how hasty humans are. It is refreshing, in a way. However, we are the appointed Guardians of the Key and remain unconvinced you are worthy to bargain for it. You must first pass a test."

'Okay, Piras. We got no weapons and they know I got no magyk. I'm not thinking they're proposing a winner take all game or "rock, paper, scissors".'

Piras sighed in Tal's head. 'I think I can handle most anything except more of your punnistry.'

'As it appears you have me between a "rock and a hard place," I'll agree to stop.'

'I'm only going to continue to help you because you know the Macedonian Realm story about The Scylla and The Charybdis is the origin of that saw. Please get your mind on the task at hand.'

"Head Paro, I wish to prove my worthiness. Name your champion and I will fight him."

Helblad's draugr laugh had a gritty gravel tenor to it. The Moai's laughter was in the same species but different at the same time. It was more like the grinding noise Tal imagined two miniature tectonic plates would make as one shifted over the other. Based on the present grinding decibel level, all three of the still verbal Moai were laughing their rock faces off.

"Oh, Young Master Quint of the Omada. You are not only hasty but you are humorous as well. 'Name your champion'," he repeated. Again, Tal heard three separate sets of plates rapidly tectonically shifting back and forth. When that noise finally subsided, Paro continued. "The test, Dust Child, is not a matter of brute force, it is a test of your spirit. You must recite for us your story, about how you came to be a student at Hunts School. The entire thing from the beginning. No hastiness. After you have finished, the Tongariki Fifteen will decide whether you are worthy to bargain for the key."

Realizing it was going to take awhile and as there weren't any pit groups or overstuffed chairs visible, Tal found a large slate slab with what appeared to be a fairly soft patch of lichen.

He sat down and proceeded to recount everything that had occurred since he was trussed up in a burlap bag and thrown out of the back of a moving pickup truck.

CHAPTER QUINQUAGINTA TRES

How did this happen? How could Mashariki have been so stupid? My last orders to him were clear. The rest of the team was to make the minimum required number of trips and, to minimize the risk, they were to seek only unimportant level three treasyre.

Kati shifted uncomfortably in her seat before reaching across her desk to grab the bottle of painkillers. It says "take 1-2 as needed." She popped two of the pills and took a drink of water. Careful, Kabila Prime, you have to maintain a fine balance between functional and fuzzy. She wasn't worried about the potential for addiction. As soon as the Hunts were over she could use her authority as Archon to be cured magykally.

The walk back to her dormitory had almost killed her. Recently pinned bones kept shifting out of place when she climbed up or down steps. Without even looking she knew blood was seeping around the stitches in several places. Thank goodness she'd worked so hard to discipline Kabila. Not a single one of them offered to assist her and they'd had the good sense to make banal chatter about what they were going to do first when Kabila won the Tyrning. Campus gossip about the remaining teams was rampant. There was apparently a sizeable gambling pool that placed Kabila a distant third. We'll show them, Kati told herself.

She had intentionally taken the long way from the infirmary to the dormitory so the entire campus would see her walking unaided and in complete control of her team. Sure she was sporting several smaller casts and had to walk with a cane, but she'd sent her message out loud and clear. It doesn't matter what rumors you've heard, Kabila has the required minimum and is confident their victory is assured.

She'd placed the tablets in her backpack. It had hurt like a son of a bitch putting it on over her beat up shoulders with the straps biting into the sewn up wounds across her chest. It was going to be worth it though. The Simurgh had promised Kabila would prevail as long as the tablets were in Kabila's possession at the time of the Final Ceremony.

Kati could taste victory. Well, what she could literally taste right now was the metallic-tinged flavor of her own blood welling up into her mouth. A sure sign her internal injuries had reopened. Fine then. She could figuratively taste the victory. Hold on, she encouraged herself. Only seven more days. Five remaining days of the last week of the Hunt and then the Coronation Ceremony two days later.

Mashariki. She'd considered offering to exchange herself as the hostage. Kabila would still have four members and possession of the Tablets of Destiny. After we won the Tyrning and were installed as the new Ruling Council, Mashariki could use his findermagyk to locate me. After that we would all rain holy hell down on the kidnappers.

But a trade wasn't an option contained in the note. You couldn't trade anyway, and you know it, she reminded herself. You're the Kabila Prime. Your primary duty is to your team, not to an individual member. The Simurgh's prophecy also said as long as the tablets were in your possession.

Call their bluff. Ignore the note. When you become Archon you can figure out how to use the Archon's additional magyk to discover the kidnappers' identities and to levy appropriate retaliation. The Hunts Rules provide for Revenge Honor although they're kind of vague about the details of when and what is allowed.

But the note says if I don't comply, he'll be lost and in pain forever. Time for the hard conversation, girl. So what if they kill Mashariki? she asked herself dispassionately. Kabila will still have four members. With the Tablets in hand we will win the Tyrning and I'll have everything I ever wanted. I'll be Archon, ruler of the known universe for the next three hundred years. Is Mashariki worth giving up the dream? I love him, she reminded herself. Ruler of the known universe, came the response.

Kati reached over and grabbed the pill bottle again, took out two more pills, and hurriedly swallowed them. Well, the directions say "as needed" and they're needed. "Practically Seeking the Center," she reminded herself right before she slumped forward, passed out cold.

CHAPTER QUINQUAGINTA QUATTUOR

Best Väst could tell, this time it was a seriously painful kink in her back that woke her. Another night spent sleeping in a chair at the library. That's just great. Her stomach rumbled. Right. Haven't had anything to eat or drink for a pretty long time.

Well, let's review yesterday's high points. Nord is torturing Mashariki and he's ordered me to "eliminate" Quint. The Big Bad has Mom and he's going to kill her if I don't seduce my boyfriend and send him to hell. Well, Five-Hells. Not sure there's a difference. I've still been on zero Journeys. Oh and I've been commanded to seek a level five artifact, which might result in me being all kinds of dead myself.

Yep, that about sums it up. It's too much, she told herself. You aren't going to be able to able to move forward in a rational manner with all of the emotional froth. Prioritize, she told herself. Sequester each issue, delineate the problem, and work on an acceptable resolution. As much as she hated to admit it, even though solving the Mom and Quint equations were easily the most important issues, they was not the most time-sensitive. I still have days before the Big Sucking Asshole kills her, she reminded herself. Big Sucking Asshole is a much better descriptor than Big Bad.

I have to go try to get that buckler first. If I remove that item from my to-do worry list it will free up some brain matter to cogitate on the other problems.

Who are you kidding, Väst asked herself. Sure you need to go ahead and knock out at least one of your Journeys, but you already know exactly how you're going to resolve the Aine-Quint dilemma. Sending Quint to Five-Hells solves two problems at the same time. Even if the BSA hadn't sandblasted you about your mother, you were already going to have to "eliminate" Quint. Thank Amarantos, Nord though he was being clever. If he'd ordered me to kill Quint I wouldn't have had any choice. As long as Quint is alive, even if he is stuck in Five-Hells, he's still alive. As for Mom, dead is dead. Period.

If Quint was here and we were talking about this decisional morass, I would probably have referred to it as a "Hobson's choice." He then would have proceeded to tell me that even though I had utilized the phrase as it is most commonly employed, I had used it incorrectly. He would have explained a "Hobson's choice" is actually a "take it or leave it" situation in which the chooser only has a single option. And, of course, he would have been right. The smartass wouldn't simply have left it there, though. In his own infuriating but endearing way he would then have told me I might have called the situation a "Morton's Fork." But then he would have told me if I had, I would have been wrong yet again, because a "Morton's Fork" requires the existence of two contradictory observations. He then would have told me that it could properly be referred to as a bizarro "Buridan's Ass" because a true "Buridan's Ass" situation involves two equally attractive choices. Quint would have finished his irritating—irritating because he so clearly loves knowledge and learning things even though they probably have absolutely squat to do with whatever the then present conversation is about—lesson by telling me there was no need for fancy words or phrases because what I had was a supercharged yet still classic example of a "dilemma." A choice between two equally undesirable options.

Still…there is no "still," you idiot, she told herself. Put aside your lovesick puppy feelings for the mortal and quit sugarcoating it. Regardless of whether you're in love with him, which you know you are, you're going to send him to Five-Hells to save your mother. Now go get yourself some sustenance so you can figure out how to obtain the buckler of Iblis.

CHAPTER QUINQUAGINTA QUINQUE

As he'd been instructed, Tal recited his story. There weren't any timepieces handy but he figured, based on the sun's movement, that he must have yakked for about an hour. After that there'd been fifteen minutes of total silence, during which time Tal came to the conclusion he'd been overly optimistic with respect to his presumption concerning the softness of the patch of lichen.

"Thank you, Master Quint, for your compelling narrative. Our conference is concluded. We believe you faithfully recounted your experiences without whitewashing the unfavorable portions. In spite of your numerous shortcomings, we believe you are earnestly attempting to Seek the Center as Amarantos has instructed. It is our considered opinion, as the Guardians of the Key, that we will treasyre-bargain with you."

"Great!" Tal exclaimed. Well, except for the "numerous shortcomings" part. Although, in all fairness, it's a fairly accurate assessment.

"You have not yet heard the bargainpryce," Paro stated.

"I trust you guys. I know you'll give me your rock-bottom deal."

'Quint—stop with the mineralogical puns!' Piras thought-admonished.

'That one was accidental. Pinkie-swear,' Tal replied to the Puca.

"The bargainpryce," Paro continued, "is two-fold. The first part is contingent and requires a guarantee of future performance. The second part..."

Okay, that's different, Tal thought. A promise now to be performed later. But I mean, hey, I've already had my ass branded with the Cult of Nyx symbol, so how bad can any "ask" be? "I'm good with it, Head Paro," Tal announced.

"Hasty, hasty human," Paro remarked. "Quint of the Omada, the Moai are dying. Where once we were thousands, we are now hundreds. Many of us who remain no longer have the lyfeforce to communicate in any meaningful manner. The barren Rapa Nui you see before you was once a tropical paradise. Thousands of coconut palm trees filled the island. Springs of fresh water were within easy walking distance of each other. Birds and creatures of every shape and color, flew and crawled here on Rapa Nui. Our makers fashioned us and, in harmony with us, lived lives of joy and laughter. Rapa Nui was an Eden."

Looking around the windswept landscape, one word came to Tal's mind—sterile. That's what Rapa Nui was now. No trees or shrubs, no birds, no insects, no creatures. Not a single one. Nothing but the Moai. Which meant none of the mysterious "makers" remained either. "What...what happened here?" he asked.

"Long, long ago, before Arthrys's Bane, it was possible for humans to voluntarily choose to be transported to this Realm by way of an Earth plane omphalos. I am the only remaining viable omphalos on Rapa Nui and our plane will only be accessible as long as I remain sentient. There was a time when each of the island's three dormant volcanoes had at least one omphalos. Rano Kau, the largest, had half a dozen."

"Mortals like me? They were your makers?" Tal asked, dumbfounded.

"Yes," Paro replied. "The youngest children of the Unfading One created the Moai. All who were here came voluntarily, through the omphalos on the Earth plane mirror Rapa Nui."

"I don't understand. You just said the Moai have lyfeforce, that means you're magyk."

"We are the only Creatures created by mortals, Young Quint. We are made sentient not by magyk, but by mana."

"Mana?" Quint asked. "You mentioned that earlier but I've never heard of it."

"It is understandable. Mana is a unique form of magyk found only on this island. Mana is a mystical energy that comes from the act of creation. When the Dust Children came, they first crafted our ceremonial Ahu on which we stand. When they lovingly and joyfully fashioned each of the Moai, they created much mana. It flowed into us and gave us lyfe. We returned the gyft by imbuing all living things on Rapa Nui with energy and lyfe. When the mortals on Earth Realm learned of this, thousands and thousands asked permission to come here to live."

"The palm trees, the birds, animals, all of it, it was the Moai dispersing mana throughout the island."

"Yes," Paro confirmed.

"You realize this raises all kinds of questions," Tal said.

"Inquire and if I can answer I will."

"Why here? What makes this place the only plane in the entire universe where human beings are kind of sort of magykal?"

"They were not magykal, Quint. They remained fully human, Children of the Divine Spark. The answer to your question is Rapa Nui is the common name for this plane and its people. As I mentioned, its full name is Te Pito O Te Henua."

"The Navel of the World," Tal mused as he repeated what Piras had told him earlier. "I get it now. The name, it's not just figurative. There's something different here than anywhere else."

"You are astute for such a rash human."

"Okay, next," Tal continued hurriedly. "You said there were thousands of human beings here. Men, women, children. Families. What happened? There's not a single person left."

The Moai's ability to convey emotion with absolutely no facial expression was proven once again. If shoulders made of rock could possibly slump, Paro's just did. "Before Arthrys, there were many atrocities perpetuated by the Folk. Against other Folk. Against Creatures. And against humankind. Slavers came. Finmen from a far away plane."

"Finmen," Tal spat.

"You know of them?" Paro asked, surprise clear in his voice.

"They caused a whole lot of trouble for a friend of mine named Helblad."

Again came the tectonic plate shifting that signaled Paro was laughing. "I do not recall your recitation mentioning you had befriended the Suzerain of the Undead."

"Sorry," Tal said, somewhat sheepishly. "I really didn't have time to go through every minor detail. There's also a really snotty Air Hose at Sol's Gas Station Crossing."

"It is fine, Young Quint, and somewhat humorous your travels have been of such import that being the only living being who is actually a friend of the Jarl is a 'minor detail.'"

"The slavers came and kidnapped them," Paro Head continued. "Every man, woman, and child, was taken, to be sold on other Realms. Sometime not long after that Arthrys's Bane was issued. Although the magyk quarantine has been a true gyft to the people of Earth plane, it was a writ of death for Rapa Nui."

"I have a feeling this brings us to the meat of the first part of the bargainpryce," Tal said.

"It does. If this Realm is to survive, mortals must come to Rapa Nui once more. Voluntarily, of course. Free will is a requirement for the creation of mana."

"Paro, you realize I'm not the Omada Prime Direction. That I don't get to call the shots, right?"

"We do, Quint. Based on your story, we believe your Borras is someone who also genuinely Seeks the Center and that if he becomes Archon and this is brought to his attention he will find a way to rectify the impact of the Bane on Rapa Nui."

"Back to that whole 'if he becomes Archon' thing. Omada is only one of three teams still trying their damnedest to win the Tyrning."

"We are aware," Paro confirmed.

"You want me to bind a contract with you, don't you?"

"Yes."

"Say the words you must say and if it is something I can do, then I will consent."

"Quint of the Omada, if Omada becomes the Ruling Council for the next Tyrning, do you freely and willingly consent, as a portion of the bargainpryce for the Key To Your Heart's Desire, to do everything within your power to see humans are allowed to once more voluntarily migrate to this Realm?"

"I do. Do you?"

"On behalf of all the Moai, we do," Paro replied solemnly.

"Great," Tal replied. "Now that the hard part is done, let's get to the easy part."

CHAPTER QUINQUAGINTA SEX

The first thing Väst noticed about the Zoroastrian plane was that her magyk level was at zero percent. There wasn't even a vestige of her gyft available. There must be something blocking it, she decided.

The second thing was the enchanting smell of the place. It was like the great outdoors had a "fresh linen" air freshener. 'Do you smell that, Ardere?' she thought-asked her Puca.

'Yes, Väst,' Ardere confirmed. 'It's lovely. It does, however, make imminent sense.' Ardere paused a moment before adding, 'No pun intended.'

Väst couldn't repress a small chuckle. Who knew Pucas had a sense of humor? The Folk's only real interaction with the Creatures was during the Hunts. We put them on, take them off, store them for however long, but really know very little about them. Other than they had voluntarily agreed to perpetual service to atone for some hideous past acts. It was comforting having Ardere along for this Journey, knowing there was at least one living being she could count on to absolutely have her back. 'Why?'

'The Peris' perfumeratic skills are legendary throughout the known Realms. On many planes an ounce of Peri scent is worth a king's ransom.'

And here I was arrogantly believing I was one of the smartest people at Hunts School, Väst thought to herself.

'I do not mean to intrude, Mistress, but you will have to ward your thoughts if you do not wish to share them with me while I cover you.'

'It's okay, Ardere, I don't mind.'

'Good. In that case, you are correct, I do absolutely have your back. And you are one of the smartest Folk at Hunts School.'

'Thank you.'

'It is my pleasure to be of service. In all of the Pucas' eons of service at Hunts School, you are one of only two students who have treated the Puca as equals, deserving of respect. Many have been deferential. Some even kind, thoughtful. But only two have accorded us equality.'

We have done these Creatures a major disservice, Väst thought. 'Wait, Ardere. The Puca have served thousands of Folk over tens of thousands of years. How can you possibility know what you said is the truth?'

This time there was a noticeable pause without a response. 'I'm sorry, Ardere. I didn't mean to pry into confidential matters.'

'It's okay, Mistress. I needed to obtain permission to respond.'

'Permission?'

"Yes, from The Piras.'

'Piras, as in Quint's Puca?'

'I thought the Hunts School students knew. The Piras is a Puca avatar. He is High King of all the Puca. His name means "elemental fire." It is why we are all named for the word "fire," in the languages of many different Realms.'

'I had no idea,' Väst replied, stunned.

'The Piras holds the collective knowledge of all Puca that have gone before and all living Puca are linked through him. It is how I seem to know so much. There is no "I" who knows all these things, it is "We".'

'That makes sense. Okay, I have to ask, the other student, who was it?'

Again the slight pause. 'The appropriate tense is "is." It is Quint of the Omada. He is a Lynchpin.'

Quint? The only munedan to ever attend Hunts School. And his Puca is High King of the entire Puca race. There is no way that's a coincidence. 'What's a Lynchpin?'

'With apologies, the Piras has advised it is not yet time to discuss that matter. I have been asked to inform you why the Peris became renowned perfumers.'

'They like smelling good?'

'They do,' Ardere confirmed. 'They really do. That was not the original and most important reason though. The Deevs wage constant war against the Peris. When they capture them they trap them in cages of cold iron. Iron is anathema to the Peris, it leaches their lyfeforce from them. The Deevs use Peri lyfeforce as a narcotic drug.'

'That's terrible. They kill them simply to get high?'

'Yes, it is their nature. The Deevs absolutely cannot abide the scent of the Peris' perfume.'

'So you're saying this place is frequented by Peris and that because of their perfume we also are safe from Deevs while we are here.'

'From Deevs, yes. Ifrits, no.'

I know that Folk, Väst thought. Ifrits are the malevolent Jinn. Extremely high level, in both malevolence and Jinn pecking order. 'What you're saying is we need to quit screwing around and get on with the business part of this venture.'

'That and that caution is warranted. If this place is warded against the Deevs it means their masters are usually not far away. Although my impression is we are safe in this specific place. The omphalos is an Asherah Pillar.'

Know that one, too, Väst acknowledged. On some planes, there is an avatar called The Asherah. On others, it might be The Astarte or The Ishtar. Good news is I can't think of any Folk Realm where that individual is considered evil. 'Good to know. Okay, let's reconnoiter.'

She began walking clockwise around the omphalos, not venturing too far away. The pillar was sited on the flat top of a rock outcropping. Walking to one edge she looked down. It was hundreds of feet down to sand dunes on the valley floor. As far as the eye could see there were sand dunes. Not just your run of the mill Sahara Desert type dunes, these dunes had to be twenty stories tall.

'I'm thinking we're supposed to be staying up here,' she thought-spoke at Ardere.

'Agreed. We might as well finish the circuit.'

Väst continued until she would have been one hundred eighty degrees from her starting point. On this side of the Asherah Pillar there were four or five rough hewn stone benches. The seating was in a small semi-circle and faced a rock outcropping, which jutted out into the void. A stone altar occupied almost the entirety of the promontory. A single object set atop the altar. A brass lamp.

"Scheherazade!" Väst exclaimed aloud.

CHAPTER QUINQUAGINTA SEPTEM

"The second part of the bargainpryce requires that you solve a riddle," Paro stated.

What the hell? Tal wondered. A riddle? Really? "Okay, fine. But when I get back to Earth plane I'm letting the Sphinx know your tuff is horning in on her turf."

Paro either ignored Tal's quip or wasn't at all amused. "I will state the riddle. One time. You will give us your answer. One chance. I'm sorry, Quint of the Omada, but the worth of this treasyre means the terms of the bargainpryce must be substantial."

"Got it," Tal confirmed. "One and done."

"One last matter. The riddle is for you and you alone. You may not consult Piras for your answer."

'You've got this, Quint,' Piras chimed in. 'You realize don't you, that the Gas Pump's prophesy has come true?'

'What? You mean that whole absolutely no pressure whatsoever statement by good old Gas Pump Unus that, "worlds depend upon me"? Thanks for not further pressurizing an already tense sitch, Piras.'

"Are you ready?" Head Paro asked, in a cadence smacking of formal ritual. Tal nodded his reply and the Moai continued.

> A deity of the liminal am I,
> I am less than he who first you will guess.

Worshipped first in Urbs Aeterna,
or Caput Mundi as some may know her.

No matter whether you be rich or poor,
my sigil that I hold, can open any door.

Where is Emet when I need him, Tal asked himself. In Five-Hells doing penance for your sorry ass for all eternity, came the quick response. Stop it, Tal. You absolutely don't have time for a deep wallow pity-party, so don't go there. No, you idiot, absolutely go there, chimed in Basal Ganglia. Deep wallow in it. I just had your subconscious throw you a softball response.

C'mon, Tal, you're supposed to be a freaking boy genius. Stop, rewind, go back to what you told yourself a few thoughts ago. You mean the part where I'm a "sorry ass?" No, not that part. The next bit. "For all eternity?" Yes. Eternity. The riddle, Tal. "Worshipped first in Urbs Aeterna." Aeterna is Latin for "eternal." Good, but "urbs?" I know it but I can't call it.

Treat it like a standardized test. Answer what you can, then go forward to come back. "Caput Mundi?" Right, that's also Latin. "Mundi" is easy, that's world. "Caput?" Think, Tal, you've heard that. Think other languages. "Caput" sounds…like "Capo" in Italian. Means, "Boss." Thank you "Godfather" movies. "Boss of the World." No, that's not right, Tal. It's one of those phrases where the word combination means something a little different than its component words. "Worshipped first in the Eternal Urbs or Boss of the World some prefer." Urbs…urbs…urbs. Work around it. Sounds like? Rhymes with? Sounds like…verbs…sounds like…suburbs. "Eternal Suburbs." Hello? We have a winner. "Urbs" is Latin for "City." There it is, "Eternal City" and the other one is "Capital of the World."

ROME! We're talking about Roman mythology. Winner, winner, chicken dinner. Don't start the end zone celebration yet, Cowboy. That's only one of the three couplets and this is sudden death overtime rules.

Next, "Deity of the liminal am I." The literal definition of "liminal" means a position that is on both sides of a threshold. Like somebody straddling a fence. We're looking for the Roman god who straddles a threshold. Easy peasy! That's Janus, the two-faced Roman god, Tal thought, as he got ready to give Head Paro the answer.

STOP, TAL! Don't open your piehole just yet. Janus is the most powerful Roman liminal god. We get January in our calendar from him because with one face he stares across the threshold to the past year and with the other face gazes into the new year. He is also the sucker punch the second line of that couplet warned you about. "I am less than he who first you will guess." A different Roman god. Not as powerful or well known. A minor one. Well, shit, how am I supposed to know that?

C'mon, this is no hill for a stepper. That's what the third couplet is for, to give you the last necessary clue to solve the puzzle. "No matter whether rich or poor, the sigil I hold can open any door." Solve that, Tal, and we're going to Disney World. Well, not really. Hey, I wonder if there is a Disney Realm? That would be way too cool, Although, I'd just as soon not run into a real life The Captain Hook…or The Cruella DeVille. Now that there is one scary bitch…

Excuse me, this is Important Quest calling Tal. Seriously? Thea should have had you tested. Like a lot. Right. Focus, Tal. Okay, eidetic memory, it's time to call up everything you can remember about Roman mythology. "No matter whether rich or poor," that's code talk for "Everyman." The same is true for "every door." The riddler is referencing "Everydoor." Everyman can open Everydoor if they hold the deity's sigil. A sigil is a sign or symbol. What kind of symbol could someone hold that would open every door? What opens every door? Damn, I must be low on blood sugar. That's easy. It's a key. A key is a sigil that can be held and Everyman can use a key to open Everydoor.

Turn the Rubik's cube, Tal. You can absolutely do this. The lesser known Roman god of doors and because he is a god of the liminal, of thresholds as well. A god who is often pictured with a key as his symbol…

"PORTUNUS, Head Paro. The Keeper of the key is The Portunus."

"You are correct, Young Master Quint of the Omada. You now have permission to touch my tuff. To initiate the omphalos, of course. With the riddle unlocked, our omphalos will forward you to the Realm where the Key To Your Heart's Desire is located."

"I'm sorry. Don't you mean there will be a Recall which will take me back to the Prime Omphalos and then the Prime Omphalos will send me to that other plane?" Tal asked.

Three sets of small tectonic plates began once again rapidly shifting. "So hasty," Head Paro said, "and so sure they know everything. It will be good to interface once more with the Children of the Divine Spark. Remember your promise to the Moai, Young Master Quint."

CHAPTER QUINQUAGINTA OCTO

Väst walked quickly toward the small promontory. After her initial steps she noticed the beginnings of a breeze. By the time she was within a few feet of the rock formation the wind was fierce and by the time she realized she was going to have to sidle around the outside of the spur to reach the lamp it was gale force. As her heels hung out into the cloudless blue sky she tried her best not to think about the sizeable drop to the valley floor.

The surface of the altar was smoothed stone, humid slick. Of course it's smooth wet stone with no handholds, she thought. It wouldn't be the least bit fun unless death (or worse) was on the table.

Not wishing to tarry she scooched around to where she could grab the lamp with one hand, leaning forward with her other arm to counterbalance her weight inward. Väst finally completed the altar circuit and began quickly walking back toward the safety of the stone benches. As she walked she began rubbing the hell out of the lamp.

Väst almost jumped straight out of Ardere when a melodious female voice cut through the wind's howl. "Thank you for polishing my lamp but it's quite unnecessary."

Väst turned her attention to the voice's point of origin. The Asherah Pillar. Well, actually a semi-transparent woman stepping forth out of the pillar.

Stunned, Väst went with her default state—smartass. "I

thought the genie of the lamp was supposed to come out if I rubbed it."

The semi-solid chick's laugh sounded like the tinkling of keyboard ivories. Not like someone pounding out "Chopsticks," more like a fun little spontaneous riff by some Liberace-level savant. "I'm afraid you have been spending way too much time listening to some trickster from the Arabian plane. Still, it's an important lesson to learn. Sometimes a lamp is only a lamp. I keep it on the sky-pedestal because it dresses up the place a little." The more solid, but not a whole lot more solid, than a wraith woman took several steps toward Väst. "I am Maymunah."

Ardere, who had been silent thus far in the encounter, spoke up. 'Väst, that is Crown Princess Maymunah, she is a Jinnayah.'

"I see your Puca has recognized me," Maymunah interjected. "Maymunah is sufficient for me, if you please. It is curious that she named you using a proper noun. Väst. Is that your Hunts School name?"

"Yes, although I'm not sure how you know…"

Solidifying a little more, the Jinnayah, raised her shoulders in a shrug. "You've been sent by the Prime Omphalos to a plane known to have superior treasyre wearing a Puca. Really, Väst,…may I call you Väst?"

"Um, sure why not, since it's just us girls here."

Again the buoyant laughter. "Am I correct in assuming the Puca refers to you by your first name because you treat her as an equal?"

"Ardere, please. Her name is Ardere. And yes, why wouldn't I? She's my friend."

"Interesting." The Jinnayah paused a moment. "I think Ardere has something else she feels you need to know."

'Ardere?' Väst thought-inquired.

'Proceed with extreme care. She has immense power. Many levels above that of even your royal-level magyk. The Crown Princess's father is Iblis, King of the Ifrits.'

Not a coincidence, Väst told herself. No way. 'But you said Maymunah was good and Ifrits are evil.'

'That is correct. Although I should have probably said "Ifrits are really, really evil".'

Princess Maymunah interjected. "It is true Iblis is my father. Our relationship is, well, let's say it is strained. The UnFading Spirit has given all of her children the freedom to choose our own path. I have committed my life to Seeking the Center."

CHAPTER QUINQUAGINTA NOVEM

Their arrival had thrown a layer of gritty dust high into the air. Either that or they'd had the misfortune to arrive on a plane where the atmospheric composition was more particulated than it was oxygenated. Tal couldn't help the paroxysm of coughing that ensued.

'I'm working on redirecting a number of things, Quint, but your cough response is really the most efficient solution to removing the contaminants from your lungs.'

"I know you're hitting it as hard as you can, Piras. Maybe if you could tone down their vehemence a little?'

'On it,' Piras responded.

While Piras was working internally, Tal pondered their status. Piras is still with me, so Amarantos hasn't shipped me off again to othertyme. We're not in the Prime Omphalos chamber in the basement of the ziggurat at Hunts School. Which means Paro was in the know and we're still on mission.

He quickly glanced around. The receiving omphalos was a time-faded, well-used oak door. More specifically, the inside of an oak door. The upper half was frosted glass. Through it Tal could see there was some type of stenciled lettering but couldn't read the words. Around the base of the door there were five or six small piles of ash. That's odd, he thought, who takes ashes from the fireplace and makes ant mounds next to their entry door?

This place looks exactly like the set of an Elizabethan-era

"ye olde shoppe" rendered straight-up out of the pages of a Dickens' novel. Not the malevolent mojo of the Rag and Bottle Shop, operated by the alcoholic, self-combusting Krook of "Bleak House," mind you. No, not that vibe at all. This was much more like the poulterers' or fruiterers' establishments, as recounted in "A Christmas Carol." If you conflated the happy Christmas joie de vivre of those shops with Disney's depiction of Geppetto's joyful workshop in "Pinocchio," you'd probably have pretty much nailed the shop's ambience.

There was a large fire burning in an oversized hearth, exporting tendrils of warmth throughout the frosty-breathed air. The establishment smelled of, what exactly? Apples and cinnamon, Tal concluded.

'And cloves,' Piras added.

'Yes, those too,' Tal agreed. "Piras, this place most decidedly is not Roman plane themed.'

'Given the security measures employed in hiding this treasyre, that makes sense, Quint. I've never heard of a two-stage Journey. All the Folk, as well as all Creatures, have been taught the Prime Omphalos is the only confluence of all the Realms. I'm thinking that is a deliberately promulgated misstatement. The reason for its dissemination being to add another layer of security to hide the Key."

' "There are more things in heaven and earth, Horatio," '

'You know who wrote that don't you?'

'Duh, Shakespeare,' Tal retorted.

'Well, in a way,' Piras replied.

Tal thought about that statement for a few beats. 'Oh no, don't you start that too. When he was that obnoxious kid, Dr. Mertin Wilt, Myrddin kept taking credit for writing all kinds of…'

'Anyway,' the Puca thought-spoke, moving the conversation back on course. 'Everyone assumes The Portunus is on one of the dozens of Roman oriented planes. If Amarantos has taken the considerable effort to set up an omphalos relay to guard the Key, doesn't it make sense it would be safeguarded in a Realm where none of that plane's denizens would ever think to look for it?'

'Yes, actually it does,' Tal thought-replied. 'You are one

smart dude, Piras.'

'Thank you.'

As Tal studied the place, he decided it couldn't be more crammed full of items if it was the home office of the five-time and still undefeated International Hoarding champion. If there was such a person and whoever that person might be. Still the establishment, while patently unruly, was not untidy.

One entire wall was occupied with floor to ceiling windows. Generationally-smudged, sporting an overcoat of frosted rime. Still, as begrimed and be-iced as they were they still gave permission to some late afternoon sun to illuminate the store's contents.

There were hundreds of glass jars and receptacles containing all manner of powders, and barks, and insect wings, as well as different sizes of claws, hoofs, and antlers. The stock of an experienced apothecary, Tal decided. Those shelves that didn't contain apothecarial items were crammed full with hundreds of hardback books. There were also wobbly shoulder-high stacks of books rising like stalagmites from the floor. Racks of books raced horizontally across every flat surface. Over all and everything was a layer of dust. Scratch that, Tal thought, as an exceptionally explosive sneeze erupted from his chest. Several layers of dust.

It was the far wall, however, that commanded his attention. The wall was behind a waist high counter that ran the width of the room. Rising the entire height of the wall was a wheeled ladder that could be used to access any item on the wall.

How do I even describe the wall's content, Tal wondered. It was glorious, and fascinating, and myriad. The entire wall, floor to ceiling, wall juncture to wall juncture, was populated with keys. Brass keys, copper keys, iron keys, keys that looked like they might actually be made of gold. Keys so large it would take two hands to hold, maybe even a hoist to lift. The humongous keys were counterpointed by teensy keys made to open the locket that contained the lock of hair of someone's True Love.

Viewed individually or in the aggregate, they were magnificent. Glinting, shining, preening, boasting, pretty much just showing off to everyone who entered the establishment.

When another couple of minutes went by and there was

still no sign of a shopkeeper, Tal turned back toward the door, slid a security bolt to the right, then opened and closed the door several times so the tiny silver bell hanging above the door jangled loudly to announce their presence.

"Coming, coming, be there in a minute. I'm all the way in the back," came a harried male voice. It was from a smallish doorway cut into the key wall that the proprietor emerged. "We're closed for lunch. I'm not sure how you got in…

"GREAT CAESAR'S GHOST!"

CHAPTER SEXAGINTA

I have no leverage, Väst reminded herself. I'm going to take the princess at her word. "Lady, I do not mean to be rude but Ardere has advised me what the Peris' perfume means. I also have no idea how Earth plane time syncs with this Realm."

"Which is a polite way to say you don't particularly trust me and you wish to conduct your treasyre-bargain and be away as swiftly as possible."

"Yes. Thank you for understanding."

"Our Realm is blessed with substantial treasyre, Väst. Each piece will, of course, have a different bargainpryce. What treasyre do you seek?"

"Your father's shield, my lady."

In an instant Princess Maymunah went from fairly solid to barely visible. It seemed to Väst as if the Jinnayah actually blanched away to a light-colored vapor.

As Maymunah gathered herself to reply, Väst watched as a little tremble shook the princess's entire form. Kind of like a small earthquake rolling through quicksand, before she coalesced once more into semi-solid form. "Long, long ago, The Solomon waged war against my father. He ultimately prevailed, using the power of his ring, his Seal as it is now known, to bend my father to his will. The Solomon ordered Iblis, as High King, to capture the seventy-two most powerful Ifrits in all of this Realm, and to imprison them in his shield."

Väst had read the Compyndium entry but it hadn't fully sunk in why a small shield with a wrist strap could be a level five treasyre. What was it Nord said to me right before he walked out the door of the team room? The buckler was only insurance, he had already obtained an artifact he believed to be the winning level-five treasyre. Why is he so intent on Släkt obtaining the buckler?

Nord must have obtained the Seal. He was right. Solomon's ring is probably enough to win the Hunt. So, why is he determined to get the buckler as well. There's more to this though than Nord trying to get me killed. "Maymunah, if someone had both items, would they have the ability to release the Ifrits trapped in the Seal?"

"No, thank Amarantos," Maymunah replied, as her shoulders relaxed a little. "There are many secrets surrounding the Seal's power. It gives anyone wearing it the ability to speak to animals as well as some extraordinary healing properties. The most closely held secret is that, regardless of widespread legend, only The Solomon can utilize its ability to control the Jinns within."

"Wouldn't all of that information have been disclosed if someone looked the Seal up in the Compyndium?" Väst asked.

"The Compyndium?" Maymunah repeated, clearly surprised. "The Seshat has allowed the Compyndium to be used by Hunts School students?"

"Yes, but that's a long story."

"Wonders abound this Tyrning," the Princess mused. "The answer to your question is no. As powerful as the Compyndium are, the Seal's ability to protect its secrets from disclosure is greater."

"Seems kind of fraudulent to me," Väst responded. "Competitors might put their life on the line trying to snag the Seal and then it's not as valuable as they thought."

"That issue has been fairly addressed. First, the Seal is a marvelous artifact, an extremely high level-five piece. Second, the bargainpryce for the Seal is ridiculously low. Anyone negotiating to acquire the ring would be put on notice something was awry."

'Anyone negotiating who wasn't blinded by avarice,'

Ardere thought-spoke.

"The Puca is correct," the Jinnayah confirmed. "Väst, let us bargain for treasyre other than the buckler. On this Realm is also the treasyre of Ali Baba. There are only two more valuable treasyre hoards in all the known Realms. The second most valuable collection is the dragon-hoard of the great wyrm, Snype. That treasyre is on a different plane, and as you may know, dragons do not generally…"

"You can stop there, Highness," Väst said, interrupting Maymunah. "There's not a single student left alive at Hunts School who would seek a rematch with that foul beast from Hell." Seeing the Jinnayah wasn't following along, Väst explained about the previous year's Snype Hunt and how hundreds of competitors had been killed or maimed.

"I see," Maymunah replied. "The single most valuable treasyre hoard is even more unavailable than the dragon's gold. The fabled treasyre of the Undead. That treasyre would guarantee victory. The trove is so large it has to be stored on many different planes. However, the Undead will not treat with anyone concerning their treasyre. It transfers only by the Last Will and Testament of their Jarl."

Ardere interrupted. 'Väst?'

'Yes, Ardere?'

'The Jinnayah's unwillingness to treat with you for the buckler is a clear indicator of great danger. Regardless, if Ali Baba's treasyre will win the Hunt, perhaps that should be your focus.'

'Agreed,' Väst thought-spoke to her Puca. 'There is absolutely no way in Five-Hells I'm collecting the buckler of Iblis for Nord.' Turning to Princess Maymunah, she said "Okay, Princess, you smooth talking salesperson you. Change of plans. On behalf of the Släkt, I wish to treasyre-bargain with you for the…buckler."

What the hell, Väst thought to herself. Try again. "I'm sorry, Maymunah, I misspoke. What I meant to say was that I wish to treasyre-bargain with you for the…for the…buckler?"

Comprehension poleaxed Väst.

"WHAT THE HELL?"

"OH, SHIT."
"DAMN YOU TO FIVE-HELLS, NORD!"

CHAPTER SEXAGINTA UNUS

The shopkeeper abruptly about-faced, clearly intending to back slang it. He suddenly pulled up short, then turned back around. "Wait a minute. You wear a cardinal Puca," the liminal god whispered.

Not sure what's up with that, Tal wondered, as he took a couple of beats to check out Portunus. The shopkeeper's wardrobe was classic Victorian mercatilian. His shirt was china colored, lightly pleated, with a club collar and puffed sleeves that were gathered around black sleeve garters. The shirt was barely restrained by a light brown herringbone patterned vest, misbuttoned one hole off correct. A fob chain ran from a middle vest button to the vest's watch pocket. The pants were dark brown, high-waisted button-fly wool trousers complete with umber suspenders. His well-worn, well-scuffed brown shoes were the perfect complement to his battered brown felt derby, which looked like it had seen more use as a seating cushion than as a chapeau.

The entire ensemble was in complete period accordance, with one exception. Over his right eye Portunus wore an anachronistic steampunkish combination spectacle and jeweler's loupe. Actually, when Tal took a second look, it appeared the apparatus might even be his right eye. The eyepiece had a coke bottle bottom main lense, with two or three little stick-handled magnifying lenses that could be rotated singly or in combination in front of the main glass. The entire thing was set in a black leather harness, with the main lens being held in place by several closely spaced brass hoops. On the outside of the small contraption was a brass engraving of a compass. A compass with five directions. North, south, east, west, and center.

Portunus, himself, was unprepossessing. Almost as round as he was tall, he looked tiny against the backdrop of his wonderful key wall. He sported no facial hair and the hairline underneath his hat appeared to be well past receding. The only "tell" of a Roman plane origination was his parish pickaxe of a nose.

'Quint,' Piras thought-spoke in Tal's head. 'It's your turn to respond.'

"Right. Of course," Tal said out loud, before continuing. Slowly. Intoning. In case it was some weird ritual. "Yes, I am Quint of the Omada, um, the anointed wearer of the cardinal Puca."

"Yeah," the proprietor said, absent-mindedly doffing his hat so he could scratch the top of his head. "Sorry, must be some other guy with a red Puca. I was told to be on the lookout for a guy wearing a cardinal Puca who was plagued with a quippish lip. No offense, stranger, but you seem to be about three horses shy of a coach and four."

"No offense taken," Tal replied calmly, even though he found himself more than a little offensed. 'Weird?' he thought-queried Piras.

'Yes,' Piras agreed, in response. 'But he has what you need.'

"Who was it who told you to be on the lookout?" Tal asked.

"Let me see," Portunus replied, before scratching a completely different place in his expanse of baldness. Then he started gesturing with a finger in the air, muttering something about "carrying the naughts." "Yes, that's the number. Some gent showed up here, I make it roughly eight hundred years past."

Eight centuries, Tal thought to himself. "This guy, do you know who he was?"

"Sure," Portunus replied quickly. "It was one of Her

Stytches. It's not every day someone appears out of nowhere all bug-eyed and asking for Chlorodyne from having an othertyme migraine."

"Did he have a name?" Tal asked, now a little frustrated with the whole pulling teeth aspect of the conversation.

"A name? Well, of course he had a name. Kind of a silly question, if you ask me. Everybody's got a name, don't they? You haven't hit your head lately, have you?"

Tal shook his head, no.

"Let's see, his name. I never can keep Her Stytches straight. Seems like they're here and then in the very next minute, it's somebody new. But this guy, he's been Her guy for quite some time now."

Tal decided he was going to have to lead the witness. "His name wouldn't have been Myrddin, would it?" Tal asked rhetorically.

"Yep. Absolutely. That's the guy," the shopkeeper affirmed, his Adam's apple bobbing up and down in sync with his bald pate. "Of course, just because you know him doesn't mean you're the guy. What proof you got?"

"I answered Head Paro's riddle and the Prime Omphalos sent me here using a previously never before heard of relay Journey," Tal replied.

"That is an indisputable fact, Quint of the Omada," the shopkeeper affirmed. "If it hadn't happened exactly as you related, you would not be arriving by omphalos on the inside of my shop while it was closed for lunch. Well, you might have, but you would have been immediately immolated."

Holy crap! Those ash piles by the front door weren't from the fireplace, Tal realized.

Still behind the counter, Portunus smiled broadly as he walked a little closer to Tal. "My shop is the second most heavily warded place in all the known universe."

"Hunts School being number one," Tal proffered.

"That is correct."

"I'm not trying to be short, Portunus, but we're on the clock back at Hunts School." Tal gestured to the wall of keys, which seemed to have somehow enlarged and brightened during his time in the emporium.

It's like the Disney World of keys, Tal thought. At which point, Subconscious interjected. Sorry, but don't you mean it's like a supersized version of the Baldpate Inn, located in Estes Park, Colorado? What? Central Processing asked. Sorry, Subconscious replied, but the Baldpate Inn is a much more appropriate reference. It has the largest collection of keys on Earth Realm, more than twenty-thousand keys hanging from the ceiling and the walls. The collection is extremely diverse, ranging from keys opening a White House bathroom, to Westminster Abbey, even Hitler's bunker. Of course, now that I think about it, every one of those keys is tagged. Not a single one of these keys has a tag on it. Funny story about how the Baldpate Inn got its name. It's actually named for a fictional inn from a 1913 novel…

CEASE! Central Processing demanded. The only useful part of that entire recitation is that not a single one of these keys has a label or tag of any nature. "Portunus, your key collection is unequaled. I noticed though that none of them is tagged. How do you know which one is the Key To Your Heart's Desire."

"That's easy," the god of portals replied. "They all are."

CHAPTER SEXAGINTA DUO

'Väst?'

'Ardere, I'm screwed. Nord used the team binding to give me a specific order. Pretty much said I was expendable and Fem wasn't. They both must have known the bargainpryce would be ridiculous.'

'If that's the case, there is no other option,' Ardere replied.

Väst approached Maymunah. "You can hear our thoughts, so you're up to speed, right?"

"Yes, little sister. If that is the only treasyre on this Realm you may seek, then I beg you to leave here empty-handed."

"I'm thinking that's not an option, either," Väst remarked before walking over to the Asherah Pillar. She stretched out her hand to touch it but couldn't get any closer than about a foot. She then backed up and sprinted directly at the pillar. Next thing she knew she was sitting on her ass, head spinning, having been bounced backward about ten feet through the air.

'I tried to cushion the blow,' Ardere told her.

'Thank you. I had to give it a try,' she replied. "Princess, I thought my Prime Direction was merely a lowlife brute. He may also be much smarter than I believed. During our Journeys this Hunt, the Recall only occurs when we make physical contact with the receiving omphalos. Nord's commandment means I either successfully bargain with you for the treasyre or Ardere and I never return to Hunts School."

"Your Prime Direction sounds very much like some of the most detestable of my father's lieutenants," Maymunah remarked. "Your choice then is to bargain?"

Väst paused a moment to give Ardere a chance to voice any further argument. Nothing. "I have no choice. What do I have to give you for the buckler?"

The Jinnayah once again became pellucid. "To fully understand what you will be paying, you must know a little more about the High King's buckler. There is not a shred of decency or compassion left in the Ifrits who are imprisoned in the shield. In exchange for great power, they long ago voluntarily gave themselves to my father and his evil machinations. So, there is that. There is also Iblis's almost incomprehensible anger. The Solomon bested him, made the great and powerful High King of the Ifrits his vassal. My father's rage has increased every day for thousands of years. Additionally, he is angry that seventy-two of his most powerful servants are trapped. He gave each of them a portion of his power and now that is also trapped in the buckler.

"That is not all. The powerful Ifrits themselves are also inflamed. Even while trapped they continue to feel the passage of time and the diminishment of their lyfeforce. Väst, the buckler brims with distilled hatred. It physically emanates their evil. Anyone, other than me, holding the shield for more than a short period of time will find their will slowly bent to the goals of Darkness. My father has designated me as its keeper to punish me for choosing to follow Amarantos. The royal blood of Iblis flows within me so the buckler cannot physically harm me, but it constantly seeks to work its evil upon me.

"I tell you this because for me to determine your bargainpryce, you will have to grant me access to everything that makes you who you are. You will be required to voluntarily agree that whatever the most horrible, terrible thing is that can ever happen to you, that you will voluntarily do that thing to yourself. Which means for the rest of your lyfe you will know you chose of your own free will to wreak that havoc upon yourself. I am truly sorry but I have no choice in the matter. The bargainpryce has been set by my father."

Väst swallowed hard. "I consent. Do you?"

"I do." With that, the Jinnayah walked toward Väst. She didn't stop when she reached her but walked right into her. Väst gasped as Maymunah flowed into and through her. All of her. She found herself unable to move. Physically, but not mentally, paralyzed.

Over the course of the next few minutes she felt the inner recesses of her mind being poked and inspected. Violated. Gently, but still violated. This must be what a medicine cabinet feels like when subjected to inspection by a non-owner. Well, if medicine cabinets were sentient. Which I guess they might be on some planes. Another few minutes went by before she felt the Crown Princess flow out of her, eventually reforming once more in front of Väst. Maymunah stood there, oscillating between nearly transparent and almost firm-fleshed.

"Well?" Väst asked, the suspense getting the better of her.

Tears were now rolling out of the Jinnayah's eyes. Well, the tears would form, then become tiny gossamer bubbles before floating away. Soap bubbles of sadness, Väst told herself. That's what they look like.

The Crown Princess finally gathered herself enough to speak. "Younger sister, I have looked through you, into your past, your present, and your future. I grieve for the terrible loss you shall endure. A loss you will choose to levy against yourself. Any bargainpryce I might exact from you pales in comparison to what I foresee you will already do. That suffering shall suffice as the bargainpryce for the buckler."

Cold shiver. Cold shiver. Get hold of yourself. It's okay, Väst told herself. Amarantos has given you free will. Just because the Jinnayah saw something happen doesn't mean it's a done deal. It is merely a possibility.

Maymunah became more solid and as she did, a small shield appeared in her hands. Dirty gray, convex, it was about a foot in diameter. In its center there was a huge black gemstone. It looked like a black diamond. A living black diamond, as it seemed to pulse. No, it was pulsing, Väst realized. The stone was flashing brilliant black in the syncopated rhythm of a heartbeat. The Jinnayah extended the shield, with the back toward Väst. There was a thin leather strap used to hold the shield.

Väst reached out with her right hand and grasped the strap. She immediately recoiled but didn't let go, as hate pummeled her. Every time the black diamond pulsed she could feel it hammer her. Meanwhile the anger undergirding the hate roiled up and over her.

"Farewell, Väst of the Släkt and Ardere of the Puca," the Crown Princess of the Ifrits said. As she began to dissipate, she added, "Remember you are a child of Amarantos and you are charged to Seek the Center." With those final words she was gone.

Hold on, Väst told herself. You only have to maintain possession of this abomination long enough to get it back to the Släkt team room. Then you never have to touch the foul thing again. Happy place, Väst. Go to your happy place, she repeated as she slowly walked toward the Asherah pillar. When she finally reached it, she stuck out her left hand and touched it. As she did, she felt the familiar tingling beginning in her feet. The Recall. Focus on that, she told herself. Focus on anything other than listening to the buckler's voices. Her last thought before being transported was what did Maymunah see that I'm going to choose to do to myself? How could anybody voluntarily hurt themselves that much?

CHAPTER SEXAGINTA TRES

"Huh?" was the absolute best response Tal could fashion.

Portunus laughed. Not unkindly. "Children of the Dust have such parochial thought processes," Portunus added, before waving expansively at the gazillion keys. "The Key To Your Heart's Desire isn't one size fits all, it's bespoke."

Tal thought he finally understood. "Each of us has our own individual goals and dreams. There is no way a key for me would fit anyone else's dream."

"That is correct," the merchant replied.

Tal took a minute to look over the massive collection that filled every bit of available space. "You made every key in this shop?"

"Yes. All but one."

That's an interesting reply, Tal thought. Focus. "One for everyone who has ever been born?"

"Yes."

"I can't even begin to guess how many hundreds of thousands of keys you have here," Tal continued. "It seems like there should be lots of empty space on the wall by now."

"That is my hope, Quint, every time I fashion a new key."

For the first time since I arrived he doesn't look like some jolly roly-poly. Now he looks, well, disconsolate is the best word. "Portunus, before Piras and I dropped in today, how long had it been since someone actually received their key?"

"There are two ways to enter this shop. A handful of individuals figure out how to cheat the relay Journey and somehow brute their way into my establishment. They never leave."

Because they end up asses to ashes beside the front door, Tal thought.

"Almost everyone comes in legitimately, through the front door. Everyone who enters has the same chance, the same opportunity to reach out and claim their unique key. There are some, a very small number, who somehow manage to find their way to my little store more than one time during their life.

"The majority of my customers, you see, well, their present heart's desire is not of the Center. Those poor souls never even see the wall of keys. Their life's focus is on the wrong things so the wall behind me looks bare to them. They see only the books and the apothecarial items. They buy a book or a trinket and then leave. They always know they left something important behind, just not exactly what."

"They missed their chance for some reason," Tal added.

" 'Some reason' comes in many guises, Quint of the Omada, but in the end it is always a variation of the same reason. They have the wrong thing in their mind as the most important thing in life. You see, it is okay for money to be an important thing, but it should never be the most important thing. It's fine for success or physical appearance to be important things, they simply shouldn't be..."

"The most important thing," Tal finished for him. It's the lesson Pell was trying to teach me in the kitchen that day, Tal realized.

"Correct. If we are truly Seeking the Center, there is only one most important thing. Love."

"I must be on the right track, then, right?" Tal asked. "I can see the wall of keys."

A smile erased the sadness on Portunus's face. "You? You are kind of a unicorn. That's a technical term among us gods. It means..."

"A one of a kind individual or thing."

"Oh," Portunus replied. "Great. I guess there must be a

website on that damnable internet now that gives away all of our secret god lingo. Probably our secret handshakes as well. Anyway, you are a unicorn. You've made it farther than most. We know that because you can see all of the keys. But your story still has a number of potential endings."

"Let's get to it then," Tal said excitedly, as he scanned the tens of thousands of possible keys. "Okay, I realize this makes me a little shallow but I hope mine is a shiny one with some diamonds or one of those keys with something cool set in the base. Which one is it?"

"None of them," the affable, rotund shopkeeper replied.

I'm apparently not as smart as I thought I was only like a hot second ago, Tal decided. "I'm lost. You said everyone has a key."

"So they do," Portunus confirmed. "Yours is the only one in this shop, which means in all of existence, that I didn't make. Well, that's not completely accurate. Yours is the only key I've ever held at a point in time when I hadn't yet created it."

'I smell othertyme,' Tal thought to Piras.

'As do I,' the Puca responded.

"This one is yours, Quint," the key maker extraordinaire said, as he pulled on the chain running from his vest to the vest pocket. The other end of the chain wasn't anchored by a watch, but rather by a key. A nondescript, boring, tired-looking metal key. Portunus unhooked it and proudly handed it to Tal. "Myrddin brought this to me when he came for his visit. Said to keep it close and not to lose it. I have done as he requested, for over eight centuries."

Tal took the key from Portunus, turned it over once, then again, not believing what his eyes were telling him. "You've had possession of this key for more than eight hundred years? On the outside possibility I might actually show up?"

"Yes. Each of us is charged to use the gyfts the Unfading Spirit has given us," the liminal god replied cryptically, as he spread his arms to encompass the wealth of keys at his back.

'Quint, what is it?' Piras thought-asked. 'Do you recognize the key? Do you know what door it opens?' the Puca queried, in quick succession.

'Yes, Piras. I do,' Tal thought-replied, before speaking once again to the key's former custodian. 'Thank you, Portunus, for keeping the key safe for me all these centuries. I understand the message. With your permission, we will take our leave now. I have the ending of a story that needs writing."

The lesser known god of thresholds nodded his head to Tal. "Godspeed you, Quint, wearer of the cardinal Puca."

Right before Tal touched the inside of the oak door, he turned back toward Portunus. "Just in case the key doesn't work, I don't guess you have a pair of ruby slippers in my size you'd sell me?" Seeing the shopkeeper was lost in translation, Tal added, "I guess it's true what they say. 'There's no place like home'."

As Tal and Piras faded from view, Portunus chuckled to himself, as he absentmindedly scratched a previously unscratched place on his forehead. "Myrddin was right after all. That boy does in fact have a serious case of the smartass."

CHAPTER SEXAGINTA QUATTUOR

Once they were safely back to Hunts School, Tal thought-answered the Puca's question. 'It's a front door key to my family's house in Nemeton on Earth Realm. A house that didn't exist eight centuries ago, Piras. A house we didn't even move into until Pell accepted the job in Nemeton right before this school year started.'

Since he planned to quick-jump his next Journey, Tal wore Piras back to his dorm suite, instead of the locker room. Once there he respectfully folded Piras, leaving him at the foot of his bed. Next came a long shower, followed by a quick trip to the cafeteria where he loaded up a small to-go crate of victuals and fluids. Including three ewers of nectar. Looked like the rest of the week was going to be a sprint and he would be needing all the energy he could muster.

About twelve hours later, the prospect of a quick turnaround Journey was lost in the rearview mirror of best laid plans. He'd eaten three times, taken another shower just because he had to do something different, and laboriously reviewed three of his textbooks.

Tal had the house key, he knew he needed to go to Earth Realm. The only thing missing was identification of the treasyre he was supposed to retrieve. The Prime Omphalos could only be used for treasyre collection Journeys. He could go through the Gas Station Crossing. That method was only a one-way ticket though. There would be no Recall and therefore no coming back if he went through Sol's Ladies' Room.

At an impasse on the Earth Realm treasyre, Tal decided to give it a break and work on some of his other requirements. He finalized the research for his thesis and got started on the rough draft of an outline before opening another one of his notebooks for treasyre ideas.

He caught a break after that and picked up two mediocre level three treasyres in one Journey to the Necropolis Realm, one of the many Egyptian planes. Freaky jackal-headed The Anubis bargained him the Book of Thoth, a grimoire with a number of notable magyk spells. The Khepri was visiting jackal-boy at the time. He was willing to part with a humongous carved star sapphire, which had been crafted into the shape of a scarab. The gemstone was as big as Tal's entire hand. The bargainpryce had been easy, except the relative time differential between the Necropolis plane and Hunts School time had exhausted about a day and a half of his quickly diminishing time inventory. The two avatars had been tickled pink to call the bargainpryce even-steven in exchange for Tal acting out pretty much verbatim the dialogue and action from the latest "Mummy" movie. Go figure.

Neither of his acquisitions was going to be of much value in determining the Hunts winner but they kept Tal as an active player. He was counting on the Earth plane trip to hit his home run. If you make the Earth trip, he reminded himself, as he threw his final textbook on the disheveled knowledge heap rising from the floor beside his bed. He normally wouldn't be so disrespectful to the written word but he'd now been through all of the textbooks with a fine-toothed comb and none of them had seemed the least bit interested in authoring any Eureka! moments.

Tal quickly glanced to the magyked alarm clock on his bedside table. Piras remained folded at the foot of his comforter. Sitting on go. Waiting for Tal to put him on for what would be their final Journey together. Which had to happen, or not, before Tal's Journey window closed in…twenty-eight hours. Damn it!

Even though being out and about was dangerous at this juncture, he'd gone everywhere looking for inspiration. Walked in and through every building on campus, looking at the buildings, looking at the artwork and sculptures contained therein. He'd spent a buttload of hours in the library. Actually, a "buttload" is a real unit of measurement for liquids. It's equal to two hogsheads. In the United States that is one hundred twenty-six gallons. Although time may sometimes appear to be fluid it is most certainly not measurable in gallons...FOCUS YOU IDIOT!

Right. Sorry. Tal knew he was dissembling because he was stuck. He looked over to the few remaining research resources laying on his coverlet. He was pretty much down to some notes he'd taken during first term. Oh well, no stone unturned.

CHAPTER SEXAGINTA QUINQUE

Hmm, Tal thought, as he scanned yet another notebook. I'd completely forgotten I learned during the first semester what "agamogenesis" means. Not sure what use the info is. File it away, you never know. Although I'm going on the record to say I'm not in favor of any type of reproduction that doesn't involve a male gamete. Hello? I'm looking right at you parthenogenesis and apomixis. Then there were his notes on the three different types of sphinx: Androsphinx, Criosphinx, and Hieracosphinx. The first has the head of a man, the second, the head of a ram. The Hieracosphinx, the deadliest of the three, has the head of a hawk and the body of a lion.

Guess there is a reason to take all of those damn notes after all. "Knowledge for its own sake," and all that. Of course when Albert E. was coining that phrase it was also coupled with, "an almost fanatical love of justice and the desire for personal independence…"

I got to shake things up for a couple of hours, he decided, as he grabbed the Compyndium, some rolls, a half-full pitcher of nectar, and the only one of his first term notebooks he hadn't yet reviewed. He stuffed them all into his backpack and headed out for what would be his last study trip to the library.

CHAPTER SEXAGINTA SEX

It hadn't taken Tal but a few minutes to get settled into his customary spot. He'd seen no one except the Head Librarian. Made sense, he decided. The only other students who should be in this library wing the last Journey week are Fem and Magharibi, the other Fifth Primes.

He'd grabbed an armful of books on his way to the table and found himself fast-flipping through hundreds of pages, speed-scanning volume after volume, hoping inspiration would leap off the page and smack him upside his frontal lobe. He was down to his last day and some change.

Tal stood up and cruised the racks, looking, hoping for anything that might suggest a treasyre that could win the Hunt. He finally found books he would have bet a thousand dollars he'd never seen before. "I've been by that shelf at least a dozen times so far this week and didn't see them," he mused to himself. A three-volume set entitled, "Alphabetical Compilation of Magykal Objects." Tal didn't know if hardback leather covers could get the mange but if so, the exteriors of those three books had a terminal case.

Someone else must have had the books squirreled away, either reading them or defensively hiding them from everyone else. Either way, Tal decided, if they'd been returned to the shelves at this critical juncture the contents must be pretty lame. Still, it's a three-volume set and I've found nothing spectacular in anything else I've reviewed.

A mushroom cloud of mold and dust erupted when he picked up the books. After a round of staccato sneezing, Tal took them back to his table. You know, it really doesn't seem like there would have been that much loose airborne nastiness if someone else had recently used these books.

He opened Volume I, which covered A-G. As he quickly paged through the front matter, he noted the copyright page listed the publisher as:

HC SVNT DRACONES
Royal Stationers & Cartographers
M. Ryss, Proprietor
777 Shamb Hala Court.

Huh. Depending on your translator that would be either, "Here Be Dragons," or "Here Are Dragons." "M. Ryss?" A random thought tugged hard right in the no man's land between conscious and subconscious thought. No time to waste, Tal decided, I have three no doubt exciting volumes to work my way through. First entry, "Areadbhar," the spear of Lugh. It's only a level three treasyre. I'm pretty sure Mom and Pell don't have it in their hall closet. And, quite frankly, I've had enough experience for several lifetimes with bloodthirsty independent minded weapons. Next.

CHAPTER SEXAGINTA SEPTEM

She'd called Kabila to an early morning meeting in their secure team room. Kati made sure she got there well before the set time, so the rest of the team couldn't see how crippled she really was. Both physically and emotionally. Once everyone was seated, Kati began. "Have you all used the time as I asked?"

"Yes, Prime," Kasini replied. "We divided the entire campus into thirds and we have searched every square inch of space. He is not to be found."

It was only with conscious effort that Kati kept her shoulders from caving inward. "Thank you. We had the time. It was obviously worth the effort but we struck out. I have decided the decision in this matter should be a team decision."

She reached into her backpack and took out five slips of paper, four pencils, and a small toboggan. She kept one scrap of paper and one pencil in front of her and slid the others to her teammates. "Write down your vote. The question is do we quit the contest to save Mashariki? Yes or no. Kaskazini, take two slips, one for your vote and one for you to exercise proxy for Mashariki. I will also write my answer down but it will only be disclosed if it is necessary to break a tie vote. Vote."

With that all four of them used their hands to shield what they were writing. When they were done, Kati motioned for them to fold their answers and put them in the hat. They did so and then gave the cap back to their Prime.

Kati reached into the hat and one by one withdrew the folded votes, announcing them as she opened each. "Yes." "Yes." "Yes." "No."

"The 'no' vote, Kaz, that is the one you cast for Masha?"

"Yes, Prime. I voted not how I felt but how he would have voted."

Kati smiled wanly. "It is decided then," she announced. "I will surrender our treasyre and announce Kabila's retirement to the HuntsMistress around noon."

"We've already voted," Magharibi stated. "Why can't we go ahead and get the whole damn thing over with right now?"

Kati's face took on the dispassionate steel gaze they were all used to seeing their Prime wear. "Because Kabila is not going down without retribution to the malfeasors," she replied. "I am going to trick the culprits into disclosing their identity. Kabila will have its revenge for this injustice. Now go on, I'll fill you all in on the details when I've implemented the plan."

Kati watched as her teammates walked single file out the door. They would have made a wonderful Ruling Council, she thought, as she tore a piece of blank notebook paper in half. On one piece she wrote a note to Nord, First Prime of Släkt. On the other, the exact same note to Borras of Omada.

Before she stood to go find a courier for her messages, she picked her vote up off the table and tore the word "NO" into a dozen indecipherable fragments.

CHAPTER SEXAGINTA OCTO

There went ten hours of my life I'll never get back, Tal thought, as he stood and stretched. No choice, I had to be thorough. Couldn't take a chance on missing the answer. Even though I'm pretty sure I'm going to get Black Lung disease.

Nothing in the "S"s. I'll finish this book, then pack up and head back to the room. By way of the cafeteria. Drum roll, please, for the first entry in the "T"s. It's the Taleria. He reached over and opened the Compyndium to its next blank page. Sure enough, a three-dimensional image of the Taleria rose from the page, and began turning in mid-air. Hermes' winged sandals, in the flesh. Well, not really. He slowly ran his finger down the lengthy entry to get to the "Location" subheading. Earth Realm. You have to be kidding me.

You know, Professor SilverTongue spent considerable time telling us about the Taleria. I took really good notes, too. Straight out of the textbook. He reached for the notebook that was still in his backpack. Turning it quickly to the right page, he read what he'd copied verbatim from the textbook:

> The Taleria is a shapeshifter. Its most common
> form is that of winged sandals, but it can appear
> as almost anything. Almost anything—with wings.

Tal closed his eyes as he closed the notebook. "Almost anything—with wings." His mind's eye rolled the year back to Atlantis plane. Where he'd met Fortuna and spun her second-rate, badly in need of a new coat of lacquer, Wheel of Fortune. Where he'd stuck his hand into a cracked Tupperware tub full of gimcrackery, and out of all the junk, static electricity only sparked between his hand and one piece. A scratched, translucent gum machine bubble. Its only contents, a little plastic pair of fake pilot's wings.

"HOW THE HELL COULD I BE SO OBTUSE?"

CHAPTER SEXAGINTA NOVEM

Tal only paused long enough to grab the Compyndium before setting off at a dead run. Down the stairway, out the library's massive front doors, making a beeline for the dorms at all ahead full.

Stupid, stupid, stupid. It was like a negative-mantra. Negantra? No, that's no good. Sure? I'm sure. Run faster. I've had one of the single most valuable artifacts in the known universe for almost two school terms and didn't know it. Unbelievable. Think of all the places I could have gone. Not to mention, Omada will be a shoo-in to win. Borras will be Archon and I'll be the hero. So suck it, Notos.

He took the stairs two at a time at the dormitory, pressed his thumb against his door until it clicked open. He carefully laid the Compyndium at the head of his bed, grabbed Piras, nabbed the house key off his nightstand, and lit out for the Prime Omphalos chamber.

CHAPTER SEPTUAGINTA

"Those idiots have conceded to our blackmail," Nord announced smugly. "Oh, and they want to make a side deal with us."

Väst knew the instant she'd received the note demanding she attend a pre-dawn team meeting that something important was happening.

"What kind of side deal?" Söder asked.

"Instead of walking away in defeat they want to salvage something out of their hard work. They want to split their treasyre with us."

Ost interjected. "It doesn't work that way. Treasyre is only borrowed in a Treasyre Hunt. Following the contest conclusion it has always been returned to its original plane."

"Is that in the Hunts Rules?" Nord asked.

"No, but it's what has customarily been done," Ost responded.

"Things change," Nord replied. "If we're interested, they want a team member to be sitting out by Fountain Flow, reading their "Creatures" textbook at eleven o'clock. Further information will be delivered after that. Fem, be at the fountain no later than ten forty-five."

"Yes, First Prime," Fem responded.

Väst couldn't stand it any longer. "We haven't talked about the single most important matter. How are we going to free Mashariki from our Compyndium before I turn it in at midnight?"

"We're not," the Släkt Prime replied matter of factly.

"What?" Väst was stunned. She was even more stunned when she looked around the table and saw none of the rest of her team seemed to care about Nord's most recent duplicity.

"I don't have any idea how to get that damn book to let him go," Nord explained. "And I'm not planning on wasting a minute worrying about it."

Väst was about to lodge a formal protest when Nord interrupted her. "Last time I checked Acting Fourth Prime, you hadn't complied with my order concerning the munedan. Do I need to repeat your orders?"

Can't take a chance on him wording it differently the second time around. "No, Prime," Väst replied quickly. "I am meeting him and it will be taken care of by midafternoon."

"I don't know what you're acting so pissy about. You get to knock some off this afternoon while the rest of us are doing the drudge work necessary to get ready to be the next Ruling Council."

"You're not planning on letting Kabila keep half its treasyre, are you?" Väst asked.

"Of course not," Nord replied, as the other three chuckled. "After the Coronation Ceremony, the new Archon will have to seize their treasyre. For failing to see it was returned in accordance with established tradition. Oh, and all of Kabila will then be placed in irons for the entirety of our Tyrning."

CHAPTER SEPTUAGINTA UNUS

Tal was totally winded by the time he made it down to the Prime Omphalos chamber. Another not so super smart move on his part. If he'd put Piras on first he would have made it faster and in better shape to Journey. Live and learn.

'I consent, do you?' he thought-queried the Puca.

'I consent,' Piras replied, right before Tal placed him on top of his head. Once Piras was firmly in place, Tal filled him in.

'The Taleria? And, of all places, it's back on Earth plane after centuries. Quint, you have no idea how big this news is.'

Tal walked down the ramps until he reached the hollowed out center of the Prime Omphalos stone. Touching its dry, cool surface he made his request. "Going to fetch the Taleria. Earth Realm, please." He felt the now familiar tingling begin in his feet and work his way up until everything went black.

CHAPTER SEPTUAGINTA DUO

"Where's Quint?" the Omada First Prime asked the rest of his team. "This is important or I wouldn't have taken the risk of having us assemble."

"I checked our floor of the library, he wasn't there," Dysi replied.

Anatolia responded next. "One of the cafeteria staff said they'd seen him a few times loading his backpack full of food. That's all he could remember."

"I knocked on his door, no answer," Notos added.

"It's fair to assume he's Journeying then," Borras concluded.

"Or screwing shit up again," Notos remarked tersely.

"I'm sure he's using his time wisely, Notos," Borras stated. "I've received a note from Kabila," he added, before passing the piece of paper to his teammates.

After giving everyone sufficient time to digest the note, Borras continued. "Thoughts?"

"What the hell is Kati talking about?" Ana asked, a split second before Dysi said, "This is some crazy shit."

"Notos?" Borras asked his Second Prime and the Omada Parliamentarian.

"Kati took great care in formulating this note, Prime."

"I agree."

"I believe the note has two purposes, neither being the note's stated purpose. One of the other two teams has somehow secured some insurmountable leverage against Kabila. Kati has no idea which team. The note is a concession to that leverage as well as bait to ascertain which team has gained the leverage."

"And the other purpose?" Borras asked.

"The note was written to inform the other team, us, that Kabila is withdrawing from the competition and that we need to be extremely concerned about a potential escalation of hostile activity by Släkt."

"I concur with your assessment," Borras confirmed.

"What are we going to do?" Dysi asked.

"First, none of us are going to be anywhere near Fountain Flow at any time today. Second, Dysi, Ana, and I are going to make ourselves impossible targets from now until the competition is completed by going completely underground." The girls nodded, acknowledged their understanding. "Notos, I hate to put you at risk but we need for you to…"

"You don't have to ask," Notos said, as he interrupted his Prime. "I'm volunteering. Second Prime is head of team security. As soon as I can locate Quint, I'll stick to him like glue."

CHAPTER SEVENTY-THREE

Piras had all the negative side effects of the Journey covered, so Tal waited comfortably until the tingling stopped. When fully present on Earth Realm, Tal looked at the building his hand was touching. 'It's the Nemeton Post Office,' he thought-remarked. 'Who would ever have guessed there'd be an omphalos in Nemeton?' The only response Tal received was some odd noise in his head. 'Oh, no you didn't?' he remarked. 'Did you just "oh sweetie" me?'

'Yes, Quint,' Piras replied. 'Sometimes your human education is sorely lacking in basic information. Do you really not know what the word "nemeton" means? Or why Sol's Gas Station Crossing is sited where it is on Earth Realm?'

When Tal didn't respond in an appropriate response period he received another sigh from the Puca. Which then prompted a response. 'Fine, I'll look into it later. If I don't get captured or killed.'

Tal looked down at the key in his hand. 'Don't know what's up with this though. I don't need a house key. I left the Taleria in my backpack. Which is hidden outside Sol's Ladies' Room.'

'I know you well enough to know you've analyzed the risk to reward ratio for being physically present on Earth plane again. You're normally quite proficient at such analyses. Still the risk of capture by the authorities is substantial, even with me to help you.'

Tal took the moment to take a small gulp of air. 'I know, I know.'

'Quint, I realize I've reminded you every time we've Journeyed this week but it seems an excellent time to re-re-remind you. There is no automatic Recall on Journeys this term. Recall is only triggered by you touching the same omphalos at which you arrived. If you are taken prisoner or killed neither one of us will be making the return trip to Hunts School.'

'I know. We'll be out to the gas station and back in a flash. Relax, Piras, this is only going to take me a moment. What could possibly go wrong?'

'There's always the possibility of the interjection of entropic forces,' the Puca replied.

"Nothing quite like traveling with a wearable word of the day,' Tal thought-spake with a quick smile before taking one last three-sixty look. 'Emet and I used to could make the trip in ten minutes. I bet we can do it in less than five.'

CHAPTER SEVENTY-FOUR

Tal was beside himself. The last time I was here, I retrieved the backpack from its hiding place. Emet had hooked the phone up to an extra battery so the phone would have plenty of power. I listened to all of the voice mails and texts from Mom. She'd been worried to death. She cried. She was angry. She broke down on the phone message. Pell finished the last message for her, asking me to please check in with them. And to tell me they both loved me. I texted Mom, assured her I was safe, and that I hadn't killed Elle.

Elle... No, Tal. No. Later. Not now. I texted them I would contact them soon. Then I removed the battery from the phone so it couldn't be pinged or used to locate the backpack and its contents. The very last thing I did was re-hide the backpack really well under dirt and leaves.

'I don't understand, Piras. I was really careful when I hid my backpack. I put a layer of dirt on top of it and then scattered leaves all over. I assumed the police would make it out here eventually, but there's no way they looked under that azalea bush. The backpack is gone, but the hiding place doesn't even look like it's been disturbed. It looks exactly like I left it, except for more leaves.'

'Proceeding deductively, Quint, it means someone took your backpack but that someone also took great care to make sure no one knew it had ever been hidden there.'

'Who? Who would do that?'

'If it wasn't for the object presently in your left front pocket, I would have to speculate,' Piras replied.

'The house key,' Tal thought, as he gently tapped his thigh. 'Of course. Mom or Pell came out here and found it. That's why I need the key to the house.' Tal was about to tell Piras it was time to haul ass to the homestead when an unbidden thought rocked him. 'I shouldn't need a key. Mom and Pell would let me in, unless…unless…'

'Stop it,' Piras demanded. 'Speculation does no good. We can get there quickly but we should not be hasty. It would be catastrophic if you were apprehended by the authorities. Even for a short period of time.'

'You're right,' Tal thought-replied, as he squelched the panic-driven nausea threatening to erupt. 'Let's go find out what's up.'

CHAPTER SEVENTY-FIVE

It was a clear, moonless night. Daffodils, spring's southern heralds, were busily proclaiming the triumph of rebirth over winter's frozen death. Running with Piras would have been glorious. Except for the circumstances.

He'd heeded the Puca's warning and they'd veered away from any and all light sources. They'd also chopped the run into small segments, stopping to hide in lightless corners only long enough to make sure they remained unseen. There had been very little traffic to contend with but they'd seen three different police cars out patrolling. The possibility of unmarked vehicles also cruising around couldn't be discounted. More than a little concerning for a town as small as Nemeton. It's only been a couple of short months, Tal reminded himself. Nowhere near enough time for everyone to completely address the trauma from the Formal. Elle… Suppress it, Taliesin. Suppress. It.

They were now within two blocks of Tal's house, standing where they remained swathed in darkness. Between their location and their objective there was one street light and a smattering of front porch lights. The City Hall clock had showed it was just before two o'clock in the morning when they'd first landed, so the amount of lighting seemed appropriate. Except for Tal's house. Mom and Pell always left the front porch light on. It was a thing. Not tonight. From two blocks away the house appeared completely dark.

'I say we stay to the curb until we get to my yard, then get between the oak and the house. We'll be invisible from the street.'

'It's a good plan, Quint,' Piras thought-replied.

'Here we go,' Tal responded, as he accelerated down the side of the street. 'So far, so good,' he thought-whispered, when they were safely leaning up against the bough of his old friend. It was because of the tree's size that he hadn't previously noticed the sign.

The big honking Sellars Realty "FOR SALE" sign in his front yard. With an oversized "SOLD" sticker on it.

CHAPTER SEVENTY-SIX

Tal realized he'd never had anything in his pockets before while wearing the Puca. 'Um, Piras, I'm not sure what the proper etiquette is when wearing a Puca for,…um…'

'You need the key out of your front pocket?' Piras asked.

'Yes, please.'

Next thing Tal knew the key had somehow been translated from within the Puca to the outside. He grasped it tightly in his left hand.

Piras adjusted Tal's optics so his night vision was enhanced. The adjustment would have blinded Tal if Piras had done it while there were cars passing them on the road or too close to the street lights, but it was perfect for scoping out the front yard.

Plywood covered all the windows on the lower floor. Tal looked up to his bedroom window on the second floor. Same. He looked down at his feet, studying the ground around the base of the huge oak. There were any number of smallish shards of glass. The assholes threw rocks through all of the windows. No wonder I needed this to get in the house, Tal thought as he angrily squeezed the key.

On the front porch there were a number of small potsherds but nothing else remained of all the homey knick-knacks his mom always kept out front. The chains were busted on one side of the porch swing, leaving it hanging at an angle.

And on the front door, "MURDERER" was spray painted in jagged red lettering.

'Quint, your heart rate just skyrocketed. I'm bringing it down to a high functioning level. I realize you're worried and you're angry...'

'DAMN RIGHT, I AM!' Tal yell-thought in response as he started up the steps.

'I'm advising caution...'

'NO!'

'Quint, I feel another's thoughts. There's someone inside the house.'

CHAPTER SEVENTY-SEVEN

'Who?' Tal asked, as he carefully stepped onto a known non-squeaky board.

'Without a binding I am unable to do any more than sense other thoughts within a close radius. I am the only one of my people who has ever been blessed with such gyft.'

'Only one of many reasons you are the Pucas' leader.'

There was a slight pause before Piras answered. 'Thank you, Quint of the Omada. Folk do not generally compliment the Puca.'

'Why not?'

'We are not seen as their equals,' Piras replied.

That needs to be addressed when Borras is Archon, Tal thought. But we have more pressing matters now. 'Proximity?'

'That I can ascertain. The individual or individuals would have to be within a fifteen foot radius before I could sense their thoughts.'

It's why Piras didn't know until we got all the way to the steps, Tal told himself. 'That means whoever it is, is in the den.'

'If that is the first room inside the door, then yes,' Piras agreed.

Tal put the key in the lock, turned it, and pushed gently until the door silently swung open.

CHAPTER SEVENTY-EIGHT

'Turn the night vision off, please,' Tal thought-asked as he stepped across the threshold, while simultaneously flipping the light switch inside the front door. Several times.

A familiar deep bass voice came out of the darkness. "Doesn't matter how many times you flip the switch, Tal. I had the electricity cut off last month."

"Pell?" Tal asked, relieved. Make that disbelieving relieved. "Mom? The twins?"

"They're safe," Pell replied, as his large bulk stepped within arms' distance. "Son," he added.

Tal dissolved. He knew it was happening, couldn't do anything to stop it, didn't want to do anything to stop it. He just melted into Pell's great big, familiar, warm, bear hug.

"Hold on there, Champ," Pell said, as he gathered Tal in close. "It's going to be okay. We need to be as quiet as possible. Even though we've done everything we can think of to convince everyone we left and never looked back...whoa, what are you wearing?"

Tal knew better than to try to explain about Hunts School. The geas would swell his throat shut. Or worse. 'Piras, is there anything you can think of to get around the Hunts School magyk?'

'Because you are bound, I am bound while we are together.'

"Tal, you're worrying me," Pell said, anxiously.

"Pell, if you give me just a second I think I can figure out how to explain what's going on, at least enough to assure you I'm safe."

'Piras, if Pell agrees to bind a contract with you, is that doable on your end.'

There was a noticeable pause from the Puca. 'It's a creative solution. At least worth a shot.'

"Pell, do you trust me?"

"Why, of course..."

"Good," Tal said, interrupting his step-dad. "I can't tell you directly. Long story. This is going to seem freaky weird. You're going to hear a voice in your head. Think of it like I'm wearing a liquid high-tech Iron Man suit. I'm going to let you try it on. You'll need to tell it that you consent and ask if it consents in return. Got it?"

"Umm, sure?" Pell replied.

Tal didn't need any light to tell him Pell was definitely not sure but that he would try because Tal had asked him to. 'Okay, Piras. Time to jump ship.'

Tal watched as Pell leapt backwards when Piras began rolling down and off of Tal. When Piras was totally on the floor, Tal picked him up, folded him neatly, and placed him on top of Pell's head.

Pell's eyes became dinner-plate sized. In a few seconds, Pell said the magyk words. "I consent. Do you?" Moments later, Piras began covering Pell's body, excepting only his head and feet.

It took about five minutes with Pell mumbling words at first, but apparently he was a fast learner at the whole telepathy thing. The final thing Pell said out loud, right before the Puca slid off of him was, "You promise that no matter what you'll take care of our child as if he were your very own?"

Tal picked Piras up, engaged the ritual, and Piras covered him once more. 'Well?'

'Obviously I could only hit the high points but he is a Dust Child whose heart is full of love and of the truth. He will communicate what he knows to your mother. Oh, and I've been invited to Thanksgiving dinner. It is apparently a feast day with which I am unfamiliar.'

Tal smiled broadly. 'You don't even eat.'

'No, but I have to admit the concept of "cornbread dressing," whatever that is, sounds appetizing nonetheless.'

Pell reached behind him and picked up Tal's backpack. After opening it and rummaging around a minute, he pulled the Taleria out and handed it to Tal. "Seems like an awful lot of hullabaloo over a scratched plastic bubble with some plastic wings."

"I know, right?" Tal replied, as he reached for the Taleria.

Pell didn't let go, he used Tal's grasp on the artifact to pull him in close for a final hug. "You promise me we'll see you again, Tal? Safe and unharmed?"

"I promise, Pell." Sorry, Baba Yaga, but sometimes white lies are a blessing in disguise.

"Off with you then," he said releasing Tal and the Taleria. "I'll dispose of the backpack and the rest of the contents in a safe place. Tal, this will be my last trip here. I don't know how you'll find your way to where we are. I guess we'll just have to trust, Amarantos, is it?"

Tal smiled and nodded.

"Go out the back door and over the fence. The alley is almost pitch black without our house lights. I'll wait five minutes and then go out the front. That way if anyone is cruising looking for you they'll hone in on me."

Tal had barely cleared the back fence and was getting ready to ask Piras to kick in the afterburner when two police cars with their full array lit up pulled up out front of the house. Piras chimed in, 'It appears we need to proceed to the omphalos with all haste.'

CHAPTER SEPTUAGINTA NOVEM

First thing Tal did on his return was to secure the Compyndium, the Taleria, and Piras in the wardrobe in his bedroom. It was everything he could do to lock the plastic bubble up. He'd wanted to run over to Borras's room shouting the news that because of Tal, Borras was definitely going to be the next Archon. He'd wanted to break open the plastic covering, put the Taleria on, go places he'd only imagined in his wildest dreams. Instead he'd gone down to the lobby common area and requisitioned a courier to send the following message to his four teammates:

> Met Minimum Journey Requirements. STOP.
> Best I Could Do Was Low Level Four Artifact.
> STOP. Sorry. STOP.

There was no question Borras was a brilliant tactician. He'd known at the start of term exactly what would happen when one of the Omada gave a "private" message to a courier. Under Borras's coding, "low level four artifact" meant Tal had acquired an extremely high value level five. Perhaps even a contest winner. The inclusion of "STOP" had been Tal's addition. He'd never ever gotten to send a telegram before and he felt like it added a certain air of intrigue to the message. Plus, without any doubt the surplus verbiage would piss Notos off. Hat trick winner!

Tal had until midnight tonight to turn his partial outline into a completed thesis and turn it in together with the Compyndium to Principal Chiron, the HuntsMistress, and Head

Librarian Seshat. As he stuffed his research notebook into his backpack, he realized he couldn't remember the last time he'd felt good. Sure, all of the terrible events of the last few months still weighed heavily on him but with the Taleria in hand, which meant an almost guaranteed Omada win, he didn't feel totally beat down.

It won't take me but a couple of hours to knock out an acceptable thesis. The grade is a pass/fail. A quick stop at the cafeteria to load my backpack to bursting at the seams and then off to the library.

Tal was about two steps away from the hallway door when he heard a scratching from out in the hall. Given the stakes involved in this Hunt he decided the smart play was to take a few steps back and out of the line of fire of the door. Not good enough, he told himself. Back behind your solid wood bedroom door, immediately.

As soon as he was there the scratching noise ceased. He peeked around the door to see what was up. What was up was down. On the floor. A sealed note. Tal took three quick strides and picked the note up.

What if it's poisoned? Screw it, you're being paranoid, he told himself as he opened the note.

Quint-

I need to see you immediately. You know where.
It's a matter of extreme urgency. About Emet.

Väst

Väst! Emet! Go, now! Do what she says, all brain components told Central Processing. All brain components excepting one. Central Processing, this is CereCort, Left Hemi.

Yes, Central Processing replied, little busy right now. We need to effectuate an emergency response.

Uh, yeah, that's just it. Do we? CereCort asked.

What are you talking about, you dolt? Väst said it was an emergency.

Yeah...so about that. One, she happens to be on one of the other two teams trying to kick our ass. Two, she knows that like her, this is our last day to get our Journeys completed and that even if they're completed, we still have to get our term paper written and turned in by midnight. Three, she knows Amygdala is round the bend loopy about her.

Central Processing interrupted. I'll finish this unnecessary conversation. Four, Väst said it's about Emet. Discussion closed.

CHAPTER OCTOGINTA

I'm sorry, Quint. I'm so, so sorry. Can a person be damned for things that aren't their fault, Väst wondered. Are there things we can say, or do, that even though Amarantos forgives us the moment we ask her for absolution, there may never come a time when we can forgive ourselves?

It was done. She had no idea what the Big Sucking Asshole intended for Quint to do with the mandated information but she'd done what had been required of her.

He'd been stunned when she'd told him about the nonexistent Rule. Then he'd been angry at his teammates for not telling him. Something else to add to my sin litany. The geas had held, just enough. Who am I kidding? she asked herself. The compulsion was negligible now. It was me using my body that sold the deal. Let that sink in, Väst, old girl. You used your body to coerce someone you love.

But if I hadn't done it Mom would be dead…

And if I hadn't done it, Notos was going to…

Rationalize all you want, Väst. While you're engaged in that exercise, remember how it felt when the spark jumped from his perfect lips more acutely this time than ever before. Think about the indisputable fact you are more in love with Quint of the Omada than you've ever been with someone, anyone, ever.

And while you sit here and finish crying so you can put your game face on and go let Nord know you've taken care of your dirty business, don't forget to spend some time thinking about the fact that Amarantos has already forgiven you, but Quint probably never will.

CHAPTER OCTOGINTA UNUS

It was all Tal could do to stagger back to his spot in the library. Physically, mentally, soully—if that was even a word—all of his components, in all respects, were well past critical overload. The fastest roller coaster in the world is the Formula Rossa. Its top speed is allegedly around one hundred fifty miles an hour. Tal's recent emotional ride made the FR look like a kiddie ride.

He'd been on the pre-rendezvous high of securing the Taleria, which in all probability was going to secure the win for Omada and make Borras the Archon for the next three hundred years. Add to that the unbelievable physical and emotional intimacy he always shared when he and Väst were together.

Those two events combined to send Tal to an emotional perihelion. How many times did Daedalus warn Icarus? Would any number of times have been sufficient for the kid to listen?

I should have known something was up when Väst cried the entire time we were congressing. Man, it was some seriously excellent congressing. Although now that I think about it, I'm pretty sure your partner isn't supposed to be openly weeping the entire time you're engaged in Paphian activity.

Afterward, when Tal was holding her close, trying to comfort her, he'd discovered why she was crying. It was for him. Because his teammates had been hiding something important from him. Important, hell, critical. What was funny about that was he'd been through the Hunts Rules a couple of dozen times since he'd gotten a copy, and he had never once noticed the rule about replacing bloodpryce equivalynts. But like Väst said, she was in love with him and wanted only the best for him and knew that he would want to know for his own peace of mind. What reason did she have to lie to him about something so important to him? None.

I can see Notos being so selfish, I never would have thought it of Dysi or Ana. Certainly not Borras. I guess you never know people like you think you do. Wanting to be Archon must be more important to the Omada First Prime than he'd let on.

Tal wasn't sure how he did it but he finally made it back to his study table, pretty much collapsing into the hard wood chair. This whole "no electricity so no keyboards and, of course, no word processors" thing was definitely cramping his style. It wasn't a problem for any of the other Finalists, they'd never written their papers any differently. At least during their hundred years at Hunts School. Tal wondered if on their home Realms some of the Folk were endowed with typewrytermagyk. Which would actually be pretty cool. Especially if when they used their magyk it made the tap-tap-tap-ding noises the old Underwoods used to make on Earth plane.

Focus, Tal, he told himself, as he quickly reviewed his outline, before gathering his notes and sorting them into half a dozen piles. Got to establish some semblance of order. You just need to go ahead and get started, the writing will come. It always does. Take a quick cruise back through all of your notes and then make a beginning. There's too much else going on this term for you to be fretting about this project. Right. Here goes nothing.

If he was going to be honest with himself, it wasn't just the lack of hardware that was holding him back. It was the paper's subject matter—females. That's inaccurate, he cautioned himself. You're getting derailed because of females, specifically Väst, and Elle, but that's not your thesis. Your paper is about how over the last three thousand years the overwhelmingly male dominated culture has rewritten Earth's oldest stories. Subverting the original role of the feminine as the mother of all creation. Tal pinched himself as his mind began to drift again to the two specific females. Come on, Tal. Channel your inner Emet and get this show started. Fine, okay,...here goes—

Amarantos. The Unfading Spirit. Female. Three of her four Elder Children. Female. The reason he'd picked this topic was because the gender of the Folk version of the supreme deity seemed to be the polar opposite of the overwhelming majority of the Earth plane religions and mythologies. It was clearly half ass backwards from all the mythology Tal had read growing up.

Weren't Zeus and Jupiter the keepers of the thunderbolt heavy artillery in Greek and Roman mythology? Wasn't Odin the indisputable big dog for the Norse cultures? It seemed like in all of the stories he'd read growing up the guy gods were inevitably the showboat peacocks, the cock of the walks. Funny, how that oft times vulgar anatomical word was used so often as a masculine descriptor.

That had been his starting point. As he began reviewing the Folk historical reference books he'd begun peeling back the layers. One by one. Removing the glittering generalities. Eliminating the smoke and mirrors. Tal kept going, layer after layer—deeper, deeper, even deeper. Until he'd finally reached, well, until he'd finally reached the heart of the matter.

It was astounding. In plain sight if you looked for it, espoused by many cultures as the beginning of everything. One constant female mytheme explaining the origin of all things—the "Great Goddess," more often referred to in human cultures as the Earth Mother.

Her names are legion. She is Terra Mater to the Romans. The Tuatha Dé Danann, the fairy folk, call her Danu. Their name even means "folk of the goddess Danu." She is Nerthus to several Germanic tribes, Nirhursag to the Sumerians, Prithivi Mata to the Hindu, Gaia to the Greeks, and yes, the list included Mokosh of the Slavs.

The Great Goddess had as many names as Babel had languages, yet her characteristics were always the same. It was to the Earth Mother that most of life's essentials were attributed; birth, life, death. Authority over the entire life cycle was given not to the testosterone-crazed male gods. No, in the beginning, in the true beginning of all things, the distaff gender was uniformly acknowledged to have primacy in the custody and control of the universe and all of its inhabitants.

She was Amarantos. The Folk had taught all of the different human civilizations about the Unfading One. Each culture understood only a small piece of the puzzle and used their own respective language to name her.

After his first epiphany, Tal experienced two others. The second came when he realized the gender replacement was systemic across the Earth plane. Whether because men have a universal inferiority complex or because they were unable to write interesting stories with female protagonists, human male authors, historians, and journalists almost universally started rewriting the ancient knowledge. With Gaia being the perfect example.

The Greek mythology Tal had read growing up was about Zeus and his pantheon of fellow gods and goddesses. Tal learned from his research this period was called the "classical" Greek period. In those myths, Zeus was always the Alpha male and All-Father.

For the first time ever, Tal read about a mythical human named Pelasgus. Depending upon your source, Pelasgus was sometimes the first man in what is now modern day Greece, sometimes he was the first man to live on Earth, period. An "Adam" by a different name of a non-Judeo-Christian culture. In every story the Pelasgians were the people who preceded the Greeks in many of the Greek territories.

The Pelasgians worshipped Nature as a deity. They gave Nature a name, Gaia, and said she was the first of the gods. Under the ancient myth it was Gaia who was born out of Chaos. It was Gaia who, without any help from anyone else, birthed Uranus. It was Gaia who then ickily hooked up with her own son, Uranus, to birth the twelve Titans. That sort of ickiness was apparently a family tradition as Oceanus and Thetis, two of their Titan kids who married each other, spawned more than three thousand children.

Fast forward through centuries of male controlled story writing and an intentional, concerted purpose became apparent. The historians diminished, reinvented, and watered down Gaia's authority. The stories now told how the Titans were vanquished by the familiar Greek gods and goddesses. That pantheon was consistently composed of stronger male gods and lesser female goddesses.

It wasn't only in Greek culture that Tal found evidence of this subversion of the power of the female aspect of God. There was also plenty of evidence in Judeo-Christian stories. The Hebrew word for "breath," "wind," or "spirit," is *ruach*. In the earliest writings of the Jewish people, when the "Spirit of God" is referenced, the word used is a feminine noun. When Moses penned the second verse of the first chapter of Genesis, "The Spirit of God moved upon the face of the waters," he was writing of the feminine aspect of God. Shekinah is another feminine noun referring to God, the word actually being of Talmudic origin. Shekinah refers to the physical presence of God. During the forty years the Hebrews wandered in exile, it was the Shekinah, the female presence of God, which went before them and led them, during the day as a cloud of smoke and as a pillar of fire at night.

Tal's third "Aha!" moment came when he realized the mythstorians' degradation of the power of the female deity was also accomplished by dividing the Earth Goddess's powers into separate, lesser goddesses. The number was usually three. Where the one Earth Goddess had encompassed birth, life, and death, those powers were now divided into a triune. The "mother" was in charge of birth, the "damsel" of life, and the "crone" generally held sway over death.

In Egypt, the female power was divided into the triumvirate of Isis, Mut and Hathor. Tal stopped writing as he realized he couldn't call the names of the three Greek goddesses that together essentially took over Gaia's singular power and authority. He reached across his paper stacks, of course the one with his Greek notes was the farthest away. It took him only a moment to find the page he needed. The Greek threesome was most commonly called Demeter, the mother, Persephone, the damsel, and Hecate, the crone. Birth, life, and death.

Tal noticed he'd scribbled something at the bottom of the page. During his research he'd been going ninety to nothing and hadn't had the chance to stop and digest all of the raw data he was accumulating. He squinted to make out the word. Damn, I know my handwriting is atrocious but it's pretty ridiculous when I can't even read it. He vaguely remembered discovering the Greeks had infrequently used other names for Demeter, Persephone, and Hecate. He picked the paper up and held it up so the wall sconce's light showed it a little better. "Persephone, representing the damsel, was sometimes alternatively referred to as Kore, which means 'maiden' in Greek."

"HOLY CRAP!"

CHAPTER OCTOGINTA DUO

Tal jumped up, then stepped to his right so he could see down the walnut paneled library hallway. In eyesight was the stairway alcove with its ornate entry table with the portrait of some really old dude hanging above it. Neither of those items held any interest for him at the moment. The twelvehourglass on the landing was the library accessory he needed now.

They have magyk alarm clocks in our dorm rooms, Tal thought as he walked toward the stairs. Why not magykally light this place up big time? I'm sure it's to enhance library ambience, he decided. Tal knelt and squinted at the hour lines etched in the lower half of the glass bulb. Right at ten o'clock. Two hours until midnight—Journey deadline for the three remaining Fifth Primes. He jogged quickly back to his study table and sat down.

Assemble the puzzle, he commanded himself. Persephone was the beautiful daughter of Demeter, goddess of the harvest. Hades, the God of the Underworld, was smitten by Persephone's beauty. He kidnapped her and took her to his kingdom. Demeter was so distraught that crops didn't grow and mortals began to starve. A deal was finally made and Persephone spent half the year with Hades and the other half above ground with her mother. Persephone is the reason for the season.

And Kore, which means "maiden," is an alternative name for Persephone. Tal sat back down at his table and pulled out the map he'd found in the Archives. Yep, just as he'd remembered, it listed Eynhallow as a pseudonym for Atlantis. While those two sirens were trying to fatal attraction me on Atlantis Realm, the rest of the team met a girl who helped them. She told them she'd taken a slave name, Kore, in place of her Earth name. What else had she told them? I need the rest of that information. Pronto!

Hold on a second, Tal, bucko, pal. Time is at a premium right now. You gotta get your checklist organized, you don't have time to be running all over the campus.

Write the paper. Doesn't have to be a magnum opus, it's a pass/fail grade. Allot a maximum of one hour.

You'll need a fail safe in case something goes terribly wrong. It's the final week, so the penalty on not timely turning in the Compyndium is basically nothing. If it doesn't get turned in at all, now that's a different story. Fine, take the Compyndium and your completed term paper to the secured team room. Oh, and Piras. Go to your dorm room, get him, and place him with the book and the paper in Omada's room. Any of my team can access the team room.

When that's accomplished, then go get your confirming information. From whom? Not Borras. He's Omada Prime. If my hunch is right, I can't put him in a position that would compromise his responsibility to the team. Notos is a no-go. He'd tackle me and tie me up until after midnight. One of the girls? Which one? Which? His neurons finished firing and printed the answer for his mind's eye—Dysi.

Which brings us to the sticking point, he told himself. What exactly is it you plan to do and what are the possible consequences?

CHAPTER OCTOGINTA TRES

There were simply too many factors, with too many second and third generation downstream consequences, for Tal to parse the options completely in his head. Tal knew it had a lot to do with his defcon five stress level. Central Processing had already sent numerous messages to both Left and Right Adrenal Gland, demanding they ratchet down the massive amounts of cortisol they were pumping into the bloodstream. Thus far they were either unable or unwilling to comply. It doesn't matter how many times I turn the Rubik's cube on this one, every choice sacrifices someone or something important.

If I choose "no further action," Omada, with the Taleria, probably wins the Tyrning, Borras becomes Archon, and Helblad eats me for dinner. The last point also means Emet will remain in Five-Hells forever.

If I knew of a specific piece of treasyre on Atlantis Realm, I could choose to use my final hour of Journey window to travel there, give the Taleria to Aislinn, the Recall would bring me back to Hunts School, and Aislinn could use the Taleria to return to Earth Realm. I personally know it's been on both Earth and Atlantis, as well as here at Hunts School. I don't know whether the Taleria has ever been to Helblad's plane, so he and Aislinn still might never be able to hook up. That option results in one of the other two teams wining the Tyrning, which means Nord may become Archon. Depending on Helblad's interpretation of our contract, I may remain uneaten, but Emet will certainly spend eternity in Five-Hells. That option is a nonstarter. I don't have any intel on a specific piece of Atlantean treasyre.

There is only one possible course of action that guarantees a reunion for Helblad and Aislinn and that also gives me a chance, somehow, someway, to find a way to Five-Hells to trade places with Emet. Although even that option has a high probability of fricasseed Tal being the main entrée at Christmas with the Draugrs.

Being angry with Borras and the rest of my team can't be the basis for my decision. My Star Trek discipline tells me, "the needs of the many outweigh the needs of the one." On the flip side, there is the possibility of salvaging True Love for a brace of star-crossed lovers. Plus, if there is anyone in this entire narrative who is absolutely, completely innocent, it's Emet.

That's it, Tal told himself. The decider. I choose the option that gives me at least a snowball's chance in Five-Hells of setting Emet free.

I still have a logistical problem, though. The Prime Omphalos will only send me to Helblad's Realm if I identify a specific piece of treasyre for the Compyndium. There were hundreds of piles of treasyre at Maes Howe, but not a singular piece to focus on. Think, Tal, think about that entire experience. What was said, what was done. As Memory rolled through its collection, Tal pressed pause. There, that's it. Helblad bargained only one of two pieces of Gleipnir. Said it was dwarf-forged from, "three impossible things. The noise a cat makes when it takes a step, the roots of a rock, and the breath of a fish." Gleipnir. That's my ticket. Quickly, now, finish your paper.

CHAPTER OCTOGINTA QUATTUOR

Term paper completed, Tal shoved it and the Compyndium in his backpack and took off down the hallway. As he started down the stairs he noticed the hourglass evidenced there was now only fifty minutes until Journey cutoff. *You have time, Tal, just be surgical.*

He flashed out the library's ornate front doors and ran straight to his dorm suite to grab Piras. It took only a couple of minutes to then go to the secured team room. After depositing Piras, his paper, and the Compyndium in plain sight on the table, he sprinted across the quadrangle toward the girls' dormitory. Dysi's window was on the far corner of the backside. *Of course.*

Tal was so out of breath when he arrived that he couldn't holler. He looked around for some pebbles to throw at her window. There were none. *Stupid perfectly manicured not a single blade of grass out of place Hunts School landscaping!* He slung his backpack around, grabbed his "Creatures" textbook and threw it hard at her window.

THUNK! Still gasping for air he tried to summon her. "Dysi!" He couldn't manage much more than a whisper. Tal grabbed another book, "An Alphabetical Listing of All Known Realms" (387th edition.) *Damn, I haven't even gotten a chance to read that one.*

THUNK!! Tal took a deep breath and tried again— "DYSI!" *Better,* he told himself. *Much more volume. Actually he* sounded a little like Stanley hollering for Stella in "Streetcar Named Desire."

He squinted as he heard a darkened window sliding open. Thank goodness, he'd guessed right and it was Dysi's window. "Quint? What is the matter with you? You're going to wake up the entire building."

"Dysi, I don't have much time…"

"Why? What do you mean you don't have much time?" She dropped her voice to a whisper, "We're not meeting until tomorrow at lunch to debrief…so why would you not have much…" Tal could tell from the change in her tone she'd realized what he had in mind. "Oh, no. No, sir! You're not getting me involved in anything. You came to me because you think I'm the soft touch. We're all done. All five of us. You sent your results by courier. There is absolutely no need for you to risk another Journey. No. No. You can't leave now. If something happens it's not only you at risk, it's the team as well. I'm not helping you, Quint, not when we're this close…"

"Dysi," Tal pleaded. "Listen, just listen to me. There's something I have to do…"

There was a pause as Dysi leaned farther out the window, giving him a harder looking over. "Quint, if you're planning on another Journey, why aren't you wearing your Puca?"

"He's back at the room. Um, taking a nap."

"I really don't want to insult you by stating the obvious but you're a human. You've already taken a number of time-proximate Journeys this week and you have no magyk. Which means without your Puca you are totally exposed on another Journey."

Damn it, Tal cursed silently. I'd hoped she wouldn't notice. Truth, he reminded himself. You learned from Baba Yaga you should always lead with the truth. Unless it's a little white lie to your freaked out stepfather. "Dysi, I can't take Piras with me."

There was a much longer pause now. "There's only one possible reason why you wouldn't take your Puca with you. Because you know right now you might not be coming back from the Journey. The only reason to Journey this term is to bring back an artifact. Not even you, at your most harebrained, would take a one-way Journey. So tell me, Quint, why can't you take your Puca on the Journey with you?"

"Because I may not be coming back."

Dysi's response was instantaneous. "I'm not telling you anything. You stay right there until I can get dressed and come down."

Tal didn't know how much time was left but he knew it was fast evaporating. Sorry, Dysi, but I'm going to have to bluff you. "I can't wait, Dysi. I can't let you stop me, either. I'm going whether you help me or not. What you tell me may help me succeed...and help me return safely."

"You're bluffing."

Tal turned on his heel and started walking away.

"Fine," Dysi's voice carried to him. "Come back. If Borras doesn't kill me, Notos absolutely will. What do you want to know?"

"Real fast, Dysi. I need for you to tell me verbatim about y'all's interaction with the woman named Kore on Atlantis plane."

"Kore? Okay, that's random. You mean Kore, who gave us our entry fee for Borras to fight in the ring?"

"Yes. Please hurry, Dysi."

"Okay, just give me a second. We ran into Kore, she caught our attention because she had circular dot tattoos all across her face and down her arms."

"Right? What did she tell you?"

"I'm pretty sure she said Kore was her Atlantean name and that she'd given up her human name. She apparently worked for the nasty fight promoter..."

"That's it," Tal replied. "Now it's coming back. Y'all described him as having gills and finlike arms."

"He did. Damn, that guy was a douchebag. After the fight, after Borras won, Ana and I found Kore to thank her and to apologize for not being able to pay her back because we probably weren't going to be able to return to Atlantis Realm. She gave us the oddest response. She said, 'Remember, whatever treasyre your mind may conjure, it all be dross compared to love. Seek the Center always'."

Confirmation received, Tal decided. It's Aislinn. "Thanks, Dysi."

"Quint?"

"Yes?"

"I'm not going to ever forgive you, or myself, if you don't make it back tonight."

"Understood. My term paper and the Compyndium are both on the table in our team room," Tal yelled over his shoulder as he swung his backpack around and took off running toward the ziggurat and the Prime Omphalos chamber.

CHAPTER OCTOGINTA QUINQUE

"DAMN! DAMN IT! SONOFABITCH!"

This is exactly like the first trip to the Ring of Brodgar, Tal thought, as his eyeballs rolled back up into his head. It may even be worse. Even Dysi didn't think about the possibility that Piras's protection on my other trips might cause a consequences amplification if I made a time-proximate Journey without him.

Tal felt like the pain was actually chewing his gray matter. Correction, Tal decided, as a new wave of pain threatened a blackout. First grinding, then chewing. Followed by more grinding.

Suck it up, Tal. You know there's a better than even money chance the only way you'll be making the return trip is on the long black train. The Recall won't happen unless I touch the omphalos stone and that won't happen if I'm deader than a doorknob. Maybe in this case, undeader than a draugr would be more apropos. You've been over all of the potential outcomes, Tal reminded himself. Amarantos knows, we don't need any more cortisol released.

He cautiously breathed in the foggy air. Only sea-haar right now. No draugr stench. Yet. "Helblad," he managed to croak, the additional auditory stimulus of his own voice causing the pain to re-crescendo. Tal stumbled backward against the damp, moss-covered menhir. "Helblad!" he managed once more before the pain drove all conscious thought away.

CHAPTER OCTOGINTA SEX

The first thing Tal heard as he roused to consciousness was the sound of papers rustling. Really loud papers. Wrong, he decided, after Olfactory contributed its two cents. It's wood crackling in a fire. A really large fire.

"Child of the Dust," Helblad said in greeting, as he threw a log the size of a small sapling on the bonfire. If you took two pieces of the coarsest grade of sandpaper in the history of the world and rubbed them together, over and over, really, really slowly, that's how Helblad's voice sounded. It was worse than fingernails ever so slowly dragging their way down a chalkboard. "Imbolc has come and gone but 'tis not yet Beltane, the due date of our contract," the draugr concluded.

"No, it isn't," Tal confirmed.

"You have not yet fulfilled our bargain by returning Aislinn."

"You are correct," Tal confirmed. "Aislinn is not yet home."

The giant draugr's shoulders lowered noticeably, as if the very air of the massive stone cairn was now actively pushing him into the earth. He bent down and picked up several sofa-sized pieces of wood, which he then casually tossed atop the now roaring blaze.

"Going to be a chilly evening tonight, is it?" Tal asked, adding a little half-laugh.

"It is my dinner fire, Quint of the Omada," Helblad replied solemnly.

"I realize I didn't call ahead and reserve a table, so I hope there's enough vittles for the two of us," Tal added.

"I warned thee," Helblad replied, the words bearing more resemblance to a minor rockslide than to actual words. "Didst I not warn thee?" he growl-added.

"You did," Tal answered, his voice thus far refraining from emulating the rampant quiver seizing most all of his other muscles.

Helblad turned his back to Tal and walked over to a full-sized oaken barrel. It was standing on its end, its top sitting on the floor, leaned up against the barrel. He retrieved a ladle from the bucket and splashed the contents on the fire, which cheered its fervent response. The now engorged flame fingers were seeking to clamber all the way through the vent hole in the ceiling. "I told thee thou couldst not return here, to this place, until thou wast ready to fulfill our bargain."

"That is correct, Helblad, that was our agreement." Tal had no idea how he was managing to appear so calm outwardly when his every nerve ending had deliquesced into neural goo.

"I specifically told thee, did I not, that if thou didst return that our bargain would be accelerated, and that I would be honor bound to fulfill its terms?"

"You made that perfectly clear." Shock, Central Processing advised. Preternatural calm may sometimes be an indicia of shock.

If possible, the air appeared to increase its force on Helblad's hulking mass, shrinking him further under its weight. "Even though I be Hogboon of Maes Howe, we have bound a contract. I have no power to alter its terms."

Helblad threw another ladle full of what was apparently the draugr equivalent of gasoline on the fire. Maybe gasoline is the draugr equivalent of gasoline, Tal thought. Focus, idiot. Focus. He's planning on barbequing your ass.

The draugr leaned to his right to grab a supersized, rust-splotched black cauldron. He hefted it easily with a hand roughly the size of a door off of a 1976 Cadillac Coup DeVille and then proceeded to hang the kettle on an iron pole that transversed the massive fire. "Art thou ready?" Helblad asked, while at the same time drawing a knife from a sheath tucked on the outside of his loincloth. Like the cauldron, the knife was rusted, the rust being overlaid with a patina of dried gradu.

If he cuts me with that damn thing I'll die from lockjaw, Tal thought. Forget tetanus, Stupid, he's planning on charbroiling you tonight, Tal reminded himself, as he felt his teeth begin to chatter involuntarily.

This is not how I planned on our reunion going, Tal told himself. Don't panic. You have a plan. Whip it out. If he doesn't go for it, then panic. "Helblad?"

"Yes?"

"If our bargain allows you to first nibble on some appetizer that isn't one of my body parts, I would like a couple of minutes to explain why I am here."

Tal could swear the jagged horizontal fissure that opened on Helblad's face had some indicia of being a smile. "Actually, I had just dined. I'm only cooking thee now to fulfill our bargain. I'll probably end up salting you away for the next rainy feast day."

Okay, maybe I might have been mistaken about the smile possibility, Tal thought, as he gulped down a mouthful of anxiety. "If conversation helps thou come to terms with your impending demise, I can indulge thee," the draugr replied. "There is nothing in our contract that prohibits me from having pre-dinner conversation with the dinner. I had thought to end thee quickly, as I have grown somewhat fond of thee," Helblad added, as he resheathed his weapon and squatted down on his heels so that he was almost at Tal's eye level. "What wouldst thou like to talk about? The weather? A game of hnefatafl, perhaps?"

"Well, a lot has happened since the last time I was here." Quickly, Tal reminded himself. Give him a recitation but quickly. Tal proceeded to tell Helblad about the Combat Challenge and about both he and Väst almost dying. He related how Omada had gone to Atlantis Realm and that they made the first term team cut. He then proceeded with some other details rounding into meeting Baba Yaga, getting branded with the brand of the Cult of Nyx, and related in detail the chronology surrounding the wytch's death. Tal found himself having to pause a considerable period of time to gain sufficient composure to tell about the events at the Winter Formal, about Emet taking his place as a blood-pryce Equivalynt, and being sentenced to Five-Hells.

The draugr interrupted him at that point. " 'Tis a fine tale indeed mortal and a shame about the golem, who be innocent."

"The torment?" Tal asked. "How bad is it?"

"There be unending pain."

Tal felt his heart actually jump into his mouth. Well, that might be a bit of an exaggeration, maybe it only climbed about halfway up his throat. Maybe it didn't actually physically move into his esophageal canal but it sure felt like it did. "Is it really that bad?" he asked.

"Oh, it be terrible indeed. Dost thou not understand? Emet be doomed to live on the Five-Hells plane until Amarantos finally calls all of her children home." Tal realized his total lack of understanding must be evident on his face because Helblad continued. "Those exiled to that foulest of Realms do not ever die while there. They suffer without ending because their bodies are as incompatible with that Realm as that of Veles and his Folk are with any of the other known Realms. It is truly unending torment, Quint of the Omada."

Tal's elation evaporated, his previous sadness at Emet's status now compounded. The permanent words on the Hunts Orientation blackboard came back to him—"Death (or worse.)"

"I am sorry to have further burdened you," the giant said as he stood and stretched. "Art thou through with whatever conversation thou wanted to have with me?" Helblad asked, not unkindly, as he leaned over to pick up Skullcrusher.

It's go time, Tal told himself. "No, Jarl of the Undead, I have told you all of those things because you are my friend and I knew you would be gravely interested in one specific part of my tale."

"Thou hast piqued my curiosity, mortal. Which part?"

"The part where Omada traveled to Atlantis," Tal replied.

" 'Twas a fair adventure but so wast your entire tale," the draugr replied. "What be special about Atlantis Realm?"

"Aislinn."

The intake hiss of Helblad's breath was substantially louder than the exhalation of the largest steam locomotive ever created. Had to be, Tal thought.

"Aislinn." The word was as close to a caress as sixty-grit sandpaper could offer. "She is alive and well, then?" the draugr asked so softly Tal almost couldn't hear the words.

"She is alive. Kore is the name she's using. I don't think I'm going too far out on a limb in saying my teammates got the impression she wouldn't mind a rescue. At your earliest convenience. In fact, now that I've had a little time to reflect, I believe even more strongly her last words to them were actually a hidden message for the two of us."

"Me and thee? How couldst she know of our friendship?"

Friendship, Tal thought. The big guy may have to chow down on me but he really considers me his friend. Heart-warming almost. Well, except for the part where I end up with grill marks. Keep going, Tal told himself. "Kore said these exact words to my squad, 'Remember, whatever treasyre your mind may conjure, it all be dross compared to love. Seek the Center always.' "

Helblad slowly exhaled the massive breath he'd been holding. "That she liveth be news most welcome indeed. While thou hast done more on her behalf than I have been able to accomplish in centuries, it still does not fulfill the terms of our bargain. No matter how grateful I am, I cannot modify our contract. It is simply not allowed."

Here goes nothing, Tal thought. "I totally understand. I would never ask such a thing of you." Tal stopped to take the opportunity to make himself smile. Sell it brother, he told himself. "As I recall, Helblad Clawfoot, Jarl of all the Draugrs and Wights of all the known Realms loves to bargain, does he not?"

This time there was absolutely no question Helblad was smiling. "The Jarl dost, in fact, truly love to bargain, Dust Child. But we two already have a bargain and its terms must needs be fulfilled."

"I'm totally good with that," Tal confirmed. "However,

since our initial contract, events have happened which could never have been foreseen by either of us at the time."

Helblad's smile expanded until Tal could see its glint in the teacup-sized black pools of the draugr's eyes. "Tell me more of these unforeseeable events."

"Well, there's Emet going to Five-Hells. I've decided I'm going there to make Veles exchange him for me. Although I have zero idea how to get there. I used up my final bit of Journey time coming here, but I'm getting the feeling Five-Hells is the one Realm to which the Prime Omphalos does not have access."

"Thou art correct," Helblad confirmed.

'Figured as much. Starting the moment the Recall returns me back to Hunts School, I'm devoting all of my time and energy to figuring out how to get there. I figure me going to Five-Hells for all eternity greatly reduces the odds of me getting Aislinn back by the appointed time and date, does it not?"

"It dost," the Jarl rumbled. "A person voluntarily going to the worst place in all of the known Folk universe dost qualify as an unanticipated event. You said events. What else?"

"Well, there is the little matter that there is a new Stytch in town. Moi," Tal added, using his best "absolutely no big deal" tone of voice.

Instead of being teacup-sized pools of inky blackness Helblad's eyes momentarily became teacup saucer-sized pools. Of inky blackness. "Odin's beard! Thy story be worthy of a song sung by immortal Bragi himself to the einherjar of Valhalla." The draugr reached over and grabbed a thirty-foot length of hardwood, which he snapped in half and casually tossed on top of the inferno. "I hope something unfortunate hast not happened to thy predecessor."

"No," Tal replied smiling. "He has successfully retired."

"Good," Helblad boomed. "Taliesin be a good man and a hero many times over. I am glad all be well and he hast finally found the path to self-forgiveness." The draugr turned his attention back to Tal. "The UnFading Spirit doth have a plan for each of her children. As her present Traveler I couldst not now enter into an agreement for your life with thee but since our contract doth precede your appointment, it dost not change the contract between me and thee."

"I'm not looking for a technicality to welsh on our deal." Tal paused a moment to cough. "The Hunt this term is a Treasyre Hunt."

Helblad nodded his head. "Several of my liegemen have made such information known to me. A Treasyre Hunt dost not qualify as an event that couldst not have been anticipated."

"Again, agreed," Tal replied. Get to it buddy, he told himself. "What could not have reasonably been anticipated is that because of everything that has happened to me I finally feel like I see the choices I must make if I am truly 'Seeking the Center'."

Helblad waited patiently for Tal to continue. " 'Seeking the Center' requires that I go to Five-Hells to see if there is something I can do for Emet. 'Seeking the Center' requires I fulfill my obligations as the new Traveler.

"Now comes the part where I may have gone totally around the bend. I have a treasyre that until a few minutes ago I truly believed would win the Tyrning for Omada."

"Something hast caused thee to believe otherwise?" the draugr asked quietly.

"Yes. A fuller understanding of what Aislinn was trying to tell both of us. If I am wrong, if I really am clueless as to what 'Seeking the Center' is truly about, I will have thrown away Omada's chance to win the Tyrning. In which case Notos will probably see that I meet a violent end. Which would, of course, make it impossible for me to return here for you to eat me."

Helblad rubbed his chin as he nodded his understanding. "I told you when first we met that Amarantos has given you two of her greatest gyfts, gyfts much greater than many forms of magyk. She has given you a clever mind and a giving heart.

"As there be no time frame specified for when I must eat thee in the event of your premature return here, thou art telling me thou wisheth to bargain a contract separate. Not a superseding contract but a preceding contract. If the proposed preceding contract dost not ultimately inure to my benefit there will be no adverse impact upon the terms and conditions of our existing contract."

The big guy just cut me some slack, Tal thought. He knows much more about the binding rules than I do and he deliberately couched what I want in terms that will satisfy all necessary requirements. "Couldn't have said it better myself," Tal replied.

"Thou hast treasyre which thou believest would be of great value to me as well?" Helblad asked.

"I do," Tal replied.

"Thou hopest that by entering into this new bargain thou might somehow attain even greater treasyre under the Hunts Rules?"

"To me? Yes."

"Before I canst decide whether to accept the proposed preceding bargain, I must first know what treasyre thou wishest to bargain."

"That's fair," Tal replied as he reached into his left front pocket and pulled out the translucent plastic bubble. "I desire to bargain this."

The Mohs scale of mineral hardness ranks the hardness of minerals by their ability to scratch other minerals. Diamonds are the hardest mineral on the list. Corundum is the second hardest. The draugr's face was now at least as hard as corundum. His voice, however, was diamond. "A child's bauble?" Helblad demanded. "This be not a good time mortal for thou to engage in flippancy."

Oh shit, Tal thought. Clearly I need a little more visual explanation. Stat. He leaned over and slammed the plastic against the nearest jewel-encrusted goblet. The plastic wings spilled out and as soon as they made contact with the outside air they morphed. Boy did they morph. Quickly shapeshifting into a glorious pair of alate slippers. Both the wings and shoes were woven, their threads containing representatives of the entire auriferous spectrum.

It's too bad there isn't a Mohs scale for degrees of facial nonplussage, Tal thought. Cause if there was, Helblad's would now be rated 'flawless diamond'."

With no immediate undead response forthcoming, Tal intentionally kept babbling to give Helblad time to catch up. "At the time of our original agreement I had no idea these wings were anything but a cheap carnival crackerjack prize."

"You hold the Taleria," Helblad finally whispered, providing further evidence that even the High Lord of the Undead could still be awed.

"Yeah, I got it, or him, or her, from spinning a Wheel of Fortune that had the design of my own personal kalachakra...

"You hold the Taleria."

"Having a little deja vu moment, big guy, but I'm pretty sure we've established that fact. Anyhoo, the person running that carnie operation identified herself only as Fortuna..."

At this point whatever measuring scale that was the visual nonplussage equivalent of the Mohs mineral hardness scale would need to go to a twenty, not merely a ten. "Mortal. You are mortal, a Child of the Divine Spark, and yet you aver the Taleria wast given to you by Amarantos herself?" Helblad asked. To say Helblad's mouth was agape would be an understatement.

"I have been Jarl of the Undead for many centuries. For dozens upon dozens of human generations. I have been a draugr for longer than the lifetimes of even the longest lived of the Folk. Never have I seen the Taleria. Never have I met anyone who hast seen the Taleria. There be none presently living who hast seen it, save mayhaps the Elder Children themselves."

The draugr stopped a moment. Tal could tell he was sorting his thoughts before he continued. "Before thou came here today thou knewest the Taleria would probably be treasyre enow for the Omada to win the Tyrning. Thou knewest the odds be thou wilt not be able to fulfill our bargain. Thou knewest I have no heart to slay thee in accordance with our contract and that were I to win our bargain, Aislinn wouldst still not be restored to me. And mayhaps most importantly, thou knewest if thou came here this day that I would probably have to kill thee. Yet still you came."

"Yes, Jarl, I knew all those things," Tal responded somberly. He watched as the draugr's amazement gave way to his previous sadness.

"I cannot accept the new bargain, mortal. As you can see, I have treasyre enow. And what you see here be only a token of my treasyre on almost countless Realms. It is accepted throughout the entirety of the known universe there be no treasyre horde that doth come close to equaling that of Maes Howe. Yea, even that of Snype, mightiest of the great fyrewyrms, pales in poor comparison.

"There must be value ere I can bargain. Even though the Taleria be a uniquity throughout the universe, it be of no use to me. The Taleria cannot transport me to a Realm, unless it has previously been to that plane."

Tal smiled. It couldn't match the draugr's earlier smile in sheer grin distance but it could, and did, in amplitude. "Oh yeah, that reminds me. I might have forgotten one perhaps relevant fact. That Wheel of Fortune that was all tricked out with the design of my destiny, you know, the one operated by Fortuna? It might, or might not, have been located on Atlantis Realm."

Helblad's laughter was a hailstorm of jubilance. It bounced and echoed and clattered throughout the vast expanse of Maes Howe. It was so joyful, so exuberant, Tal could have sworn it raised the roof by several feet. " 'Might have forgotten one perhaps relevant fact.' I think mayhaps you did, human." The laughter and its accompanying smile left the building as fast as they had arisen. "Before we continue, there is a fact you must know about the Taleria. The information is intentionally not contained in any of the sources of Folk lore."

"What?" Tal asked.

"A person may possess the Taleria only once in their lyfetime. If we make this bargain, it may never return to you, directly or indirectly. Ever."

Which means there's no possibility of rebound treasyre for use in winning the Treasyre Hunt, Tal realized. It doesn't matter. I hadn't really been counting on that possibility anyway. Apparently the leap of faith on "Seeking the Center" requires trapeezing without a safety net. Thanks for that, Amarantos. "I didn't know that, Helblad, but it does not change my decision. I wish to bargain with you, Jarl of all Draugrs and Wights."

Helblad's bargaining face quickly rearranged his facial muscles. "It is not allowed for there to be only one side to a bargain. There must be consideration. I cannot bargain the saving of your life because we already have a contract that addresses that issue. I can and wilt, however, bargain information worthy of thy trade in fair return. Dost thou accept, Quint of the Omada?"

No need to even ask, Tal immediately decided. If Helblad thinks the intel is worthy, then that's going to have to be good enough. "I accept. Do you?" Tal replied formally.

The draugr finished the contract ritual. "I accept."

Tal handed the Taleria to Helblad, who nodded his thanks before turning and reverently placing, on the seat of his throne, the only sentient creature in all of creation woven of golden thread.

Turning back to Tal, he said, "In fulfillment of my portion of the bargain I advise thee of two discrete pieces of information. The first is that a ploutonion exists on the grounds of Arianrhod."

Wow, Tal thought, that is some random data. Baba Yaga told me about Arianrhod, Luna's Earth Realm home back in the day when she created the Cult of Nyx. It had no fixed location, appearing wherever Luna's moon avatar was closest to Earth. Which meant the moon was always full at Arianrhod. As Tal reflected, he recalled the wytch's exact words—"There were moonbeams wider than the boulevards of great cities."

After giving Tal a minute to consider the information, Helblad continued. "Second, under the Moiety rules governing bargains, if either party should be gathered to Amarantos before completion of the bargain, honor is deemed satisfied and the bargain deemed fulfilled. It applies equally to the living and the undead."

Wow, Tal thought. And I thought the first fact was random. Just goes to show when you're bargaining with a draugr anything can happen. Seems like that lesson should be on a Hallmark card. Hell, it probably is.

"Do ye accept my information as sufficient for our

bargain, Quint of the Omada?" Helblad intoned.

"I do," Tal replied.

"Good. I must remind thee our original bargain remains intact—unless one or both of us be no longer in corporeal form before its completion."

"Understood," Tal confirmed. "And good talk. A bit on the depressing and morose side but I guess that's only to be expected with you being Supreme Leader of the Undead and all of that. Are we done here? If so, I could use a lift to the omphalos so I can hurry up and get back to Hunts School so that one or all of my teammates can be disappointed in me beyond all belief."

Helblad laughed. As usual, it sounded like truckloads of scree sliding down a mountainside. "Yes, we be done. Before I depart to fulfill my vengeance, there is one detail I must attend." With that Helblad walked to the far side of his throne and bent over, rummaging around in some Brobdingnagian-sized saddlebag. He withdrew a draugr-sized piece of vellum and matching pen. I'd like to see the specialty stationer that carries those products, Tal thought. He watched as Helblad scribbled a few sentences, before folding the paper and stuffing it into his loincloth.

Aughh! Would it kill him to add a fanny pack or something similar to his ensemble, was Tal's first thought. It was followed closely by his second—sometimes it's better to remind yourself to just shut the hell up.

"Done," the draugr stated. "It be time for leave-taking," Helblad continued, as he retrieved the Taleria. "When the Hunts are done I predict binding thee as Omada's replacement Fifth Prime will have been the wisest decision the new Archon ever made. Art thou ready?"

"What do I need to do?" Tal asked nervously.

"I would suggest thou firmly shut thy porridge-hole so thou dost not choke on gravel whilst we sojourn together."

Tal immediately closed his mouth. He couldn't have squeezed his jaws closed any harder even if he had tetanus. From Helblad's rusty knife or otherwise.

"Let us be away to our respective tasks," Helblad said, as he effortlessly picked Tal up in his left hand.

Afraid to open his mouth, Tal nodded, right before they both fell through the cairn's stone floor.

CHAPTER OCTOGINTA SEPTEM

Time at the Maes Howe on Helblad's home Realm moved faster than at Hunts School. Even with that disparity, Tal made it to Principal Chiron's office only fifteen seconds before midnight. The other two Compyndium were already stacked on Principal Chiron's desk. Tal handed his term paper to the principal and the Compyndium to Head Librarian Seshat. She gave it a thorough look-see to make sure it was undamaged before opening the book and ascertaining the pages were once again blank. She nodded to Chiron, picked up the other two books, and headed out the door. Tal was out the door himself only a moment later.

On his way back to the guys' dorm Tal swung by Dysi's building and yelled underneath her window until she appeared. More than half-asleep she appeared to be genuinely pleased to see he hadn't gone and gotten himself killed dead.

Tal didn't have the heart to tell her what he was about to do next.

CHAPTER OCTOGINTA OCTO

Now what is the human doing? Notos hadn't been able to sleep so he'd staked out Quint to make sure he returned the Compyndium in a timely manner. He did. After that, though, he'd hidden in some shrubbery, watching the human as he stood outside the girls' dormitory conversing with Dysi while she hung out her window.

The mortal should have headed straight back to his dorm suite to grab some shuteye and get ready for the final team meeting tomorrow. But he didn't. Instead, Quint was now walking around the side of the main building, walking toward Fountain Flow, toward the front of the campus. There's only two places he can be going. Forest Fell...or the Gas Station Crossing. Damn it! He's veering toward the left. Why the hell would he be going back to the Gas Station Crossing now? There's no crisis like last time. If anything, there's less pressure on him now than anytime since he first signed on with the team. We gave him the bonus Earth Realm Journey. If he'd wanted to visit Earth plane he could have Journeyed there. Wait a minute. He's not wearing his Puca. He wasn't wearing it for his final Journey either.

Why? Why would he screw this up for us now? Borras thinks we have a good chance of winning the Tyrning. But we have to have four unmaimed members present at the Final Ceremony. Granted, we have five now but if Quint gets lost on

Earth plane proper and Släkt finds out we're down a person, Nord wouldn't hesitate to try to kill one of the remaining four.

I really don't need this. I only have a couple of days left to make a final campus search. Sure, if we win I'll have another three hundred years. Quite frankly, though, I don't know if that will help. I've looked every place possible. If my binding didn't prevent me, I'd get Quint to help me. I'd never admit it to him but he's easily the smartest of us all.

Notos looked up to see that while he was deep in thought, Quint had traveled two-thirds of the way to the far end of Grass Grow. Gotta double-time it, now. After what happened earlier this term, I'm not sure what the "I'm with him" rules are. I may have to be practically hanging on his arm to follow him through the Crossing. I promised Borras I would bird dog him so that's the plan. If he goes to Earth Realm, I'll be with him and can use my magyk. I'll zap him and carry him back if I have to.

CHAPTER OCTOGINTA NOVEM

Tal stopped as soon as the portal door appeared. You've already been over this with yourself. If I walk through that door, I may, or may not, be able to save Emet from Five-Hells but Omada will for sure be down to four members. Four is all we need to show up for the Final Ceremony. The Journeys are over. The treasyre has been collected by the teams. I'm easily the shortest lived of all my teammates. It's not like I would make it the entire three hundred years anyway. Bottom line, I'm pretty much dead weight here.

Emet is in Five-Hells because he sacrificed himself for me. Amarantos, if you're listening, I realize I have that whole Traveler gig I signed up for, but surely if I'm doing my best to "Seek the Center," you'll make special arrangements for that, won't you? Maybe a few centuries in Five-Hells will be enough time to forgive myself for what I did to Elle.

Motor Cortex interrupted Tal's contemplation. Legs are ready. Is the mission a Go or No Go?

It's a go, Central Processing replied, as Tal began reaching for the doorknob.

CHAPTER NONAGINTA

Now he's stopped. The portal door appeared when he got within a foot of it, and then he stopped. What's he doing? Notos wondered. I'm totally exposed out here on Grass Grow but that can't be helped. I have to close the distance in case he opens the door. I can't take a chance it might close behind him and disappear.

Okay, that's it, he reaching for the doorknob. It's sprint time, Notos told himself, as he took off at a dead run.

CHAPTER NONAGINTA UNUS

"HEY, NEW GUY! GET YOUR HEAD OUT OF YOUR ASS AND GET OVER HERE."

Tal shook his head in a failed effort to clear it. He couldn't see a damn thing and there was a faint repetitive ringing in his ears. Did some idiot explode a flash grenade? Maybe they lit a pan full of phosphorus. It was bright enough to be a flash grenade but those normally had some loud, concussive element to the incendiary device. Loud, as in close to two hundred decibels, invariably resulting in tinnitus or busted eardrums loud. Definitely not a faint background ringing.

Seems more likely it was phosphorous. Phosphorous wouldn't make a noise, well, no more than a noticeable sizzling, but it would certainly be bright enough to momentarily blind my ass. Lots of different allotropes of phosphorous, though. Yellow, scarlet, violet, even black of all things. No, if some asshat was flaming phosphorus at me, it would have been white or red. Most probably white.

Unknown and Potentially Life-Threatening Reality calling Tal! Focus, you numbskull. What the hell difference does it make what caused it, your eyes are gonna need a minute. Fine, he told himself, back to the matter of the annoying ringing sound. He shook his head again. Nope, still there. It was a ding-ding-dinging. Ding-ding-ding. ding-ding-ding.

Sounds like, what? Quantify it, he told himself. What's a

similar noise? Well, it's kind of, sort of, like one of those obnoxious little servant's bells from a period English drama on BBC America.

DING-DING-DING!

"HEY, YOU! I GET IT YOU'RE SOME HIGH FALUTIN' BIG SWINGING DICK SABRAGE SPECIALIST BUT THIS IS MY KITCHEN AND YOU'RE WORKING HERE TONIGHT. THIS IS THE LAST TIME I'M GOING TO SAY IT. AFTER THAT, I DON'T CARE ABOUT NO FANCY-SCHMANCY SPECIAL OCCASION REQUEST. YOU'RE OUT ON YOUR ASS. *DING-DING-DING!* NOW PICK UP THOSE TWO CAESAR SALADS AND GET THEM OUT TO TABLE 10, PDQ."

Whoever that jackass is hollering at better get his fanny in high gear, Tal thought, as he reached down to tweak-straighten his bow tie. Hello? Since when in my entire life was I wearing a bow tie? He scanned downward, assessing the rest of his wardrobe. A conservative black tuxedo. Clearly a well-used, much abused secondhand tuxedo, but a tuxedo nonetheless. Well, damn, that ringing is one of those stupid, annoying service bells…and I'm the new guy, he suddenly realized.

A hard elbow to his right slab of ribs knocked the breath out of him. "Dude! What's the matter with you? You stoned or something? Pick those two damn salads up and get them out of here before the Chef comes across the prep table and fillets everyone of us. I got kids at home to feed."

"Uhhh, sure. Right away," Tal mumbled, his brain trying to process the unquantified data. Othertyme, he told himself. That's the only thing that makes sense of this nonsense. Starburst light show, a freaking cranium-splitting headache, and momentary disorientation. As soon as I touched the Gas Station doorknob, Amarantos sent me othertyme.

On this particular trip I'm apparently a waiter at some snooty foo-foo establishment where the wait staff has to dress formal. Which plane? When is it in realtyme? Why has Amarantos sent me here?

"Umm, Table 10?" he managed to stammer to the air at large.

The not unfriendly fellow waiter with kids to feed, who probably didn't know he had exceptionally sharp elbows responded. "It's the two-top. Second from the left as you go past the main bar area."

Tal leaned forward, snagged the two salad plates from the chill row on the prep table, placed them on a service tray, and headed toward the double-swinging doors. "On it," he said cheerily to the chef.

"Hurry up, you idiot," Chef replied. "The potatoes for Table 12 are coming out of the oven now."

As Tal entered the dining area he realized snooty was nowhere near an accurate description. The ballroom sized dining area had thirty-foot tall ceilings, with numerous cut-crystal chandeliers providing the mood lighting. The floor to ceiling windows were draped in venetian silk velvet, the fabric ripples flashing all the way from darker port and crimson to the lighter shades of red. A string quartet of two violinists, a violist, and a cellist were providing lovely, whispering white noise, ensuring that conversation at any of the widely spaced tables was completely confidential.

One of his fellow waiters came flying by him, holding a large tray full of steaming vegetable dishes over his head. "I'd quit dicking around if I were you. Full house tonight and the chef is already on a tear."

Right, Tal thought, as he moved forward. Table 10. Two-top. Second from left as you go past the main bar area. He quickly located the two-top, occupied by a gaudily dressed couple who didn't even deign to acknowledge his presence as he dropped off the salads. As he rushed back to the kitchen he caught a glimpse of himself in one of the multitude of mirrors decorating the walls. I look like crap, he thought. What am I, a rode hard fifty year old? My tux looks about two complete holiday seasons too small for me. Clearly, I haven't made getting to the gym a priority. For decades. Why am I not in my own body?

When Tal blew back through the swinging doors, it seemed as if the kitchen was even busier than it had been less than five minutes before. He found himself the only discordant note in a well-orchestrated dance involving dozens of participants. Sous chefs, junior waiters, bus boys and drink waitresses. The place was a crazy busy hive. Chef had already tired of waiting on him for Table 12's potatoes. He'd sent the side dish with some other poor unfortunate and now looked like he was getting ready to tee up on Tal.

Tal was saved by none than the maître d' himself. Well, Tal assumed he was the maître d' because he had a pencil mustache and the crease in his tuxedo pants looked sharp enough to cause paper cuts. Well, because of those two things and because the smile on the man's face looked like it had been indelibly tattooed.

"When we called the service they said you were the best in town. Are you on the drugs or something?" the man asked.

I know that tone from my limited sports career, Tal thought. He wants to know if he needs to scramble for a sub to play my position. Amarantos put me here for a reason. Got to bring my "A" game. Tal quickly shook his head no and professed his readiness.

"Good, because no one else here has the faintest idea how to do your job and we have never once failed at fulfilling any guest's special request. The reputation of Le Roue de Temps as the finest dining establishment in the entire region is at stake." The man paused and gave Tal a hard stare. "Why are you looking at me like you are on the drugs? You **are** a sabrage expert, aren't you?"

Sabrage? Play along, Tal told himself. It'll come to you in a minute. "Sabrage? Sure. I've performed sabrage only like about a billion times. I'm pretty sure I've sabragated in my sleep before."

"In your sleep? I think you are on the drugs. Well, you're all we've got," the maître d' replied, as he gently dabbed his brow with a handkerchief that disappeared into his vest pocket even faster than it had appeared a split-second before. "The gentleman seated at Table 24 is proposing tonight to the lady seated with him. He has ordered a bottle of Dom Pérignon Rosé 1959." The maître d' pointed at an already chilled bottle nested in a sterling silver wine chiller. The chiller was inset in a table on wheels that also contained a smallish salver holding maybe a dozen strawberries, freshly dipped in intricately swirled white and dark chocolates.

"You know the drill. Take the bottle to the table, ask the gentleman if that is what he ordered. After he confirms, make sure everyone is out of the line of fire, then open the bottle. Do not leave the area, simply back out of the alcove but remain where he can summon you if he needs anything. This is an exceptional bottle and we want to provide service well beyond that of even our normal high standards. Do you understand?"

Tal nodded.

"The champagne was a special order for this occasion and we only have the one bottle. Do you understand?"

Tal nodded again.

The maître d' clapped his hands twice in rapid succession. "Excellent. Then, vite! Vite! What are you waiting for? Your instrument is in its sheath. Over there," he said pointing to a hook hanging against the far wall. "Be careful, you've never found a sharper edge on a blade." As he turned and flew back out of the swinging doors, the maître d' clapped his hands twice as he yelled back over his left shoulder, "VITE DE VITE!"

Tal looked to where his boss for the evening had pointed. There was a sheathed sword hanging on the wall. Champagne? Sword? Holy hell, Tal thought, as he stepped toward the hanging instrument of death. Sabrage...sabrage is the art of opening a bottle of champagne using a sword to knock the end off the bottle. Thanks, Amarantos. No really, thanks. Sometimes I think you may be the one "on the drugs."

Tal took the sword and sheath off the wall and carefully strapped it around his waist. He didn't have a clue how one went about slicing the top off a bottle with a razor-sharp sword without creating a billion glass shards. First things, first. How the hell was he supposed to know which table was Table 24?

He scanned the kitchen looking for assistance. There was a cluttered work desk over in one corner, the topography of its entire horizontal surface comprised of taller mesas of stacked paper products broken up by rounded mounds of kitchen flotsam. On the wall there was an old school yellow landline telephone with a curlicued cord that had to be at least fifteen feet long when extended. Thumbtacked supply orders littered a large corkboard—which also happened to have a calendar pinned to it...as well as a yellowed copy of the seating chart. Bingo.

Tal took possession of the chiller cart and started pushing it toward the board. When he got there he pinpointed Table 24 and was just heading out the swinging doors when the calendar caught his eye. Somebody had taken the time to mark off each day as it passed. The grease-begrimed record showed today was June 30, 1996.

How about that? Amarantos sent me pre-millennium. Well, barely. 1996. Only a couple of years from now and they'll all be freaking out about the Y2K bug. 1996? Funny, that's the same year I was born, Tal thought, as he turned and backed through the swinging door pulling his cart behind him.

CHAPTER NONAGINTA DUO

Notos paused momentarily. What's he doing now? He acted like he was reaching for the doorknob and now it's like he's frozen. Like some department store manikin. I'm still too far away, he told himself as he geared back up.

CHAPTER NONAGINTA TRES

Table 24...table 24...the seating chart showed it to be by itself in a little alcove, set off from the main dining room. Tal searched the crowded main dining room. Ah, over there, behind that column. I know a smattering of le francais from ninth grade French. That should help sell my fakery. Surely this place is tony enough for a French-speaking waiter.

As Tal wheeled the cart in and around the jam-packed dinery, he wondered. Why am I here, Amarantos? Whose tapestry is being woven that requires a Stytch?

Tal heard the happy couple at Table 24 before he rounded the pillar. Heard them. Laughing. Uninhibited, free to be yourself, all is right with your existence because you're with the person you love laughter. Tal knew that kind of laughter...because his mom had laughed like that with Pell. Because I've laughed like that with Elle, he added.

The woman's voice, sprinkled with that wonderfully refreshing laugh, seemed familiar. As Tal trundled his cart closer to the alcove Central Processing indicated it wanted to begin its rolodexing procedure. That's ridiculous, Tal told his brain. You saw the calendar less than five minutes ago. You're not even born yet. How could some strange lady's voice be familiar? Analysis responded it couldn't possibly hurt to process the work order. Tal felt the familiar mental whirring as Analysis began its work.

Focus, you knucklehead. You never know what's going to

happen on one of these trips. Upon reaching his destination, Tal paused to get his best French phraseology voice together before pulling back one of the privacy curtain's floor to ceiling panels.

As he tugged on the curtain, the female portion of the duo happened to be in his direct line of sight. Before Visual could process the new information, Speech proceeded as planned. Smiling broadly, Tal opened his mouth to frenchily announce the arrival of the champagne. "Mademoiselle et monsieur, je suis arrivé avec le Dom Pérignon Ro…MOM?"

CHAPTER NONAGINTA QUATTUOR

Come on, Notos chided himself. You've gotten accustomed to relying on your Puca. Run, damn you. Run! You have another fifty yards before you're close enough to the human.

CHAPTER NONAGINTA QUINQUE

Crickets…

Crickets…

Crickets…must be thousands of the little bastards.

Still more crickets…revised estimate—perhaps tens of thousands.

"I'm sorry, what did you say?" Thea finally asked him.

Damn, the crickets are back, Tal thought to himself. Okay. Sure. Get your shit together. It's okay. It's not okay, that's my mom. You're going to be fine. I'm not going to be fine, in case you hadn't noticed, that's my mom. Hello, Medulla, get off your stem and bring the heart rate down. Stat!

Central Processing tacitly acknowledged the ambient hushed babble of casual conversation from other parts of the restaurant. Cerebrum Temporal Lobe reported it was unable to verify that status because the abject silence in its immediate vicinity overwhelmed any other aural information.

Say something you idiot, Tal told himself. Quick! Say something. You're the deus ex machina in this scene, for heaven's sake. Remember she has no idea it's you in a different body and she doesn't even know othertyme exists.

"Uh, er, I'm terribly sorry. I was more than a little nervous because I knew this was a special occasion for you both. I'm afraid I overestimated my command of the French language. I sometimes get a frog in my throat when I get nervous. What I meant to say was your bottle of Dom Pérignon Rosé 1959, monsieur and mademoiselle. As requested."

"Ce n'est pas un problem," he heard the male portion of the couple graciously respond.

Analysis inserted itself once more. What now, Central Processing asked crossly. Sorry to interrupt old chum but the man's voice. It is also familiar. Stop it. It can't be. It's impossible for the guy who is out on a date with my mother before I'm even born to have a familiar voice. I've got enough on my hands trying to figure out how you can fake decapitating a bottle with a sword.

"Entrez-vous," Tal heard, as he found himself stepping forward in response to the man's request, and to his hand beckoning Tal the rest of the way into the alcove. "Ne vous inquiétez pas de la sabrage. Pourriez-vous nous verser un verre," the man added.

Hallelujah! I'm pretty sure he just said I'm off the hook for the whole sword bottle-slashing ritual. Tal's hand was visibly shaking as he reached for the hand towel to dry off the bottle. His mom was the person still squarely in his sight, her unknown male companion remained just outside of Tal's left peripheral vision.

He couldn't help but stare at Thea. His mom, well his mom almost two decades ago, was absolutely mind-blowing drop-dead lovely. She was dressed to the nines in a full-length black evening gown, with a plunging neckline and an empire waistline that both obscured and emphasized her status as...a soon to be mother. And cue, crickets.

"Just a little in both glasses for a toast, please," the man said.

Tal began twisting the cork off the bottle, holding it firmly so it would gradually release the carbon dioxide gas without an eruption.

"Pour vous, Madame," Tal stated, as he poured until her glass was half full. With that he turned square toward the man, "Et vous…"

Paralysis. Full and complete, total in every respect. Tal's tongue swelled in his mouth. His hands became open, outstretched claws. Tal saw, with eyes that couldn't even move to follow its fall, the bottle spilling everywhere as gravity did its thing. His ears heard the crash as the heavy champagne bottle shattered against the formerly pristine white marble floor.

Tal found himself frozen. Staring. At his mom's boyfriend. A boyfriend who in scant moments was about to become her fiancé. Analysis had been correct, the man's voice was familiar. As were his multitude of names. Memory gladly supplied the litany. The first time they'd met he'd called himself Dr. Mertin Wilt. The Alfar called him Myrddin. The Folk most often referred to him as the Traveler. He had been renamed Munedan by a former lover, who just happened to be one of the Principes. Many, many human lifetimes ago.

As Tal's synapses slowly began to fire again, Memory added one more name to the list...the man's psuche name...Taliesin.

CHAPTER NONAGINTA SEX

Faster, you simply have to run faster. You can do it. Twenty-five more yards.

CHAPTER NONAGINTA SEPTEM

Without the courtesy of an advance warning Tal's knees went wobbly and he staggered against the table's edge.

"Sir?" his mother asked suddenly. Tal looked behind him to see who else had shown up. No one. Thea was talking to him. She reached over and tugged gently on the French cuff of his shirtsleeve. "Sir, are you alright? You look as if you've seen a ghost."

One of these days I'm going to laugh about that time Mom was about twenty-years younger than me and called me "Sir." I just know I am. Well, maybe. Of course, she would call me "Sir." I'm old enough to be her father. Okay, stop that whole othertyme Conundrum thing, it's going to drive you crazy—or crazier—as the case may be.

"Yes, Mademoiselle. I am so very sorry. I'm not usually this clumsy. I'll go get a broom and pan and get this cleaned up. Oh, and I'll get you another bottle of champagne." *Well, there's a lie,* Tal told himself. *First, there ain't another comparable bottle on the premises and second, there's no way I have the money to replace that one. It's okay, Tal, you're merely making an excuse to get out of here so you can regroup.* "I'll be right back," he said as he stepped through the privacy curtain and headed for the nearest column, which he promptly leaned against to make sure he didn't unexpectedly crater again.

What have I just done, he asked himself. *Did I further Amarantos's purpose in sending me here? Did I thwart it? How* am I supposed to know the difference?

Thank goodness the maître d' told me I had to hang out here, I couldn't do anything else right now anyway. Suck it up, Tal, he admonished himself. Amarantos sent you here, there must be an important reason. Stop gasping for air, you'll hyperventilate. Slow things down so you can think. Deep breaths, take deep breaths. Better. Much better.

Review the known data. It's 1996—the year I'm born—only about three months before my actual birth date. So, that's clearly me cooking in the oven. Nothing new there. I knew Mom hadn't ever been married before she and Pell got hitched. What I didn't know was that Mom's boyfriend was Myrddin and that he had intended on asking her to marry him.

What did Myrddin say about his final othertyme trip the last time I saw him? We were in the Ladies' Bathroom. He was no longer the Traveler because I had taken his place as the Stytch. He said he'd been in othertyme for over three years, which was an unusually long period of time. He also said his trip had been abruptly terminated. There's something else, Tal. He said something else important. His brain began sorting the short-term archives. What was it? Bingo! Myrddin said he hadn't realized it was me who was the new Traveler.

Oh shit! This is all on me. To help Baba Yaga I used my last wish and asked to be **the** Taliesin. That choice resulted in Myrddin being relieved of that role and caused the precipitous termination of his final othertyme trip. Which then left my pregnant mother abandoned and broken hearted. It also resulted in her spending my early years scratching and clawing as a single mother to barely eke out a living for the two of us.

No time for a pity party, Tal, he reminded himself. Your decision also resulted in she and Pell meeting by chance in a coffee shop a few years down the road from right now. Which allowed them to fall in love, get married, and bring your two little twin brothers into the world. And if it hadn't been for Pell's work, we would never have ended up in Nemeton and I never would have gone to Hunts School. Tal stopped himself just as the endless permutations of the "chicken or the egg" paradox threatened to overwhelm Central Processing. I can't believe I ever seriously questioned what difference one person can make.

He stuck his hands in his front pockets, hoping Billy kept some Tylenol handy. There was absolutely nothing in his left pocket, not even a piece of lint. He rummaged quickly in his right pocket, before making contact with a small, rectangular scrap of paper.

What the hell, he thought, as he pulled it out and unwadded it. It's the business card Myrddin gave me. It's here, in my work pants pocket. Why? Why would it be the only object sent othertyme with me?

Tal solved that softball immediately. It's the reason I'm here. The note triggers Myrddin's departure. Which results in my mom being left completely alone, right when she needed him the most. Or does it? Maybe the purpose of the note is to tell Myrddin his othertyme is about to end, so he can make a proper goodbye to her.

Analysis interrupted once more. Apologies to the NonClear Reaction portion of our brain, wherever that is, and I hate to be a bother, but Tal, you might want to take a beat to recognize the white elephant in the china shop. That's not even a real metaphor. Doesn't really matter, Analysis replied. I just needed to distract you long enough for the thermonuclear conclusion you've been subconsciously suppressing to be allowed to erupt. If you'll just take about one more beat...

Taking Analysis's suggestion, Tal took one more beat. And then a couple more. What? What is so important that I should have recognized it immediately?

OH, HOLY CRAP! CRAP! CRAP! CRAP! This means that Myrddin is my—

CHAPTER NONAGINTA OCTO

Ten yards. Thirty feet. You have to get right up on him to make sure. It would only take him a quick turn of the wrist to be inside the doorway.

CHAPTER NONAGINTA NOVEM

My father? Warring thoughts commenced fire.

He should have told me.

He didn't know.

Mom should have told me who my father was.

Right. She should have told her minor child she got knocked up by some time-traveling wizard who ran off and left her when she was super pregnant.

Well, when you put it like that. Besides, what did she even know about his backstory?

Right. What did she know?

Looking at them tonight one thing is clear. She knows Myrddin loves her very much. I think she's also going to know that if he could possibly have chosen to stay with her, that he would have.

How could she possibly end up knowing the last part?

There's only one way she could know. He would have to have told her.

Correct. He's been at the Traveler gig long enough to know there is only one Traveler at a time. Which means he'll know he's being retired effective immediately. Back to now. How is he going to find out he only has a couple of minutes to make a decision and to tell Thea whatever he wants her to know?

He won't. It will be a complete surprise to him, unless… unless you tell him, Tal.

How? It's not like we're pals and I can ask him if he wants to step outside for a drag.

True.

She's sitting right there. I can't let her know I'm her as yet unborn son. How do I warn my not quite yet father, moments before he's about to ask my mother to marry him, he only has a couple of minutes to make what will be a life-altering decision? Hello? I'm sorry Inner Voice, were we done with our conversation? If not, it's time for a response.

Sorry. I was processing. Simply do what he asked you to do the last time you saw him. Give him the business card.

Of course. Why didn't I think of that?

Well, you really kind of just did.

I don't want to do it to him. To either of them. He's clearly in love with Mom and she's obviously gaga about him, too.

You're not doing anything to anyone, Tal. You're simply presenting him with a choice. It is up to him to decide whether to stay or go.

I see what you're doing. You're making this situation analogous to what he said about the "EXIT ONLY" sign on the door in the Ladies' Restroom.

Exactly. It's why he said those words to you. To prepare you for this moment. Plus, it's not like he hasn't already made the choice. You've had a conversation with him about this sequence of events.

Please don't start that again, Tal begged himself. We've already ascertained there's no Tylenol available. Let's get to the nuts and bolts. How do I get the card to him?

Tell him there's no more Dom. Give him a wine list and tell him to pick out whatever he wants. On the house. Slip the business card into the wine list.

Great idea.

A few minutes later, safely ensconced in the kitchen broom closet, Tal had time during his translation back to realtyme to think about the look on Myrddin's face when he saw the business card inside the wine list. It had been an unusual progression of sudden   realization…staggering   loss…long   overdue   self-forgiveness, all of which finally metamorphosized into a beatific grin reflecting the ineffable redemptive power of True Love.

CHAPTER CENTUM

Oh shit! I'm not going to be able to hit the breaks before impact. Sorry in advance, Quint. No, really. Terribly sorry.

CHAPTER CENTUM UNUS

"DAMMIT!"

That was all Tal could get out as some heavy-ass cannonball hit him in the middle of his thoracic vertebrae, propelling him through the open doorway and into the Ladies' Room. Where he landed spread-eagled, his jaw jammed into the tile floor. With the cannonball laying atop his back.

Thank goodness Sol believes in keeping clean bathrooms at his fake gas station, was Tal's first thought. His second was cannonballs don't typically squirm and moan. Not that he'd had much firsthand experience with cannonballs. "Who the hell clipped me?" he yelled. "I'm calling a flagrant foul which is going to result in ejection. As soon as you get off me and I can get up."

"Sorry. Sorry," came the mumbled response, together with some frenzied extricational movement.

"Notos?" Tal asked in disbelief, as he freed himself from being the bottom pancake in a human short stack. "What the hell are you doing here?" Which was immediately followed by, "Why are you blindside tackling me?"

"I said I was sorry," Notos replied. His tone indicated he was rapidly getting over the entire being sorry phase, and was now moving to the offensive—becoming a little more offensive with each sentence—phase. "The real question is what in Five-Hells are you doing here? Our Journeys are over. The Coronation Ceremony is in less than forty-eight hours. Why? Why in Five-

Hells are you going through the Gas Station Crossing to Earth Realm?"

Tal started to explain. "It's kind of a long story…"

Notos cut him off. "You can tell it to me back on Hunts School turf." Notos grabbed Tal and turned them both around until they were facing the back wall. The back wall that usually held a door, or an aperture of some nature for ingress and egress.

The back wall that was currently a backdrop for a festive going away party. There was a huge multicolored banner that arched up and across the entire wall that spelled out, "BON VOYAGE, QUINT!" A long table was festooned with helium balloons, noisemakers, and little obnoxious totally a waste of money pointy hats. There was a large white sheet cake centered on the table, with red icing-lettering, "Worlds Depend Upon You." Next to the cake was a punchbowl. It looked like a gilt-edged Venetian glass bowl, the kind they make on the island of Murano. The bowl, complete with ladle, was full of red punch, garnished with sliced oranges, raspberries, and a few mint leaves.

Confetti began spewing from a non-existent confetti making machine. Numerous best wishes were scrawled in marker across the wall's surface. Even though the penmanship was atrocious, as in worse than the stereotypical doctor's indecipherable handwriting, Tal could read the inscriptions from several feet away. One signed by Gas Pump No. Unus read, "Read the cake." A second, authored by Gas Pump Duo read, "First, dust yourself off a little." Having been brought up to respect his elders, even if they were inanimate objects, Tal brushed himself off a little before reading the next inscription. "D-d-don't s-s-screw this-s-s up." That one wasn't signed but he'd know that smart mouthed Air Hose's handiwork anywhere. The final writing merely said, "Wash your hands, and please turn the light off on your way out. Thank you, The Ladies' Room."

"Umm…human…care to explain what this ridiculousness is about?" Notos asked, waving his arms all around. "Oh, and please include a precise description of the location of the back door so we can get out of here."

Tal responded nonverbally by gentling grabbing Notos's shoulders and turning both he and his teammate around until they were now facing the front door. The vivid red neon sign was still there. It still read, "EXIT ONLY." The only difference was that it was now stuttering. Like the ballast was going out, or it was low on neon. "Do you see a sign?"

"Of course," Notos replied crossly.

"When you read the sign, what does it say?"

" 'EXIT ONLY.' Why?"

"I was hoping that might only apply to me," Tal replied.

"Okay, Fifth Prime, I'm totally lost and I really don't like that feeling so I guess you'd better fill me in on what in all the known Realms is going on in this bathroom."

Tal gripped Noto's left elbow and pointed over to the quaint little seating area. "We might as well sit. This is going to take awhile. Would you like some cake and punch?"

'NO, I WOULDN'T LIKE ANY CAKE OR..."

"Myrddin is my father," Tal interrupted, in a calm, measured voice.

Many times during Tal's youth, he'd played Star Trek after school with the neighborhood kids. Of course none of them had ever volunteered to be tagged as the security guy with a red shirt. They normally stuck the new kids with the high mortality rate gigs. There was a kid who moved to town for only about a year. Gregorious Hopkins. Small kid, big name. His parents were like Welsh-Russian or something. Kid was a freaking genius. Never forgot anything he ever learned. Anyway, whenever that day's late afternoon peace mission failed and the inevitable intergalactic war broke loose, everyone always wanted to be the first kid to shoot G-Hop, because he held the title of "Best Face Ever When Shot By A Phaser Set To Stun." He was undefeated through a hundred campaigns. Until now, Tal decided. Notos just claimed the title belt from the former champ.

After another couple of moments the phaser blast wore off enough for Notos to speak. "Why yes, thank you," Notos replied in a subdued voice. "Just a small piece of cake though. I had a late dinner."

CHAPTER CENTUM DUO

Two generous portions of cake...each, with three glasses of punch...each, later, the teammates both sat back in their comfy armchairs. Tal had summarized everything, beginning with the Moai on Easter Island, Portunus's shop, the Journey to Earth Realm to retrieve the Taleria, his interaction with Väst, his decision to free Emet, and his subsequent visit with Helblad.

"Okay, human, I think it's time you told me why we're here. What's so important you've risked Omada's chances to become the Ruling Council?"

"Helblad told me there is a ploutonion at Arianrhod."

As Tal watched, Noto's chronically wan face became substantially more pallid. For once it didn't seem like it was because the Omada Second Prime was angry at Tal. It seemed almost as if Notos was scared. Which couldn't even be possible. Could it? "Five-Hells? Quint why would a human voluntarily want to go to Five- Hells?"

"Because Väst told me something my own teammates were too selfish to tell me," Tal replied curtly.

A flush of anger returned Notos's face to its regular cemetery white as his upper lip retreated into a take no prisoners snarl. It was a sufficient harbinger of the threat of immediate violence that Tal involuntarily recoiled into his chair. "She is the enemy, Fifth Prime. It is well-established she has tried to kill you on at least one occasion. You assured all of us you would have no further interaction with her. Yet now, now when we are closer to winning this Tyrning than at any previous point, you are fraternizing again? Please, please tell me all-knowing Dust Child, what great secret has the she-devil imparted to you that your loyal teammates conspired to withhold from you."

Being mocked by Notos was enough of a regular traffic pattern that Tal's flight response was quickly cancelled. Amygdala initially sent Embarrassment to replace Fear but after a couple of beats benched it and sent Righteous Anger up to bat. "There's no need to play dumb, Notos. I realize Emet's life isn't as important to any of you as being in charge of the universe for the next three hundred years."

Somehow Notos's nose, mouth and eyes formed a blank. "I have absolutely no idea what you're talking about."

"Right, sure. Like I'm supposed to swallow that. You're the damn team Parliamentarian and you're going to sit there and deny to my face that the Hunts Rules permit anyone to sub in for a previous bloodpryce equivalyn..." The look of disbelief on Notos's face stopped Tal cold. It proved the lie. It proved Väst had lied. "There is no substitution rule?" he asked rhetorically.

"Nope, you've been had," Notos confirmed. "You dumbass," he then added, because he was Notos.

CHAPTER CENTUM TRES

There are many infamous traitors recorded in the annals of history. Marcus Brutus, Ephialtes of Traxis, Vidkun Quisling, Dona Marina, Mir Jafar, and of course, Arnold "Eggs" Benedict. Eggs had been Tal's bestie since pre-k. One day in second grade, when Tal was wearing khaki shorts and both he and Eggs were in the washroom, Eggs intentionally splashed water all over Tal's crotch. When they got back to class, Eggs told Ms. Myers, in front of the entire class, that Tal had wet his pants. All because Eggs was jealous that Mabel Sharlee Brannigan had asked Tal to walk out with her on the playground at lunch that day.

Mabel Sharlee never again asked Tal to walk out with her. Ever. Tal never uttered another word to Eggs. Ever. Tal never wore khaki shorts or trousers again. Never. Ever.

It's time, Tal decided, to pencil in the latest addition to history's rogue's gallery of traitors—Väst of Släkt.

CHAPTER CENTUM QUATTUOR

Tal slumped into the chair, every muscle group defeated by the breadth of Väst's betrayal. "But why, Notos? I mean we were all naked and well, you know, and she told me she loved me, and because she loved me she had to tell me…"

"The 'why' is easy, Quint. To help her team win the Tyrning. Every time this year that it looked like Släkt might win, it was always you that somehow pulled the rabbit out of the hat. She had the necessary weaponry to take you off the board and she used it. It clearly didn't bother her that both you and Emet might end up trapped in Five-Hells for all eternity."

"That fucking bitch. Up until now she's only tried to kill me. Now she's trying to send me to hell." You gotta draw a line in the sand somewhere, Tal decided.

"Five-Hells to be precise," Notos said in agreement. "You dumbass," he added. Because he was Notos. "The only reason I'm not beating the snot out of you right now is because you've doing an excellent job of doing it to yourself."

"What do we do now?" Tal asked, as the entire undergirding of his plan had just been blown to smithereens.

"We need a new plan," Notos replied. "First we have to nail down a few things. I'm going to try to keep my cool because me having an aneurism at this point isn't going to help anybody. I fully intend, however, to kick your stupid ass from here to kingdom come once we get everything settled out. Capisci?"

"Capisco," Tal replied.

"Buono." Notos turned around in his chair, then back to the front door, before continuing. "After looking at all the swell going away decorations, the nonexistence of a back door, and the 'EXIT ONLY' neon sign on the front door, am I correct in concluding we're not going back to Hunts School through the Gas Station?"

"You are," Tal replied.

"I'm not sure that one ass-kicking is going to be sufficient," Notos said, his voice beginning to rise.

"I'd like to remind you that you didn't want to chance an aneurism…"

"Shut it!" Notos barked. "Unless at least one of us makes it back to Hunts School, it won't matter what treasyre Omada has. One of the other teams will win and possible Archon Nord will get to wreak havoc throughout the known universe for the next three hundred years."

"I know three squad members isn't sufficient, Notos," Tal admitted. "But I never planned on you being along for the ride. Even with me gone, Omada would have four and Borras would be Archon. I figured whatever route I took to Five-Hells that Emet could walk it in reverse and get to live out his life on Earth plane proper." Tired of taking punches, Tal added, "For the record, I'm not the one that tackled us both into the Ladies' Room…"

"For the record, that's not a winning argument," Notos replied, as he stood up. "Doesn't matter. We don't have the luxury right now of addressing how badly or in how many different ways you may have cost Borras his chance to be Archon."

Okay, that one hurt, Tal thought.

Notos began pacing around the seating area. "The Gas Station portal will be closed to us. You have no magyk and mine won't help us jumpstart any omphalos located on Earth Realm."

Notos stopped pacing and took a moment for a really big sigh. Then another. Followed by a half-dozen more.

CHAPTER CENTUM QUINQUE

Now I'm the one lying to him. Or at least not telling him the entire truth. But it's different, I'm not doing it to him voluntarily. I'm stuck in this human form until I return to Five-Hells. The specifics of my binding with my father prevent me from telling Quint or anyone else who I am, what I can do, and most importantly, why I came to Hunts School.

Quint has taught us to think our way around problems. He calls it "turning the Rubik's cube." Maybe there's something going on with the girl we don't know about. Maybe she's not acting voluntarily either.

I mean Quint is the kind of guy that girls go all sappy over. She's got to be into him. Leave that lay, Notos, you have a bigger problem to solve.

If Quint steps across the threshold into Five-Hells, he and Emet are going to be stuck there forever. No way Veles is letting either of them go. He'll think it's enormously funny someone could be so stupid they would try to sacrifice themselves to save another person.

As it stands, neither one of us has a mechanism to effect our return to campus. Quint is the new Traveler but I don't think that an othertyme trip can solve our present problem. Even if Amarantos sent him on one.

The Unfading Spirit. Borras is always reminding us that we are supposed to win by Seeking the Center. If it's true for the Hunts, it must also be true for all of the rest of our endeavors.

Omada has to have four to remain in the competition. Which means at a minimum either Quint or I have to get back to Hunts School. As it stands, if I don't make it back the search is over for the key words to free my mother and she and her companions will be trapped until the end of time. Sentient but frozen, unable to move. It's way worse than Five-Hells.

Quint is smart as hell. I know I've been rough on him but he has screwed up monumentally. He's come through monumentally as well, Notos reminded himself. He has an exceptionally quick mind. If I could tell him my problem, he could probably solve it. If not in the next couple of days, then if Omada wins, most certainly in however long he lives of the three hundred years that Borras is Archon.

How, though? How can I fix this so Quint has time to figure out how to resolve my problem? What can I do?

There is only one thing, in all of the known Realms Veles might bargain for in exchange for both Quint and Emet.

CHAPTER CENTUM SEX

"Notos?" he asked worriedly. "Yo, Mr. Catatonic, are you still with me?" Tal watched as Notos shook himself before answering.

"Problem solved," Notos announced. "There is only one option that has even the slightest prospect of returning Omada to the minimum number required to stay in the competition."

'Minimum number?' Tal wondered. Seems kind of odd phrasing. Of course Notos is more than a little odd.

"How were you planning on getting to Five-Hells?"

"Through the Arianrhod ploutonion," Tal replied.

"That's what I figured. Okay, human, how in Five-Hells were you planning on getting from this bathroom to Luna's demesne?"

"That's the easy part," Tal replied. "Through a junkyard."

CHAPTER CENTUM SEPTEM

"Aine, thank Amarantos, you've returned."

"Where? What happened?" she whispered. "How long, Alberich, how…"

"Ssh! Not a word, you're too weak," the Archon of the known universe told his spouse. He repositioned her in the chair a little before materializing his wand. He began at her feet, focusing every ounce of his available lyfeforce to repair her. He slowly worked his way up her entire body, finishing with the top of her head.

It's not possible, he told himself. She's been away from her body for days. Who could possibly marshal the magyk to keep her alive? Why? Why would they do this to her? It had been everything Alberich could do not to let their daughter know what had happened to her mother. He couldn't though. The Hunts Rules. It didn't matter the personal cost, he wasn't a dictator. It was not his place to interfere with the choices freely made by all of the Hunts contestants. Or anyone else for that matter.

He gazed at his consort, his partner in every sense of the word. She'd fallen asleep. He waved his wand once, just to double-check. No, she was home and she was safe. It would take a few days, even with his magyk, before she would be even a semblance of her old self.

He was spent himself, he realized, as he pulled up a chair right next to hers. The next few days transitioning are going to be hectic and will require me to be completely recharged.

The end of our three hundred year reign. Thank you, Amarantos. It has been such a gyft and we have tried to be your faithful stewards every day. Thank you for our lives and for the thousands of blessings you've bestowed upon us. Thank you for bringing Aine back to me. Please watch over our daughter and keep her safe. The next few days may prove to be exceptionally dangerous.

CHAPTER HUNDRED EIGHT

Tal followed Notos out the bathroom door. The door probably didn't close any differently than normal, but Tal could swear it felt like the door slammed shut with an air of finality. Of course he also thought he heard the sound of about twelve different locks being thrown and a drop bar being engaged. Okay, did that really happen? Doesn't matter, he decided. One door closes...

Walking toward the gate he thought back to his first impression of the junkyard fence. Had it really only been a little more than six months ago? The sharpened tips of the seven-foot tall, rusted wrought-iron risers still looked like spear points. The padlocked gate still wore its zip-tied large hand-lettered sign.

LUNA'S TIMELESS TREASYRES
KEEP OUT! DON'T COME IN HERE! I'M NOT KIDDING!
TRESPASSYRS WILL BE ~~DRAWN AND QUARTERED~~
~~DISEMBOWELED~~ SLAYN!

He'd arrogantly ascribed the odd spelling with extra "y"s to rustic ignorance. Turned out he'd been the ignorant one. He still wasn't sure what was up with "Slayn." It undoubtedly meant some particularly hideous form of magykal death.

Notos walked up beside Tal, reached forward and tugged at the lock. "Magyked. There's not any Folk strong enough to undo a Principe's magyk. No way we're popping that lock."

They both stepped closer to peer through the space between two of the uprights. "Same as before," Tal remarked. "Junked cars and refrigerators. Never ending crap piles."

"It's an illusion," Notos replied. "Has to be. The Elder Children do not commerce in human leftovers."

"I'm really sorry," Tal replied, as they stood there peering through the fence. "I was counting on punching a one-way ticket only for myself."

Tal's experience was that a Notos smile was even more rare than a blood moon eclipse, but there it was. "There are absolutely so many things wrong with your assumption, human. There's no need to go into how many different ways your plan is idiotic. One will suffice. There are various means by which persons may enter Five-Hells but unless you're Five-Hells royalty there are only two ways out. One way is if Veles opens the Gate of Anguish and the second, well, no one has made it back that way for centuries. The bottom line of this lesson, Quint, is that it doesn't matter if you're a regular run of the mill dumbass or a noble dumbass, you're still a dumbass."

"Okay," Tal replied. "I'm pretty sure I'm not supposed to say 'thank you' to that last comment, so let's just move on. On the positive side, one of the ways into Five-Hells is through the hellmouth located at Arianrhod?" Tal asked.

"That is correct," Notos confirmed.

"Our only choice then is to go through the junkyard, find Luna, and try to convince her to take us to Arianrhod."

CHAPTER HUNDRED NINE

After they both clambered to the top of the extremely mean and pointy fence spears, Tal watched as Notos dropped first. We have to be every bit of ten feet up in the air and he landed like a cat. Sometimes I'd swear he's not human, Tal thought. Well, he's not. He's Folk, but I know what I meant…focus, Tal, he told himself. Ten feet is enough to do some serious damage to your bony ass.

Although not the least bit gracefully, Tal successfully lowered himself a couple of feet before negotiating a tuck and roll. The instant his feet touched the ground his ass-brand erupted with scorching heat. From the moment when he'd first been branded, pain had radiated nonstop from the Nyx symbol but its regular pain level had become part of Tal's white noise of simply existing. Part of the human condition, Tal thought. The unbearable somehow becomes bearable so that life can go on.

But this shit right now is ridiculous. It hurts every bit as bad as when Baba Yaga bent me over the sofa and seared me with the branding iron. Maybe worse. His physical distress was sufficient that he was unable to immediately stand up. When he was finally able to stagger to his feet he figured he was about to get one of Notos's patented smartass munedan putdowns. When nothing was forthcoming, Tal first looked at his teammate before turning his gaze to whatever had rendered Notos momentarily mute.

"Holy crap!" Tal exclaimed, albeit in a very hushed tone.

CHAPTER CENTUM DECEM

Gone. All gone.

The seemingly endless sea of carelessly stacked heaps of wrecked Pintos, Tauruses, Gremlins, and Matadors. The klatches of broke down Maytags, Frigidaires, and Whirlpools. Every last scrap of the rusted out metal detritus of humankind.

All of it. Gone.

When the wytch Baba Yaga had been telling Tal about Arianrhod his focus had been more on figuring out how to keep he and his team alive than on the details of her narration about Luna's Earth Realm home. As the pain supernova on his ass cheek began to lessen a little, Tal began to see with his own eyes just how accurate the wytch's description had been.

Moonbeams wider than the boulevards of great cities. Check. Immaculate grounds. Check. No question that if he made it to the lunarium there would be moonflowers so finely sculpted they had the appearance of glazed porcelain. Precheck. And everywhere there was the multi-hued silver light Baba Yaga had described.

The moon shining upon Arianrhod was not the limpid light of ten thousand love poems. It was brim to bursting, quicksilver shimmering, every bit as refulgent as the golden light of Luna's twin brother.

For the first time in Tal's life, silver wasn't an accurate description of silver. He realized there are a seemingly endless number of hues under the big silver tent. Silver would never again be a monolithic one-note shade. From now on he would remember silver is a rainbow. Silver chalice, silver pink, silver sand, sonic silver, old silver, and roman silver. Now enlightened, Tal felt pity for pedestrian colorists who casually denominate silver as only one color of gray.

When Borras had recited the Luna-Munedan-Corcra love triangle story, he'd said Luna began refusing to teach mortals about Amarantos, and she'd hidden her face and dimmed her light as night's liege so that darkness and evil could stake their claims on mortals. Now, now that Tal had seen the full brilliance of Luna's light, he began to understand the enormity of mankind's loss.

"Damn," Notos finally said under his breath.

"Double damn," Tal agreed.

It was at that moment the howling began.

CHAPTER CENTUM UNDECIM

"What the hell?" Notos asked, as he methodically checked from left to right. "I got nothing. Where's the racket coming from?"

Tal looked over his shoulder, to where their escape route back up the fence should be. But wasn't. Somehow they were squarely in the middle of Arianrhod, its landscaping stretching as far as they could see, behind them as well as in front. "Again, double damn," Tal finally responded.

Both the frequency and the volume of the howling—which upon further listen was actually a miscellany of howling, yipping, and yowling—increased. Baba Yaga told me something else important about Arianrhod, Tal reminded himself. I need that info. Central Processing sent an urgent demand down to short-term memory—mission critical information needed. Stat. Memory promptly responded—Rougaru. Baba Yaga said there were Rougaru, also known as "Loup-Garou."

"Oh hell, I forgot," Tal stated matter of factly. "Arianrhod's guards, they call themselves, 'Loup-Garou'."

Notos's stance and face retreated to his usual "angry with the idiot mortal" posture. "Freaking werewolves? Are you kidding me? You didn't think it was important to mention lycanthropes guard the one place in the entire known universe where the moon is always full? You saw what's behind us now. Arianrhod as far as the eye can see. We can't jump the fence back to Earth Realm because there's no fence. Werewolves? Really?"

Before Tal could respond, new sounds were added to the auditory mix. As the new noises continued to swell, so did the variety of werewolf sounds.

"Music?" Notos asked, now with an entirely new category of disbelief. "The werewolves are cranking tunes?"

Tal had to smile, just a little, before he responded. "Not just any tunes, Notos. I do believe the werepack done dialed up 'Boogie Wonderland' by Earth, Wind and Fie–yer."

CHAPTER CENTRUM DUODECIM

Tal stared down the well-manicured silver sward that ran between the immense boughs of Arianrhod's forest. "Great, a new form of death (or worse.) Being rent limb from limb to a thumping bass beat."

"There's no need to panic at the disco, mortal," Notos responded.

"Wait, did you just make a…"

"No," Notos replied curtly.

"Hey, what about your magyk? Even though Arianrhod is anchored to Earth Realm, you're with me. So, Alberich's Bane doesn't apply." When Notos didn't immediately respond, Tal pressed the matter. "C'mon, I'm sure you got some major magyk chops. Let's see you pull a rabbit out of the hat."

Notos stared daggers at Tal. "What is the matter with you? Why would we need a magykal pregnancy test? He took another quick look around, then sniffed the air. "We're upwind. As retreat isn't an option and since they're carousing, now's a good time to try to find the hellmouth."

It only took a few steps for Tal to realize it was a good thing the Loup-garou were caterwauling. Notos moved silently down the path between the trees, as if his substance was shadow not flesh. On the flip side, Tal felt like his sneakification quotient was nigh on to nada. Which, of course, earned him numerous elite level stink eyes from his teammate.

The forest path gave way to a large clearing. In its center was a bonfire. Nestled deep in the cross-hatched logs, the ember bed smoldered silver-blue. On the fire's periphery, the colors were...well, if the moon had lunar flares like the sun has solar flares, then that would be an accurate description of the flickering tongues of an Arianrhod bonfire.

As Gloria Gaynor began stridently confirming she would survive, Tal was desperately wishing he could say the same. After a few seconds of parsing the clearing activity, he glanced at Notos and saw the Omada Second was performing the same sitrep. Borras had trained them well. It was hard to get a precise count, what with all of the cavorting and intertwining, but it seemed like there were several dozen individuals twirling clockwise around the blaze.

The werewolves weren't the least bit Lon Chaneyish. Or Teen Wolfish, either. Tal's initial thought was they looked basically human but then his optics started sending up all of the minute differences between them and humans. Humanoid, yes. Human, definitely not.

Baba Yaga said there were both male and female Rougaru but there were no males in evidence at the bacchanal. Everyone cavorting was most definitely female. Best Tal could tell, they all appeared to be about his height and their bodies were covered with a sheared silver fur. Well, what he could see of their bodies. Everyone was wearing sports bras and either booty shorts or yoga pants. The clothing contained the same logo as the brand on his ass. Which was now throbbing in rhythm to the music. It's like they all shop at the Cult of Nyx equivalent of Lululemon. Of course, Luna would spell it "Lululymoon."

Their sinuous terpsichorean movement appeared part feline and part lupine. Even from several hundred feet away, Tal could see their feet and hands looked like long paws, with talons instead of fingers. Which brought him back around to the whole dying by tearing and rending thing.

He felt Notos tap him on the shoulder, signaling they should step back a little. They retreated maybe twenty feet back into the trees and got low to the ground, with their heads right next to each other.

Notos started the whispered conversation. "Luckily, the wind direction still holds. For now, anyway. I think we should assume the lycanthropy augments all of their senses."

"Agreed," Tal replied. The initial strains of "Dancing Queen" began, the song loud enough they could feel its reverberations through the ground under their feet.

"We know the hellmouth isn't behind us," Tal stated.

"My bet is it's near the manor house."

"Baba Yaga said there was a lunarium," Tal added quickly.

"That's our best bet," Notos announced. "We'll skirt the clearing, hope the party keeps rocking, and once we're on the other side, resume course dead ahead."

"I'm good with that," Tal replied.

Just as he started rising to a crouch, Tal heard the screech of a stylus sliding across a now ruined vintage record. "Holy shit," he whispered. "The weres have a turntable. They're spinning real vinyl." After the screeching echo of the needle scratch there was total silence.

"Damn," Notos added. "The wind changed and we're downwind now. Quick! We have to get a move on."

Substantial growling in surround sound advised the teammates the "get a move on" option was no longer an available selection. Another anxious heartbeat and they were able to visually confirm they were completely encircled by fang and claw.

CHAPTER CENTUM TREDECIM

There were several dozens of the weres but three of them were standing several paces in front of the remainder. "Well, I didn't know we were having barbeque," the center one said. "Did you Billie Jo?"

"No, I never did, Bobbie Jo," the one to Bobbie Jo's left, replied. She looked across Bobbie Joe to address the third of the triumvirate. "You, Betty Jo?"

"Well, I hadn't realized it until right about now but we must have forgot it's potluck night," Betty Jo responded. "I see what I'm bringing."

Wait, what? Tal said to himself. Those names, those names are from…Petticoat Junction. Maybe I can ease some tension. "Hey, so we just got off the Hooterville Cannonball down at the station house. Where's Uncle Joe? I hear he's been moving kind of slow," Tal quipped, as he chuckled to prime their laugh pumps.

"What the hell is that supposed to mean?" Bobbie Jo growled.

Write it down in your diary, Tal. If you survive today and ever buy a diary. Loup-garou most decidedly do not have a sense of humor. Also write down there are simply way to many Folk and Creatures that seem to want to eat me.

"They is trespassers," Billie Jo added, growling a little deeper than her sister.

"They is trespassers making fun of us," Bettie Jo stated, growling deepest of all three.

"Lady give us permission to do what we will with all trespassers," Bobbie Jo declared. "What says the Meute?"

"Eat them!" "Eat them!" "Eat them!" came the resounding chorus.

The three ringleaders walked right up to Tal and Notos and began sniffing them, starting with their crotches.

"Hey, shoo! Shoo!" Tal said, making the accompanying hand gesture.

Billie Jo lingered, smelling Tal's hip extra long. "Something's not right, Bobbie Jo. This one smells like a human. But he smells like he's already been cooked."

"A human? Here?" Bobbie Jo asked in disbelief.

"Smell for yourself," Billie Jo added.

Bobbie Jo took her up on it and began to sniff Tal all over, including what seemed like forever in his crotch and his ass. "You're right," Bobbie Jo concurred. "Bettie Jo, you want a sniff?"

"No, thanks," Bettie Jo replied. "But y'all better come smell this one. He smells like he's already gone bad."

Tal watched as Notos remained totally impassive and silent as they smelled him all up and down and in between.

"There's something wrong about both of them," Bobbie Jo agreed. "Let's cook them anyway and we can see if they're edible after."

Anything, Tal. Absolutely anything. "Um, I can do every single dance from 'Saturday Night Fever.' And the hustle," he added.

"Eat them!" "Eat them!" "Eat them!" came the even more resounding chorus.

"Notos," Tal whispered. "I got nothin'. Is there anything you can do to get us out of this mess?"

CHAPTER CENTUM QUATTUORDECIM

I could easily stop them, Notos thought to himself. Except the contract I bound with Veles won't permit me to use my magyk to do anything that might reveal I am the Crown Prince of Five-Hells. The only time in the last hundred years I could use it at all was that first time we were all together on Earth Realm. In Quint's bedroom, when he and his family were being threatened by the Crestfallyn. Wait a minute. Why? Why then?

It suddenly came to him. Because the only conversation that was had was about sleepmagyk. It's a common form of magyk. I used a minimal amount on Quint's parents. Casting that spell didn't in any manner indicate I had royal-level magyk, particularly not deathmagyk.

Quickly, he told himself. What has to happen to recreate that situation without there being any indicia of the strength of my magyk? Got it. I'll knock us all out, including myself. If I hit Quint the least, he'll wake up first and think he's helping me wake up. I'll whammy the weres a lot more, enough to allow us a few minutes to escape.

Now! He commanded, feeling his magyk flow out and through the entire group.

CHAPTER CENTUM QUINDECIM

Central Processing was pretty much shut down. The largest portion of higher processing functions would be unavailable until the red light of Unconscious gave way to the yellow of Subconscious. There was barely enough processing to even recognize it was still a long haul from the yellow caution light to the green "go" light of Conscious. Right now, Subconscious was trying to find the word to complete the following sentence, "Damn! I feel _____ as hell." It kept turning Tal's lexicon Rubik's cube, searching, searching, for the word.

For some reason, Subconscious was lost in the weeds of Mount Vernon. That's right, George Washington's Mount Vernon. Yeah, but discard the George Washington arc. It's not relevant. Turn the cube. Mount? No, mountains as a geographical feature are also a dead end. Turn the cube. Vernon? Yes, that is a partial match.

Hmm. "I feel Vernon as hell?" Nope, keep turning. Well, George named Mount Vernon after a famous British naval officer, Admiral Edward Vernon. That's it, now we're creeping toward the green light. What about him? He first became famous because he always wore outer coats made of a heavy ribbed fabric, grosgrain. Grosgrain is a derivative or bastardization of the French word, 'grogam.' That's it. Getting warm, let Conscious know green light initiation is imminent.

It was Vernon's outerwear that caused his sailors to nickname him, "Old Grog." Nailed it. Only one last connecting concept to correctly align. Bingo! Vernon was the naval officer who first ordered that all of his sailors' daily rum rations were required to be heavily cut with water. To keep the sailors from getting knee-walking sea-legged. Central Processing immediately pressed the button to engage the solenoid of nerves responsible for waking up.

"Damn!" Tal exclaimed. "I feel groggy as hell."

CHAPTER CENTUM SEDECIM

Tal shook his head a couple of times trying to clear the unusually sticky cobwebs. No need asking, he decided. I'm sure Luna has zero Tylenol in Arianrhod. What happened? Whatever it was it zapped every one of us.

"Shit!" he exclaimed louder than he probably should have. This is our chance to get away from the weres. Never look a gift coma in the mouth. I'm sure that's a saying on some Realm.

"Notos," he whispered, as he shook his teammate. Nothing. "Notos," he whispered somewhat more urgently, while shaking him somewhat more urgently.

"Ugggh," Notos muttered. "What the hell happened? I feel...I feel..."

Tal finished for him. "Groggy, you idiot. That's how you feel. Come on. Whatever happened, this is our chance to get out of here."

Notos slowly looked around before leaping to his feet.

Damn, Tal thought. That's a quick recovery. "Plan?"

"Sprint your ass off toward the main building. As soon as we see the lunarium, head for it," Notos replied, by then already four steps ahead of Tal.

CHAPTER CENTUM SEPTENDECIM

They were only several hundred yards away from the lunarium when she arrived. And man, did she know how to make an entrance.

Either Luna stole Glinda's entry sequence from the Wizard of Oz, or the scriptwriters somehow met a Principe. Either way, it was impressive as hell.

Tal watched spellbound as a translucent silver sphere floated groundward until it kissed the grass several arm lengths in front of he and Notos. As the sphere dissipated, Luna stepped forth, flowing toward them like the quicksilver of a full moon's beam.

Words. Central Processing was generating lots and lots of words but they were all jumbled together, bumping into each other in their lame efforts to adequately descriptivize a Principe. Pale. Radiant. Patrician. Glorious. Mythical. Captivating. Subzero. Regal. Steel. Elvish.

Wait, what? Like Arthrys and the Alfar? Little bit. More like Arwen in "Lord of the Rings." Except with regular ears. Luna was dressed to the nines, like every day in Arianrhod was black-tie optional. Without the optional.

The Lady Aurora had spoken to Tal telepathically when she'd appeared to him in her rainbow avatar form. Tal realized now she'd been showing him a significant kindness, to keep his human senses from being overloaded. The same probably held true for Sol, with him choosing only to present as his Gas Station avatar.

Luna clearly wasn't concerned about frying all of Tal's mortal circuit boards. As all the spinning words slowed, became more coherent, an inescapable conclusion punched him right in the face.

In every possible respect, the Principes were as far above mankind as were all of the gods and goddesses from hundreds of different Earth cultures. Hell, why shouldn't they be? The Principes were the gods and goddesses of many of the oldest stories of the Children of the Divine Spark. Luna, by appearing in this form, was making sure Tal and Notos understood they were barely even insects to her.

Damn, Tal suddenly realized. This is what Luna looked like centuries ago when Myrddin first saw her. Before she broke up he and Princess Corcra. This person is the single most important factor in him asking to become Amarantos's Stytch in Tyme. Now that I think about it, probably better steer clear of any family tree discussions.

CHAPTER CENTUM DUODEVIGINTI

"Your lives are forfeit."

Welp, we're back to that whole my life being forfeit pattern, was Tal's first thought. I guess I should be grateful this is the first time this term that particular topic has come up. Oh, and that the (or worse) option isn't on the table. Yet.

"Uninvited to my Sanctuary you have come, sullying its perfection with your presence."

Luna has the slightest hint of an overbite lisp. The superhot kind, like Bernadette Peters. More specifically like Bernadette Peters in the movie, "Pennies From Heaven."

She turned her gaze to Notos. It was then Tal noticed her eyes were entirely silver, except for tiny crescent moon shaped pupils. "You, Prince, have additionally committed multiple counts of felony assault by magyk against my subjects." With that she waved a wand over her head and Tal heard the formerly napping weres commence howling and hauling ass toward them.

If Tal hadn't been totally overwhelmed, he would have first wondered where the wand came from. Then, second, hopefully he would have been smart enough to keep his mouth shut.

He was. Overwhelmed. So, he wasn't. Smart enough to keep his mouth shut. "Now see here, Ms. Know It All Principe, er, Ma'am. We needed to speak to you and didn't have your contact info, so, yes, we did. We totally jumped your fence.

Which by the way could use a little maintenance and you'd better make sure your premises liability insurance is all paid up, but…" Audio playback was completed at that moment. "Wait? Did you say, 'Prince'?" Tal asked, turning to stare at his teammate.

"Quint, I,…Quint…"

Laughter devoid of mirth interrupted the Omada Second Prime's attempt to explain. Not devoid of mirth, Tal decided. Laughter from which joy had been surgically removed. "Silence!" Luna commanded.

Tal tried to move his lips and he couldn't. He looked over at Notos. His teammate was doing his best with only his eyes to communicate something. What? It wasn't the normal "if you don't shut up right now I'm going to kill you myself" Notos look. It was different. His eyes were begging Tal to stop making things worse. Okay, if Notos is begging me, we're in truly desperate straits.

Luna, who it was becoming apparent with every passing second, was not the least bit Glinda-esque, waved her wand over and around Notos. "Ah, a binding. It's quite cleverly crafted as well. Veles did always like playing games. I see he's gotten much better at it." Again, there was the short bone-chilling laugh. "Well, I'm not going to interfere with that little exercise. But just to make sure you play by the rules," she said, before moving her wand left to right. As the wand moved, silvered stitches wove themselves from left to right across the width of Notos's mouth.

Damn, that's got to hurt, Tal thought, as he watched his teammate struggle.

It's your turn," she announced, as she turned her silvered gaze toward Tal and waved her wand over and around him. Suddenly, the silver leached from Luna's face, leaving her shock-white.

And then she began a scream. Not screaming. One singular scream that began softly, shrilly but still softly. It was enough to silence the werewolves, who now surrounded the two teammates. It continued well past when human, probably even Folk, would have had to draw breath. It kept going until the glass in the manor house windows exploded inward, and still it didn't stop. Tal could see that even the mortar between the bricks of the mansion was beginning to crumble and flake away. Luna was nowhere near done, perhaps the most primal of primal screams every voiced continued until it finally, it finally turned into, it became words.

"NO!
IT CANNOT…
YOU CANNOT…
IT'S NOT POSSIBLE!"

CHAPTER CENTUM UNDEVIGINTI

There was silence, except for large gasping. Everyone, Tal included, was falling over, doing whatever they could to find oxygen. Notos was having the hardest time because he could only breathe through his nose. Tal could breathe normally, he wasn't paralyzed. That wasn't the problem.

The air was impotent. It was as if Luna had vacuumed up every molecule of free oxygen in Arianrhod. Other than everyone choking out, it was eerily quiet. As if Arianrhod was afraid of its own Mistress.

Luna waved her wand once over her shoulders and the windows were good as new. The second wave restored the integrity of the manor house exoskeleton. Finally, with a delayed third wave, Luna restored the breath of life to the barren air. We were last, Tal thought. Even her weregirls. All of us, our continued existence, meant less to her than having her windows replaced.

"You," she barked, pointing her wand directly at Tal. "You may now speak. What is your psuche name?"

More than a little scared, Tal shook his head from side to side. He couldn't comply. The Hunts School binding would not allow him to say his true name until the Hunts winner was announced. Luna was angrier than he'd ever seen anybody be angry.

"Right. Asinine rules of an imbecilic organization. I'll just take the information I want." She stretched her right arm, the one holding the wand, out toward Tal. A silver beam erupted from its tip, crossing the space between them before physically striking Tal in the forehead.

"Son of a bitch," he exclaimed.

The beam continued drilling. Central Processing reported the chain of command had been disrupted and all kinds of "eyes only" confidential information was being copied to an off-site location.

"It's true, then. You are his bastard whelp." She laughed. Again, it was that kind of fey to gangrenous flecked laugh.

As the silver in the beam brightened, her expression turned grim. "And you, you are guilty of the murder of my handpicked leader of my Cult of Nyx."

Tal knew he should keep quiet, he knew he should hope for the Principe's anger to run of out steam. The bastard comment was technically true but he couldn't let her call him a murderer and let it go unrebutted. Rebut respectfully, Tal, he chided himself.

"Due respect, your Ladyship, I am not a murderer. Baba Yaga pleaded with me to end her life. It was she who made the decision to choose True Love over Hate. It is because of her that I am Amarantos's present Traveler."

The beam vanished. It didn't flicker and die. It didn't gradually fade. It vanished. With a pop. One look at Luna told Tal the beam hadn't yet bored into the part of Tal's brain where that information was stored. "This is true?" Luna asked quietly. You are Mother's present Stytch?"

"I am," Tal confirmed.

Luna flicked her non-wand bearing hand at Bobbie Jo and Tal watched as the pack turned and raced back into the crystal forest.

"Surely you have not dared come to Arianrhod for some trivial Hunts purpose?"

Tal knew with certainty if that had been the case, he and Notos would never have been allowed to leave Luna's home alive. He proceeded to explain to her about Emet, about his volunteering to be Tal's bloodpryce equivalynt, and finally, about

Väst's perfidiousity. Luna seemed to find the entire tale interesting, but the last part where he was tricked into going to Five-Hells, that part totally snagged her attention.

"This Väst, you believe you love this Folk woman?"

"Yes."

"Ah, but you hate her right now, mortal. Don't you?"

Tal paused a moment. Baba Yaga had taught him when in doubt that honesty was the best option. "No. I'm pretty pissed off at her but I think I still love her."

Luna's laugh this time was a little different. It held a little more rabid edge to it than the other laughs in her repertoire. She looked at Notos. "You haven't told him, have you?" Notos grimaced as he shook his head no. "Of course not. You couldn't because of the binding. Oh this is good, this is really good." Turning back to Tal, she whispered. It was a venom-laden whisper but a whisper nonetheless. "That feeling you call Love is no such thing, Child of the Dust. It is merely Hate which has not yet blossomed."

Luna crossed her arms across her fulsome chest. "You have my permission to utilize Yggdrasil to travel to the boundary of Five-Hells. It will be someone else's decision as to whether you die there or continue onward."

Surprised, Tal looked to Notos. He was trying to stand still and act like nothing was amiss but it was obvious the stitches were causing him substantial pain. Notos immediately understood, based on Tal's past performances, that Tal planned on doing something about the situation, and he started violently shaking his head from side to side.

Tal gave Luna a deep head nod. "Thank you for your courtesy, Lady Luna. Now would you please remove the stitching from my teammate's mouth."

Without a beat, Luna responded. "I think not. It pleases me that he suffers."

STOP, DON'T DO IT, Central Processing barked its order to Amygdala. I'M TELLING YOU TO DESIST. STOP. DON'T. SAY. A. WORD. Amygdala, acting true to its amygdalactic self, paid absolutely no attention to Central Processing.

Tal exploded. "I see you clearly now for who you are, Luna. You think you're one of the high and mighty Elder Children and that that makes you better than everyone else. You think we should all be scared shitless because you're so gosh-darned powerful.

"Well, you know what? You ain't shit. You're just another sorry-ass, dime a dozen schoolyard bully. Myrddin told me…you know him, right? The Traveler? The original Munedan? The guy who was totally in True Love with Princess Corcra until you selfishly showed up? You remember, the one you didn't love enough for the Kiss of Lethe to work? Yeah, that guy.

"Anyway, he told me the first time I met him. Well, I'm pretty sure it was the first time, but he was maybe…probably in othertyme because you see, he was this really irritating, pain in the ass, know it all pre-teen. Standing in a roomful of colored sand that turned out to be…well, none of that matters, what does matter is Myrddin was right. He told me there is a Barton Sellars, or worse, in every universe. Oh, and in case there's any doubt, in this particular scene, you're playing the part of 'or worse.'

"You're not doing what Amarantos has called all of us to do. You're not 'Seeking the Center.' Full confession time. I'm still pretty clueless about what that actually means, but whatever it is you aren't doing it. Best I can tell, you haven't been since you f'd Myrddin's life all to hell. You're just a soured up old Elder Child bully. That's all you are."

Luna said nothing and remained completely stationary. Her only reply was that the Nyx symbol branded on Tal's ass began burning, hotter than ever before. Even hotter than when Baba Yaga first seared his flesh with the red hot branding iron. This time, for the first time ever, it was burning downward, burrowing deep into Tal's body, the heat feeling like it was about to reach nuclear meltdown status.

At the point Tal felt like it was going to char its way through his hipbone, Luna finally hissed her reply. "Such a bold, insolent Child of the Divine Spark. I wonder, would your words have been so brazen if you didn't know I cannot kill or permanently maim you while you wear my totem on your body?"

Wait, what? Tal asked himself. I got a "get out of death

and/or maiming free" card and didn't even know it?

Luna watched Tal's face, gauging his response. "Oh, that's rich. You didn't know that either."

Note to self. Never, never have that damn Nyx brand removed. Not lasered, not tattooed over into a cool dragon, nothin'. No, Tal, not even a super-cool dragon. All high and mighty can't do shit to me as long as it's on me.

"I weary of your stench in my Realm. Yggdrasil is inside the Lunarium. If you both survive the climb down, you will arrive at the boundary of Five-Hells. It will then be up to The Morrigan to decide whether you live or die. Begone," she commanded as she waved her wand in an arc back toward the center of Arianrhod.

CHAPTER CENTUM VIGINTI

If you want to initiate a heated discussion at an arborists' convention, wait until everyone has already invested in a couple of happy hour priced rounds down in the convention hotel bar. Then say you'll pay a hundski to whoever can name, "the most famous person who is/was an arboriculturalist." Everyone who guesses wrong has to take a double-shot of mescal.

At least a dozen folks who think themselves quite clever will name Francis Bartlett. He was the founder of Bartlett Tree Services, which now has over a hundred offices worldwide. That Mr. Bartlett is not to be confused with Enoch Bartlett. The American who named the Bartlett pear after himself, even though an Englishman named Williams had already beat him to the pear naming game by probably half a century or more. To each and every one of them, you'd say, "Drink up, Losers!"

The Barlettinians would then be outyelled by scads of arborihistorians, who would doggedly plead their answer—John Chapman. Who? Ah, if the gentleman's legal name isn't immediately recognizable, his nom de abre should be. Johnny Appleseed.

"Wrong, again," you would state casually. "Drink up!" There would be much grumbling, but after all they are already more than half-lit in a convention hotel bar at three o'clock in the freaking afternoon, so they'll follow instructions.

Next you would state you have the correct answer and if

there is unanimous agreement you have the correct answer, you'll utilize the previously said hundred-dollar bill towards buying additional double shots of mescal. There is a general huzzah from the attendees, who are now hanging on your every word.

You tell them you didn't ask who the most famous arborist in the history of the world was, you asked them who the most famous person who is/was an arboriculturalist. That person happens to be an Officer of the Order of the British Empire, Dame Commander of the Order of the British Empire, and Member of the Order of the Companions of Honor. Dame Judi Dench. That's right. Dench. Dame Dench. The person who even filmed a documentary, "Judi Dench: My Passion for Trees," to document her arboristerial affection. There would be stunned silence. Then uproarious applause. Followed by a hundred dollars worth of mescal double shots.

If, however, you simply wanted to instigate a riot, you would ask the impaired arborist collective to name the "biggest tree" that every existed. The current tallest single trunk specimen is Hyperion, a coast redwood, right at three hundred eighty feet. The biggest giant sequoia alive now is "General Sherman," who is a little over a hundred feet around at his base. The biggest tree, anecdotally, was the "Crannell Creek Giant," who was felled in the 1940s. If multi-trunk species are considered, then there are some eucalyptus, baobab, and Montezuma cypress specimens that could arguably…

Tal suddenly realized someone had been steadily shaking his sleeve for about five minutes past. That someone was now about to rip the sleeve off his shirt. "Notos!" he exclaimed.

Notos stopped sleeve-tugging to give him an exaggerated "what the hell is going on" shoulder shrug.

"Sorry. I'm sorry. I know those stitches hurt and it's a terrible time to lose focus," Tal said apologetically. Get your head in the game, he told himself, as he looked forward and upward. To the reason his brain had been ruminating on the subject of gargantuan trees.

CHAPTER CENTUM VIGINTI UNUS

Yggdrasil was the giant centerpiece extending through and overreaching the entirety of the etched crystal Lunarium, as well as the adjacent manor house. The massive tree was almost an entire forest unto itself, Tal thought, as he craned his neck, looking all the way to the top. The canopy must be all of a quarter of a mile high. Needless to say, if the arborists got a gander at Yggdrasil, drunk or sober, they would unanimously agree it was both the tallest and largest tree in the world.

Who would have guessed Luna was the custodian of the World Tree? Check that thought, Tal told himself. She's the custodian of Yggdrasil. In all probability this is only "a" World Tree, not "the" World Tree. The concept of a World Tree is common in many Earth plane cultures, so some incarnation of it must exist on many Realms. On a Magyar plane it would be called Világfa, Modun on Mongol Realm, and on one or more of the Japanese planes it would undoubtedly be named Jian Mu.

Hold on a minute, World Trees are often referred to as Axis Mundi. An Axis Mundi, by any other name, is a Navel of the World, or a...wait for it...omphalos.

Notos pointed to a Lunarium entry and they walked briskly toward it. The entry was a large crystal arch, decorated with glyphs.

When they walked through the entry, they saw, carved into the World Tree itself, a winding staircase. The stairs wrapped all the way around the tree. Somewhere on the far side of the tree—which if Tal had to take a guess, was an Ash—the stairs went below the floor of the Lunarium. The portion of the staircase they could see was also totally covered with symbols and glyphs.

Tal had a flashback. Well, he wasn't sure an experience could be called a flashback if you had no independent recollection of the remembered event. It could be called any number of other things. Like a psychotic break, Central Processing offered. Shut it, Tal told himself.

In the maybe memory, Tal was really young. Both he and his mother were young. There some old dude named "Keeper." He had a lantern and he accompanied Tal and Thea down a spiral staircase. Which was covered with many of the same glyphs carved into the present staircase. Keeper told Thea they protected against internal magical attack, from things such as poison. Tal also remembered the trip down the stairwell seemed to take forever.

"I feel like I've been here before, Notos. On this stairway. Crazy, right?" The Omada Second Prime's only response was to push Tal in the back, urging him to get a move on.

CHAPTER CENTUM VIGINTI DUO

At the juncture where the stairs sank beneath the surface, there'd been a large alcove. No food, no water, but there were oil-burning lanterns. Real oil lanterns, not magyked lamps made to look real. They'd had to fill the lanterns from an oil reservoir and then light the lamps by shoving a stick into a brazier and then lighting the wick.

That had been what seemed like hours ago. Hunger and thirst gnawed at Tal. He felt certain Notos was starving as well. There'd been no way to bring spare oil so both teammates flinched every time one of their lanterns flickered.

Round and down they monotonously went. The bole of the tree steadily increased in diameter. There was considerable open space between the tree and the surrounding earth. Tal had made the mistake of looking out and down several times. There wasn't the slightest indicia of a bottom.

Both the temperature and the humidity had begun inching up as soon as they'd left the surface. Fog appeared shortly thereafter. It seemed to Tal the "smother" factor was now growing perceptively with every downward circuit of the World Tree. The unpleasant environment also caused the carved wood to become slick. They'd each lost their footing several times and were now making sure they were within a hand's grasp of the other.

Every few feet a massive branch would bisect the stairs.

Going up and over wasn't too tough but it was much harder holding onto the warm, moist wood coming down the far side. The cross-branches had finally gotten large enough that they were now having to relay each other up and over. Tal would first give Notos a foot up, then when Notos was on top he would give Tal a hand to assist in pulling him to the top. They reversed the process climbing down. Now, not only were they hungry and thirsty but they were both scraped all to hell.

Their lanterns only provided sufficient light to plan their next two or three steps. It wouldn't take but one small misstep to plunge them both into, well, Tal didn't know what was at the bottom, or even if there was a bottom. A myriad of different animal noises sounded from the surrounding blackness. Birds, he wondered? Robins, maybe? Right, Tal told himself. Because lots of robins want to live deep underground. They're probably some prehistoric leather-winged carnivorous raptors. There were other noises too, like insect buzzings. But there were also whizzings and croakings. Tal decided the possibilities ranged from mosquitoes to poisonous tree frogs.

Down, down. Ever down, the ancient staircase took them. On the rare occasions when the staircase had a landing like plateau, they'd both stop and lean against the tree. It was during one of these respites that Notos's lamp flickered for the last time. They'd kept talking to a minimum. Notos couldn't and Tal was both beat down and out of breath. Communication was necessary now. Tal spoke as he stood. "No telling how much longer mine is going to last. We have to go faster, with less light." Tal saw Notos nod his agreement.

One interminable flight of steps followed another. The air now felt—and smelt—like a steamy teenage boys' locker room after a day's worth of gym classes. Every time they reached another landing Tal would think they were finally to the bottom. He was wrong. Every time.

At some point all of the animal rustlings and random noises disappeared. Tal wasn't sure whether it was a good portent—or an evil one.

It felt like every hundred feet down raised the temperature an entire degree. The humidity factor was now off the chart. Whatever the defined level of humid was beyond super-dank, that's what it was. His clothing was drenched, his skin chafed raw pretty much everywhere.

Just as he finished telling himself for the umpteenth time to buck up it couldn't get any worse…

His lamp went out.

CHAPTER CENTUM VIGINTI TRES

Great, this is just f'ing great, Tal told himself. They were miles beneath the surface, with no food or water, on a wood staircase with no handrails that was now basically a slip-n-slide. And now add "could it be any darker" darkness.

We can't turn back now. It's as dark upward as it is downward. If I hadn't given the Taleria to Helblad, I could go get help.

They now had to hold one hand out to touch the tree itself and the other where they could make occasional contact with each other. Tal would say something periodically so Notos would know where he was.

It was too much, cumulatively, simply too much. The small remnant of Central Processing still functioning was telling Tal he had only a few more moments of holding on to his sanity. In a few seconds the dam would burst and gibbering lunacy would seize him. And odds were, it was never letting go. Hold on, Tal, try to rationally parse your way through this. C'mon buddy, you got this.

Just as Tal felt the remaining motes of his sense of identity dispersing into the aether, Notos gently pulled on his sleeve. Once, twice, three times. "What?" Tal asked, his voice harsh after so little recent use. Tal heard a rhythmic tapping. He listened a minute more. It's Notos, tapping his foot on the stairs. No, wrong sound, he quickly realized. Not wood. Harder, different. Grabbing Noto's arm, Tal shuffled forward a step. Then another. "It's stone, Notos. A stone patio," he added.

In the next minute the coffin of dead air surrounding them was cleft by a breeze. A putrid, rancid breeze, but at least it held life within it. Choking back the bile climbing up his throat, Tal saw a half dozen bobbing balls of light chastening the darkness. So, again, that has to be an improvement. Doesn't it? he asked himself.

As the lights approached, his ears were assaulted by a cacophony of sounds. The noise seemed deafening after the prolonged silence. More animal noises, Tal decided. No, he thought, as he listened several seconds more. Not animals. Birds. Raucous, like a bunch of crows gathering to feed. Hey Tal, he asked himself, what's the name for a group of crows? C'mon, Tal, he replied, that's a no-brainer. The proper word for a group of crows is a murder. Stop internal dialoguing with yourself and focus, you idiot. Death, or worse, he added, may only be a couple of hundred yards away.

The cawing ceased as the lights encircled him. As they formed an almost complete circle, Tal noted there were six separate lights. The light emanated from dusky glass globes. Not glass, he decided, they look more like they're made of light colored smoky quartz crystal.

The globes weren't floating either. They were being carried by robed figures. Damn they're tall, he thought. At least seven feet. The robes and matching hoods were a nondescript gray. The colorless material completely swathed the figures— except for their faces. Which looked like dirty-white cracked porcelain masks.

"So, the rumor from the surface-dwellers is true, then."

Central Processing quickly catalogued the voice. Feminine. Deep. Throaty. Sexy. Lauren Bacallish. It was at that moment Tal realized his dick was hard as a rock. Really? he asked Impulse Control. You do understand I'm pretty much standing at Death's door? And you still decided now would be a good time to redirect my blood flow to sporting major wood?

Now there was rolling laughter. Deep. Throaty. And, yes, almost unimaginably, sexy.

As Tal watched, the gap in the lights of the surrounding circle was filled by a figure stepping forward, occupying the space clearly left open for her. Boy, was it ever occupied. Her face was whiter than her handmaidens' porcelain masks, with heavily penciled eyebrows. The shade of her lipstick and matching nail polish must be called "Dried Blood Black." Please, please, please let that be lipstick and nail polish.

The new person was statuesque, but nowhere near the height of the wraith-like torchbearers. His first thought was she was wearing a type of long-sleeved, full-bodied cat suit. He quickly realized she was wearing feathers, so black they read as blue-black in the dim light cast by her minions' lamps. What does she have on under her feathers, Tal wondered.

"Mortals are such charming creatures," the woman said. "Even when they are near their heart's last beat they still have the desire for one last throw."

Damn it, it's true, Tal told himself. Either that or I have a hitherto undiscovered feather fetish.

The woman turned her attention to Notos. "And you, Prince, Moon got your tongue?"

Notos, of course, couldn't answer and chose to stand completely still.

What's up with this whole "Prince" thing anyway, Tal wondered.

"What have you brought to me for your offering, little mortal?" the woman asked Tal.

"P-P-Pardon?" Tal stuttered.

"Your companion is free to come and go from Five-Hells as he pleases. Rather, as Veles pleases. You, on the other hand, must have significant payment for your crossing...and to keep your lyfe."

Need some information up here, Central Processing demanded. Yesterday, if not sooner. Lampades came the initial response. Torch-bearing maidens of the Underworld. That's the willowy porcelain-faced apple dolls. And the leader? Need another moment, that information is stored in a different department. Got it. Luna said it would be The Morrigan's choice whether I lived or died. In Earth plane mythology, The Morrigan, also known as the Phantom Queen, is in charge of death and war. Oh, and she often appears as a crow. Nailed it.

The Morrigan closed the distance between she and Tal and reached forward with her left hand. The nails were long, sharp, and extremely well-manicured.

I mean, really, where would you go down here to get your nails done, Tal wondered. Is there some type of franchised chain that caters to subterranean demi-goddesses?

The Morrigan extended her left index finger and drew it all the way down Tal's right forearm, from inside the elbow to the wrist. Blood welled the entire length of the slit. She collected some inside her fingernail and brought it to her lips, sucking the blood into her mouth.

Well, ick, and I guess that resolves the issue of whether it was lipstick or...

"Just when you think there are no surprises left in all of Creation, some strange mortal shows up at your door. Blood tells all. Seems you have already made a binding with the Jarl of the Undead for your lyfe."

"Um, yes ma'am."

"Did I taste that you are also Amarantos's present Traveler?"

"That's correct, as w-w-well," Tal replied.

"Well, I guess that takes killing you off the table."

Until that exact moment, Tal hadn't realized how close he'd been to crapping in his pants. He'd been that scared. "Well, that's good news, isn't it?" he asked, trying his best to display a convincing smile.

"Sure," she replied, with a truly scary smile, a mouthful of Hollywood-white teeth framed by her blackened lips. "Of course, that leaves, 'or worse'."

Damn it, Tal thought to himself. I completely forgot about that possibility.

"Seems you do have one thing bargain-worthy on your person," The Morrigan said, softly this time. Again, with plenty of teeth but no smile this go round, Tal noticed. "Something that might prove quite useful to me, that will finally afford me the opportunity to walk with impunity above ground once more."

Tal had zero idea what the Goddess of Death and Destruction was talking about. Notos, who had been still throughout the entire conversation, was neither still nor silent any longer. He jumped up and down, moaning loudly behind his stitches. Doing whatever he could to get Tal's attention to tell him not to bind the bargain.

"I'm sorry, Notos," Tal told his Second Prime Direction. "I can't stop here and it's not like there's a damn thing you can do to help get Emet out of Five-Hells."

At this Notos cranked all of his indicia of displeasure into overdrive.

Tal turned back to address The Morrigan. "I'm sorry. You'll have to forgive my teammate. He's obviously out of his league here. Please state the terms of your proposed bargain."

"You will give me one designated item from on your person. In return, I shall provide safe passage for you to the boundary of Five-Hells."

"I consent to the bargain. Do you?"

"I consent," she replied. With that, The Morrigan lifted her arms wide.

Holy mother of pearl, Tal thought to himself. She's going commando underneath those freaking feathers.

The goddess turned and shrugged as if to discard a robe, and the feathers fell from her shoulders.

"Baseball, baseball, baseball," Tal muttered. "Winter league baseball. In Antarctica."

"Come forth," The Morrigan commanded. The mists swirled and cleared from in front of her, revealing a river. Slowly crossing the river was a small, seemingly self-propelled raft.

"Ha," Tal said lightheartedly, "I guess Charon is on strike."

"I killed The Charon hundreds of years ago, Dust Child. He displeased me in bed."

Okay, Tal, your new mantra is, "Shut the fuck up! Shut the fuck up! Shut the…"

The raft bumped up against the shoreline, causing a small wave to advance in front of it, almost to Tal's feet.

"Careful, human," The Morrigan advised. "River Styx has

not been fed in quite some time. She is thirsty for new lyfe."

Tal found his stutter had returned, albeit for a different reason. "The R-r-r-iver S-s-styx?"

Death's maven motioned to Notos. He'd calmed down now that Tal had done the deal, and following The Morrigan's prompt walked slowly up to the raft, before stepping onto its surface. The Morrigan next turned to Tal, who also started forward. "Not so fast. There is the little matter of your payment, Child of the Dust," she stated, as she pointed to Tal's buttock.

No," he exclaimed. "Wait, I thought something 'on my person' meant like my shirt or my pants. Yeah, I'm going to need that brand. Luna is gunning for me and if she ever catches me without it she's going to kill me all kinds of dead."

The Morrigan motioned to the Lampades. Three of them closed in a tight circle around Tal. He watched as the lamp-staffs of the other three turned into spears with thin sharpened blades. They approached Tal, who now found himself immobilized.

One at a time they dug their spear points, all the way to the blade hilt, into Tal's ass cheek. He was crying, blood was flowing down his leg, pooling in his shoe, before running over and out onto the ground. They kept going around, taking turns until The Morrigan waved her hand in Tal's direction. He watched, frozen, as a chunk of his flesh, together with skin containing the intact Nyx symbol floated away from his body and into The Morrigan's outstretched hand. Upon receipt, she raised her hand to her right breast and affixed the flesh with symbol to her own skin. As her body absorbed Tal's flesh her nipples got hard, she closed her eyes, then shuddered several times before opening her eyes and smiling broadly.

Did she just, did that freak just get off on my...

Still naked, The Morrigan waved her arm, first toward Tal and then toward the raft. Tal quick-stepped onto the raft, which promptly left the shore and began its way back across the River Styx. On its way to Five-Hells.

CHAPTER CENTUM VIGINTI QUATTUOR

"I'm terribly sorry, Quint, but I can't take a chance on you and your mouth screwing my plan all to hell."

CHAPTER CENTUM VIGINTI QUINQUE

County Wicklow was the last to be formed of Ireland's thirty-two counties. Legend has it that sometime early in the seventeenth century, in a small village in that county, a local farmer was having a tough time with a neighboring bully. For years the mild-mannered farmer put up with the ale-stealing and the fence-wrecking and the sheep-killing. Until one day he decided enough was enough.

The mild-mannered farmer went out to the nearest blackthorn tree, cut him a stout branch, carved it to a suitable length, and then he shoved it way up in his cook hearth chimney for the entirety of the long Irish Winter. When the spring thaw was fully engaged, the farmer retrieved his well-cured stick, sanded it, lacquered it up, particularly the knobby end, and wrapped leather around the thinner end.

The farmer waited until the next feast night, until the malignancy that was his neighbor was ólta at the town social, harassing all of the young maidens. He called out his huge, belligerent neighbor telling him to "Stad!" A gleam came into the bully's eye as he advanced upon his small, timid neighbor, asking "Who is it exactly that's going to make me?"

The neighbor waited until the cad was within striking distance before responding, "Mise, you fecking gobshite!" He then whipped his stick out from behind his back and with one blow split his asshat neighbor's head wide open, é a mharú marbh right on the spot.

The farmer was subsequently unanimously elected as the first Mayor of that tiny village. Shillelagh. His club spawned millions of descendants, known by dozens of different names, depending on their size and other optional modifications. Blackthorn, cudgel, truncheon, blackjack, and when used by law enforcement, billy club.

Central Processing interrupted. First of all Subconscious, you totally made that origin story up. What? Don't start that shit with me, we can't have anybody relying upon that ridiculousness. Second, and more importantly, you're almost up to speed, push the pedal a little harder and you'll hit the green light to Conscious status. Sure, it's going to hurt but it's like pulling a band-aid off. Do it fast and you probably won't even feel it. Pretty sure.

CHAPTER CENTUM VIGINTI SEX

"HOLY MOTHERS OF INVENTION!" Tal yelled as he awoke and sat up. A fistful of nausea jammed itself down his esophagus, so he immediately retreated to totally prone status. Somebody is using my head for a freaking bodhrán. He barely turned his head to the left, then back to the right, before closing his eyes as the least painful option. It's not the end of a school term, so I'm not in the f'ing infirmary. There's that. Wherever I am, I'm sure there's no Tylenol. Dammit!

What happened to me? I remember that freak Morrigan getting her rocks off absorbing my Nyx branded piece of ass. Tal felt his gorge rise again at the memory. Then she put me and Notos on that self-propelled float. While we're on that subject, how come they got a damn self-propelled aquatic device and absolutely zilch for a hangover?

It's not a hangover, Central Processing reported. We're experiencing short term amnesia, so I'm putting us into the concussion protocol. Concussion? That's right. We stepped off the raft on to Five-Hells Realm proper, I started to turn to check on Notos...and...some guy that looked an awful like a mini-me of that sorry rat bastard Veles jacked me with a shillelagh. Or his fist. One of the two. Or both of the two. Pretty sure.

Tal reached up and gingerly tried to ascertain the parameters of the billiard ball-sized lump on the crown of his head. You know what, I think the best thing for me to do right now is to pass out again.

CHAPTER CENTUM VIGINTI SEPTEM

"Quint! Quint, wake up. I only have a few minutes before someone comes to get me. Quint! Wake up!"

That's got to be the loudest whisper ever, Tal thought. I mean, whoever is doing the whispering is really terrible at it. That whisper is loud enough to wake the...me, he realized, as he was jolted back awake. And cue, migraine. Damn, damn damn, he repeated as he tried to sit up, finally succeeding.

When Tal was finally able to open his eyes he found himself looking at...the Veles copy who bludgeoned me? "Hey, asshole, I don't know who you think you are, but..."

"I am your teammate, Quint. The Omada Second Prime formerly known as Notos. Now that I have returned home, I have been restored to my body and my psuche name. Crown Prince Arawn, heir to the throne of Five-Hells."

Nonplussed, Tal told himself. Look that word up in the Google and you'll see a picture of me at this exact moment in time. Of course, you'll also see it under the entry for "man whose head is about to explode."

Moving on, Central Processing announced. Additional data is needed. Once they started, Tal's fount of questions seemed unending. "Notos? Arawn? Crown Prince of Five-Hells? I mean, what the hell? Can I even say 'hell' when I'm in Five-Hells?"

"Stop, Quint. Please stop. I'm sorry but we simply don't

have time for me to answer your questions right now. The major domo is on his way right now to notify my father I'm home. I'll be summoned immediately for a private audience."

"But you're the Crown Prince of…"

Notos waved his hand and Tal found his mouth no longer functioned. Still had the skull-pounding headache but his mouth was offline. It wasn't just his head either, his entire body was now sending in pain messages.

"I'm sorry but I have things I need to tell you. Fast. First, I am sorry for having been such a complete and total bastard to you this school year…"

Unable to talk, Tal had no choice but to listen. Wait a minute, Notos is apologizing? To me? A munedan?

"You're now experiencing some of the pain I felt every single minute of the last hundred years. Not the headache from where I clocked you, the full body pain. Because I'm Five-Hells royalty it was magnified hundreds of times beyond what you're presently feeling."

Hurts pretty damn bad, Tal thought. Chilblains followed by flesh broiling, in an asymmetric pattern. I guess I'd be an asshole too.

"I agreed to terms with Veles before I was allowed to leave Five-Hells. This whole thing has been a huge game for him. Until I stepped back across the Styx and reassumed my proper form, a geas prevented me from telling you or any of the rest of our teammates why I was at Hunts School…"

Damn, this pain is awful. Has Emet been putting up with this since he's been here? What about Kentro? He's been here almost an entire year. Tal couldn't stop his brain from serial questioning. It was probably just as well Notos had used his mojo on him.

"Everything I've done was to try to save my mother. My mother is…"

Mokosh, Tal realized. Veles's wife is Mokosh, so she's Notos's mother.

"Mokosh. She and my father held joint rulership over Five-Hells. This Realm wasn't always like this. Veles seized a moment when Mokosh was weakened, after expending most of her magyk helping our subjects following a tragedy. The son of a bitch imprisoned her."

What a coincidence, Tal thought, there's a statue of Mokosh in Fountain Flow.

"He used his magyk to make her a living statue in Fountain Flow. My mother and her principal loyalists."

Now I know it's a good thing Notos whammied my mouth, Tal decided. So many questions, so little time. One of which is just how many millennia-old is Notos?

"Veles has bragged for eons that he'd left, in plain sight on Hunts School campus, the magyk phrase that would release Mokosh."

Things are starting to make a little sense now, Tal thought.

"I...I was arrogant, Quint. I made a bet with Veles to obtain Mokosh's freedom."

I was wrong before, Tal thought. Right now is when Notos absolutely made the right decision to keep my yap shut.

"I bound a contract with Veles. I agreed if he would allow me to be the first Five-Hellion to ever attend Hunts School that if I couldn't find the magyk phrase and release Mother before I was required to return to Five-Hells, I would never mention her ever again and no one from Five-Hells would ever again be allowed to attend Hunts School."

Which means Mokosh and her friends would be imprisoned forever, Tal realized.

"I looked everywhere, Quint. Two and three times. Knowing my Father wasn't above cheating, I looked in every private place as well as the public spaces."

The door opened and the major domo appeared. "The King requires your presence, Prince Arawn." When it appeared Notos might try to continue his conversation with Tal, the functionary continued, "His Highness emphasized the word 'immediately,' Prince."

Shoulders slumped, Notos turned to Tal, waved his hand in front of Tal's face, turned and slowly followed the Chief Steward out of the library.

Tal felt the muscles in his jaw regain functionality and

decided to try them out.
"HOLY CRAP!"

CHAPTER CENTUM VIGINTI OCTO

Tal had been sitting, cooling his heels for what he could only guesstimate was about an hour. He'd cracked one of the double-doors and stuck his head out. The two guards facing him uncrossed their halberds to unambiguously illustrate he should wait inside until further notice.

One of the doors finally opened. Guess, Notos got the lowdown from his daddy, Tal thought, right before one of the footmen sporting the house livery and bearing a tray with a pitcher and a glass on it, walked into the library.

"I've brought you some water, sir," the servant said somewhat loudly, as the door closed shut behind him.

"Thank you, put it there please," Tal replied in his indoor voice. "I'm not deaf. In lots of pain but not deaf."

"Hopefully your stay will be brief, Quint," the man said smartly, as he placed the tray on a side table.

Quint? How does he know my name. "I'm sorry, have we met?"

"No, we haven't but we have some mutual friends," the man said, a big smile appearing on his face as he stuck out his hand. "Hi, I'm Kentro."

CHAPTER CENTUM VIGINTI NOVEM

"Wait, what?"

Kentro quickly closed the distance to Tal and beckoned him to follow him to the far corner of the room. "The walls have ears," Kentro stated by way of explanation. "I only have a few minutes before they notice I'm not at my post outside the kitchen. Is everyone well?"

Tal nodded, figuring if the walls had ears then body language was better.

"You're obviously still in the competition. Who else? Slākt?"

Tal nodded, before adding, "And Kabila."

"Could be worse," Kentro stated. "Mitt and Kati are decent enough Primes."

"Mitt is dead," Tal replied.

"Not good. Not good at all. Nord is a bona fide psychopath."

"You have a gift for understatement."

"How's Borras holding up?" Kentro asked.

"Please don't take this the wrong way but it's hard to imagine Omada having a better leader than Borras."

Kentro obviously didn't take it the wrong way. "I knew he'd do great. One of the finest beings I've ever met. Amarantos was watching over all five of us, actually over the entire universe, when we ended up on the same Hunts team. Quint, I have to ask, before I go, about, well about…"

"Dysi misses you, is still crazy mad in love with you, and would move heaven and earth to have you back with her."

Kentro's entire body language changed, became more relaxed. "Thank you for that kindness."

A rapid-fire cycle of freezing and burning hit Tal. "Kentro, you've been here an entire year. How does anybody stand the pain?"

"Well the Hellions are natives of Five-Hells, so they're okay. The rest of us, well, it's pretty tough. I lucked out and got a job in the palace. The Hellions have medicines and drugs they can use to relieve our pain. It also makes punishment easy. They simply withhold the medicine."

"Classic carrot and stick," Tal replied.

"I had absolutely no idea Notos was from Five-Hells, much less that he was the Crown Prince," Kentro added.

"Neither did the rest of us," Tal replied.

Kentro glanced back toward the door. "They're going to check on me in just a minute, so I have to go."

"Don't go far. The deal includes springing you, too," Tal offered.

Kentro's face tightened. "I can't go."

"Sure you can. We'll get Emet and the four of us will head back topside."

"You know that…" Kentro mumbled, before catching himself. "It's easy to forget none of the rest of you know what I know. Quint, I'm in Five-Hells voluntarily."

Stunned, Quint shook his head side to side. "No, that's not right, Kentro. Dysi explained it all to me. She said Väst is responsible. That Väst somehow used magyk to seduce you last year and she tricked you into a confrontation with the Snype. Which somehow got you thrown into Five-Hells."

One of the doors started to open. "Yes, sir," Kentro stated in his uber-loud obsequious servant voice. "I'll see if there are any fresh seedless pomegranates in the kitchen. Is there anything else I can get you?" They both watched as the door slowly closed.

"Quint, listen to me," Kentro whispered. "What

happened is not Väst's fault. She's not responsible for her actions in our entanglement. I imagine she mistakenly carries the burden of me being here, but listen closely. I am here of my own free will. Because of the Snype's prophecy. I am prohibited by our bargain to talk about the specifics but it's critically important I remain here until the Hunts are over and the new Ruling Council is installed. Repeat that back to me, it's important."

"You have to stay in Five-Hells until the Hunts are over and the new Ruling Council is installed," Tal repeated.

"Good. Last thing," Kentro said, as he took Tal's arm and started walking toward the double doors. "You have to make it back to Hunts School, Quint. You have to. The fate of worlds is on your shoulders." With that, Kentro shook Tal's hand, marched quickly the rest of the way to the doors, and slipped out of the library.

Great, Tal thought. Someone else telling me the fate of worlds depends on me.

CHAPTER CENTUM TRIGINTA

Tal wandered from wall to wall, pulling out a volume, reading for a few minutes before moving on. There were no clocks nor windows in the library, so it was hard for him to gauge the passage of time. His best estimate was that when both of the grand doors swung inward, it had been twice as long since Kentro's visit as the waiting period before that visit.

This time, however, his visitor was Crown Prince Arawn. Yep, not Notos, Arawn. Thankfully, Arawn, looked like his mother's side of the family. Also, thankfully, Tal noted, he was more modest than his father. Either that or the King was the only one who got to be half-nekkid for formal occasions.

Arawn was decked out in full dress uniform, like the pictures you see of the British royals on Trooping the Colors Day. Except that instead of the bright reds and yellows and blues that garbed the Mountbatten-Windsors, shades of black were the predominant colors. Carbon black, coal black, obsidian, every nuance of the black of a cloudy, moonless night. The several rows of medals and the obligatory sash were a deep purple. I've seen that shade in paint books before, Tal thought. What's it called?. Xiketic. Yes, that's right. Xiketic. I've got to give it to former Notos, Tal thought. He looks every bit the part of a Prince of Darkness.

The heir apparent was only one of Tal's two visitors. The other, a respectful two steps behind the Crown Prince, was the major domo. It was obvious Tal and his teammate weren't going to be left alone anymore. Notos made the right call earlier in making me shut up so he could tell me then what I needed to know.

"Honored servant," the Chief Steward began.

Honored servant? What the hell? Tal was a muscle twitch away from jumping down the chief lackey's throat before he caught himself. This whole freezing/scalding pain cycle has me on my last nerve. Let it go, he told himself.

"The entire Realm is appreciative of your efforts serving as Prince Arawn's dogsbody on his long trip home."

Dogsbody, my ass! Let it go, Tal, just let it go.

"However, now that your master has safely returned, it is impermissible for you to remain in this sovereign kingdom. You will be escorted to the throne room immediately for leave taking."

Wait, that's not the deal. We're trading me out for Emet. He and Notos are supposed to head back to Hunts School.

The major domo turned his attention to Arawn. "Prince, I believe the King instructed you to do an inspection of the castle's walls…"

"In a minute," Arawn said brusquely.

"But your father…"

"The last time I checked, heir to the throne outranked major domo. Now leave us alone. I promise I will be about my father's make-work business in a few minutes."

The head of household looked like he was going to take another crack at enforcing Veles's orders but apparently decided he'd done enough to cover his ass. Particularly since the Crown Prince undoubtedly had the ability to say "Off with his head!" In any event he turned and hightailed it out of the library. Arawn curtly motioned for the two guards to take themselves and their halberds outside and to close the door.

"I'll promise to listen a little better if you'll promise not to zap me again," Tal said lightly.

"I am truly sorry for that, Quint."

"It's okay. It was the right call."

"Thank you," Arawn said, clearly relieved. "I've only bought us a few minutes. I really don't like putting the staff in harm's way by disobeying Veles."

"I get that," Tal replied. "By the way, Kentro dropped by for a visit."

Arawn's eyebrow arched. "Really? Things must have gotten a little lax during the last hundred years. Good, that'll save me some of my explanation. Emet is being released."

Tal couldn't remember the last time he'd had such a weight lifted from his shoulders. It was huge. "Awesome, thank you. You and Emet will be making the trip back to Hunts School. Of course, you'll have to leave the whole 'I'm a super big deal' ensemble here or else everyone will figure out who you are."

Arawn gripped Tal by both shoulders. "I'm not going back, Quint. You are."

Although he still hadn't fully processed the ramifications of Arawn's last statement, Tal felt the heavy ass burden land right back on his shoulders. "That's not right. I'm Emet's bloodpryce substitute."

"You know there's no such thing," his former teammate said. "The only way either of you was leaving this Realm was to trade Veles something, someone, he wanted more."

Tal now knew exactly what the renewed shoulder weight was all about. "You."

"Yes," Arawn agreed.

"But your time as Notos isn't up. The Omada need you to win the Tyrning. If they win, you'll have another three hundred years to find the magyk words to release your mother and the others…"

"Quint, the only way Emet or you were leaving was for me to stay." Before Tal could interrupt him again he yelled, "Stop! Just stop!" Tal complied.

"You're a good man, Quint, and for whatever reason you have mad human skills that seem to be even more powerful than royal-level magyk. It's a hard thing, humility. For anybody, but particularly for someone who's spent eons as the only son of the ruler of a powerful Realm.

"I looked for a hundred years and couldn't solve Veles's puzzle. You can, though. I know it deep in my heart. You are the key to Omada winning the Tyrning, just as you are the necessary instrument to achieve my mother's release. Whether you understand it or not, Quint, at the heart of every decision that you make, you somehow instinctively Seek the Center."

Arawn glanced back to the door. "I have to go. You are expected in the throne room right now and it would not do to anger Veles. It doesn't matter that he bound a bargain, this is his Realm and he can do whatever he pleases.

"Quint, the Omada need for you to make it back for the team to have the four-person minimum. You have to do whatever it takes, fight however hard you have to fight, to win your way back to Hunts School. Seek the Center, Quint, it is the only way you'll make it home."

Tal was too close to the breakdown verge to speak. Lots and lots of tears were bucking to jump over and out.

"I admire you, Child of the Divine Spark. I admire everything about you. Now, shake the hand of someone who counts you as one of his dearest friends and walk through those doors. The guards will see you to the throne room."

Tal wasn't going to do it. He was going to argue or talk longer or try to figure out something he could do. In the end, he decided the best way to declare his mutual friendship was to honor Notos's sacrifice. So, he shook his friend's hand. A long, firm, "I won't drop the ball, buddy" handshake. And he walked out the library doors.

CHAPTER CENTUM TRIGINTA UNUS

Hurry up and wait. I should have known, Tal told himself, about thirty minutes later. He and his escort of two guards were the only occupants of the enormous throne room. There was no way the Big Dog of the Damned would be cooling his heels waiting for me to show up.

It was then that Veles entered the throne room, surrounded by an enveloping shroud of both steam and icy mist. The Lord of Five-Hells remained as daunting as when Tal had first seen him in the Great Hall of the Ziggurat. As tall as Borras, Veles was again wearing only a fancy loincloth, but this time had accessorized with a golden arm cuff on his right arm and a matching golden torc around his neck.

Absolutely no question, the dude is ripped, Tal reminded himself. In a weird doctor's anatomical chart kind of way, as Veles had no skin covering his musculoskeleture. His soft tissue was made of interwoven strands of red ice and black fire, which as they moved exposed portions of his bones of sparkling crystal.

As the throne room doors closed slowly behind him, Veles turned his attention to Tal's group. The dead sockets which operated as his eyes were only partially visible, as tendrils of oily black smoke continuously appeared, only to move slowly across his face before continuing on down his back. Emet, escorted by two armed guards, walked ten paces behind the king.

Veles snapped his fingers one time and the doorway began to take form on the far wall of the throne room. Damn, Tal thought to himself, Veles really is the best finger-snapper ever. The door to and from Five-Hells was as large as Tal remembered. Vertical planking of blackened oak, each plank being thirty feet tall and five feet wide. The planks were tightly bound by horizontal black iron bands, with the door attached to the wall with massive hinges of the same material.

I don't know how Notos withstood the pain for a hundred years, Tal thought, shifting from foot to foot. It grinds at you relentlessly. It's different from the pain of the Nyx brand. Except for the occasional throb, that pain was static, so my brain could mostly ignore it, kind of like white noise. But this, one minute I'm frostbite-achy from the cold, the next minute it's like all of my fingers and toes have gotten burned on an oven rack. I can't wait to walk through that damn doorway.

Veles broke the silence. "Voluntarily through the Gate of Anguish the simulacrum golem did enter my Realm, so shall he depart," Veles intoned, snapping his fingers twice. The door began opening, grayish smoke enveloped the portal as the terrible high-pitched screams began. Veles motioned for Emet to approach the portal.

As Emet reached the threshold, he turned back toward Tal. "I am going to see you on the other side, aren't I?"

"I'm right behind you, brother," Tal replied with a grin, watching as Emet walked through the doorway.

Veles snapped his fingers a third time. The smoke and screaming surrounding the Gate of Anguish dissipated as the door began to swing closed.

"Hold up there!" Tal yelled, as he ran toward the portal. "You made a deal. Two one-way tickets are supposed to get punched today. Remember?"

Veles did nothing to even acknowledge Tal's existence until after the door completely closed and dissolved. Only then did he turn to address Tal. "Oh, I intend to keep my bargain, munedan," he said with an ugly smile. "Voluntarily you did enter my Realm across the River Styx. Luna has banned you from Arianrhod, so you may not climb back up Yggdrasil."

"Just show me my exit and I'm out of your hair for good," Tal replied, determined not to let Veles know he was creeping him out big time. And I realize the dude's got no lips, so maybe I was being a little judgey about that whole "ugly smile" thing. Nope, Tal told himself a split-second later. It really was an ugly, ugly smile because he's doing it again.

"As it is through your own choices, freely made, that you may not leave the way you entered my Realm, your path home shall be through the Well of Souls." The ugly smile was now accompanied with an even more ugly laugh. "Take him to the chamber," he told his attendants before turning back to address Tal. "This audience is ended. Bon Voyage," he said spitefully, before turning and striding out of the throne room.

CHAPTER CENTUM TRIGINTA DUO

The guards left him at the entrance to a dimly lit tunnel, silently pointing for him to enter. "Thanks for everything, guys," Tal said. "And you can tell Mr. High Muckety-Muck, he's not half as smart as he thinks he is. You only say "bon voyage" when it's a water trip. So, there." Now that I think about it, the Ladies' Room said the exact same thing to me.

Two spears were lowered toward his midsection. "Fine," Tal said. "I'm going. There's no need to go all medieval on me." Tal entered the passage and found himself walking down a moist, twisty corridor. After he'd walked a pretty good ways it began to shrink around him. It finally reached the point where Tal had to turn sideways and stoop to keep from scraping his shoulders or banging his already brutalized head.

The tunnel ended abruptly when Tal found himself facing a hobbit-sized door. It looked like a miniature version of the Gate of Agony. The door creaked in vehement protest as he pushed it inwards with both hands, before getting on his hands and knees to crawl through. "Alice never got treated liked this," he remarked out loud.

On the other side of the threshold was a rough-hewn granite chamber. It's about the size of a high school basketball gymnasium, Tal decided. An immense cistern occupied the center as well as most of the room's floor space. There was only marginally enough room to navigate all the way around the pool's edge.

A large waterfall flowed down the rocks of the wall farthest from the entry door. The cascade's terminus was the cistern. Oddly, even though Tal estimated there were hundreds of gallons careening down into the pool every minute, the pool's surface was serene. Not a single ripple marred the surface and the water level didn't rise even an inch. It was as if the pool swallowed all of the water's momentum energy as well as its cubic volume.

This is all well and good but that asshole Veles promised me this was my only way out of his Five-Hells hellhole. Fine, maybe a little redundancy there but this place is definitely not on anybody's bucket list. This room looks more like a Five-Hells Waterpark than an exit. Yeah, you're a funny son of a bitch, Tal Smith, but you're in a tough spot, so how about some focus for a minute or two.

"Taliesin Smith."

"Holy crap!" Tal yelled, stumbling backwards a couple of steps before conceding he was going to bust his ass. Which he did. A second later. He listened for a few moments but the only noise in the chamber was the sizeable rushing noise generated by the waterfall. "Umm, yes? To the party whom I believe may have just possibly spoken to me. You seem to know my name but I don't know yours."

"I am the Well of Souls."

There's a first, Tal told himself. *Now I'm talking to a small body of water. And it's not even think-talking. How does a pool of water have vocal cords?* "Great, so what do your friends call you, 'Well'?" There was no response. "Well?" Still no response. "Fine, I give up. It wasn't that funny, anyway." He pointed at the water cascading down the walls and feeding the pool. "Is that the Styx?"

"It is."

"There's a shit ton of water pouring in but you're not getting any bigger. Where does the water go?"

"The Land of the Living."

"Yahtzee! That's where I want to go."

"You wish to bargain with me, Child of the Dust?"

"Maybe. What exactly is it you're offering?"

"The barest possibility you might return alive to the ones you love, to those who care for you."

The WOS ain't much of a salespool, Tal decided, but it gets points for honesty. "Yeah, that's not gonna be good enough. I'll need the absolute guarantee of a safe return."

"That bargain cannot be offered."

"Why not?"

"Because it is up to each individual whether they successfully complete the Journey."

"And if I don't? 'Successfully complete the Journey,' I mean?"

"Your mortal form shall perish and your soul will be trapped within me for all of eternity." With that, the entire surface of the pool was suddenly lit by thousands of will o' the wisps, blinking off and on. Probably looked like the audiences did when Sir Elton closed his encores with "Candle in the Wind." Interesting fact, conventional wisdom holds the first time candles or matches were held up during a concert was during Melanie's set at Woodstock in 1969. Really, he asked himself. You're probably about to die, Tal Smith. You really are. Right over there in that damned-soul lit sump hole if you can't get your idiot brain on task.

Well, it's a frog-strangler of a bargainpryce, Tal told himself. "As long as we're playing for keepsies, you might as well show your hand. I don't have any leverage do I? This really is my only option for getting back to the real world?"

"No, you don't. Yes, it is."

"Is there a blueprint for a safe trip?"

"Yes."

Holy hell, it's like pulling teeth to get a straight answer out of this subterranean mere. "Will you please tell me what I have to do to make a safe trip?"

"Your mind must not remove from constantly Seeking the Center. Do not be distracted by any false light promising life."

"Said every religion ever. Is that all?" Tal asked facetiously.

"No. You must also be able to hold your breath longer than is generally considered humanly possible."

I shouldn't have listened to those stupid Gas Pumps, Tal told himself. And if I ever get the chance I'm going to wring that Air Hose's skinny little hosey-neck. Well, it appears I got no choice. "I consent. Do you."

"I consent."

What do I do first?

"Take off all your clothes."

CHAPTER CENTUM TRIGINTA TRES

"Wait, what?" Tal thought he was pretty much stutter-proof after the year he'd had at Hunts School. He was wrong. It was apparently not enough that he was going to have to dive into the literally life-threatening inky black waters of the Well of Souls and attempt a low-percentage of completion trip trying against the odds to make it back to the real world. No, the Well had to humiliate him by making him do it butt-naked. "That's a joke, right?"

"Does not one of the many holy books of the Children of the Divine Spark say that naked you were born and naked you shall return?" the disembodied voice asked.

The Well of Souls is remarkably well-read for an entity made out of H2O, Tal thought. "Well, yes, but this isn't the same thing. Not at all."

"Are you so sure?" the Well asked. Before Tal could respond, the Well continued. *"In any event, you seem to be making a very big deal out of a very small matter."*

"What? Hello? Did you, the keeper of lost—or whatever euphemism is appropriate—souls just make a 'small dick' joke? At my expense?"

There was no response. Tal waited a few more minutes. The absence of further communication was clear. Time for talk was over. It was go time.

Lack of oxygen is rarely the most pressing problem when

trying to hold your breath. The buildup of carbon dioxide triggers autonomic action before oxygen is actually depleted. Based upon numerous youthful bottom of the swimming pool contests Tal knew he had good lungs and could go a solid two minutes, maybe two and a half, if he was trying to beat that sorry rat fink Eggs Benedict. Swimming for his life it was probably one minute forty-five seconds tops. Based upon the Well's comment, that probably meant he needed to last at least two minutes. No hill for a stepper? Right?

Tal bent over and untied his shoes, then removed them. Shirt, pants, and underwear quickly followed. Naked as the day he was born, he took a couple of minutes to take steady calming breaths to help get his heart rate down. When he felt as calm as he was going to get under the circumstances, he took several deep preparatory breaths before completing exhaling, then filling his lungs to capacity.

Start stroking immediately, he reminded himself as he dove in.

CHAPTER CENTUM TRIGINTA QUATTUOR

For the first few strokes Tal squeezed his eyes closed tight. That's not going to work, he decided, and was relieved when he opened them to find the damned Well of Souls wasn't chlorinated. It was, however, Stygian. Look at you, Tal, you are just so damn funny. Of course, it's Stygian. Hello?

You need to focus, boyo, or you're going to end up as an eternal floater. As Tal concentrated he noticed there was a slight pull of the water against his naked skin. Bingo! The current will lead me to the Well's exit point. Swim as fast as you can with the flow. Which, by the way, I might not have felt if I was still fully clothed. Central Processing notified him after only a couple of more breaststrokes the water seemed to be cooling a little. Okay, that's good info. Swim with the current and let the temperature help guide you. Time alert, Tal, you've been swimming about fifteen seconds. Maintain good form and pull hard with your arms on the strokes. About every fifth stroke, exhale a tiny puff of air. Not too much. Only enough to clear a little of the carbon dioxide. Concentrate on your stroke, not on the fact the clock is ticking. Distance, Tal. You simply have to cover as much distance as possible. You've been underwater no more than thirty seconds. Now, let go another small puff. Just a little to ease the chest constriction. You know that's next up. Lungs are going to try to make you exhale completely to force you to take a breath. Come on, Tal, stay the course. If Central Processing can suppress the autonomic contraction, the spleen will kick in immediately thereafter. It has a reserve of oxygen-rich blood cells specifically for this kind of emergency. Another small exhale-puff to eliminate a little more carbon dioxide.

Tal felt the current speed accelerate at the same time a phalanx of will of the wisps appeared in a hundred eighty degree spread in front of him. Except these were will of the whispers, each speaking to him in an immediately recognizable voice. Thea, Pell, the twins, Myrddin, Borras, Väst, Emet. Each of the lights were simultaneously speaking blandishments, all giving legit reasons to follow one of them in their various trajectories.

The water grew colder still, its pull greater. What if I'm supposed to follow them, he asked himself. I could be going the wrong way. These people love me, surely they are here to help. They're all the people who love you, Tal, but they're going helter skelter. His strokes faltered, their efficiency level dramatically reduced. NO, TAL! he screamed in his head. They are phantasms sent to distract you. None of those people are dead so there is no way their spirits are in the Well of Souls.

Problem solved. In a blink, the dozens of lights were all gone. Save only one. 'Tal, it's me.'

Elle. She's dead, Tal. Remember? You're responsible.

'Yes, it's me. You tried as hard as you could to save me and I'm here to help you now. Follow me, Taliesin, I will show you the way,' the light whispered in his mind, as it veered only a few degrees to his left.

"Elle," Tal silently mouthed. "You're here to help me, I know it."

'Hurry, Tal. Come with me. You only have about forty-five seconds.'

As he turned to follow Elle's wisp there was suddenly a new light on his right periphery. Floating on the original course. 'Every choice bears consequence, Taliesin. At some point all who truly Seek the Center must stop talking and listen. To me.'

That voice, who is it? Everyone else had been immediately recognizable.

'If you wish to live, my son, you must turn and follow

me.'

Got it! It's Fortuna. Er, Amarantos. Well, both of them, Tal told himself as he turned to follow. The contractions hit him right then. Hard. Really, really hard. He was having to chuff inwards to rebuff his body's repeated attempts to draw breath. I've got about fifteen seconds before I'll have to blow out the last of my air. After that, ten seconds, at most.

CHAPTER CENTUM TRIGINTA QUINQUE

Swim harder, Tal.

Time's up, buddy, Central Processing reported. Hypothalamus has the "fight or flight" emergency code and it's punching the required authorization in right now.

Harder.

Amarantos's light. It changed, he told himself. It's brighter now. Five more seconds, Tal told himself, as he stroked forward.

Just a little more.

Cue lungful of water. Drowning. Choking. Drowning. Is there really a difference?

Five more seconds.

Something's changed, damn it. The light, it's almost blinding now and the current is propelling me forward.

I can't do it anymore. It's too hard.

This is Hypothalamus, I'm commencing higher function shutdown. I failed, Tal told himself. I'm so, so sorry everybody, I let us all down, Tal thought, as he closed his eyes to the now incandescent light and rushing water.

NOT IF YOU'LL TRY BREATHING ONE MORE TIME, Central Processing yelled. Fine, Tal decided, what's a lungful of water going to hurt. He cough-vomited water as he expelled, then inhaled.

More racking coughing. Why? Because it wasn't water, it

was a misty spray. Central Processing reported there were some water droplets, but it was mostly oxygen. And oh by the way, your trajectory has changed to rocketing skyward.

Skyward? "Holy crap!" Tal yelled. I'm on top of a pillar of water carrying me straight up into the air.

Still vomiting water, Tal bent his head to look. Below him air, then ground. Not just ground. That's Fountain Flow down there. With like several hundred people hanging out around it.

People? I'm naked. My junk is flapping everywhere. Hey, all of you down by the fountain. No judging. The water is cold. It's really cold, I tell you. Like, super frigid.

This is Central Processing, Tal. You're at best still only semi-conscious but I feel like I should remind you that what goes up must come down. As in right about now.

Tal glanced downward again. Shit. It has to be at least five hundred feet to the ground. Even if I miss the fountain, I'm dead on impact.

The Well of Souls is a liar. It promised me I stood a chance. I mean, really. If you can't trust uncarbonated water, who can you trust?

Well, hello, sunbeam. Thanks for flashing right into my eyes. Might as well be blind, too.

Hold on, the light just danced sideways. Sol's ray is now shining straight through the jet of water below me. Now there's a rainbow shining through the water...and across Mokosh's sword.

The inscription, there it is again—*'cor aut mors.'*

That's it, you idiot.

What's it?

The key phrase that asshole Veles hid from Notos.

What are you waiting for? Start screaming.

"COR AUT MORS!"
"HEART OR DEATH!"
"COR AUT MORS!"
"HEART OR DEATH!"
"COR AUT MORS!"

It worked. The statues. They're all moving. Surely they'll do me a solid.

Tal, Logic here. It takes about twelve seconds, with a vertical fall of about fifteen hundred feet to achieve terminal velocity. We don't have anywhere near that far. Bottom line, there's about three seconds to impact.

The former statues still aren't helping.

Three...

Damn, they can't. They're Folk so it's against the Hunts Rules.

Two...

Then I'm a goner.

Looks that way.

One...

Damn, this is going to hurt.

Yes, but only for the briefest of moments.

CHAPTER CENTUM TRIGINTA SEX

'NOOOOO!'

She screamed so loud inside his head it ruptured his eardrums from the inside out. Only seconds ago he'd been watching the commotion by Fountain Flow from his first floor office window. Now he was prostrate on the floor, his hands trying to staunch the flow of blood from both his ears. "Please, Mistress," he begged out loud.

She was still screaming in his mind now. The physical rupture of his tympanum did nothing to reduce the volume of her telepathy as it raped his mind. 'THIS CANNOT BE HAPPENING. HE WAS TRAPPED FOREVER WHERE HE COULD NOT AID HER CAUSE. WHAT IN FIVE-HELLS HAPPENED? VELES HAS NEVER, NEVER LET SOMEONE LEAVE HIS REALM WHO ENTERED VOLUNTARILY. NEVER.'

He could feel additional pieces of his hearing apparatus crumbling to dust. "Please, Mistress. Please, you're killing me."

'Yes, that will have to do for now. Thank you, Malebranche for giving me the answer. Whatever it is She wants, whatever Her plan. It will slow Her down, give me time to figure out another path.'

"What will, Mistress?"

'You, you dolt. Get your sword and go kill that damned mortal.'

"But it's daylight and there are hundreds of witnesses."

"You have been begging for your revenge for centuries. This is it. You finally get the chance to be the Hero and rid the Folk world of that munedan canker. I WILL PROTECT YOU!"

Hero, Malebranche thought, as he ran his index finger down the puckered scar on his face. *The day has finally come when I get to avenge all the wrongs done to me and mine. With impunity. She says she'll protect me. She's so much more powerful than any of those fools out there, more powerful even than that imbecile Arthrys.*

Malebranche found himself a little wobbly when he first stood to retrieve the thrice-blooded sword from the false bottom of his lowest desk drawer. His anger steadied him once the blade was in his hands.

'GO NOW. HURRY BEFORE YOU MISS YOUR CHANCE TO BE A HERO!'

She watched as Malebranche ran out of his office and out the front door before she began floating upward. First through the ceiling and then dissipating completely from the Hunts School campus. It wouldn't do to leave any evidence she'd ever been there. In case the fool failed them both.

CHAPTER CENTUM TRIGINTA SEPTEM

Slowly—

    —ever—

       —so—

          —slowly—

Tal opened his eyes, treating his eyelids with the same consideration he would have used in sliding open an antique roll top desk that had been shoddily treated for the better part of its existence. Ever…so…slowly…rolling them open.

There was absolutely no doubt in his mind unimaginable pain was lurking, waiting only for an opportunity to unleash blitzkrieg upon his nerve endings. At which point the completely unimaginable real-pain, which until only a split-second before would have been only unimaginable possible-pain, would no doubt rise up to bitch slap him. Hündinschlagenkreig!

After successfully opening his eyes Tal elected to otherwise remain motionless, not willing to risk further stimuli until he could access more data. Central Processing sent instructions to Hippocampus to call up all recent memory. HipCamp, as it was called at Brain Lobe extended family picnics, was attempting to respond but was currently moving at a pace slower than wine cellar stored molasses.

Tal felt like his brain was operating on dial-up internet speed. The images, lining up in single file, were only low-res jpegs appearing only one pixel at a time. C'mon HipCamp, start with something easy.

I dove into the Well of Souls. Swimming. Swimming harder and faster than ever before, breast stroking through the squid ink dark, with the certain knowledge that if I drew breath in the Styx I was a goner.

Then there was a light. After that, HipCamp's procession ended. Nothing, I got nothing else, he told himself.

Without moving his head, Tal rolled both eyeballs through their full range of motion. So far, so good. Still no pain. Not yet, anyway. Well, there's the only clue I need. I obviously drowned. I must have made the cut to take the stairs leading up. This has to be heaven, Surely to goodness heaven is a designated no-pain zone. Sorry, Amarantos, looks like you're in need of a new Stytch.

Seems kind of odd though. Hypothalamus is still sending "breathe" signals to Lungs. Apparently heaven must be oxygenated, Tal decided, as his Lungs took another slow, deep breath.

Well, shit! I know that smell. Tal took another breath— actually it was more of an exploratory sniff this time. If that isn't a kick in the teeth. Heaven smells like the damn Hunts School infirmary. Who was it that said, "Every time someone opens a bottle of formaldehyde, an angel gets his wings?" Nobody, Tal. As in no one. No one ever said that.

This won't do, Tal decided. Not at all. My first order of business needs to be hooking up with the Manager on Duty to arrange a transfer. Elysian Fields would be okay. As long as it's not any earthier than extremely high-end glamping. Maybe like those treetop safari places. It also wouldn't hurt my feelings too much if a couple of Valkyries swooped in here and carried me off to Valhalla. I could do mead and rough-hewn wood décor for a couple of eons. As long as they have wool socks. Eternally cold feet is not on my list of favorite things.

Still staring at the sterile white ceiling, Tal drew yet another breath. Okay, I need to know what's going on, he decided, before turning his head a smidgeon to the left. Bingo. A row of linen sheeted barracks style beds. He turned his head an equivalent amount to the right. What a surprise. Same view.

Damn it. Damn it! DAMN IT! Why am I the one who freaking always ends up mortally wounded and in the hospital? It's like my final exam every term is a near death experience. The trend is not my friend.

Might as well find out how bad it is this time, he decided, as with no small amount of trepidation he carefully sat up. If the pattern holds, I should be hurling within about a minute. So he leaned over to prophylactically sight-in the expectoration receptacle. No vomit bucket this time, he noticed. Must be a rookie physick on call.

Still no pain registering, Tal reported to himself, as he finished easing up into a sitting position. I'm not nauseated either, just unbelievably weak. I feel like some energy vampire has sucked every bit of go-juice out of my bony ass.

He looked up and down the row of cots with their precise hospital-pointed sheets. Figures. Per normal operating procedure I'm the only one in here.

Tal's reverie was interrupted when the stainless steel double doors at the far end swung inward. This time, instead of physicks draped in medical garb, it was some lady in street clothes. She walked lithely toward him. His first thought was her graceful steps were like those of a classically trained dancer. Tal quickly amended his impression. The gait was more feral, less balletic. Yep, he decided as she walked closer. Exactly like the self-assured stalk of a natural predator.

Her bright russet hair was shorn clean to the scalp on the left side. The remainder, on the right side and down her back, was waist-length, falling freely except for looping outer strands that were elaborately interwoven with thick black ribbons into cascading knots. You know what those type of hair knots are called, Tal told himself. Really, he questioned himself, your most recent near death experience has rendered you a hair fashionista? Focus, Central Processing demanded. Right, fine. I have seen the design before.

Where? Here, Memory reported. At this school. That's it, it was in one of the Hunts history books. A picture of Ruling Council members from about six or seven Tyrnings past. What's it called? C'mon, c'mon. It has a distinct cultural name.

Celtic braid? Atta boy!

As the woman came closer Tal saw she bore faded robin's-egg blue tattoos across her face and neck. Not tattoos, he decided after she took another couple of steps. It's body paint. There were a number of calligraphic-looking whorls stenciled vertically on the outside of both her cheeks. On the right side of her neck there was an intricate graphic. Tal couldn't quite make it out but it looked like a flaming arrow bent into a z-pattern, with the z-pattern image superimposed on a double disk. Her closely fitted, full-length long-sleeved obsidian dress was sans adornment. Even the buttons were coal-black.

Her expression was grim. Not grim like resting bitch face. Pure undiluted grim. Look at the corners of her eyes and the downturn of the soft parentheses brackets around her mouth. She's sad. Very sad. As the strange woman finally made it to his bedside Tal noticed her eyes were a light green. Fern green, he thought. Tal realized he was staring but he couldn't help it. Everything about the stranger was unusual, mesmerizing.

She finally spoke as she glided into a chair next to his bed. "Aye and finally be ye waken then," she stated.

What the hell kind of accent is that, Tal wondered. It has a little of the sound and nuanced cadence of some weird combo Scottish burr and Irish brogue. Tal would have shaken his head to clear the cobwebs but as it had become obvious he was in the infirmary and not in heaven, his fear of the possible return of overwhelming pain had returned. Keeping his head motion to a minimum he moved his lips. "Please excuse me but I've apparently been knocked senseless. Again. I feel pretty sure I would remember if we'd ever met. I don't guess Hunts School is hosting the Scottish version of Riverdance?"

The young woman's face morphed as her green eyes twinkled and laughter lilted outward from her beaming smile. If I thought she was mesmerizing before, I was mistaken, Tal told himself. This is what mesmerizing looks like.

"Aye, as if it were not suffice ye be reborn into this world from Annwfyn shouting a magyk spellye that didst turn the River of Death into the Uisce Beatha, freeing those long held captive.

Every bit of it all as if thee 'twere Manannán mac Lir himself, come to walk once more amongst the sons of man."

She paused a moment while sadness renewed its assault on her smile. Sadness lost, for the moment anyway, Tal decided.

The woman continued. "No, apparently not enow. The wailing of the bean sidhes hast close ringed thee round this past fortnight and yet the first thing thou dost upon awakening 'tis seek to strathspey me with your gilded tongue. Sooth, I be fortunate indeed to have been forewarned thou art not only a Hero, but that thou hast also received a full portion of the gifts of Ogmios."

Tal simply stared, entranced by the radiant stranger. "Okay, I'm going to fess up. I don't have the faintest idea in hell what you just said, and I'm going to have to google the word strathspey. Well, and Ogmios too. When I get to a Realm that has electricity. And the internet.

"I'm not hitting on you, I'm really not, but you are smoking hot." Down boy, he told himself. This woman clearly has the ability to tear your heart out and show it to you before you die. I realize you've been through a traumatic event. Traumatic event, my formerly branded ass. That far exceeds understatement. It was a near death, should have been death, experience. Yet again.

Still, Tal counter-pointed to himself, that doesn't give you the right to go full-on lecherous over any attractive young woman you happen to meet. "Let's start over," he said to the young woman. "I'm Quint. Please excuse me for not getting up but at the moment it seems I am ill-disposed."

His words were rewarded by a renewal of her infectious smile. "As if the entire known universe dost not now know thou by thy psuche name, Taliesin Smith."

Tal couldn't stop his involuntary recoil. After all, the use of psuche names had been verboten for his entire school year at Hunts School. The woman apparently saw his reaction as she reached over and lightly patted him on the shoulder. "Be thee at ease, Taliesin. The Hunts be over."

As she paused, Tal thought he saw a hint of major sadness race through her eyes. "I have requested that the Folk at

Hunts School call me as I hast named myself for many centuries now. Kore," she added, her smile returning. If possible it was even larger than it had been seconds ago. "Since thou art the instrument of my salvation, I thought between thee and me that thou couldst call me by my Earth Realm name…"

A glass chock full of liquid comprehension splashed across Tal's conscious thoughts. "Aislinn. You are Helblad's Aislinn."

All of Aislinn's former smiles paled in contrast to the one she now wore, its only restraint the hint of moisture rising in her eyes. "Thou speakest truly. Arnfinn Skullcrusher, War Chief and eldest son of Ragnar, first Earl of Orkney, vassal to King Erik Goldenhair was mine and I wast his."

Tal slumped back against his pillows as the weight of returning memories, and their unanswered questions, drop-slammed him all at once. His broken contract with Helblad, having to leave Kentro in Five-Hells, his decision concerning the Taleria that had no doubt cost the Omada a certain win. And still there were so many other blank spaces that needed filling.

Aislinn gently took his left hand, "Taliesin, do not sorrow." Tal watched as a cold cloud of sadness moved across Aislinn's face, only to be pushed away by the warmth of her returning smile. "'Tis a day for joy, Amarantos hast returned thee to us. With the Tyrning done, your teammates be tasked with responsibilities most grave and urgent. Having no duties I didst beseech the Archon for the privilege of attending thee until thou didst awake."

"When? When will I get to see them?" Tal asked.

"The Archon magyked the infirmary so all of Omada would be alerted when thou didst wake. I have little doubt they chafe even now to finish their required chores so they might hasten here. I have been asked to answer what questions I can until they arrive."

Tal kept trying to get his brain back into its normal groove but it kept refusing. "I do have a lot of questions but I'm afraid they will seem like a random scattershot right now."

"Make the beginning, Taliesin," she invited him.

"You said I've been out of it for two weeks?"

"Yes. Thou hast been in an unconscious state for fourteen days of Earth plane time."

"What the hell?" Tal asked. "Two weeks? Why didn't somebody immediately abracadabra me brand spanking new?"

Aislinn shook her head and smiled. "I hast lived with the Folk so long I sometimes forget that we mortals be strangers to magyk. A Hero you mayst be but thou too art a Child of the Divine Spark. Magyk dost not a panacea be for every problem.

" 'Tis only by Amarantos's divine hand that even with help thou didst make it through the Ruling Council's declaration of Omada as the winning team."

"Omada won...," Tal mused. "That's wonderful news but I don't remember a thing. Not any of it."

"It was expected that if thou didst survive, thou wouldst remember but little. Thou didst collapse immediately after the declaration of the Hunts winner.

"Lord Alberich had already summonsed the seven strongest Folk physicks in all of the known Realms but they could not treat you magykally prior to the official announcement. Immediately after the ceremony ended, the Archon didst transport thou here, where the physicks were waiting to attend thee. They didst work without surcease for seachtain amháin efforting to negate the remainder of the foul poison from thee. When those seven were depleted to the point where their lfyeforces were almost completely drained, the next seven strongest took over. During it all, the Archon used all of the magyk given to him as Archon, until he was forcibly restrained because of the danger to his own lyfe. At that, it still took all of the front door sentries to remove him from the infirmary. It was clear he intended to expend all of his lyfeforce trying to save thee. The new seven physicks worked until earlier today, when they too wast almost totally drained."

It was a lot of information but Tal was trying to keep up. Like, what kind of poison is that terrible? "I'll thank Alberich first thing when I finally get out of here." When he saw Aislinn was about to interrupt him, he hurriedly continued, "Okay, I have some stray fragments of memory but they're all jumbled up in my brain. I need some help filling the blanks chronologically from the last thing I remember. Which is almost drowning in the Styx. No, that's not right," he corrected himself. "I remember blowing out of the top of Fountain Flow and being sure I was going to die when I came down. Then I saw the sunbeam created rainbow display the words on Mokosh's sword. I yelled them as loud as I've ever yelled in my life and then…then all of the statues came to life? Is that right?"

"They wast not statues, Taliesin, they wast living beings."

"That's right. Notos told me that in Five-Hells. Dammit, there is so much I can't remember. But that means that Fountain Flow…"

"Yes. It be the continuation of the river Styx, although it be not part of the Hunts School campus proper."

"Okay, I'm lost," Tal admitted.

"The river Styx remains part of Five-Hells as it travels up from the hellmouth. As long as it doth flow, however much or little, the river be magyked to prevent passage of all non-Hunts School beings, whether Creature or Folk. It be one of the most powerful magyks protecting the school. Lord Veles, however, didst use the powers of Styx for an additional purpose."

"To turn those Folk into living marble for tens of thousands of years. Seems especially shitty, even for that lowlife. He was going to leave them there for all of time?"

"Until all be gathered to Her when Amarantos hast decided it is time for eternity to begin."

"Eternity," Tal mused. "Never thought about it but eternity pretty much means no more time." Central Processing threw a random thought up for discussion as revelation began ordering his potpourri of jumbled thoughts. "River Run is the Styx. It's one of the Hunts School's most powerful wards. Students can cross because they belong on campus. That's why the Keres couldn't cross to the other side to kill us during first term."

Aislinn nodded.

Tal's brain ran with the current thought-thread. "That can't be right. The Cooshies were able to cross the water."

"Didst Arthrys not tell thee they were 'summoned to battle' by your act of self-sacrifice?"

"Yeah, he did. Just something else I didn't understand at the time. You're saying the Cooshies could cross because their presence was an extension of my action to protect the students?"

"Thou be correct."

Tal replied before his brain hopscotched on him once more. "Wait. Fountain Flow sits on top of a ploutonion? So what Emet read in the history book was true." There were so many questions spinning in his head, Tal couldn't make them queue up. His stream of consciousness was now split into a multi-tongued torrent of thoughts. "Damn it! I completely forgot. Emet. Did he? Is he?"

"Fret not, Emet be safely returned to Hunts School. He shall attend thee shortly."

Emet is safe, Tal thought. I did something right. No, not me, his memory reminded him as his shoulders drooped low "Notos. He gave himself up for Emet and me. Someone else paid the debtpryce for bringing us both home."

A wry smile quirked Aislinn's entire face. "Thou be correct. To a point. "Notos had no choice but to honor the agreement made with his father to remain in Five-Hells, helping to rule over its subjects and the damned until Time's end."

"Well, at least I kept my promise to him." Tal repositioned himself on the pillows, overwhelmed as the sudden and complete recollection of the events in Five-Hells flooded his brain. "That sourpuss curmudgeon may have been the best of us all," he finally mumbled. "Hold on," he said sitting up straighter, "I'm not trying to be rude but you were big big smiling just now and this doesn't seem to be even a little little smileable subject," Tal replied. Again came the smile. "Ah, there was a proviso. You said 'to a point'."

"Aye, I did," Aislinn said, as her smile grew exponentially. "Thou mightst have heard 'tis said, 'Five-Hells hath no fury like a wife imprisoned for millennia by her husband before finally being set free'."

"Oddly specific proverb, and quite frankly, no, I haven't heard it before," Tal replied. "But I like where this is going since it seems like at the end old Veles is going to get something shoved up his fire and ice ass."

"Turns out there be a significant number of denizens of Five-Hells who favor Mokosh over Veles. Something about him being a 'humongous arse,' if I understand correctly."

"We're talking coup," Tal replied.

"Verily. There apparently might have been a successful one if Mokosh and Veles had not come to terms."

"They bound a contract," Tal interjected.

"That they did. The contract had several terms which thou might find of interest. First, Veles remains Lord of Five-Hells but Mokosh is now co-ruler. Both have plenipotentiary powers."

"Beyoncé was right," Tal mused.

Aislinn pursed her lips before responding. "I do not understand."

"Sorry, pop culture reference," Tal stated. "I think you said there were several matters I might find interesting."

Aislinn's smile returned. The current generation was even smilier than the iteration from only moments before. "Yes, yes, yes." She stopped and clasped Tal's arm. "Arawn will be allowed to remain part of the Ruling Council and to come and go from Five-Hells for his official duties for all of this Tyrning." Aislinn almost squealed. "Isn't that wonderful?"

Tal hadn't realized how assiduously guilt had been squishing his heart with its mean-ass bony claws until he felt it relax its grip. Positive outcomes. First, Emet and now Notos. "That's wonderful news. Thank you."

"There be more," she added gleefully. "The Hunts have now been concluded. Any person who might have voluntarily Journeyed to Five-Hells because they were truly Seeking the Center hast been released."

Central Processing was still struggling upstream toward normal but the current was now flowing somewhat swifter. "Kentro," Tal breathed. "Kentro has been set free."

" 'Tis so," Aislinn confirmed.

"But the Snype's prophecy, Kentro himself told me while we were in Five-Hells that…"

"Aye," Aislinn said, interrupting him. "The Hunts now be over and the Tyrning won. The great wyrm's prophecy wast fulfilled and be now concluded."

Tal felt gladness, a too-long absent friend, greet him. At the same time he started feeling a little, well, stretched. Like taffy that's been pulled to the breaking point, he thought. Chills overtook him. Chills and a brutal lethargy.

Aislinn obviously noticed his physical change because she leaned over and picked up a washcloth to dab his forehead. "Thank you," he responded. "I'm sorry, I'm feeling really wiped out. And there is so much more I can't remember that I need for you to tell me. Like what happened immediately after I hit the ground. The only other mental images I keep seeing make no sense. I see Principal Chiron...and a long knife or sword, and then...and then for some freakin' reason he stabbed me."

"In truth it wast not Chiron. Chiron wast murdered sometime ere Hunts School reconvened, more than a hundred years ago."

"I don't understand. Then who..." Tal stopped, both because he was feeling dizzy and because he'd heard a noise from the far end of the infirmary.

Aislinn glanced quickly in that direction, then returned her attention to Tal. "My time with thee be almost done, Taliesin. Unlike thee my name wast never in The Book. 'Twere only by special leave of the Archon I wast permitted to remain until I could bring you my tidings." Seriousness seized control of her beautiful face. " 'Tis the rightful place of others to tell thee the remainder of all thou seekest to know."

It wasn't until then Tal realized he'd forgotten to ask about someone. Someone very important to the both of them. "Helblad. I've broken my contract with Helblad. I was supposed to deliver you to the Earth Realm's Maes Howe before the Coronation Ceremony."

A shudder of sorrow rocked Aislinn. It took her a handful of heartbeats but she finally shook it off, squared her shoulders, and proffered Tal a beatific smile in its place. " 'Twas only fitting the most important message I bear to thee be saved for last."

Tal watched as Aislinn stood erect, tears in both eyes but her head held high, her shoulders back. "It 'tis my very great honor and privilege to tell thee that because of your selfless act, Arnfinn Skullcrusher, War Chief and eldest son of Ragnar, first Earl of Orkney, vassal to King Erik Goldenhair, one of the mightiest warriors that hast ever walked the mortal Realm, he who wast the love of my life, hast finally died. He hast now been properly burned on a funeral pyre so his spirit mightst be carried to Valhalla, where he shall one day be joined with the UnFading Spirit."

It finally occurred to Tal that it wasn't only his rational thought processing that was jacked all to hell, his emotional controls were severely out of whack as well. Maybe it was an unintended side effect of two weeks of magykal healing. Overcome, he said the only thing he could think to say, "I am so, so sorry, Aislinn."

She smiled even more broadly than before. Wiping the tears from her eyes, she continued. " 'Tis no need for any to be sorrowful this day. I have remained that I mayst personally give thee my lord's message of thanks and to bestow upon you his blessing."

"I don't...I don't understand," Tal replied. A frown appeared across his forehead as he tried his hardest to process the data. "I don't understand how that can possibly be good news. Even though we started out a little rocky, Helblad ended up being one of my closest friends. Sure, there was that whole thing where he would have had to kill me and eat me if I failed to hold up my end of our bargain, but I'm pretty sure he wasn't going to enjoy it. Hell, Aislinn, I don't understand what there is to be thankful about and my brain isn't helping me out much right now."

"Soothe thyself," she replied, as she leaned forward to grasp his hand. "There be things worse than death."

That warning, Tal thought. That warning was on Luna's junkyard and on the blackboard in the Hunts classroom from the very first day of school.

Aislinn continued. "Things such as my forced servitude over the many centuries Arnfinn spent trapped as a draugr. Be assured that both of those be things worse than death. Arnfinn spent wasted centuries having been misled into believing that hate had power enow to preserve him so that he might save me."

Tal began to understand. A little, anyway. Please, he begged all components of his gray matter, let me finish this conversation with Aislinn before you slingshot me to the next topic. "I was right, then. Your message to my crew in Atlantis—it wasn't just for me. It was for Helblad, wasn't it?"

Aislinn nodded, smiling even as her face prepared itself for the inevitable thunderhead of tears. "Aye, thee hadst the right of it. 'Tis a lesson we each hae to learn—or fail to learn, as the case may be—in the time Amarantos hast gyfted us. Of a surety, Hate doth be bold and brash. It strutteth about as if it 'twere the cock of the walk, sparkling with false light. Brassy it be as it clangs loudly for attention, making empty promises for those who wouldst be seduced into following its path. Mark thee, Taliesin—Hate be a scabrous liar, Death's willing vassal. Hate hath no real substance, it be only the mephitic reek of the voluntary corruption of a heart.

"Love alone must be our Lyfe's liege. Only Love be enow to sustain us as we wander this mortal plane, 'tis only Love will see us to our home with the UnFading Spirit." Aislinn stopped a moment, the tears now flowing from underneath the shimmering green of her eyes. "It 'tis only in Love's service that we be able to find the way from our heart to that of another."

As she took a moment to wipe her face, she looked at the moisture on her fingertips. "Taliesin, these be tears of joy and gratitude. Joy for him…and gratitude to thee. 'Twas only when Arnfinn found me on Atlantis plane that he didst realize it wast his True Love for me that wast paramount. He had the opportunity to exact vengeance upon the Finman and the blackguard Harald but he chose to turn his back on Hate, and in so doing, opened his arms to Love. It 'twas at that moment he became mortal once again."

"Mortal? But when he was last mortal…his injuries?" Tal asked softly.

Aislinn nodded. "They claimed his life. But not until I had the chance to comfort him. Not until we hadst the chance to hold each other and to swear one last time our undying love for each the other." She leaned over and kissed Tal on his forehead.

"Because of thy generous heart I will see Arnfinn once more when it comes my time to be gathered unto Amarantos."

Tal knew he was about to break down himself so he changed the subject. "Where will you go now, what will you do?"

"There is another who finds himself no longer 'mortal suspended.' Another like me whose tyme on Earth Realm has past."

"Myrddin," Tal whispered.

"Aye," Aislinn confirmed. "Your father. His name be not in The Book either so 'tis impossible for him to cross River Run now to bid thee farewell. At the Lady Aurora's invitation, I go from here to live in the Pentacle."

Tal was back to being clueless. "But the last time I saw Myrddin…well, actually the next to last time I saw him…well, I guess it depends upon whether you are going in strictly chronological order or whether you put othertyme before realtyme, even if the othertyme happened after the realtyme… anyway, he said I would see him once more."

"Mayhaps you shall then," Aislinn replied. "He be very proud of his son. As are we all. Proud, and grateful. Slán abhaile, Taliesin Smith. Safe home," she concluded, as she turned to leave.

As Aislinn gracefully exited the infirmary, Tal found himself crying. Again. Damn, maybe I'm not healed after all, he thought. Physically or mentally.

The metallic swing of the double doors recalled him from his reverie. Tal quickly used a corner of his bed sheet to smear the moisture off his cheeks. As he watched, he saw the second unknown beautiful woman of the morning enter the infirmary.

CHAPTER CENTUM TRIGINTA OCTO

As Tal watched, a blonde-haired vision floated into the room. He rubbed his eyes. No really, she's floating, he reassured himself. The woman took her time wafting down the center aisle. She was dressed in an unadorned midlength blue gown. The simplicity of the dress provided a perfect background for a necklace of flashing fire opals. In her right hand she carried a clear glass chalice full of pink liquid.

There's something familiar about that necklace, Tal thought. C'mon brain, there's way too much going on for you to still be AWOL on me.

As the woman arrived at his bedside she lowered herself until her feet gracefully touched the floor. "This is for you," she said, proffering the glass to Tal.

Okay, Tal, told himself. Even in your mentally debilitated condition, you know you don't throw back a glass full of sparkling Pepto-Bismol without asking some probing questions. You mean probing questions like what color was the hemlock tea Socrates drank, one area of his brain asked. Random, some other part of his brain chimed in response. "Umm, what is it?" he finally asked.

The woman laughed as she sat in the chair recently occupied by Aislinn. "It's an energy drink I made just for you, silly." Tal realized he must have still had his face formed in a skeptical format because she quickly added, "It's okay, Quint, the

Archon authorized me to administer it to you once you awakened on your own."

Tal took a sip. Okay, it looks bilious but it tastes like a double chocolate malted shake. A really odd pink double chocolate malted shake but a delicious shake nonetheless.

"How is it?" the woman asked.

"Not too shabby. Hey, look, I'm going to be honest. My memory is a little whack right now and your voice sounds familiar and everything but…do I know you?"

More laughter. Gentle laughter with a much needed soothing echo. It was fun laughter. Like one could imagine a small rivulet making as it burbled while playing hopscotch over shiny river stones. Wow, Tal, your brain really is out of control, see if you can get a grip on the rampant metaphoria.

"I am so sorry," the young woman replied. It's been unbelievably busy these past two weeks and you've been unconscious every time I've been able to shake loose to come check on you. Hello? It's me, silly. Anatolia. Well, actually, I'm going by my psuche name now. Aphrodite."

Wow, Tal thought. Ana was beautiful before, but now? Wow. "Yeah, that avatar selection was a no-brainer," Tal replied, as he took another big slug of his drink.

Anatolia smiled broadly. "Clearly the elixir must already be working."

"I do feel a little better," Tal said, as he began to move around on his bed a little, checking his energy level.

"Good. Finish that and it should temporarily get you back up to semi-restored. It may only last a few minutes. Time is still going to have to do most of the heavy lifting to get you completely healed." She motioned for him to take another swallow, which he did. "Dysi, well, she is now The Mielikki, sends her sincere regrets. The Archon has already sent her as part of a two-person team to appraise a new Realm that has sent an envoy through the Prime Omphalos. Everyone is beside themselves at the news. They are the first new Folk in many years."

"Let me take a wild guess. The other member of her team is Kentro?" Tal asked.

Ana smiled in response. "You know?"

"Yes, Aislinn told me."

"We were all so excited when he came through the Gate of Anguish with Emet. Dysi, of course, more than anyone else. They've been inseparable since his return. The next three centuries are going to be extremely rewarding. Hectic but rewarding."

Tal was definitely starting to feel much more like himself. "What about me, Ana? When is Borras going to give me my first team assignment?"

Anatolia glanced quickly down at her hands before raising her head to make eye contact again. She then leaned over and kissed him on his right cheek. "Well, I see we're going to need to work on our names and titles. Borras is now The Atlas. Actually, Lord Atlas, as he is the Archon. He is on his way now to visit with you, Tal. It would be better if you had that conversation with him." She paused a moment before leaning forward and kissing him quickly. On the lips this time.

"Hot damn! What was that for?"

"That was for thank you. That was for good luck. That was for...goodbye, Quint of the Omada, who is now both Taliesin and The Taliesin. May Amarantos guide your steps and be with you always." With that, Anatolia turned, first walking and then rising in the air to float back down the aisle, her hands covering her face. Even from the back, Tal could tell her chest was heaving from sobbing.

What's up with that, Tal wondered. Sure, I'm still mortal so I won't last as long as the rest of them but I have a few good decades ahead of me. Tal chugged the rest of his drink. "I'm tired of laying here doing nothing," he finally said, just to break the silence. He thought about what had just happened. "And now I'm talking to myself. Clearly, I have to get out of here." He swung his legs over the edge of the bed. Much better this time. Of course I have no clothes. He looked around the infirmary. Surely there's a locker around here where they keep some clothing. I should have one with a nameplate on it by now.

CHAPTER CENTUM TRIGINTA NOVEM

As Tal was bent over looking under the bed for clothes, or shoes, or pretty much anything wearable, his search was interrupted.

"Hey sport, if you're thinking about going out in public, I would suggest somewhat different attire. Bareass isn't really a good look for you."

Tal looked up to see the voice's owner was already only about ten feet away from him. He was a trim young man. Short. Really short. Less than five feet. The man was wearing a natty royal blue pinstriped suit, a light pink wing-collared French cuffed shirt, glossy black wingtips, his ensemble completed by a matching pink patterned tie and pocket square. Actually, it looks like he's an escapee from the set of "Honey, I Shrunk the Extremely Dapper Accountant." That voice, Tal thought, that voice is familiar.

What else do you notice, Tal asked Optics. Well, he's carrying a shopping bag. What else? His skin is a light blue color. Right. Anything else that might be important? Anything at all? Oh, right. There's the whole he's wearing a crown thing

The speaker reached Tal's bed. He set the handled bag on the floor before reaching in and pulling out some jeans and a black t-shirt. He put those on the bed before reaching back into the bag and retrieving a pair of white Chuck Taylor high-tops, which he placed on the floor. He then sat down in the guest chair next to Tal's bed. "Gotta admit, it kind of wigged me out when I found out you're The Taliesin."

The guy's voice finally clicked for Tal. "Borras? I mean…The Atlas, is it?"

"That's Lord Atlas, if you don't mind," Borras said, grinning broadly, as he stuck his hand out for Tal to shake. Just like when we first met Tal thought, as he gripped Borras's hand.

"But, you're so…so…normal sized."

"Surely after all you've been through this year, you're not going to engage in the fallacious assumption you can judge a book by its cover?"

Tal laughed and shook his head in the negative.

"And for what it's worth," Borras now The Atlas, continued, "I'm pretty much a giant as far as my Folk are concerned."

"For what it's worth, you're pretty much a giant as far as any of us are concerned," Tal added.

"Thank you," his close friend and now the brand new leader of the known universe, replied. "Did The Aphrodite give you her elixir?"

Tal nodded.

Borras motioned for Tal to sit back on the bed before laying his right hand on Tal's forehead. Tal felt a sudden flush emanating from that spot outward. It kept going and going until it reached all of his extremities.

"There," Borras finally said. "That healing should heal you as much as magykally possible. Your body will have to heal itself through the passage of time."

"Wait a minute," Tal exclaimed. "The Archon who was here for days and nights, the one that had to be removed by force. That wasn't Alberich, it was you."

"Yes," Borras said. "After everything you've done for me, for the Omada, for all of us, how could I do anything less in return? You need to cut yourself some slack for awhile, Tal. You're not going to be one hundred percent back in the game, physically or emotionally, for some time. It's at least seven times seven miracles you even survived. I can't begin to describe how much healmagyk has passed through your mortal system these past two weeks."

"I'm completely lost. I don't have the faintest clue how we even ended up winning the Hunts after I, well, after I..."

"Slow down, buddy. I'm here to bring you up to speed on everything. Well, everything that I can. I was kind of hoping you might be able to figure out one important thing for me. How much did Aislinn cover with you?"

"I'm pretty clear about everything that happened while I was in Five-Hells. I remember holding my breath for as long as I could, certain I was going to drown in the River Styx before I apparently shot out the top of Fountain Flow. Aislinn told me a little about Mokosh. She gave me the good news about Notos, Emet, and Kentro...and she told me about Helblad. Everything else keeps getting tangled up with other memories and thoughts. It's like all of my thoughts are triple-knotted shoelaces and my fingernails are too short to get them unknotted."

"Like I said, you're going to have to give it some time," Borras said kindly. "With mental matters there's a fine magykal line between compulsion, which is taboo, and repair."

Tal sat up as straight as he could while sitting in a bed. "My head doesn't hurt, Borras, it's just not working correctly. My memories are only partially backfilling and in a completely random, non-logical sequence."

Borras patted Tal's arm "It would be kinder to wait for all of this until you weren't still at risk mentally. I'm sorry but I don't have the luxury of waiting. You need to know everything that has happened, so you can help me figure out something extremely important."

"Got it," Tal said firmly. "I want to help. For what it's worth, I feel like my brain will be more damaged if I leave it like it is more than it could possibly be from knowing everything that's happened. Plus, it keeps jumping around on me. Before it moves on to something else, please give me the complete chronology. All of it."

The brand new Archon of the entire known universe looked compassionately at his human friend. "It's a lot, Taliesin, and it's going to be tough to hear. I'm going to give you the whole story. Then you're going to have to help me. I am now responsible for the lives of every living human, Folk, and

Creature. I desperately need to find an answer. I know that special brain of yours can find it, but to do so you have to know absolutely everything first.

"We'll start with the last thing you independently remember. Not from Aislinn or from me, you on your own. What was it?"

"Being shot out of Fountain Flow and hitting the turf."

Borras continued. "I got to admit that whole sequence was pretty damn cool. Well except for the 'you were close to having every bone in your body broken' part. The force of your expulsion shot you several hundred feet higher than the top of the plume. I'd say you were well above the top of the spire on the main building."

Tal whistled a little through his teeth, "That's almost as tall as a forty story building."

"There were hundreds of us gathered around the fountain, waiting to be called to the Great Hall. It took a couple of seconds for us to even realize it was you coming out of it. Even then we didn't know whether you were alive or dead until you began screaming hysterically…"

Tal couldn't help but interrupt at that point. "It's not like I had just been shot out of a hellmouth in a water coffin. Naked."

"Point taken," Borras agreed, smiling. "Anyway, right before you started your free fall you began repeatedly shouting a phrase in Latin."

"That's right. It was, '*cor aut mors*'," Tal confirmed. "The literal translation is 'heart or death.' It essentially means live with honor or else you've never really been alive. Funny, the first time I saw it was when some random sunbeam happened to refract the water on the sword. This time, this time, as I looked down towards the ground, right when I was about to abandon hope and close my eyes, a rainbow from the spray drifted across the sword. Huh. First time it was a sunbeam that showed me the words. This time it was a rainbow."

Borras tapped his finger against his chin. "You're thinking it wasn't a coincidence either time? That it might have been a brother-sister Principe act?"

"Principes and Creatures aren't bound by the Hunts

Rules restrictions, only Folk. I guess we'll never know for sure," Tal concluded.

"We looked your phrase up, Tal. 'Cor aut mors' is the Latin translation of the original Slavic incantation that would release Mokosh. On the outside chance that Notos might see the sword's inscription Veles wrote it in Latin to make it almost impossible for Notos to figure out."

"Veles," Tal practically spat the name. "You know that guy is really not a very nice person."

"Agreed," Borras replied. "The second you yelled the words Mokosh sprang to life, along with every other entity that was trapped with her in Fountain Flow. Tal, they weren't in suspended animation for all those millennia, they were completely conscious…"

"I know, Notos told me," Tal added. "Like I said, Veles is really not a nice guy."

"It was clear Mokosh and every one of her crew wanted to help you, to catch you but…"

"Folk are prohibited from interfering in any of the Hunts and the Treasyre Hunt wasn't over. So, why am I alive?"

"Turns out if you're sufficiently worthy to survive the passage from Five-Hells there is complementary magyk on the Hunts School end to ensure your survival. The magyk only guarantees survival, not a pleasant landing. Even with the magyk and the lawn being completely water-soaked, your head made a pretty good bounce. Three bounces actually."

Tal felt around the back of his head. "I thought I felt something new back there sufficient to commission a phrenological study."

Borras continued. "Omada was on the far side of Fountain Flow from where you landed. As soon as you hit, you were surrounded by the former prisoners and several hundred students. That's when Principal Chiron appeared at the front doors of the school. He came running down the steps, two at a time, screaming for everybody to get back. At first we thought he was only trying to make sure no one violated the Hunts Rules by helping you. Even though we were running toward you, none of us were close enough to help. I really don't know how you did it but you managed to stagger to your feet. It was clear to us all you were major jacked up, both physically and mentally."

"Aislinn said something about this before she got all weird and non-talky. Something like Principal Chiron wasn't really Principal Chiron?"

"No, he wasn't," the new Archon confirmed. "Fake Chiron started screaming about how he'd waited hundreds of years to take his vengeance and today was your day of reckoning. From nowhere he drew a sword and before anyone even knew he had it, he thrust it all the way to the handguard through your stomach."

Tal rubbed his abdominal area before pulling his shirt up to take a look. The scar was sizeable and just to the right of his navel. It was still pinkish but fully healed.

"Chiron pulled the sword out and started screaming that the sword's magyk should finish you but he had been promised your head and he was taking it. He swung the sword behind his head in a great arc and was just starting to bring it forward to cut your head off when…WHAM!"

Tal jumped as Borras yelled his last word.

"In less than the space of time that exists between two heartbeats, a shuriken struck his sword arm knocking it backwards. A second throwing star then struck his right thigh collapsing him downward and just as he started to fall forward, a third shuriken buried itself halfway into his skull. Right between his eyes. He died instantly."

"Wow. There's only one person whose fashion sense heavily favors instruments of death."

"Yes. While everyone was focused on you and Chiron, the HuntsMistress had also hauled ass from the front of the school. Tal, she was still more than a hundred yards away when she made those three throws."

"This entire year, all the times she seemed to have it in for me, I had her pretty much pegged for the bad guy in this whole narrative."

"Nope," Borras, said as he shook his head in the negative. "Another important lesson learned."

"What's that?" Tal asked.

"Some people are just born assholes," Borras replied, smiling.

"Word," Tal confirmed. "Again, why aren't I dead?"

"You need to be prepared, Taliesin, the story only gets tougher from here."

Hundreds of memory fragments were still careening in Tal's head. For a moment, two or three that belonged together would hit and stick and Tal would get a partial visual. Then they'd fly apart and seconds later perhaps another four or five would momentarily align. A pattern began to emerge, well a partial pattern. Tal knew he knew something. He also knew what he knew was bad, really bad. He felt himself becoming steadily more agitated as he began to remember. One image kept reappearing. Piras!

"Borras, where's Piras? I can remember he was at Fountain Flow at some point. He was talking to me. Well, think-talking, you know. He was trying to help me. Is he hurt? If he was injured he should be in here too." Tal felt frustration as well now. "Is it just some more ridiculous Folk bigotry that Creatures and Folk can't all be treated in the same infirmary?"

Tal couldn't stop himself moving beyond agitated, into frantic. His hands began clenching and unclenching and he couldn't stop them. "I know it wasn't a dream, Borras. I have a recollection of Piras whispering in my mind. He was telling me he could save me." Tal gave all of the beds in the infirmary another quick look-see. "Where is he? You know he can't get here on his own power. Can someone bring him? I need to put him on. I need to talk to him, to thank him."

A single, wide furrow wrinkled the width of the Archon's forehead as he leaned forward and placed his hand on Tal's forearm. "Taliesin, stop," he said softly. "Your heart knows the answer. Piras is gone. He sacrificed himself to save your life."

"No!" Tal exclaimed, reflexively trying to jump up and out of the bed. Okay, still physically jacked up, Motor Control reported.

Borras paused a moment. "Taliesin, time is short and we have much to discuss. Please sit back," he said patting the bed. After Tal complied, he continued. "I told you, with the unprecedented amount of healmagyk you were administered, you're going to be pretty messed up for awhile.

"I don't want to do this to you but I have to find out who has been trying to disrupt the Tyrning Cycle. And why. I think you can help me but only if you remember everything. I have the power as Archon to join our event memories together. We will each see, hear, and think the thoughts of each other. Together we should be able to reconstruct what you presently can't remember. Tal, this is dangerous Archon magyk."

"Do it!"

"You're not only human, you're not completely healed…"

"Do it! Now!" Tal demanded vehemently.

Borras took his teammate's left hand. "You have to let me finish. This is going to be all kinds of bad, for both of us. We will each feel everything the other was feeling during the event."

"I don't care," Tal quickly replied. "I'll do whatever it takes to get the asshole who's doing this. I consent. Do you?"

"I consent," Borras responded, as he clasped right hands with Tal. "Focus on the events immediately following your stabbing."

Tal did as his Prime directed.

"Now, take us there."

Even though his eyes remained wide open, Taliesin watched as the infirmary simply went away, replaced by what appeared to be a movie screen.

'Quint,…'

"Piras? Is that you? Where are you? Hey, guys. You know what's funny? I think I hear Piras talking to me. From far away."

'Quint, you must focus. We have only moments before it will be too late.'

"This is bad," Anatolia said, as she knelt next to Tal. "He's already slipping into delirium." She quickly bent over, ripped a strip off the bottom of her skirt and dipped it into Fountain Flow. "Quint thinks his Puca is talking to him."

"That's impossible," Borras replied. "All of the Pucas have been stored in our gym lockers since the last Journey."

Anatolia laid the cool, wet cloth on Tal's forehead with her left hand, while she reached out and placed her right hand over his heart. "His heartbeat is weak and arrhythmic." She looked up at her team leader. "He has maybe a handful of minutes, Borras. I might could help but I have no healmagyk here on campus."

Dysi angrily looked around, staring at everyone in the burgeoning crowd. "Someone has to do something, anything." No one did.

"We're not officially done with the Hunt, Dysi," Borras replied. "You know they can't assist us in any way."

'Quint—command Borras to send someone to the team room. You left me there, not in your gym locker. Remember?'

Tal gave a little laugh, which led to a large sputum-filled cough. When he was finally able to speak again, he replied to the Puca. "Command Borras? That's crazy talk. He's the Omada Prime, I can't tell him what to do. Wait, what? Hey, everybody. Piras just reminded me I left him in the team room after our last Journey and before I..." Tal watched as Memory Tal began writhing on the wet grass, muscle spasms preventing him from continuing with conversation.

Without a beat of hesitation, Borras looked to Dysi. "Faster than the wind, Dysi. As you've never run before." Dysi was fifty yards toward the back of the main building before Borras even finished his order.

As Tal started to thrash violently, the Omada Prime lowered himself to one knee so he could firmly grasp both of Tal's shoulders with his massive hands. "Hang in there, Quint," he said. He then motioned to Anatolia to pick up a pencil from the school supplies scattered all over Grass Grow. When she handed it to him, he placed it between Tal's teeth.

Dysi returned only moments later and wordlessly laid the folded Puca under Tal's head. Tal hard wretched several times in quick succession causing the pencil to explode from his mouth, followed immediately by a cascade of blood.

The Puca whispered in Tal's brain. *'Tal you must now say the words to me.'*

"'Piras?" Tal asked wanly, the red blood now turning to a pinkish froth at the corners of his mouth. "Is that you, buddy? Wait a minute, you said my psuche name, didn't you?"

'Yes, Tal, I know everything about you. Remember, Pell used your name when we retrieved the Taleria. Say the words to me, now!'

"Fine, but first I'm going to take a short nap."

'No, Tal. You must not sleep, not until you say the words.'

Tal tried to speak, but his tongue had grown so thick in his mouth he began choking on it.

"Borras, we're losing him," Anatolia said, crying as she stood up.

The Omada Prime put his arms around both she and Dysi. "Pray to the UnFading Spirit for strength and healing for Quint," Borras replied.

'Tal, I cannot bring you back from death itself. Your muscles cannot make the sounds now, you must think-say the words to me. Now. Think, "I consent".'

'I-I-I con ... con...sent.'

'Now you must ask me. "Do you?" Tal, think it quickly. "Do you"?'

'Do ... you?'

'Yes.' With that the Puca began to swell from under Tal's head, beginning the process of enveloping him. *'Goodbye, Taliesin Smith. It has been my great honor to be your friend. Remember, worlds still depend upon you. You may sleep now, Child of the Dust. My brethren and I will take it from here.'*

The Omada watched helplessly as Tal's facial muscles went slack.

Dysi was the first to notice something different about the Puca's actions. "Wait a minute. Stop him! Stop the Puca! He's covering all of Quint, including his head and feet."

Anatolia quickly knelt and tried to grab a handful of the Puca to stop its progress. "If he covers Quint completely, he'll kill him."

Borras reached down and gently pulled Ana to her feet. "Let the Puca be, Ana. It is Quint's only chance."

The process continued until Tal was completely covered. A few minutes later the Puca suddenly lost its iridescence and slid off of Tal, flopping onto the close-cropped surface of Grass Grow. It lay there, inanimate, looking like a wrinkled, washed out old red silk blanket. Tal, now naked, also lay unmoving on the manicured lawn.

"What just happened?" Dysi asked.

Borras stood there, humongous tears rolling down his cheeks. "I think the Puca just sacrificed himself trying to save Quint."

The movie reel blurred, then stutter-framed away. Tal blinked as the infirmary reappeared. One quick look to the Omada Prime and he could see that Borras was again weeping. "Borras, you saw, did you see what Piras did?"

Stunned, the Omada Prime said nothing, did nothing. For a few moments. Then for a few more moments. When he started talking, it was clear he was himself just then putting facts together to form conclusions. "So, that's why they...why all of them..." He stopped and pulled focus to Tal. "It wasn't just Piras. He was the High King of the Puca. All of the Puca in service for the Hunts must have consented to..."

A wave of nausea bitch-slapped Tal. "No, Borras, please, don't..."

Lord Atlas clearly didn't want to continue but felt he had to. "To give you even the barest chance of surviving, it cost the lives of all of the Puca on Hunts School campus."

Tal felt like someone had stomped on his chest. No, that doesn't adequately describe it, Logic replied. The not being able to breathe could be the result of someone stomping on your chest. The bone deep ache in the middle of your heart is in an entirely more substantial pain category. "Why?" Tal pleaded. Both Ana's elixir and Borras's magyk must have worn off, he thought, as he realized he once again had barely enough energy to sit upright. "Why? Why would Piras sacrifice himself and his people for one human?"

Borras used the sleeve of his fancy, tailored jacket to wipe his own eyes, before taking a deep breath to continue. "When Notos made the deal with his father to free you and Emet, that left Omada with only four members for the remainder of the contest. For the Omada to remain in the Tyrning competition we had to present our treasyre with all four of the remaining members alive—and in a non-maimed status. Because of the connection you and Piras shared, he knew, even though the rest of us were clueless at the time, the precise nature of the weapon used to strike you down."

"Which was?"

"A thrice-cursed blade, Tal. Multiple Folk sacrifices are required to make such a weapon. It is one of the most vile misuses of magyk that has ever been imagined.

"He knew you were going to be dead within minutes and that the Hunts Rules prohibited any of the Folk from interfering in the Hunt. Tal, even if Anatolia had been able to utilize her royal-level healmagyk, it wouldn't have been enough. You would have died."

"The Puca are Creatures and therefore not bound by the Hunts Rules," Tal confirmed, his voice trailing off toward the end.

"Piras must have asked every single one of the Puca on-campus for their consent. Good thing, too. As it turned out, it took the lyfeforce of every one of them to give you enough healing and energy to make it through the Hunts Ceremony. Even then we needed some timely help from Väst. After that you collapsed and remained in the coma for the last two weeks."

"I still don't get it. Piras was the leader of all of the Puca. His life was important."

"Said the Dust Child who has taught us all that every life is important. Human, Folk...and Creature," Borras said, a sliver of a smile emerging. "It's a lesson I will never forget. A lesson the Folk will never forget."

Tal rubbed his free-flowing nose with the corner of his bed sheet. "Sorry," he added. "Apparently there's no generic brand of magyk Kleenex."

"It's okay," Borras replied, reaching over to grab another corner of the sheet for his own nose. "To answer your question, Piras and his brethren gave their lives because in this place, in this time, because you have so assiduously sought the Center, you are the Lynchpin."

"Me?" Taliesin asked. "Why am I the Lynchpin?" He paused a moment before adding, "And what the hell is a Lynchpin?"

"A Lynchpin is someone who by their choices, for good or evil, becomes a fulcrum upon which an entire future balances. Do you think it a coincidence that both Gas Pump Unus and Piras told you the same thing?"

"That whole 'worlds depend upon me' hyperbole?" Tal asked.

"Right. Not so hyperbolic, huh? In either the physical or metaphysical meanings. Time and again during this school year you repeatedly made the difficult choice to Seek the Center. The results of your choices have already effected change in all of the known Realms. Because of the respect you gave all Creatures during the Hunts—and their reciprocity of that respect—I've already obtained commitments from a majority of the Areopagus to vote in favor of acknowledging that Creatures are also children of the UnFading Spirit. Invitations for all of them are being prepared and addressed as we speak."

"Invitations?" Tal asked.

"Yes," Borras beamed in response. "Invitations to formally join the Moiety. Those Creatures who elect to join will then be allowed to send student representatives for the next Hunts School session."

"That's huge, Borras. Sorry, Lord Atlas."

"Huge? It's a fundamental change in the order of the whole freaking known universe, Quint."

"And the Puca?"

"I have issued a full pardon for all past crimes, they have been released from any further obligation to serve at Hunts School, and they also are being invited to join the Moiety."

Tal couldn't stop the renewed tears. Clearly he was going to need some fresh linens for his bed. He gave up trying to stop them. Borras had told him his emotions were still yo-yoing big time and that this would be his life for a presently indeterminate amount of time.

More facts, Tal. If you had more facts it might help stabilize you, he told himself. Agreed, he agreed with himself. "If you'll start catching me up a little, I think it might help me settle." Now that he was down to only sporadic sniffling Tal went ahead and released his death grip on the now thoroughly besnotted sheet corner.

Borras took a deep breath and began the tale of the past two-weeks. "Piras and the Pucas gave you enough lyfeforce to keep you alive and on your feet. You were pretty much a zombye, though. Concussions by themselves are not a disqualifying event. Lots of contestants have received multiple concussions during the Hunts. It didn't matter that you were a few clowns short of a circus. As long as we could keep you upright until the winner was announced, we had the minimum four. All four of us knew we were racing the clock.

"As soon as you were able to stand on your own two feet Alberich materialized out of thin air. He took a long look at you. I'm pretty sure he knew things were not good because he asked Dysi and Ana to assist you while he took my arm and walked me back over to fake Chiron's corpse. After a moment of looking at the scene he waved his hand in the air and several moments later, Queen Aine materialized by his side.

"The Archon knew he couldn't interfere to assist you or the Omada in any manner, so he turned his attention to an Archon responsibility—finding out how magyk and a thrice-blooded sword had gotten around the Hunts School wards. Tal, the dead guy was Malebranche..."

CHAPTER CENTUM QUADRAGINTA

"Malebranche?" Tal asked in disbelief. "Arthrys's Mordred? The one I helped defeat during Arthrys's Hunts? How could that be? How could magyk be used on Hunts School campus?" Tal felt Chaos begin chewing on the fabric of his nascent understanding.

Borras must have seen Tal was losing it because he quickly added additional information. "Tal, the magyk used to glamour Malebranche was that of one of the Elder children. The same Elder magyk was used to help forge the thrice-cursed blade."

Tal felt like his reasoning ability was mired in quicksand. The more he struggled trying to comprehend the chain of events, the more his logic was sucked into a one-way morass. "Borras, I don't understand, I don't understand. Borras, please..."

"Hang in there with me, brother," Borras said, reaching over to grip Tal's upper arm. "Armed with that new information, Alberich authorized Queen Aine to use her awaymagyk to trace everywhere the blade had been during this school year. It turns out Malebranche perverted the binding of the rest of his teammates and used it so he could murder them to allow the blade to be magyked. Tal, Malebranche had to have known that even if Alberich could have interfered, even with all of his power as Archon, he couldn't have saved you. Not against a sword thrice-blooded with Elder magyk."

It's too much, Central Processing told him. It's simply too

much. Tal felt all of the partially formed images dissolving. Go ahead, Chaos. Chew away.

No damn it, he scolded himself. Fight. Amarantos has given you a wonderful mind. Use it. Do not concede to insanity. Don't do it. You know why you're teetering right now so deal with it.

"Come on, Tal. You got this. We're almost done," Borras said encouragingly before continuing. "I don't know how he did it but Alberich magyked every single member of the Areopagus and all of the Hunts contestants out onto Grass Grow. They had already been assembled and were waiting in the ziggurat for the determination of the Hunts winner and the Coronation Ceremony. Alberich had Marid, the Seneschal, call the Ceremony to order and directed HuntsMistress Empousa to call up the two remaining teams for presentation of their treasyres. That sequence of events is a whole different story. Ultimately, we were adjudged the winners. By acclamation of the entire Areopagus, I'd like to add."

Borras's explanation had given Tal's brain a chance to focus, to let the wave of madness crest and roll over the surface of his gray matter. Better, I'm better, he told himself. I can do this. Keep moving forward, fill in more of the blanks in the puzzle. "Archon, something tells me you have left out some extremely critical information. You intentionally skipped over the treasyre presentation. Who presented what treasyre? I know Lilith Empousa wasn't okay with Omada winning. And how did that all happen in the apparently brief period of time before I ran out of the lyfeforce the Puca gave me?"

Tal watched as a much smaller version of Borras's trademark grin passed across the Archon's face. Has to be smaller, Tal realize. Borras is about a tenth the size he used to be.

"Before you start, though. I need to get something off my chest. I'm sorry about the Taleria. In my heart I knew the right thing to do was to give it to Helblad. He'd been in pain for so many centuries. Trying to find his way back to Aislinn." Tal paused to look directly at Borras. "I don't know how to explain it to you but he needed it to save himself. He was so lost in his lust for vengeance he was unable to see the truth." Tal stopped for a moment to recollect all of the details. "I'm not sure there is even an instrument that can gauge how mad Notos was when I told him I'd had the Taleria almost all of the school year and that I had given it away right when the team needed it."

Borras grinned before responding. "Trust me, word of that epic fit has made its way all the way back to and around the entire campus. Tal, we are each called to win the Hunts by Seeking the Center. None of knows exactly what that entails, we certainly don't know what decisions we are going to be called upon to make in our quests. Giving the Taleria to Helblad was a tough call but you did what you thought Amarantos has called upon us all to do." Borras paused a moment as the grin broadened, turning the corners of his mouth upward. "As it turned out, even the Taleria, with the other pieces of treasyre that Dysi and Anatolia and I collected wouldn't have been sufficient for Omada to win the Hunt."

"I don't get it," Tal interjected. "That should have guaranteed a Släkt victory." Tal was feeling faint again. Not ill, simply washed out. Maybe this is what Superman would feel like if he had super mono, Tal thought. Actually, super mono would feel like regular mono to him. So, what you're saying is that it would be more analogous to what Superman's mono would feel like to a regular human? But how could Superman transmit super mono to a…focus, you mullet!

"Tal?" Borras asked. "You still with me?"

"I'm sorry. I'm alternating between manic and deathly lethargic."

"I'll finish this up. We all have things to do. The entire thing couldn't have been more dramatic. Släkt presented an impressive smorgasbord of items. Overwhelming might be a better description. They had a dozen level three pieces, five level fours, and two off the charts level five pieces. Each of those pieces by itself would have been enough to win.

"Väst brought the buckler of Iblis. Nord saved for last what he'd obtained. Solomon's Seal. An elite level five piece which ranked even higher than the buckler. You should have seen Nord's face when he tried to show off by using the ring to command the horde of jinn trapped in the buckler. Very definition of a hard fail."

"That's a pretty tough treasyre collection," Tal agreed.

"Exactly. Then it was our turn. We had your two pieces, ten more level threes, a couple of level fours, and three level five artifacts: a golden apple from the Garden of the Hesperides, the Celtic Cup of Truth, and a pearl teardrop from a Firebird."

"Sounds like a lot."

"It was and in any normal Hunt it would have put us over the top, but it clearly wasn't going to be enough to win against the buckler of Iblis and the Seal of Solomon."

"I knew it. The Taleria would have cinched it."

"I told you it wouldn't have been sufficient," Borras added firmly.

"There's no way we will ever know for sure, is there?" Tal asked.

"Au contraire," Borras replied. "We most certainly do. Omada was about to conclude our presentation when, Bam! Aislinn, wearing the Taleria on her feet, appeared in the middle of the conclave. She begged leave to address the Areopagus. Empousa was getting ready to shut her down when the Archon gave her leave to speak.

"She told the assemblage what you had done, that you had chosen to relinquish the Taleria, and that only because of your gyft was she freed from bondage and Helblad finally at peace. Dysi was so moved she stepped forward and reminded everyone the Hunts Rules require that a team win by Seeking the Center and that's what you had done on behalf of Omada.

"Even though metaphysical treasyre had never previously been considered in a Treasyre Hunt, the Ruling Council appeared to be swayed by Dysi's argument, until…"

"Until what?" Tal asked, impatient to know the outcome.

" 'Until whom,' would be a better question. The HuntsMistress. She stepped up and reminded the Ruling Council the decision of treasyre valuation in Treasyre Hunts was clearly within her discretion and they had no authority to overrule her or interfere with her decision.

"Her exact words after that statement, were, 'And I'm not counting any damn draugr True Love mumbo jumbo bullshit as treasyre. Omada either has sufficient qualifying real treasyre or they can pack their shit up like the rest of the losers and head on home.' It was clear from her comments even if we'd had the Taleria, she was going to use her discretion in Släkt's favor. The only way to win would be for us to have indisputably better treasyre."

"She's a real peach, that one. And?" Tal asked.

"It was Aislinn who answered her. She turned to Ms. Empousa and said, 'Helblad knew you'd say that. So he asked me to give you two things before you made your decision as to the Treasyre Hunt winner—a private message and a scroll'."

" 'How lovely,' the HuntsMistress replied. 'A private message from some dumbass undead nobody who is now finally and with good riddance a dead nobody. There's no need for the message to be private, draugr-lover, you may deliver it to the entire Areopagus.'

" 'If such be your will,' Aislinn replied, before drawing a deep breath. 'Lilith Empousa, you are a loveless, cold-hearted bytch, more heart-dead than even the most forlorn of my subjects'."

"Ouch!" Tal interjected.

"While Empousa was still sputtering that Aislinn couldn't talk to her like that, Aislinn approached her and handed her a sealed scroll. Written in extremely large letters on the outside were the words: 'To Be Opened Only By The BytchMistress.' Ms. Empousa looked like she wanted to tear the scroll up without reading it but there was no way she could get away with that in front of the entire assembly. She unrolled it and began to read. As she did every tinge of color blanched from her face.

"At that point, the Archon interrupted. 'Please do us the courtesy of reading the scroll's contents aloud for all to hear, HuntsMistress.' When she didn't immediately comply, he said one more word, 'NOW!'

"She took a deep breath and complied. 'I, Helblad Clawfoot, Hogboon of Maes Howe, Jarl of the Draugrs and Wights, Suzerain of the Zombyes, and High Lord of the Vampyres, hereby make my Last Will and Testament. In the probable event the stone-hearted HuntsMistress denies True

Love is the greatest treasyre in all of Amarantos's creation, I give and bequeath—in its entirety and without exception—the entirety of the treasyre of Maes Howe to the Omada.' "

"Something tells me Empousa wasn't going down easy," Tal said.

"You're right," Borras agreed. "She scurried over to where the Ruling Council was standing and started yammering about 'this is bullshit' and 'the treasyre wasn't physically present and couldn't be included as found' and 'that's only scribbling written on a page by some bullshit self-proclaimed High Potentate of a bunch of no-account Undead Creatures.'

"You should have seen it, Tal, no sooner did those last words pass her lips than a sonic boom rocked Grass Grow. A large oval portal opened horizontally in the ground and hundreds upon hundreds of draugrs and wights and zombyes began rolling up wheelbarrow loads of gold, jewels, weapons, coins, and armor out of the ground. It was unbelievable. By the time they finished and the portal closed behind them there was a hillock of treasyre forming a wall almost twenty feet high all the way around Fountain Flow."

"Boom!" Tal found enough energy to make that one word echo throughout the infirmary.

Borras was smiling from ear to ear. "Game, set, match! I wish you could have seen it, Tal. The crowd went crazy. Absolutely bonkers. Ms. Empousa stood there motionless, completely stunned. The episode apparently broke her because after about a minute of doing that whole Madame Tussaud's thing, the Archon realized Empousa's circuits were totally fried and she wasn't going to be able to reboot on her own. He waved his scepter over his head and two physicks appeared with a straight-jacket. A black leather straight-jacket. Which probably helped keep her calm as they put it on her, before they ushered her around to the back of the main building.

"The members of the Areopagus were hooting, hollering, roaring, and squeaking. A finer example of pandemonium has never existed. Everyone was staring at the treasyre, talking about the unprecedented events of the day. Everyone, including Ana and Dysi and me. Understandable I guess, since we were on the cusp of being rulers of the known universe for the next three hundred years. Everyone…except Väst."

"Väst." Tal practically spit her name. "That conniving, low-life harlot. I wish…"

"Careful, Taliesin. Even on Earth plane wishes sometimes have lives of their own, with or without a magyk ring. Omada was about to snatch defeat from the jaws of victory. While we three were prematurely celebrating, having forgotten how precariously balanced you were between life and death, it was Väst who remembered.

"Out of the thousands of Folk present, she was the only one who had eyes only for you. She was the one who recognized you were seconds from crumpling. The only one focused enough on you to realize if you became incapacitated before a formal declaration of victory that Omada would only have three qualifying team members and we would be disqualified."

"Väst?" Tal asked. "It was Väst that sealed the win for Omada?"

Borras nodded. "She stepped forward and began yelling at the top of her voice. 'Enough of this ridiculousness. Släkt treasyre is clearly superior. In the absence of the HuntsMistress the Ruling Council should declare us the winners of the Treasyre Hunt and of this year's Tyrning.'

"It was like a switch had been flipped. There wasn't even the whisper of a breeze on Grass Grow. Thousands of members of the Areopagus were present and there wasn't the slightest rustle. Alberich looked to each of the members of his Ruling Council, who nodded affirmation to him. The Archon then inclined his head to the Seneschal. Marid banged his staff of office once on the dais floor and said, 'By acclamation of the Council, Omada is declared the winner of the Tyrning and the Hunts are officially concluded.'

"The instant following Marid's declaration you pitched forward face first to the ground. The Archon saw it happen and waived his scepter above his head and you dematerialized. It wasn't until later we learned you'd been magyked here to be attended to by the physicks." Lord Atlas paused and tiredly rubbed his face. "It's been touch and go, these last fourteen days,

Tal. There were some days it looked like we were going to lose you."

Tal thought a moment as he absorbed the fact that it wasn't an exaggeration, his life really had hung in the balance for two full weeks. "There's more you haven't told me, isn't there?"

"I'm afraid so," Borras replied grimly. "When Väst pulled basically the same end around for the second time Nord finally put the pieces together, that she had helped Omada win on more than one occasion. He went berserk and attacked Väst. Tal, he had every intention of killing her with his bare hands, even with the entire Areopagus as witnesses. I was able to grab his left arm long enough to pull him off of her but he pulled free. He took a couple of steps backwards and started yelling a command…to Väst.

"Before Nord could finish his order, there was a dull thud and a dagger appeared in the middle of his throat. It had been thrown from behind Nord and the point was sticking out the front. As Nord made some horrible wet gurgling sounds, still trying to finish his curse, a sword was shoved from his back, between his ribs, up to and through his heart. Killing him instantly."

"Who the hell?"

"Mashariki."

"I noticed you referred earlier to only two teams but there's obviously a major dynamic I'm out of the loop on," Tal remarked.

"I'm sorry. The events of the last few weeks could easily fill several volumes of Hunts history," Lord Atlas responded. "The short version is Mashariki somehow ended up trapped in Släkt's Compyndium."

"The Compyndium have that much magyk?" Tal asked in disbelief.

"You saw for yourself part of what our book was capable of. Luckily for everyone in the known universe those books rarely see the light of day," Borras replied. "You can bet they won't be out of the super-secured reserve area for the next three hundred years.

"Apparently Mashariki was being tortured by the book's

self-defense magyk every single minute he was stuck in the book. We got a strange note that Kati must have sent to both teams in an attempt to ferret our the culprit. Next thing we know, Kabila unexpectedly withdrew from the Hunts. When Head Librarian Seshat was checking all of the Compyndium prior to placing them back in the secured reserve area, she found Mashariki and somehow obtained his release.

"Quint, Seshat checked every page of all three volumes. Thousands upon thousands of blank page after blank page. If she wasn't so anal retentive, he might have remained paginated and tortured for eons."

Tal found enough energy to let out a low whistle. "Borras, you and I both know Nord somehow arranged for Mashariki to be trapped in Släkt's book. Why weren't they kicked out of the competition?"

"When Empousa questioned Kati, she feigned ignorance about the entire matter and only said thank you for the return of the Kabila Fourth Prime."

"What happened after Nord was killed?"

"Everyone was kind of in shock. The Hunt was over and Mashariki's action was technically murder. As everyone else stepped away, the other four Kabila members joined Mashariki. Kat jerked the dagger out of Nord's throat and one by one they each stabbed him in the heart. Kati went last. When she was through, she wiped the blade clean on Nord's shirt and said, 'Kabila claims Revenge Honor,' before nodding her head at her teammates, at which point they all lined up single file behind their Prime. Kati then bowed her head to Alberich and said, 'Pardon, Archon, for the interruption. Kabila stands ready to be appropriately punished for our actions.'

"Alberich nodded in return. 'You saved another contestant's lyfe just now, Kabila Prime. That will be taken into consideration by the Ruling Council in rendering judgment.'

" 'We will place ourselves under house arrest and await your decision in our respective dormitory rooms,' Kati replied. She then made a swift hand motion to her squad and the five of them moved fleetly across Grass Grow toward the dormitories."

"Revenge Honor? Tal asked. "Murder? What's the

punishment?' "

"Alberich said, 'The Släkt Prime committed numerous major violations of the Hunts Rules. He even confessed to one of the violations when he advised the HuntsMistress and other Hunts contestants last semester of his "deal" with the wytch Hecate. Immediately before his death he committed another violation of the Hunts Rules, one which constituted a major criminal act.' "

"Crime?" Tal asked. "What crime?"

"It was the words Nord was muttering. Kabila were the only ones to realize in time that Nord was invoking the Släkt contractual binding to order Väst to immediately stop breathing."

"WHAT?" Tal would have leapt out of the bed if he had the energy. "He could do that even though the Hunts were over?"

Borras nodded gravely, before continuing. "Yes. For centuries, Malebranche had apparently done the exact same thing. Exploited the continuing contractual binding of his teammates for his own purposes. It was never envisioned a Prime would use the binding in such a manner. From this point forward, the binding contract magyk will be modified to provide the contract dissolves immediately when a team is eliminated from the Hunts or when the Hunts are declared over, whichever first occurs.

"It has been left to me as the new Archon to determine Kabila's punishment. Kabila has the right under the Hunts Rules to claim Revenge Honor. The parameters of Revenge Honor under the Rules are amorphous and some Folk see their actions as cold-blooded murder. The problem is that whatever decision I make has to not only be just, it has to appear just to all the known Realms."

Tal's subconscious pulled up a factoid. "Archon, would it make any difference if their claim for Revenge Honor saved not only one life but four lives?"

"Certainly, but I'm not following," Atlas replied.

"A little something I learned from my old pal, Helblad. The death of one person to a contract, living or undead, prior to time of performance, extinguishes the contract."

"Now I must be the one who is a little slow," the new

Archon said.

"Nord's death extinguished the contract he made with Hecate."

The new Archon paused as the information sunk in. "It absolutely does, Quint. In claiming revenge, Kabila secured the freedom, if not the lives, of all four of Nord's surviving team members. Nice work, Omada Fifth. Sounds to me like banishment from the Hunts School for the rest of their lives should be sufficient punishment for Kabila."

"And the fact they would been going home the next day, anyway?" Tal asked wryly.

Borras smiled. "But they won't ever be able to come back. For you know, class reunions and things like that. I'll write the Decree of Banishment as soon as we're done."

Tal's mind skipped again, this time returning him to Väst. Omada won the Tyrning because of Väst? Why would she put herself on the line for my team? Clearly, if I hadn't received the magykal intervention when I did I would be dead right now. I'll finish processing about Väst when I have some alone time. "Tell me what else transpired."

That brought a small chuckle to Borras's face. "What else? What else? Only about half a million things thus far. You have to remember, the Hunts are now over. After the Coronation Ceremony there was the Beltane Feast, and then many more feasts, with nonstop celebrating along the way. Way too much feasting and celebration but now all of that is finally over. Graduation occurred, with thousands of students walking the line to receive their diplomas. I have also already individually commissioned several hundred of the new graduates and they have received their duties and their official seals as representatives of the Archon.

"The Prime Omphalos has been going nonstop for the last few days, returning the graduates to their home planes to lead their respective worlds for the next three hundred years. Apparently, it is a requirement that the new Archon shake the hand, paw, or tentacle of every graduate before they leave."

"That's a lot of appendage grasping."

"You have no idea," Borras confirmed.

"It seems I have a long list of to-do items as well," Tal added. "Beginning with thank yous. I guess I should start with Lord Alberich."

"A thank you is most definitely in order. First he saved your life and then King Alberich and Queen Aine sat vigil by your bedside, with Aislinn, for several days. They wanted to personally thank you for saving their eldest daughter. As the new Ruling Council has assumed authority, they could no longer remain at Hunts School and have returned to Tir Na nÓg Realm."

"I'm sorry to have missed them. Wait, what? Their eldest daughter?"

Borras laughed softly and shook his head. "Clearly you still aren't back to full processing speed yet. Yes, their eldest daughter. Fand. Crown Princess of the Tuatha de Danann. You know her better by her Hunts School name—Väst."

Tal found himself speechless. Well, for a few seconds anyway. "Yeah, totally didn't see that coming. Wow! Just when you think things couldn't take another turn, boom! You're headed in a right angle to your previous trajectory."

Tal noticed that with his last statement, Borras shifted uncomfortably in his chair. "Tal, I only have a few more minutes. Departures have been placed on hold while I'm here and there are some other things we need to talk about before I have to leave."

"Go. I'll try not to interrupt," Tal replied.

"First, I've already sent word to all of the Realms that I believe Alberich's policies with respect to Earth plane are sound and should be continued."

"Which means no boogey monsters under the kids' beds?"

"Now that the Crestfallyn are all dead, that's correct."

"What's to stop the next Archon from being a dickhead like Nord and enslaving all of humankind?"

"Actually, Ana and Dysi and I have already begun working on that issue. I'm appointing a Commission that will spend the next century familiarizing themselves with all of Earth's cultures. Once their report is completed I will have it disseminated to the entirety of the Moiety. I intend to call a vote to decide whether mortals should be invited to join the Moiety."

"First Creatures and now Dust Children. Methinks, the new Archon is bent on revolution. That should be a huge footnote for you in the history books, the farsighted leader who floated the idea that lowly mortals might also deserve to be part of the Moiety."

"Actually, Arawn will be receiving all of the credit for that one."

"Notos? Really? Old Smiley came through for the human race? Who would have ever thunk it?"

Borras's face reshaped into its serious configuration. "He and I had a long sit down the night before he followed you through the Gas Station portal. He brought the issue up. He said he'd realized how important it was and he wanted me to make it happen if Omada won."

Notos, Tal thought to himself. Back to that whole "don't judge a book by its cover" thing. "Which means by the time the next group of students arrive at Hunts School, there may be both humans and Creatures admitted as students?"

"If such is their choice freely made and their names are in The Book," Borras replied. "It will require major changes in the Hunts curriculum, as well as a substantially shorter Hunts School term."

Tal watched as a shadow passed over his friend's face. The universe will never know how lucky it is to have that man leading it for the next three centuries. "Well, go ahead. Spit it out. Whatever is sticking in your craw. I know you have Grand Poobah duties that are backing up while you're here."

Borras smiled thinly in return. "There is one final unpleasantry I need to discuss with you. But first, I need your help. We've all put our heads together. All of us and we're stymied."

Tal raised both his eyebrows in response.

"Who is it?" Borras asked. "Who was pulling Malebranche's strings? Who interfered with this Tyrning? Who repeatedly tried to have you killed? Is the sabotage going to continue? How are we going to stop it? Tal, I need that fine brain of yours to get back in the game and discover the answer for us. If we don't find the Big Bad I fear the known Realms may not survive this new Tyrning."

"You're sure it wasn't the HuntsMistress?"

"Positive. She's gyfted, wouldn't have gotten where she is if she wasn't, but she doesn't have the magykal juice to make it happen. And being a natural born asshole doesn't automatically make you Lex Luthor."

"Got it. Maybe Malebranche was a lone wolf."

Borras shook his head each way several times. "Nope. I've had several long discussions with Alberich, Archon to former Archon. Now that the Hunts are over he could share with me information he and Aine learned through their investigations. Plus it doesn't add up, not with Malabranche's comments right before he died and the fact magyk was utilized on the heavily warded Hunts School property. None of the Folk could have accomplished that. I wish I'd had time to debrief Väst about what happened to her, before she had to return to her home plane. There were too many other things to be done."

Tal felt like he'd just about gotten the old noggin back into responsible cogitation mode, but the mention of Väst's name in connection with the Large Evil derailed it again. "Why? And what do you mean 'about what happened to her'?"

"Tal, somehow—and none of us has the remotest idea how it could happen—somehow between the time Väst left her home plane and the time the Prime Omphalos delivered her here to attend Hunts School, an unbreakable reciprocating compulsion geas was placed on her."

"W–w–w–what?" Yep, he was completely derailed. Wait, Kentro told me something about that in Five-Hells. C'mon, Brain, get with the program.

Borras's present look could only be described as "grave, extremely worried adult facial configuration." "Every single one of her interactions with Kentro was involuntary. Because it was an unprecedented reciprocating geas, Kentro's interaction with her was also compelled."

Tal still couldn't get a grip around all of the possibilities of this revelation. "M–m–me?"

Borras tapped him lightly on the shoulder, several times. Efforting to bring him around. "Yes, Tal. You too."

Tal could feel his brain trying to shift from neutral back into first gear. "H–her and me?"

Borras nodded. "Yes. Well, at least until you used your first wish from Aurora's ring. By accidentally using the precise words you used, you healed her. It took quite awhile to remove all of the spell's tendrils but she finally regained control of herself earlier this semester."

Come on, Tal, told himself. Start isolating all of the constants, ascribe tentative algebraic values to each of the variables, use some deductive reasoning. Do it. Do it! DO IT! "That means even if everything she did before doesn't count against her, what she did this term does. Borras, she tricked me into going to Five-Hells. Where, apparently, I was supposed to remain for all eternity. In pain. All of her actions toward me this term, those were all her? Her using her own free will?"

"If by free will you mean that even though her mother's lyfe was being held hostage by the Big Bad, that she had been ordered by her Prime Direction to "eliminate" you from the competition, that she found a way to save all your lives by sending you to Five-Hells, then saved your life yet again at the Ceremony, and by choosing to save your life ensured that Omada would win the Tyrning? Then yes, Taliesin. All of her actions toward you this term were all of her own free will."

Tal mentally disengaged his brain clutch and shifted up into second gear. Little less torque, faster processing speed. "You're right. No one knows who did that to her?"

"No," Borras replied. "The conspiracy was an extremely well-planned malignancy, over a hundred years in its gestation and execution."

Good work, Tal told himself, let's try a little faster. Shift it into third. There were still hundreds of mental images flashing across his brain screen. He was, however, beginning to once again be able to rapidly sort them into fractile groups. As soon as an image appeared he made a decision as to whether it was relevant or irrelevant. If relevant he made the further decision as to which data subset it should be assigned.

There was one extremely diverse mélange. Its images didn't seem to have anything to do with any of the others and yet his brain kept repeatedly dropping them into that one large bucket. Väst's compulsion geas that was placed on her decades before he was even born. The Crestfallyn, the faceless spook that had haunted him since birth, and that had tried to take his face on his eighteenth birthday. His initial meeting with the pre-teen Dr. Mertin Wilt. His ability to pass through Sol's Gas Station Crossing. Borras binding the Omada contract with him. The attack by the Keres that seemed to target Väst, although the shadow nemesis had somehow known Tal would go to her rescue. The Lady Aurora giving him a ring with three wishes. The Journey where he initially met Arthrys. Elle's death at the hand of Malebranche. All three school terms of wonderful nakedness with Väst. The first part had been involuntary on her part but after that she had maintained their relationship either to fool their mutual opponent, or maybe because she actually, genuinely loved…no, don't go there right now. Stay on task.

Tal's brain ceased whirring. The known data all pointed to a consistent result—there had been multiple attempts to try to stop Omada from winning the Tyrning. False, he told himself. That is a false result-based conclusion premised upon a subjective, biased analysis of the totality of the available information.

Rev the engine, Tal, he admonished himself. Either find the answer or blow a gasket. He double-clutched through fourth and placed his brain into overdrive. I have to add to the large composite bucket my wish that both saved Baba Gaga and made me the new Traveler and Luna's response to me together with her somewhat involuntary assistance. What else? he asked himself. So many other factoids. Which, if any, are material to this inquiry?

Suddenly he remembered the stark lighting made by the single naked bulb in Utopia. In the background, Tal heard the refrain from one of Pell's favorite Three Dog Night tunes, "How does the light shine in the Halls of Shambala?" Fine, he mused, but if it had been up to me I would have picked something from Vangelis's "Chariots of Fire" soundtrack. Although I guess the other is more appropriate. Collate and synthesize. Analyze, then recapitulate. Now, again. Once more.

"AAAAHH!" Tal cried, grabbing at his temples. When his subconscious finally deciphered the answer it truly felt like lightning had flashed, searing across the length of his skull. Like there had been some ablation action that revealed the answer. "WHY COULDN'T THAT SON OF A BITCH HAVE JUST OUT AND OUT TOLD ME?"

"Who, Tal? Who could have just told you what?" Borras asked. As Borras leaned forward, he passed his hand across Tal's brow and Tal felt his pain recede.

"Myrddin. The last time I saw him. Good old Pops." Seeing the new Archon was confused, Tal continued. "That's right, I haven't even had a chance to tell you my big news. Turns out, Myrddin is my biological father." Tal realized that even though Borras was now Archon he was still stunned. Time to return the favor, he decided. "Lord Atlas, you might want to close your mouth. Mouth-breather really isn't a good look for you."

Remembering their very first meeting, Borras smiled. Tal continued, "The last time I saw Myrddin, he gave me the answer to our problem. Well, gave it to me in his whole jacked up puzzle within a puzzle lame ass Socratic method of not giving answers when he's giving answers.

"Anyway, I didn't realize it. Actually, he gave me the answer the first time we ever met and simply reminded me of it the last time we saw each other. That's not quite accurate. He reminded me of it the second to last time I saw him. Actually, if you go in chronological order, disregarding whether it was othertyme or realtyme..."

"Time, Tal," Borras said, politely interrupting, then looking back over his shoulder at a magyked wall clock at the far end of the infirmary.

"Exactly, Lord Atlas," Tal replied. "That's what he told me. It's all about Time."

At the very millisecond in which Borras realized Tal wasn't giving him some flippant answer, Tal saw the drama of the realization play out all the way across the Archon's face. Even though it was obvious they were alone in the infirmary, Borras glanced quickly over each shoulder before whispering through closed lips. "Chronos? You're saying the eldest of the Elder Children is our Enemy?"

Tal nodded. He still didn't have all of the details parsed. Not yet, but he'd get them lined out. His subconscious was now fully engaged and was hurtling at Mach one down the neural autobahn. "I think we can safely say, Time is not on our side."

CHAPTER CENTUM QUADRAGINTA UNUS

Borras bore a combo frown-tension smile as he began to assemble the pieces of the humongous jigsaw puzzle. Frown suddenly stepped squarely in front of tension. "Why, Tal? Why? There's no motive. Chronos is the oldest and most powerful of Amarantos's Elder Children. She is the Unfading One's Seneschal. There is absolutely no reason for her to try to kill you or to fix the results of this particular Tyrning."

"Now that we know who, the 'why' is pretty easy. Väst gave me the answer."

"Okay, I'm back to totally lost," Lord Atlas replied.

"Sure. She taught me the Folk origination story, the one that is taught to all Folk children." Seeing his friend still didn't get it, Tal continued. "Recite it, please."

Without any hesitation, Borras spoke the litany. "Before even the breath of a beginning, the UnFading Spirit is. She first created her Seneschal—When."

"Stop there. Myrddin told me the reason Amarantos has a Traveler, why She has always had a Stytch in Tyme, is to hasten the day when all of Her children have been given the opportunity to Seek the Center. At that point, She will be able to gather all of Her children to her for eternity."

"Makes sense," the Archon acknowledged. "Still doesn't get me to your conclusion."

"Then riddle me this, Batman. What happens to Chronos when eternity is brought to fruition, when time is no more?"

"I don't know," Borras replied, clearly not getting it. "I've never thought about it before. One of two things I guess. Either she ceases to exist. Which although possible is doubtful, as there is no reason to think Chronos is soulless."

"And the other possibility?" Tal prompted.

"I guess, Chronos simply becomes another one of Amarantos's Elder Children, no more or less than any of the rest of her siblings."

"Perhaps even no more and no less than the Folk...or Dust Children...or Creatures," Tal added.

Borras finally saw the completed puzzle. "That's it, Tal! "There's your motive. If Eternity never arrives, then Chronos remains top dog."

Tal continued. "Which still leaves a missing piece. There have been instances in which it appeared Chronos knew the future, but also instances where she was clearly caught off-guard. How would Chronos know the future? Myrddin told me that never, in all of the hundreds of trips he made at Amarantos's behest, did She ever send him into the future. According to him, Amarantos alone knows the future. Sure there are prophets and oracles but none of Her children, including the Principes, know with certainty what lies ahead."

"Which creates a huge problem with our theory," Borras agreed. "If Chronos isn't omnipotent she couldn't possibly have known you'd show up at Hunts School or be given a magyk ring. Which means she certainly couldn't have known you'd use one of your wishes to take Myrddin's place as the Traveler..."

WHOOOMP!

That's the noise Central Processing heard as hundreds of messenger neurons kamikazed one another pursuant to orders from Prefrontal Cortex. Central Processing quickly interpreted the neuron implosion. "Bingo!" Tal exclaimed. "Chronos didn't and doesn't know the future but Chronos is the only one of the Elder Children who would know every detail of the past. She would, however, only know a past event if the past had already actually occurred."

"I'm still not seeing it," Lord Atlas replied.

"Right," Tal said. "Sorry, I wouldn't have gotten the answer either if I hadn't experienced first-hand all of the vagaries of othertyme. Damn, that's probably why Amarantos has a Stytch. To keep Chronos from being able to affect the future by knowing the past."

"I don't guess you have any Earth plane Tylenol do you?" Borras, asked, while rubbing his forehead.

"No," Tal answered with a brief smile. "I know exactly how you feel. Look, there's realtyme and there's othertyme. Travelers go backward chronologically to alternate tymelines that may or may not be our own."

"I think I'm starting to get it," Borras said, as he continued to worry his forehead with his left hand. "All of us Folk, as well as the other Principes, only know what has happened in our own past tymeline. We wouldn't know about what happened in any of the alternate tymelines. Chronos would though."

"But only if it is an alternate past that has already occurred," Tal explained. "Chronos knew someone, maybe even a mortal, gave Excalibur to Arthrys hundreds of years ago. That fact wouldn't have even been a blip on her radar until…"

"Until you were actually born hundreds of years later," Borras added. "Since you're a human and since you made an appearance hundreds of years before you were born, Chronos knew that one day, somehow, you would become the Traveler."

"You nailed it. Deductively that meant she knew some day I was going to show up at Hunts School."

Borras nodded in agreement. "It also explains why the Lacy Aurora allows Myrddin to reside under her protection in the Pentacle."

"That makes sense," Tal agreed. "Chronos can't take Myrddin out while he's in the Pentacle. She wouldn't know when he was Traveling in othertyme until it was history. He'd be done and gone before it came to her attention."

Tal paused as he continued to work through all of the ramifications. "I guess knowing who the enemy is may be of some assistance. Knowing she is the second most powerful being in the entire universe, who knows every moment of every past action, and who is never going to stop trying to take me out as the Traveler is more than a little daunting."

"Agreed," Lord Atlas said, as he stood and straightened his jacket sleeves. "It also confirms I've made the smart call on the hardest decision I've had to make since I became Archon."

"Which is?" Tal asked.

"You can't remain at Hunts School."

Tal began assembling the energy and recruiting the muscles necessary to get up off the bed. "I totally agree. Hit me with a little more of your Archon juice to wind me up a bit and then we can both go get to work..."

"No," Borras, now Atlas, said quickly and kindly but still pretty damn firmly. "What I meant is I am banishing you from Hunts School. You must return immediately to Earth plane proper."

Tal wasn't even sure there was a designated combination facial/entire rest of the body muscle configuration for extreme chapfallen. If there was, his entire body just used most of his remaining energy to try to assume that position. "But, I'm Omada. I'm part of the Ruling Council. I mean sure, I won't last until the next Hunts School class shows up, but..." As Tal raised his head to look at one of his two best friends in the entire world, the rest of his energy was leeched. Given in service to being beyond extremely chapfallen.

Because Tal knew the look on the Archon's face. It was the same look Borras had given Anatolia when he'd told her she had to try to make a simulacrum golem even though there was a pretty decent chance it might kill her. It was the same look he'd given Tal when Borras couldn't leave the far side of the creek to help Tal fight the Keres. It was the same look he'd given Tal when he'd told Tal he had no choice but to remain as Omada Champion in the Combat Challenge. When Borras was Omada Prime Direction, he had always made the choice for the good of all of Amarantos's children. It was clear from his face he would not shirk from making those tough calls now as Archon.

"I would have moved you off-campus sooner but you were simply too ill. Now that you are almost healed you must leave the Hunts School campus."

Tal was at a complete loss. "Is it because I'm mortal? I mean you're the head honcho now. You get to make the rules. Right?" Tal asked, his attempt to engender hopefulness quickly replaced by the feeling he was going to be sick to his stomach.

Borras smiled a little. More specifically he gave the barest glimpse of the tiniest hint of a little bit of a smile. "Not all of them and certainly not anything contrary to the Lex Immortalis. That's not why you have to leave, Tal, and you know it."

Nausea was now accompanied by Dread. "You can't protect me from Chronos here at Hunts School. I get it. Totally. I really do. I gotta run and hide. Although I'm not sure how you hide from Time herself. Do you know how long…how long it's going to be before I can come back and visit y'all?"

There was a long pause from the very first person who'd welcomed him to Hunts School. The kind giant with a broken landscape for a face and hands the size of large hams. The individual who'd clasped his hand in friendship and took a chance on him in binding a contract that would affect the entire universe for at least three hundred years. The man who was, without any doubt, the best non-clone of himself friend Tal had ever had in his entire life. "Never, Tal," Borras finally answered. "You can never come back. No matter how long your lyfe may last."

Thunderstruck, Tal couldn't even put the pieces together to ask the questions he wanted to ask, to tell Borras the things he wanted to tell him. "And V-V-Väst? Will I get to see her before I go? To get some answers, to figure out how I really feel about her? How she really feels about me?"

Borras shook his head. "The reason Väst already left for Tir Na nÓg Realm is because the lengthy and very formal investiture process involved in installing her as High Queen of the Tuatha Dé Danann has already begun."

Don't cry, Tal told himself. Not right now anyway. You can cry all you want when you get home. Well, when you're not running and hiding from Time…and from the inevitable police dragnet that's going to be looking for your alleged murdering ass. Buck up, though. It's not like you're going to be totally alone.

Emet will talk you through it, just like old times.

"Tal, I'm sorry. There are some final details that need to be discussed but even though I am now Archon it is not my place to have those discussions with you."

Tal didn't say anything. He couldn't say anything to Borras without breaking down. And he wasn't going to do that, he couldn't do that to his friend.

Borras now Atlas stood. "I have to go, hundreds of students still remain waiting to be transported back to their own planes. For most Realms, that will be their last contact with the Ruling Council or the Hunts School for almost two hundred years. Until they choose their representatives for the next freshman class to be sent through the Prime Omphalos."

"I am Archon," he spoke aloud to the room, "and it is my will I now assume the form in which I first met the Child of Dust." With that, Lord Atlas waved his hand over his head and there was a small closely contained yet still riotous explosion. After Tal blinked several times he saw Borras, as he had appeared on Tal's first day at Hunts School standing before him.

Atlas now Borras took a deep breath. It was a breath of such dimension it seemed to capture all available oxygen in the infirmary. "I want you to know, Quint of the Omada," and as Tal looked, he saw tears sizeable enough to overflow two-ounce shot glasses rolling down Borras's face. "I want you to know that what you have done for the Moiety, for the Creatures, for the Omada," there was another significant pause as Borras collected himself, "and what you did for me, will never be forgotten. Your name will be written large in the histories of ten thousand Realms. Songs of the Taliesin and his wondrous deeds will be sung at every Moiety gathering for millennia to come."

Don't cry, Tal told himself.

Borras knelt down on one knee, making him almost the height of a normal person, before reaching over and gathering Tal in the biggest bear hug Tal could possibly have imagined. While still on his knees, Borras leaned back upright and stuck out his right hand. Tal grabbed the first two-fingers with his much smaller hand.

"For the rest of my life—and for as long after that as

Amarantos may permit—I bind myself in friendship with you, Taliesin Smith. Do you consent?"

Phalanxes of tears, impatiently waiting their signal to forward march, were compressed against the insides of Tal's lower lids. Don't cry, he told himself. This is hard enough for Borras as it is. "I consent, Lord Atlas. Do you?"

"I consent," came the response, the Archon's two short, simple words spoken between rippling sheets of new tears. With that Borras stood to his full height. He snapped his fingers one time and was once again the nattily dressed Lord Atlas, Archon of the entire known universe. He clapped his hands. Once, then twice. "I have just summoned Emet. He has been waiting anxiously to see you and is authorized to answer your remaining questions. He should be here in a couple of minutes. When you are through talking, you must proceed apace back to the Gas Station Crossing. Hunts School is not safe for you anymore and every second you are on campus is a danger to you and to the Unfading Spirit's plan."

The Archon produced his scepter from an inside coat pocket and waved it over Tal. "That should return you as close to normal as magyk may accomplish. Goodbye, Taliesin Smith." With those parting words, Lord Atlas turned and strode briskly down the long hallway.

That aisle is like a runway of despair, Tal thought, as he closed his eyes so the tears would had no choice but to be reabsorbed from whence they'd come.

Could be worse, he told himself. It's not like I'm going to be totally alone. Emet's on his way. We can make our plan for the future before we get to the Gas Station Crossing. So, there's that.

CHAPTER CENTUM QUADRAGINTA DUO

Some unidentified noise woke him. Must have passed out for a minute, Tal told himself, as he opened his now tear-tacky eyelids in time to see Emet walk through the swinging doors.

I've been stuck here in this bed far too long he decided as he slowly got out and stood up. Energy level seems acceptable, he decided. As Emet reached the bed, Tal stuck out his hand. Emet shook his head in the negative, opting instead for a hug. For a long, long time. When they'd finished, Tal spoke first. "Don't think I'm ever going to get used to it, Em. It's like looking in a mirror."

Tal noticed Emet's eyes were now intently studying his own shoes. "I know what you mean," Emet replied.

"Lord Atlas told me I'm banished for my own good. As in right now."

Emet was still looking down. "I've already been read in on that decision. Tal, I ran every possibility for him. It almost killed him to make the call but it's the best chance of keeping you alive. It's clear the Hunts School wards can't protect you." Emet finally looked up at Tal. "Still sucks though."

"Well, I guess there's no time like the present," Tal said as he put his hand around Emet's shoulder and turned him so they were both facing the exit. "I've only had a couple of minutes to start working out the logistics of our existence but surely between the two of us we can promulgate a winning plan. Since I wasn't actually born as one of two twins, I don't guess there's any way we can finagle being college roommates. Of course, that's downstream of the fact that me being wanted for murder means you will also be wanted for murder. Fake identities need to go at the top of our to-do list. It might all work if we go somewhere far away from any place where we might be recognized. Then there's also the option of plastic surgery, but that would take capital…" Tal noticed Emet was back to staring a hole in the tops of his tennis shoes.

Central Processing promptly informed Hypothalamus there wasn't enough surplus energy for Tal's autonomic system to permit Tal's breath to repeatedly catch. "Em! Look at me. Is there something you need to tell me?"

Emet looked up as he took two steps backward. "I didn't know how to tell you, Tal. It's why I didn't come earlier. Why I had to be the last one to see you."

Central Processing informed Hypothalamus that hyperventilating was every bit as inefficient as chronic breath catching.

"I had to be last because I'm the one who has to disappoint you the most. I'm not going back to Earth plane with you."

Tal felt a piece of his heart fall out of his chest. There didn't seem to be anything metaphorical about the event. He could have sworn he felt a significant portion of his heart rip free from his chest and fall to the infirmary's pristine tile floor where it smashed into a zillion crimson splintereens.

"You mean not coming right now, right?" Tal asked, knowing that wasn't at all what Emet meant. "You're coming later? When things have settled and we've thrown Chronos off my trail?" Wow, Tal, that's a new record. Three rhetorical questions in a row. Try something else. Like, begging. "I just got you back Emet. I'm not sure how much more I can take. Please tell me there's a plan to fix things so you can come later?"

Emet shook his head slowly side to side. "We both know there can't be two of us on the mortal plane. It would never work. Particularly since we are now living separate lives."

Suck it up you selfish bastard, Tal prompted himself.

Emet's you just as much as you're him. That means this is every bit as terrible for Emet as it is for you. Don't make it any worse. "I get that, I guess," Tal replied. "Not happy about it, but I get it. Where will you go? What will you do?"

As Tal asked the questions, he noticed Emet's shoes once again seemed to hold great interest for their owner. "Tal, it wasn't my idea. I've already told him no five times…"

What's he so embarrassed about, Tal wondered. Who asked him what that he turned down five times?

Hello, Tal, this is a representative of an *ad hoc* committee consisting of your Temporal Lobe, your Prefrontal Region, and your Parietal Lobe. We have a question for you—is anyone in this entire cranial establishment planning on engaging in logical thought on a consistent basis today?

Yes, Tal replied to himself, I'm capable of doing that. Actually, this should be easy, Tal told himself. Whatever would embarrass me in this situation would embarrass Emet. So, what is it? Think!

And then it came to him, together with a surge of anger-infused resentment prompted by what must have been an all hands on deck claxon from his entire Limbic System. No, that's not fair. It's not right. It's…

Tal, this is your Temporal Lobe speaking now. This was not Emet's decision, it was that of Lord Atlas. Who, for the record, has again made the right call.

Fine, you're right, Tal grudgingly conceded to his own logic.

Please don't interrupt me, the Temporal Lobe said. I'm not done reasoning with you. Well, you is me but you get the point. Or should, as you're the one having this lengthy internal dialogue with yourself.

What action are you suggesting, Tal asked himself.

Nosce te ipsum, his Temporal Lobe responded.

Latin? Really, I'm in crisis mode and your advice is in Latin.

It means…

I know what it means. If you know what it means then I know what it means. "Know yourself." That's it? That's your advice?

Really, Tal, this isn't that hard, TempLobe replied. You've just acknowledged Emet is basically your carbon copy. We both know, and by "we" you of course realize that "we" is "you," but anyway, we both know what you have to do, that there's only one way this entire thing can play out if you want Emet to have a happy ending. I do, he told himself. I want Emet to live an incredible, fulfilling, and happy life.

It has to be my idea, Tal suddenly realized. Otherwise Emet is going to live the rest of his life feeling guilty about a decision that wasn't his to make. But it can't be a pity okay, I need to think of a legit underlying reason for him, something important...

Exactly, his Temporal Lobe replied. It needs to be your idea. Quickly. As in now would be good. As far as a reason, I realize we're all operating under difficult circumstances here, but there is one contract binding you haven't yet made good on.

Binding? What binding? Tal wondered.

TempLobe sighed before responding, I'll take, 'David Byrne was the lead singer for what new age band for $200, Alex.'

What the hell?

Talking Heads, Memory interjected. The name of that band was Talking Heads.

That's all you the help you're getting, TempLobe replied. Now, if you don't mind, I have some other areas that require my high functioning capacity, it concluded snippishly, before abruptly closing the conversation window.

"The Moai," Tal said out loud. "How could I possibly have forgotten? I bound a contract with Head Paro."

"I'm sorry," Emet interjected. "Are you okay, Tal? Do I need to get a physick?"

"I'm okay," Tal said reassuringly. "Everything's going to be okay. It really is. Em, I have something to ask. Two things, really, although they're connected. It's a lot to ask with everything going on but it's very important to me."

"Sure, whatever I can do, you know I'll do it," Emet replied.

"First, when I became the Omada Fifth Prime it meant

Kentro's binding was severed. He's out and can't come back. Hunts Rules you know. Notos will apparently only be available sporadically. With me being back on Earth plane proper, the Ruling Council is extremely short-handed. I need for you to do me a really big favor…Emet, I need for you to stay at Hunts School and take my place with the Omada."

Emet's face rearranged from morose into quizzical. From there it slowly rearranged once more, this time into understanding. There was then an immediate but subtle change into grateful understanding. Which culminated in a nod of acquiescence. "Lord Atlas told me it wasn't just to give me something to do. The Ruling Council apparently has an unbelievable amount of responsibilities and duties. Way more than enough for even a minimum of four people to handle.

"He also told me both Dysi and Ana are having an extremely difficult time focusing on all of the work that needs to be done. Even with Kentro's return, they're taking your leaving really hard. The Archon said I would be doing all of them a favor if I would say yes, that it would almost be like having you still here. Almost."

Righteous decision notwithstanding, Tal suddenly felt the weight of leaving Hunts School. Even though it had only been one school year and he'd faced death (or worse) innumerable times, he realized he'd come to love the school and the friends he was being told he had to leave behind.

Don't let Emet know, Tal told himself. Finish this conversation strong, this is probably the last time you'll ever get to see him. He clapped Emet on his back. "Great. That's a load off my mind."

"There's a second thing?" Emet prompted.

"Yes. On one of my Journeys I went to Easter Island. It's the home of the Moai."

"That's the word you said a minute ago."

Tal nodded. "Long story short. They're stone talking heads that get their energy from mana."

"Magyk, then?"

"Kind of. Te Pito O Te Henua is the only Realm on which nonmagykal humans can help create a specific form of magyk."

Emet whistled. "That's pretty cool."

"I know, right?" Tal replied. "One of the unintended consequences of Arthrys's and Alberich's Banes was that humans could no longer voluntarily travel to that plane. As a result, the Moai are dying."

"What do you need me to do?"

"When you leave here, go find Lord Atlas, and tell him you're in. Then tell him about my binding with the Moai. Please ask him to let your first official act as a member of the Ruling Council be a trip to Te Pito O Te Henua. When you go, please give my regards to Head Paro and tell him the new Ruling Council will be working on a solution to their problem."

"You have my word," Emet said solemnly.

"Thank you, Em, it means a lot to me." Tal paused a moment as he suddenly realized there was something else the two of them needed to discuss. "I guess if we're going to go our separate ways, has anybody, well has anybody discussed the whole, you know, what happens when I finally…"

When it became evident to them both Tal was bogging down, Emet stepped in to finish. "You mean the whole 'will I will die when you die' thing?"

Tal smiled gratefully at his former simulacrum golem. "Yeah, that little detail."

"Lord Atlas has asked Lailoken his thoughts on the matter. No one knows for sure but their best educated guess is that I am now my own stand alone sentient being. For whatever lyfespan the UnFading One sees fit to allot me. That said, it won't hurt my feelings—for a lot of reasons—if you do everything you can to make sure you live an extremely long and prosperous life."

"Deal," Tal replied.

"Want me to walk you to the Gas Station Crossing?" Emet asked.

Tal thought about it for a moment. Better to have a clean, surgical break. "Thanks for the offer but no. I'd better take this victory lap by myself. I have a lot to think about."

"I understand," Emet replied.

Tal stepped back close to Emet and hugged him. Even longer this time than the long, long hug scant minutes before. Much longer than two teenage boys would normally countenance before deciding that things were getting "weird." Emet reciprocated the hug. Neither one wanted to be the one to let go of a best friend, a confidant, a piece of themself they would never see again. Not in this world anyway.

Finally, they did. Let go. Fittingly, it was at the exact same moment, each sensing the world was turning and it was time to begin their separate Journeys. Their words all used up, Emet nodded once. Tal turned, walked down the aisle, and through the swinging metal doors.

Damn, I really hate that infirmary, he thought.

CHAPTER CENTUM QUADRAGINTA TRES

"My Queen, you are aware that if you ask for and receive the privileges and responsibilities of the new position, it will make you the target of an extremely powerful enemy?"

Väst nodded in the affirmative.

"You consider your choice to be of the Center?"

Another quick, decisive nod.

Her mother stepped forward to clasp her hand. "You realize, Daughter, if you are chosen, and if your actions are successful it will mean...he is the one...and that you do, in fact..."

She nodded again, doing everything she could to hold back the tears.

Her mother stepped into her, pulling her close. "If I could take this pain from you, I would. Any parent would. It is one of lyfe's hardest lessons that we must learn to trust our children and let them make their own decisions."

Alberich joined the family embrace. "We do not, however, have to let you make them alone. We love you, we will support you any way we can, and we couldn't be any prouder of you."

"You will honor my request?" Väst asked.

Alberich and Aine kneeled in unison, before Aine spoke for the two of them. "Yes, High Queen Fand. We will serve as your Regents for the care and governance of Tir Na nÓg until such time as you are able to return and safely take up your orb and scepter."

CHAPTER CENTUM QUADRAGINTA QUATTUOR

Tal skipped going back to his suite at the dormitory. There wasn't anything there he could take with him. Apparently all copies of the Hunts Rules, together with any other Hunts School artifacts, dematerialized if you tried to take them off campus at the end of a term. As the old saw goes, "What's in corporeal form at Hunts School stays in incorporeal form outside of Hunts School."

Tal walked slowly through the different portions of the main building. As he walked, he reflected on his time at Hunts School, fixing sights and assigning them memories so he would never forget any of them. Starting at the back of the main building he first stopped by the Omada team room. For the first time, the door to the secure room was ajar. Why wouldn't it be, Tal asked himself. The Hunts are over, the new Tyrning has begun. It will be two hundred ninety-eight years before some new Finalist team needs to use it.

As he moved forward through the minaret section, Tal recalled the first time he'd walked that specific hallway. It had been his initial procession with the Omada. The other three team members had been furious at Borras for binding him. That was even before they found out he was a Dust Child. Now, as then, he felt awed by the artistry of the Folk who had created the vibrant tiled floor mosaics and intricate filigreed wood window coverings. He slowed every ten feet to admire the wall fountains. Heads of mythological beasts with water spilling from eyes, mouths, fangs, tails, and claws, and their reciprocal floor fountains which contained water lilies exploding with every variation of reds, blues, and yellows.

His tour brought him to the multiple hallway hub that also lead into the cafeteria. The stencil above the door made him smile. Yes, he reminded himself, it is almost always a good idea to keep your hands to yourself. He took a quick peek inside to see if there might be any ambrosia to go. Nope. Chef had locked the place down secure. After a hundred year school term, she was no doubt on a well-earned vacation.

Next on the farewell tour was the entry to he and Väst's hidden trysting alcove. He paused with his hand on the bust that activated the secret door. Nope, he decided. I can't handle it right now. I'm just going to hold tight to the positive memories of the two of us. The conversations on every imaginable subject that provided such wonderful mental intimacy. The unbelievably fun nakedness. The leap of static electricity every time our lips touched, caused by our biological differences, me being an electrical being and her being magykal. The Divine Spark, the Folk called it.

It seemed strange, the halls being deserted. Everyone else had either gone home, was in the process of going home, or was going about their new duties as functionaries of Archon Atlas and his Ruling Council. Everyone except me, Tal mused.

Quiet. The school really was deathly quiet. Always before, the sound of music had echoed throughout the entire building. Music was a required course, apparently every year. Some of the most fun he'd ever had playing and singing was with the Folk musicians who had befriended him here. As the building had changed from one plane's cultural style to another, so had the type of music. In the Eastern quadrant there had been drums, cymbals, and riqs. As his steps took him into the gothic portion of the main building he remembered hearing baroque tunes, heavy on the organ, as well as the beautiful harmonies of *a cappella* Gregorian chanting.

He was now well into the cathedral portion, nearing the front entrance. He looked upward, admiring the leaded glass windows and the ribs of the ceiling, arching away into blackness.

Finally, he was to the double-wide front doors, still completely ajar.

As Tal shuffled past the door sentries, he couldn't help good-naturedly jacking with them one last time. "Goodbye, guys. It's been fun chatting with you—you're brilliant conversationalists, one and all." He'd only taken a couple of steps down the stairs before he heard six separate voices. Separate and distinct, but somehow also a singular six-part harmony:

"Fare thee well, Child of the Dust, ..."
"this school..."
"and those who protect it..."
"will forever..."
"be in your debt."
"May Amarantos guide your steps always, Taliesin Smith."

Tal turned back as quickly as he could but saw zilch evidence the sentinels had actually spoken. As always, they were impassive monoliths. When he got to the bottom of the broad entry stairs he took the time to slowly walk all the way around Fountain Flow. It was entirely different visually, without the dozens of living sculptures. It somehow seemed even more imposing as a single central jet exploding hundreds of feet in the air.

Tal was about halfway across Grass Grow when a reflected ray of sunlight momentarily blinded him. As he shielded his eyes from the glare, he saw the beam came not from the sky but from across River Run. From the edge of Forest Fell.

As his eyes readjusted he saw Myrddin, Perun and Arthrys standing motionless on the far embankment. Arthrys was holding Excalibur high in the air—deliberately catching the sun's light and sending it to wash over Tal.

In the next second, Tal saw hundreds of Alfar and Cooshies flow from out of the brambles of Forest Fell. As they emerged, a shimmering rainbow provided them a moving backdrop, all the way from their feet to as far up in the heavens as Tal could see.

Aurora, Tal thought. She, too, has come to see me off. Tal watched as a narrow, multi-hued ray of the rainbow split off, twinning with the sunbeam all the way to him, to his right ring finger. His dull, gray magyk ring became a living rainbow once more. Tal heard the near boundless force that was Aurora, in his head. *'Taliesin, I intend to fully honor what will now be known as Atlas's Bane. This precludes granting you any more magyk wishes, Child of the Dust. But you are well deserving of a parting gyft, so I have imbued your ring with a tiny piece of myself. I will be with you always, little brother. Whenever the ring turns on your finger, gladness and joy shall be your portion as one who Seeks the Center. May the Mother of us all guide your steps, until we are all finally gathered unto Her.'*

The rainbow and the sunbeam dissipated. Suddenly and in perfect unison each of the elves smacked their right fist over their heart, the report of their salute echoing across the entire front lawn of the campus. Perun then bent his right foreleg, kneeling to Tal. The multitude of Cooshies quickly mirrored their chieftain's obeisance. Next it was Arthrys's turn. He lowered Excalibur before reversing the sword point downward and also taking a knee. As their leader kneeled, so did all of the Alfar. Last was Myrddin, bowing low from his waist and remaining in that position for several seconds.

Overwhelmed, Tal first nodded his gratitude to Aurora, and then to Arthrys, hand-motioning for him to stand before placing his hand on his hip to indicate Arthrys should return Excalibur to his side, where it rightfully belonged. Tal then popped his right hand crisply over his heart, returning the salute to Arthrys's men. Finally, he bowed his head, before also bowing from the waist, first to Perun, and then once to all of the other Cooshies. He knew Myrddin couldn't hear him but he sent his thanks to him as well. He knew we would see each other one more time, he even knew that it would be in farewell. How? Nobody knows the future, not even him. Well, maybe he's been othertyme so it's not the future to him, Tal thought, as his father stood and smiled broadly. Tal then watched as Aurora flowed around the entire company so that they disappeared in a glorious burst of color back into the dense brambles of Forest Fell.

Tal realized he was weeping. Again. He wasn't even sure why. The Omada had succeeded—Right had prevailed. Borras, Dysi, Ana, Notos, and Emet were the Ruling Council. The Folk universe would be governed for another three hundred years by those who followed the Center, who strove every day to do as Amarantos would have them do. Mortals would be protected by Atlas's Bane and both they and all of the Creatures were going to be given the choice to be part of the Moiety. Mokosh and all of the other Folk wrongfully imprisoned for thousands of years had been freed. The Moia would survive.

Piras and his kinsmen gave their lives for me, Tal thought. I think he knew their sacrifice would be a catalyst for change, that with his help the prejudices of millennia would begin to disappear.

That makes everyone accounted for, all major issues resolved, he told himself. Well, everyone…except for her. Every issue wrapped up in a neat little box…except for us. Tal realized he'd been dragging his feet as he crossed the lawn, slowing down, hoping she'd show up, despite what Borras had told him. He finally reached the edge of Grass Grow. The door in the Gas Station Crossing appeared. Another step, a turn of the doorknob, and he would be back in the Ladies' Room. Which was interesting. The front door had said "EXIT ONLY" when he and Notos went through it. How was he now going to be able to once again access the Earth plane through the Ladies' Room?

Doesn't matter, I guess. Even if Väst hadn't already gone home, she couldn't go into the Gas Station unless she was with me. Tal slowly scanned the expanse of Grass Grow and what he could see of the rest of Hunts School campus. He saw nothing. Meaning he saw absolutely everything, except her. So, nothing.

Drawing a deep breath, Tal turned the doorknob, opened the door, and glumly stepped across the threshold…

CHAPTER ONE HUNDRED FORTY-FIVE

"HAPPY BIRTHDAY, LOSER!"

Tal had the eerie sensation of feeling like he was in zero grav, his body momentarily suspended in space. Like an astronaut on the space station. Well, at least what he imagined it must feel like to be an astronaut on the space station.

Momentarily proved to be a period of extremely brief duration, as he both heard and felt the "OOOMPH!" as his head bounced off the ground, the impact knocking the air from his lungs. Pain centers were reporting distress from all quadrants. Both optic nerves were reporting zero visibility.

"WHAT THE HELL?" he yelled, after sucking in his first great gasp of air. His cochlear nerves chimed in, reporting the sound of tires squealing. It was right about then Tal felt his entire body being pummeled by sharp-edged flying projectiles. As he continued to gulp for oxygen he realized there was a nasty smelling fabric covering his face. He seized it with both hands, desperately scrabbling to get it off.

"WHAT THE HELL?" he yelled again, as his fingers finally found purchase and ripped the covering up and off the top of his head.

He pulled the cloth down to eye level. A burlap bag? Seriously? A burlap bag? "This is some seriously jacked up shit," Tal muttered to himself, experiencing the first tremor of a little episode of *déjà vu*.

Tal had expected to walk through the portal door and find himself in the nicely appointed Ladies' Room. Instead he was standing out in front of Sol's Gas Station. Take three calming breaths, he told himself, and assess your situation.

One. Blood was throbbing in his left ankle as it swelled to three times its normal size.

Two. He had gravel imbedded in both his palms.

Three. His clothes were torn and as he checked out his right elbow he could see it was oozing clearish body fluid.

Stop, Tal, he told himself. Stop and think. This is exactly what happened to you when Barton and his goons threw you out of the back of his truck on your eighteenth birthday.

What are you saying? he asked himself.

What I'm saying is that somehow you're on the Earth plane proper side of the Gas Station Crossing without having gone through the Ladies' Room.

Hello? I realize you hit your head buddy but hasn't this exact same sequence of events already happened to you?

So, what you're saying is...

"Othertyme," he whispered aloud. "Amarantos has sent me othertyme on another mission." Triangulate the data he told himself. He looked to the mouthy Air Hose. Nothing yet except the hiss of escaping air. He turned to look down to the far end of Sol's Gas Station. Yep, there it was. An envelope stuck on the glass of the service bay door, flapping in the breeze like a tiny white flag. He quickly glanced to the Gas Pumps. Nothing yet. But they didn't speak to me the first time around until after I'd retrieved and read the Hunts School note.

Steady, old chap, he told himself. You've been down this road before. Actually both literally and figuratively. It's the same drill as when you hooked Arthrys up with Excalibur. Amarantos has sent you here to help someone make a choice.

You already know what the Gas Pumps are going to say, as well as all the choices you made the first time. Surely I'm supposed to make the same decisions. So that Gas Pump Unus can tell me that worlds depend on me. Tal quickly replayed in his mind all of his movements from the first time he was in this situation.

However, this time I really, really need to pee. Surely there won't be a problem with using the facilities before I go get the envelope. Tal hobbled toward the front corner of the station closest to the bathrooms. Damn, I forgot how much it hurt to be kicked out the back of a moving truck. As he reached the Ladies' Room door, he stuck out his left hand, grasped the knob, and began turning it.

"HOLY CRAP!"

CHAPTER ONE HUNDRED FORTY-SIX

As Tal turned the bathroom doorknob, a winged goddess had stepped into his left peripheral vision, coming from around the backside of the Gas Station. The woman's skin was a vibrant chartreuse, somehow both glowing and sparkling in the noon day sun. She was wearing a long-sleeve full-length diaphanous gown which shimmered as it playfully danced around her body. First clinging, then releasing, before repeating, the garment scarcely concealing lean muscles which were rippling as she glided toward him.

She was bedecked, head to toe, with emeralds. Large, small, cabochon, faceted. Big honking solitaires adorning rings on most of her fingers with similar jewels hanging pendant from her ears. Her necklace and matching tiara, each of which had hundreds of individual stones, looked like they should be with the rest of the Crown Jewels in the Tower of London. She's not only a ripped goddess, Tal concluded, but a royal ripped goddess to boot.

Wait a minute, did I say wings?

Wings seemed much too pedestrian a descriptor for her, well, for her wings. Translucent-gossamer-feather–touching–the–floor–and–rising–a foot–above–her–head wings. That's better, he decided, as he stood mesmerized as they slowly motioned forward, before opening in reverse, all the while softly thrumming the air around her. As the sunlight refracted off of the wings, Tal could see they were the color of green rainbows, if there was such a thing. The sun's rays showcased every imaginable nuance of green, from the darkest jade to the lightest teal.

The woman's blonde hair was captured in several intricate weaves on or near the top of her head, leaving bare the nape of her neck. Set securely in the perfectly coifed hair was a filigreed green-gold tiara, which was inset round its entire circumference with alternating quarter-sized emeralds and chatoyant green tiger-eyes.

Tal was staring at a vision stepping out of fantasy into reality. One look at the smile on her face and Tal knew with certainty he would have known this woman. At any time. In any place. No matter her physical configuration. "Väst."

The responsive smile was spellbinding in its authenticity. "Thanks to the new Archon I am happily well shed of every association with the less than honorable Släkt. Including my Hunts School use name. My psuche name is Fand."

Tal found himself stupidly grinning from ear to ear, because Fand was so clearly her name. It was absolutely her psuche name. It fit her. Everything about her—including her name—kept stealing the breath out of his lungs. "Fand. You…you're…you are…unbelievably…gorgeous."

She blushed, her cheeks blooming a hunter green against her lighter skin. "Thank you, Taliesin. You do not find my birth form strange? Alien, perhaps?"

"No. I mean don't get me wrong, you were beautiful before. But now, you're—well, now you're magnificent."

"Thank you," she replied again, lowering her eyes, clearly both pleased and embarrassed at his compliment.

"I thought I wasn't going to get to see you. Borras, I mean Lord Atlas, well…anyway, he told me what happened and that you had returned home to be Queen."

"The Archon was correct. However, an unexpected opportunity presented itself for a soon to be vacant position. I applied and was accepted," Fand replied, her wings beating a little faster, even though her speech slowed a bit. "My parents have agreed to serve as Regents of Tir na nÓg until I am discharged from my new duties."

"That's great!" Tal exclaimed. "I knew Borras would figure out how to get you back into the game. So, now you're going to help the Ruling Council in some type of advisory capacity?"

Väst, now Fand, paused before continuing. "I won't be working with the Ruling Council, Taliesin."

Stymied, Tal paused a moment. "Huh. I thought the only way Folk could leave their home Realms between Tyrnings was if they were working with the Ruling Council. So what else…"

Tal realized midsentence he needed to stop talking and try to get Central Processing engaged. Since he'd given up on any chance of ever seeing Väst again, he hadn't spent any time preparing a three-point enumeration framework of what he needed to tell her.

Unquestionably first on the list would be apologies, many apologies, for all of the truly terrible things he'd said about her before he understood the reasons she had lied to him. Then, after he hopefully had made her understand he was genuinely sorry, he would tell her he'd realized he was crazy in love with her. That he would do anything to be with her, whether it was here on Earth proper or even if it was being a servant in her palace on her home plane. Anything, everything, was on the table if only he could be with her from now on.

Fand took his several moments of silent reflection to quickly close the gap between them. She grasped his face gently with both of her beautiful hands, tilted his head down to meet hers…slowly…until there was less than an inch distance…until the static spark leapt from his mouth to hers.

The "Divine Spark," the Folk called it and Tal concurred. He was beyond himself. This kiss was as unbelievable as the first time he and Väst embraced. It was every stolen moment's kiss throughout the entire school year, all of their intimate moments rolled into one, and it was…it was enormous…ridiculously enormous…and it was intimate…really ridiculously intimate, and it was everything he'd ever dreamed could happen between two people who were in love with each other.

"And the girl is crying," he noted, as he finished the Best

Kiss Ever. "Not exactly the response a guy wants when he lays an epic lip lock on his best girl," he added with a wry smile.

Tal licked his lips a couple of times as Parietal Lobe sent the results of the preliminary taste analysis to Cortex. "On the positive side, your Highness, you either naturally taste like licorice or y'all have some funky flavored lipsticks in Tir Na nÓg." Without even thinking, he quickly ran his tongue over his lower lip again. Central Processing responded by quickly sending the new sample downstairs for some in-depth micro-analysis.

When Tal focused his attention back on Fand he saw her tears were now free-flowing. "What in the world is there to cry about?" he asked, trying his best to generate an infectious smile. It didn't work.

"Come on, Gorgeous. Amarantos hit it out of the park sending me to othertyme for this trip." He pointed at the nasty, rusted exterior of the Ladies' Room door. "This time when I walk through that door I'll know exactly which choices to make. We know who the Big Bad is. I'll warn everybody about Principal Chiron, well, about Malebranche. That means Bati won't be killed by the Keres. The jig will be up about Chronos from the get-go. We can save Emet, Piras, Kita, Elle and lots of others. The Omada will still win, the bad attitude Släkt will still go down in flames." Tal paused in his recitation to give Fand his best cocky smile. "And in this version the boy and girl will live happily ever after. Game. Set. Match."

Looking for confirmation that his positivity had spilled over to his companion he saw Väst's tears had in fact stopped. Well, not quite. There was a single ginormous tear welling ever so slowly to the surface of her left eye. As he watched, it finally spilled over and began leaving a fresh quicksilver trail, quickly tracing its way down her cheek.

"I'm so sorry, Tal," Väst said haltingly, trying to act as if she was all composed and everything, when she was clearly agitated. Her wings gave her away, they were cycling faster and faster.

C'mon genius, Tal told himself. This may be the most important problem you've ever solved. Fand is beyond upset, she gives every indicator of being full-on distraught. Why? Why would she be crying when we are finally together, when Amarantos has given us the mechanism to solve every problem we are ever going to encounter?

Right, he assured himself, those must be tears of joy.

You're an idiot, he replied, you know that? Look at her body language, those aren't tears of joy. Talk it through with her, he decided. More data may solve the problem.

"I'm a little lost here, I guess," Tal began. "I'm the Traveler. Amarantos has sent me on a mission to othertyme. I'm here to present someone with the opportunity to make a choice, to exercise their free will. While I'm doing that, I just so happen to be getting a mulligan on all of my prior actions..."

Motor Control stopped his mouth midsentence on a Level-Five priority directive from Central Processing. Establish and synthesize, Taliesin. Establish additional data and synthesize it with already quantified information.

He started over. "You and me, we are both physically present on Earth Realm?"

Fand nodded yes.

"Right. Since I haven't walked through that bathroom door for the very first time, your Pops is still Archon and this Tyrning's Hunts haven't even begun because I haven't even met Borras yet to bind the contract."

"That is partially correct, Taliesin," she whispered in whatever voice the softest category of whisper falls within.

His synapses were now operating with machine gun rapidity, not even waiting for her responses. "Which means you and I haven't even met in Hunts Orientation...

"Which means, because of Alberich's Bane you can't possibly have come through the Gas Station Crossing because we weren't on the same team...

"Which also means...which also means it is logically impossible for you to know my name is Taliesin." There were no words in his personal lexicon to fully describe the blackness of the dread cloud that was beginning to form in his mind's eye.

She nodded her head to answer his last question, before hugging herself tightly as her wings slowed to an almost standstill. This time it was Fand who took the small step away from their reunion.

Turn the Rubik's cube, Tal, he told himself. There aren't that many variables. Assign them values and then you can solve the equation. "Okay. I know I'm the Traveler and I'm in othertyme. This trip is kind of sort of like when I went back and helped Arthrys with Excalibur. Except, you're here. So, it's kind of like I'm in bizarro othertyme…"

'HELLO, DUMBASS!'" he yelled at himself, except this time he actually vocalized the words. "Fand, I'm not in othertyme, **we're** in othertyme."

More tears companioned another small nod.

The dark cloud grew larger, blacker, and added a new sense component—an acrid biliousness. Tal felt like he was going to vomit. But not the contents of his stomach. He was going to hurl tears. Is that even possible? Can you become so sad you become nauseous and vomit tears?

Of course, you can't, Tal. Get your shit together. It's your subconscious avoiding resolution of the problem. "Sorry, lost my train of thought. I've almost got this," Tal said, as he swallowed about a tablespoonful of what tasted like, well, like bilious tears. "There is no Principe or Folk magyk that allows for time travel."

Fand slowly shook her head to the left, then to the right. "No," she replied slowly. "Neither backward nor forward. It is beyond both the Folk and the Principes. Amarantos is the only one who is not constrained by tyme."

Tal could tell Fand was doing everything she could to hold it together so she could answer his questions. She knew him, she knew how his brain worked. She knew he needed to be able to parse the truth for himself. "What I learned from Myrddin was that only the Traveler moves through time and then only at the will of the UnFading Spirit."

Another nod.

DAMMIT! Tal's Amygdala hadn't been able to restrain itself, and had had to blow off some steam. Everybody feel better now, he asked all of his brain components. Taking silence as an answer, he forged ahead. "That has to mean that you too are a Traveler."

Fand waited a beat before she replied, slowly and clearly.

"No, Taliesin. You know Amarantos has only one Stytch at a time."

This time it was Hippocampus in full-scale rebellion. But it still managed to comply with established protocol by notifying Central Processing it was filing an emergency complaint and demanding an immediate hearing. The gist of the complaint was Hippocampus had been a team player this entire school year. More specifically the last portion of the present term and even more specifically had voluntarily exceeded its normal operating capacity in regulating Tal's seismic emotional shifts over the last few hours in the infirmary, but that the present discussion was simply one horrible revelation too many. It was the proverbial straw that broke the Hippocampus's back. As Hippocampus reminded everyone in its emergency petition, it was also responsible for "spatial navigation" and as time is often referred to as the fourth dimension, the initial assessment and quantification of the plethora of vagaries involving the concept of time travel had also been automatically assigned to the undersigned complainant Hippocampus.

Being a kingbossdaddy in all things nerdist, Tal was, of course, fairly well-versed in most of the general theories and story lines concerning time travel. When he was little, his mom had checked out all of the classics for him from the local public library in whichever town they were living. He'd devoured Washington Irving's "Rip Van Winkle," Dickens' "A Christmas Carol," and Twain's "A Connecticut Yankee In King Arthur's Court." As he grew older, he'd even read mushier themed books, such as "The Time Traveler's Wife." He knew all of the actors who played the different incarnations of Doctor Who, had watched reruns of shows like "Star Trek" and "Quantum Leap," and was seriously into the "X-Men" and "Terminator" movie franchises.

Tal decided it might be his knowledge about time travel that was causing the Hippocampus overload. More specifically, his knowledge of Einstein's theory of relativity as it applied to what is commonly referred to as the "grandfather paradox." Simply put, if a person time traveled into the past and killed his or her grandfather, would that person cease to exist? One line of thought said absolutely not, the mere fact the person existed in the present meant the past couldn't be changed, so his grandfather couldn't be killed. Another theory held that parallel universes are created by each and every event, large or small, in our main universe.

It was Einstein's work that provided what appeared to be the most consistent explanation. Well, it was Einstein's theory of special relativity but it was Albert's former professor, Hermann Minkowski, who translated Einstein's theory into a graphic four-dimensional "world line." Which was basically a trajectory except that it traced an object in four-dimensional space-time. Oh, and Minkowski postulated that such world lines had an external existence. Which is where the "Boom!" came in for the "grandfather paradox." The Minkowski view of world lines, accepted by Einstein, is that they are never-ending. As in eternally never ending.

Hippocampus was finally pushed past its breaking point. 'STOP IT! ALL OF THE REST OF YOU JUST STOP IT. Don't you see what you're doing? I'm in charge of emotions up here and you're knowledge-dissembling to avoid what you know to be the only rational conclusion. Just deal with it, please. And one more thing—I'd like to job swap with Hypothalamus. Autonomic functions are a breeze compared to the shit I have to put up with.

Fand had stood silent, no doubt watching the emotional slideshow that must have crossed Tal's face. "Are you done doing your overthinking thing?" she asked him softly.

Tal looked at her. She really was so gorgeous it was difficult to look directly at her. "I think so," he replied haltingly. "At least a good beginning on being done. Amarantos has only one Traveler at a time. For a really long time that role was filled by Myrddin. Until I asked for the gig."

"That is correct, as far as it goes," Fand replied. "Amarantos forgives each of her children the moment we each realize we need to repent. Sometimes, however, we have reached a point where we are unwilling—and therefore incapable—of forgiving ourselves. Myrddin's self-hatred was so strong he was stuck in the loop of unforgiveness for centuries. You and your mother helped Myrddin to move past that impasse to a place where he could accept as Truth that the UnFading Spirit had forgiven him long ago. To the place where he could finally understand all that remained for him to be made whole was to forgive himself."

Tal sorted through Fand's addition to the time equation for a moment before continuing. "Myrddin told me othertyme wasn't linear like realtyme. We're here in othertyme together but since I am still the Traveler in my present realtyme…"

Fand said nothing, not wanting to interrupt the maturation of his understanding.

"You must be the Traveler in what for me is still a future realtyme." Tal stopped there, looking to her for confirmation, which she gave him with a sad smile and a nod.

"When, Fand? When in our joint realtyme future did you ask to become the Traveler?"

"It was the moment I learned the Archon was going to have to exile you from the Hunts School. The second I realized how lonely your life would be, the constant danger you would face from an unstoppable foe. Both of which were also the exact same moment I realized if Amarantos granted my request, it meant I would never see you again," she replied, before stuttering to a halt once more.

She stopped herself short, Tal thought. She had something else she wanted to say but she stopped herself. "Next question. When in my realtyme future did Amarantos send you othertyme?"

She started crying again. "It was the instant before you would have stepped off of Hunts School campus and into the Gas Station Crossing."

In other words, only moments ago in my realtyme. Possibilities whirred through Tal's brain. Faster, much faster than Tal could seize and hold them for analysis. The maelstrom of images reminded him of Baba Yaga's feelings swirling all around her before they became part of her once more. One particular conclusion, the one shepherding the cloud of bilious inky blackness, circled his head several times in a holding pattern before coming in hot for a fiery crash landing.

"NO! NO! ABSOLUTELY NOT!" Tal yelled. Not at Fand, although he saw her immediately recoil from the vehemence of his outburst. Not at her, but yes I am absolutely yelling at anyone and everyone else but her. At the UnFading Spirit, Tal? he asked himself. Are you actually yelling at the architect of all the universes, known and unknown? Hell yes, he responded to himself. Yes, I am most definitely yelling at my Creator. Sorry, but not sorry, Amarantos. It's my life. Mine. You gave it to me. You told me I had both the privilege and the responsibility of making my own choices. I accept it. Both the privileges and the responsibilities.

Fand took a tentative step back toward him. Before she could completely close the distance, Tal stuck out his right hand, warding her off. "No. I know the rules of this game very well now. I have to consent before we can bind a contract. And I most certainly do not consent. End of conversation."

Fand grasped his outstretched hand and placed it softly against her breast. "This is not a contract, Taliesin. It is a gyft."

"A gyft?" Taliesin asked, while he tried his hardest to fully understand. "Well, why didn't you say so earlier? Can't possibly be any big thing if two people who are crazy in love with each other want to exchange tokens of their affection. I mean, c'mon, why should we wait until Valentine's Day to cycle through before..."

Tal stopped joking when he noticed tears had made their reappearance on Fand's cheeks. "Whoa! Gyfts are happy things. What's with the crying?"

"You know the answer, Taliesin," she replied. "That wonderful, unique brain of yours has already dissected the matter. You and Atlas talked about it, about Chronos and the geas. You only think you feel the way you do about me because of the compulsionmagyk."

Tal was stunned. He actually felt like someone had sucker punched him so hard his eyes were wobbling in their sockets. Each one wobbling independent of its bestest eyeball pal. "No, ummm, No. That's not true. I love you because you are you, and you are sufficient, and you are enough..."

Fand removed Tal's hand from her breast and reached up

with her other one to gently clasp it with both of hers. "Think, Tal, think back to the first time you saw me. Describe to me what you thought. Moment to moment, as you thought it."

Tal sent word to Short Term Archives that he required the requested information. The response came promptly. "Your eyes," he replied. "I noticed they were blue. Then I corrected myself that they were 'flawless cerulean blue.' Then I had to immediately correct myself again to reflect they were 'flawless—insert here every ridiculous over the top poetic descriptor ever used to describe blue eyes—blue'."

"Oh, Tal," Fand cried.

"I'm not done," he interjected. "My final interpretation was you were, 'quite simply, a honey-butter-blonde-gleaming-white-teeth-undoubtedly-preferred-by-ten-out-of-ten-dentists-small-rounded-breasts-that-strained-against-her-polo-shirt-as-they-stood-up-proudly-to-say-no-thank-you-we-can-support-ourselves walking dreamfest. Come to life.' "

"No one has ever spoken such beautiful words to me, Taliesin," Fand sobbed. "But that was not your initial impression. As much as you believe they were, those were not truly your first thoughts. I was there. The two-way nature of that horrible geas kicked in when it made me make eye contact with you. Think harder," she demanded.

Tal sent an angry message back to Archives. Is there an earlier impression? Did something come before? Why didn't you send it with the other? The response came swiftly and his face fell as he scanned it with his mind's eye.

"I see you remember now, Tal," she continued. "Tell me. With what is about to happen it is important to me that you fully understand."

"No," he refused. "That's not what I really think, it's not how I feel about you."

"It is important. Say it aloud."

"My first thought…my very first thought when I looked at you, I thought…" Tal quickly realized it was his turn to be overcome.

He felt Fand gently squeeze his hand, helping him to finish. "It is okay, Taliesin. Say it."

"I thought…I thought you were, 'a petite, attractive dishwater blonde.' Until you made eye contact with me and then I couldn't look away."

"That's right. It was the compulsion geas that wouldn't let you look away, that replaced the images in your head. It was the magyk that wrote those poetic words in your mind."

Tal realized there was no denying it, it was the truth. "Fine," he replied angrily. "That was the truth then. It's not the truth now. Don't you see, the compulsionmagyk doesn't matter. Borras already told me all about the geas. He told me everything. How Chronos blackmailed you to make sure I'd go to Five-Hells. He also told me what you did, how you saved my life, what you did for the Omada. Fand, I don't think…"

"It doesn't matter what you think or feel now," she sobbed, letting him go and placing both hands over her face. "It was and it wasn't…but it is part of how we came to be, and it was—and it remains—evil."

"Stop," Tal said, moving her hands so he could place his fingers to her lips. "Just stop. I forgive you. Everything. I am not under any compulsion now, and I love you and you love me."

"Yes, I do, Tal, but it matters not. It was darkly begun between us and it cannot be made right now." She looked at him, the tears again welling over, and coursing down her face. "My gyft for you was a kiss, Tal."

"Now see, that's what I'm talking about," Tal said smiling, trying anything he could to lighten the conversation. "Swapping some spit with the Dust Child. I'll be happy to pay the gyftpryce for that one."

Fand laughed for about a split-second as she wiped her tears away. "That's just great. It's the last time you're ever going to see me and I wanted to look perfect for you, even though you won't remember how I looked, or who I am, and now my eyes are all puffy, and I'm a wreck, and…"

"Stop it, Fand. This is crazy. We're just getting started. I forgave you and now that we're through with the teams and competition, we get to be us. We get to be together. You're going to go back to your realtyme, no harm done, and I'll go to mine. I'm going to walk through that Ladies' Room door and we'll end up catching up with each other. It will be perfect…"

Tal stopped, his tongue tied by his belated recognition of Fand's use of tense. "Wait, you said your gyft **was** a kiss." He took several staccato steps backward before rubbing his fingers across his lips. "It wasn't licorice I tasted. Similar, same family. It was…anise. Fand, you…"

Fand interrupted him, swiftly closing the distance between them as she brought her wings forward to envelope them both. "Yes, Taliesin, thanks to Amarantos, my gyft to you is your life. All of it. Every choice and possibility. Every victory and defeat. Every chance for True Love and for heartbreak."

Even with Fand enveloping him Tal felt chilled. Shock, he told himself. Recognize it. Deal with it. "How long do we have?"

Fand took a breath and ran her fingers through Tal's hair. "Moments. The Kiss of Lethe has about a ten-minute window between administration and effect."

Some smartass quip began to form then evaporated in one beat of Tal's heart. And in the microsecond space before the next beat his heart seized up so tightly he wasn't sure if it was ever going to fire again. "Fand, this is crazy. There's no way in hell I could ever forget you."

Tal reached out to her left side, so he could touch the gossamer of one of her wings. Whatever is smoother than silk, he quickly decided. That's what it feels like. Except it's warm, and I can feel her heartbeat in it. He looked back over to Fand's tear-stained face. "Magyk requires that a commensurate gyftpryce must be paid. This is a huge gyft. What gyftpryce has to be paid for me to forget?"

Tal watched as Fand's face morphed quickly between portrayals of ineffable sadness and limitless joy. "The gyftpryce is the penalty Princess Maymunah foresaw I would impose upon myself. It is remembrance, Taliesin. I will remember every moment you and I have shared. How you selflessly risked your life several times to save me. The way the Divine Spark leapt from your lips to mine that first time we kissed and every time since. I will remember how your skin felt touching mine, the perfect completeness I felt the first time I let you inside me. I will remember how you make me feel far more than I can possibly hold within my heart and yet somehow I still do. I will remember every moment of our time together, Taliesin."

She must have seen the unasked question in his eyes because she continued. "Yes, Beloved, going forward I will also know when your mortal span comes to its end. I will remember all of these things and I will hold them here," she lifted her right hand to her breast, "and here," this time placing the hand on her temple, "for all of my life. I will remember us for many generations of the Children of Dust after the UnFading One has called you home to be with Her."

Tal couldn't stop crying. For her, for himself, for them. How could anybody bear that kind of pain? Alone. The one you love within your reach, watching them live their life—without you. While you love them forever. "Someone can fix this. Atlas, maybe. If not, then one of the Principes. Amarantos? Can't I give you the Kiss in return?"

Beginning with both ends of the tips of her wings, Fand seemed to crumple in on herself. "No, Tal. I am Folk so the magyk will not work on me." She looked directly into his eyes, "I consider this a very small gyftprice for the privilege of loving you."

He reached around her waist, pulling her close. "You are everything I ever dreamed of. You are every wonderful thing out of every dream all rolled into one. In any of the Realms the UnFading One has created, we should be together."

Her face was both a smile and a disintegration. "In any of the Realms she has created, save one—the world you must live in Taliesin."

Tal rocked a little back on his heels as Central Processing received an urgent message from Cerebellum that things were getting a little wonky up there, something was interfering with fine motor control. "Fand, I'm feeling a little dizzy. Kind of faint."

"That means our time has ended." She leaned in, her mouth almost touching his. The spark leapt between them for the last time as she pressed her lips to his and breathed the words into his mouth, "Forget now, Beloved. I release you. My blessings upon you for a long life full of joy…and laughter…and love. Always remember to Seek the Center, Taliesin."

A few seconds later, Fand untwined from him. She placed her hands lightly on his shoulders and turned him back toward the bathroom door. As she stepped back around the rear corner of the gas station, she whispered, the words barely crossing her lips before a soft early summer zephyr picked them up and swirled them away.

"I choose your Love, Taliesin Smith. Always."

EPILOGUE

Tal. Hello? Central Processing to Tal. Report visual data. TAL!

As Tal's optic nerves finally processed the now vehemently repeated instructions, Tal found himself staring at a wall of gray. Well, actually it was a door of gray. More specifically, a rusted out gun-metal gray door with a sign that read, "Ladies' Room."

He next performed a quick visual and physical assessment—torn jeans, sharp pain and obvious swelling in his left ankle. Both palms were pretty well ripped to shreds. Where the hell am I? he wondered. Then his stomach growled and he remembered. He remembered everything.

It's my eighteenth birthday. I was kidnapped by that sonofabitch Barton Sellars and his goons when I was supposed to have lunch with Elle. Central Processing confirmed with Cerebrum that auditory functions were now back on line a split-second before he heard tires spinning on gravel.

HOLY SHIT! He screamed at himself as he pulled himself in to a ball, making himself as small a target as possible. It must be that jackass Barton and his posse coming back for round two of wishing me happy birthday.

Run, he told himself. Where? He looked to his left. There was a back fence. Hmm, somebody out here goes kind of crazy with their "y"s. "Luna's Timeless Treasyre," what's up with that? Anyway, it's too tall to scale quickly and looks like a major tetanus incubator. If they catch me behind the gas station they could murder me and no one would ever find my body.

Footsteps. I hear footsteps. He looked back at the bathroom. I'd be trapped, he told himself. Hello? You can at least go in there and block the door. That entire bunch has short attention spans, they'll get tired and move on.

Fine. Good idea. Well, best of all of the bad ideas. Decision made, he reached for the doorknob...

"Hey, Tiger! You're not really going into the Ladies' Room are you? I mean, come on, at least knock first. You never know who might be in there. Even at a run down, abandoned gas station out in the middle of nowhere."

Startled to hear a female voice, Tal jumped sideways before looking back over his shoulder. And there she was. Driving her spit-shine polished, candy apple red, four-wheel drive Jeep. Top down and doors off. She was wearing a pair of bright blue reflective Aviators, which perfectly complimented her broad grin. A Nemeton Fighting Oracles ball cap was tilted jauntily backwards, exposing her well-tanned forehead.

Whatever mental fog Tal had been mired in dissipated in a flash. "Elle!" he exclaimed, jubilantly—until he remembered about the missed lunch date. "Elle, I'm..."

"Ya know, why don't you hold that thought for a moment as we pause to summarize," she said, interrupting him. "Today had the potential to be a category five shitstorm of a day. I stayed up really late last night baking a cake for this guy, because I thought he might be interesting. Different. But then that guy, well, he stood me up for our lunch date..."

"Elle," Tal said, this time being the interruptor. "I can explain."

"You're still on hold," Elle said, waving her left hand in the air, as she continued with her narrative. "I had previously specifically cautioned this young man about my strong feelings concerning punctuality. So, when he was fifteen minutes late I started to get really pissed."

"Elle, please..." Tal tried again, while she was drawing her next breath.

"Still paused," she interjected, as she held her palm out toward Tal. "One part of me said just sit there in the cafeteria. That way whether he shows up or not, you can be righteously indignant about it. Later—much later—after you've made him grovel for what will seem to him like a lifetime, you can allow him to try to explain. After that you can decide if you think he still has the potential to be legit or whether he is merely the newest incarnation of a snake oil salesman in what seems to be a never-ending line of various iterations of snake oil salesmen."

This time when it came time for her next breath, Tal let it go. He'd learned in Physics there are four generally recognized fundamental forces of nature. Gravity, electromagnetism, strong nuclear force, and weak nuclear force. He also recalled there had been some recent scientific chatter about a possible fifth force of nature. Tal could now empirically confirm there is in fact a fifth fundamental force of nature. And that FFFoN was now executing a perfect half-pirouette and walking back to her Jeep, no doubt to continue her verbal filleting of sole de Tal.

When she was firmly ensconced in the driver's seat, Elle continued. "I finally decided I had two choices. I could sit there getting aggravated and continue to participate in my own victimization. Or I could exercise my God-given free will and choose to empower myself by getting up and finding out what the deal was.

"It was a close call, actually, whether to stay or go. If the same sequence happened twice, I might choose differently each time. This time I chose 'go.'

"I grabbed my fancy homemade cake—and the really fun card I'd bought to go with it—and left the cafeteria in search of an explanation. Which I found almost immediately out in the hallway, in the form of my asshat brother and his two sycophants. Based on their sniggering juvenile attempts at humor, it quickly became apparent they'd successfully pulled one of their favorite routines this morning—the 'dump a chump'."

Elle stopped, pushed her mirrored lenses down on her nose a little and peered over them. "In case you're having a difficult time following along, in every possible point of view of this scenario you occupy the role of the 'chump'."

Tal felt like a miracle had happened and he was lucky enough to momentarily find refuge in the eye of a hundred year weather event. "Totally got that."

"Sol's is their favorite dump site, which made this the first stop on the chump rescue tour. It being an absolutely gorgeous day, I took a quick trip to the house, stripped the Jeep down, loaded it up with the fancy homemade cake, the really fun birthday card, snagged all of the leftover barbeque and fixins' from Williams' Restaurant out of the fridge, then drove out here to chivalrously rescue your sad ass."

Tal stood silently, completely at a loss as to what to do—or to say—next.

Elle slid her sunglasses all the way down to the tip of her nose and peered at his right hand. "Pretty ring. Birthday present?"

Tal looked at his ring finger. Last time he checked he didn't own a ring and he'd never worn jewelry. But there was this incredible looking ring on his finger. He turned it, looking for some inscription. The colors spun and leaped, almost as if they were dancing. They'd form a pattern with what would be their next door neighbors on a color wheel and before that combination could even register, they would make a rainbow twist, with their color opposites momentarily becoming their new besties, only to once again quickly call it quits and move on to another pattern. Tal suddenly felt content, happy.

For a split-second he felt like the answer to Elle's question was on the tip of his tongue. Just as quickly, it wasn't. "You know, I'm really not sure," he replied, before turning the ring a couple more times.

"Fine, keep your secrets," Elle said, as she pushed her sunglasses back into place. "You don't have to tell me everything about yourself. Not yet anyway. Well?"

Tal realized his mind was still fuddled. Way too much unusual stimuli. Even after several moments cogitation, "Well what?" was the best he could do.

"For somebody who is reported to be an uber genius you sure are dwarf star dense sometimes. As I recapitulated for you only scant moments ago, we had a lunch date. I don't have even the slightest vestige of Southern traditional ridiculousness about girls not asking guys out, but I'm not that hip on having to make multiple requests. Fair warning, this is your last chance—are we picnicking or not?"

At the same time that his mental resources in charge of all things relentlessly geeky squealed in delight that this unbelievable woman was ignoring his elite caliber nerd status, Central Processing issued a whispered reminder he had "family obligations." Tal took a quick peek at his phone to see what time it was.

"I saw that," Elle noted. "Taking medicine? Or maybe you had a couple of dates stacked up back to back today?"

"Neither," Tal replied. I'm pretty sure I recently learned an important lesson about truthfulness, he thought. What was it? And why is the phrase "naked truth" inserting itself now when I think of being truthful? Maybe I've misunderstood that phrase my entire life. Is it a double entendre? Never mind you idiot, there's an intelligent, attractive woman who wants to dine al fresco with you. Now.

"No," he laughed. "Little known fact. Wearing a rancid burlap bag and getting booted out of a moving vehicle apparently jacks with your sense of time." Honesty now, Tal. "Seriously, Elle, you have no idea how much I want to take you up on your offer but my mom is going to flip out if I'm not back at school in time to be picked up. Plus, she's worked her ass off on organizing a family birthday dinner…"

"Not a problem. I dropped by Principal Davis's office to let her know Barton and his brace of sniggering nitwits had pulled another one of their patented dumbasseries. You now have an approved absence for today. While I was in her outer office I logged into the confidential student database, got your home phone number, and then I called your mom to give her an update."

Tal found himself gulping air. "You, um, you called…"

"Sure. I introduced myself, brought her up to speed, and asked her if it would be alright if I picked you up for a late lunch date. She said it sounded like a perfect eighteenth birthday activity and that she'd see you at dinner."

Tal was finally able to translate oxygen into a few squeaky syllables. "She, um, she really said, um…you talked to…my mom?"

"Thea, Tal. She asked me to call her Thea. Wasn't that nice? I think she and I are going to hit it off great. Anyway, she thanked me for being willing to give you a ride home." Elle paused, this time to cock her hat back on her head, before giving him an even bigger smile. "She moved family dinner to 7:30 p.m. Oh, and I'm invited."

Tal stood motionless, now paralyzed both bodily and verbally. All of the different parts of his brain were competing to put their two cents in without being willing to wait their turn and the result was Central Processing was experiencing system gridlock.

Elle took his silence as an opportunity to continue. "So, Champ, looks like you have two discrete choices. I can take you home, drop you off in your driveway, and you can continue the journey on your apparently well-orchestrated and most probably monastic existence. Or…you can go on an anarchical adventure with me."

Central Processing authorized Front Parietal Lobe to take its best shot at responding. " 'We must be willing to let go of the life we planned so as to have the life that is waiting for us.' I pick door number two."

Elle laughed pleasantly. "Excellent choice. Extra points awarded for the Joseph Campbell quote. It's settled then, we're having a double feature. A sumptuous picnic lunch combined with an adventure. Who knows, Taliesin Smith, maybe the world needs saving this afternoon and the universe is depending on us to be the folks to do it."

Tal was starting to get his game back. A little bit of it anyway. "I don't know, Elle. I'm thinking nobody in their right mind would pick me to be the go-to guy to save the world."

In response, the class valedictorian laughed yet again. "Well, you're wrong there. I'd pick you, Mr. Smith. I think you got major Hero potential."

It's such an easy, honest laugh that fits her face perfectly. It's because she wears laughter often, Tal realized.

"If you'll get your ass over here and hop into the co-pilot's seat, we'll get this adventure started."

"Roger that," Tal said, as he walked behind the Jeep and carefully slid into the doorless front passenger seat.

Elle's beatific smile slid downward until it was gone. "I'm really sorry about my brother, Tal. Really." She motioned to the rear seat where there was a large plastic kit sitting in the floorboard beside the picnic hamper. "Planning ahead, I brought some bandages and Neosporin. Oh, and some extra-strength Tylenol. You can never have enough of that on hand. I'll doctor you up when we find a more scenic venue. Ready?"

"I think I may be," Tal replied, feeling the corners of his own lips tugging upward.

"Good," she replied. "Navigator is in charge of tunes."

"Okay," Tal replied, as he began pushing buttons. On about the third radio station he paused when he heard some familiar chords. "That's 'Collide'," he said.

"It most certainly is," Elle replied, the smile firmly ensconced once more beneath her Aviators. "It's my favorite Howie Day tune and one of my most fave songs ever. So crank it up...and you should be prepared for some car karaoke," she added right before she began singing along.

"It's one of my favorites too," Tal replied, before turning the volume up and harmonizing his tenor to match her pitch perfect soprano.

As Elle shifted into first and the Jeep slowly began easing forward through the deep gravel of the driveway, Tal turned back over his left shoulder for a final look at the broke down, ratty ass abandoned gas station stuck out in the middle of nowhere.

As he looked at the broken gas pumps and the paneless windows, Tal thought about his well-honed plans for college and about his pre-diagrammed life plan. The life he'd begun planning out in micro-detail beginning when he was only about eight. He also thought about how it really wouldn't be much of a life if he jumped to his preplanned ending without exploring the middle. Like what Dr. Mertin Wilt was talking about this morning. Man, is that guy ever a weirdo.

Never again, he decided. Never again will I take for

granted one minute of my now because I'm in such a hurry to get to my then.

Between the tires crunching on the gravel, the song on the radio, and their duet, they were both unable to hear the Air Hose as it hissed its farewell—

"Enjoy your birthday, Taliesin S-S-S-Smith. Perhaps we'll s-s-s-see you both again s-s-s-soon."